SHADOWS ON A SWORD

THE SECOND BOOK OF THE CRUSADES

KARLEEN BRADFORD

HarperCollins*Publishers*Ltd

For Rachna Gilmore, Jan Andrews, Caroline Parry
and my editor, Marie Campbell, who all helped me to
chip away the stone and find the story

http://www.harpercollins.com/canada

First published in hardcover by HarperCollins Publishers Ltd: 1996
First HarperCollins Publishers Ltd mass market edition: 1997

Canadian Cataloguing in Publication Data

Bradford, Karleen
  Shadows on a sword : the second book of the Crusades

ISBN 0-00-648054-3

I. Title.

PS8553.R217S53   jC813'.54   C95-933326-6
PZ7.B73Sh

97 98 99 ❖ OPM 10 9 8 7 6 5 4 3 2 1

Printed and bound in the United States

THE FIRST CRUSADE 1096–1099

IRELAND
SCOTLAND
WALES ENGLAND
NORMANDY
FRANCE
NAVARRE
LEON & CASTLE
DOMINION OF THE
ARAGON
CATALONIA
ALMORAVIDS
DOMINION OF THE HAMMADITES
SWEDEN
DENMARK
POMERANIA
LITHUANIA
Prussians
POLAND
HOLY ROMAN EMPIRE
Bouillon
HUNGARY
CROATIA
SERBIA
Rome
RUSSIAN STATES
Cumans
Khazars
BLACK SEA
Seljuk Turks
ARMENIAN STATES
Jerusalem
MEDITERRANEAN SEA
EGYPT
FATIMID CALIFATE

PROLOGUE

In the year 1096, Pope Urban II responded to the Byzantine Emperor Alexius's plea for help in recapturing the lands that the Seljuk Turks had conquered. The pope called for a holy crusade to liberate Jerusalem.

A monk named Peter, also called Peter the Hermit, set out in April of that year from Cologne, Germany, with over twenty-thousand followers. This People's Crusade, as it came to be called, was destined to end in disaster. Peter's motley band included only a few nobles trained in the art of war, and their foot soldiers. For the most part, it was made up of pilgrims anxious to liberate Jerusalem, and criminals released from prisons upon the pope's promise of pardon for the sins of all who took part in the crusade.

The People's Crusade swept across Germany, Hungary and Serbia on its way to Constantinople in Turkey. The travelers soon ran out of supplies and resorted to looting and pillaging villages as they passed. Other small groups of crusaders were also making their way across Europe and they, too, were causing havoc. Villagers, at first supportive, became fearful and resentful of these roving bands. Battles broke out between Peter's followers and the soldiers and villagers of the towns through which they journeyed. In the town of Semlin, in Hungary, which had already suffered at the hands of crusaders following Walter Sans-Avoir, Peter's followers killed four thousand people after a dispute over a pair of shoes. A final ambush by the Turkish army, just outside Constantinople, ended Peter's hopes. He settled down to wait, with the few survivors, for the First Crusade to catch up with them.

The First Crusade was composed of some of the greatest princes and knights in Germany, France and Normandy, with their well-trained armies and their followers. One of the most noble and respected leaders of this expedition was Godfrey of Bouillon, who set out in August of the same year to meet up with the others in Constantinople and, with them, march on to Jerusalem.

ENGLAND

NORMANDY

FRANCE

Bouillon

HOLY
ROMAN
EMPIRE

One

Theo raised his eyes. The sword flashed in the sunlight above him. His hands clenched into fists, and he pressed them hard against his thighs as he knelt on the sweet-smelling grass of the meadow. He willed himself to stay absolutely still, his face to remain impassive, but a singing excitement rising inside him threatened to burst out at any moment.

A touch on his shoulder; a light blow to the cheek.

"Rise, Theobald." Count Garnier's deep, slightly husky voice rang out.

Theo stood. All of the count's men were there to witness the knighting of a boy they had known for most of his life. The count lowered the sword and held it out before him, flat on the palms of his hands. The priest, robes stirring in the slight summer breeze, made the sign of the cross over it.

"Bless this sword, Holy Lord, Almighty Father, Eternal God . . ." His words resounded so that all assembled could hear.

The count then fastened the sword around Theo's waist. His movements were deliberate, solemn. Theo forced himself to stare straight ahead, even though his eyes squinted in the sun's glare. He was determined that his knees should not tremble as the count's oldest squire, Hugh, knelt to fasten gleaming new spurs to Theo's soft leather boots.

Hugh finished and stepped back. He caught Theo's gaze and held it for a moment. He had been Theo's instructor throughout all the years of his youth, and his eyes shone with pride. Theo grasped the pommel of his sword. It felt cold in spite of the heat of this late summer's day. He took a deep breath and, with a quick, determined movement, unsheathed the weapon and held it high. Cheers shattered the silence.

Three times Theo brandished the sword, and then he returned it to its scabbard. The cheers redoubled. The count's face broke into a smile, cracking the weather-beaten skin into unfamiliar creases around his eyes and mouth. Now, finally, Theo relaxed. He let out the breath he had been holding and stepped forward to receive his foster father's embrace. His own smile, wide as it was, was still only a shadow of the great happiness that welled up within him. He was a knight. At last.

Overflowing with eagerness to fulfill his duties, to prove his faith and courage, he had stayed alone at prayer all the night before in the church, dedicating himself to God and to his master. Earlier this morning, he had attended mass amid the smoke of incense and the glow of candles. And now it was over. He was a knight, pledged into his foster father Count Garnier's service. Although he had as yet seen only seventeen summers, the war that loomed ahead of them promised to be the biggest, the grandest yet, and the count had need of him.

I will not fail him, Theo vowed. He had been sent to the count by his father as a boy of seven years, according to the custom of the time. He had served him first as page, then as squire. Now he could take his place beside him as knight. His head swam with the heat of the day and with magnificent visions— visions of the battle to come, and of the joy of fighting side by side with his master for the glory of God. They would be invincible, he was certain of it.

They were assembling and making ready for a holy crusade to liberate Jerusalem from the heathen. Pope Urban himself had called for it, and the nobles of all the Frankish and German lands were gathering. In less than two weeks—just after the Feast of the Assumption—they would set out. It would be the greatest war the world had ever seen, and he would be a part of it. When Jerusalem was Christian again, he would be there. He would be among the heroes who set it free.

A trumpet sounded, closely followed by another.

"Master?" A low voice brought him back. "Your horse, if you are ready?"

Theo whipped around. His groom, William, stood waiting, eyes averted as always. To Theo's annoyance, the man never seemed to look him in the eye. William had been sent to him by his father, however, and Theo could not reject this generosity. His father had also presented him with the sword and the spurs, the embossed shield, the metal-ringed leather tunic and helmet that weighed so heavily upon him, and the magnificent warhorse whose reins the groom now held. Fine gifts, but Theo's mouth quirked down, a momentary pall cast over his triumph. His father had provided for him well, but Theo knew that, in return, he was expected to acknowledge that he would receive nothing else. The manor, the land—all would go to an elder brother he scarcely knew. It was up to Theo now to provide for himself for the rest of his life. He forced a civil reply to the groom.

"My thanks, William," he said.

He is a very good groom, he reminded himself. I should not be so ungrateful.

At the servant's side, saddled and caparisoned in a crimson blanket, the massive warhorse snorted, stamping his enormous hooves and tossing his mane as if to jerk the reins out of the man's hands. The groom gave the horse a light impatient slap. The animal's eyes rolled wickedly.

Theo raised his eyebrows slightly. Good groom or not, William treated the charger in a way that didn't seem quite right. Theo had not yet had a chance to ride the horse, but he had spent a few minutes with him the day before. Enough time to realize that the shining, roan-colored warhorse was worthy of respect—and also had a healthy liking for turnips.

There was a sudden cry from William, then a quickly suppressed curse. Theo saw that the charger had shifted his weight and planted one plate-sized hoof on the groom's foot. William was pushing at the animal's haunches, trying vainly to move him. The groom's face was contorted with pain. The horse stared into the distance as if totally unaware of the havoc he was causing; then, with a heaving sigh, he casually shifted his weight again. William leaped back. He hopped on one leg and raised the other foot to massage it, glaring all the while at the backside of the charger. Theo took the reins from him and hid a smile. Yes, this horse was definitely an animal to be reckoned with.

More trumpets. Theo looked out at the meadow in front of him. Ringed with the ancient, towering trees of the Ardennes forest, the fields lay flat, then sloped gently upward. Count Garnier's castle was situated at the top of the rise, silhouetted black against the deep blue sky. Today, the count was hosting the last great tournament planned before their departure. The vast green expanse between Theo and the castle on the hill was dotted with brightly colored tents and flying streamers. Seats had been arranged for the ladies and their retinues. Knights with their warhorses, squires and grooms gathered in knots around the edges of the jousting grounds.

A commotion at the far end announced the arrival of Godfrey of Bouillon, Duke of Lower Lorraine. One of the greatest and most honorable princes in all of France, he would lead Count Garnier and the other Lorrainers on this crusade.

Godfrey rode up to where the count and Theo stood. His charger was a dapple gray, but so hung with gold and jewelled trappings that little could be seen of its original hide. The sunlight glinted off all the adornments in dazzling shafts. The duke saluted Garnier, and inclined his head toward Theo.

"A noble knight you make," he said. "I shall be honored to number you among my party."

Theo dropped to one knee. "It is my honor to serve you, my lord." His blood was pounding through his veins so hard that the sound of it in his ears blocked out everything else. He felt it rush to his cheeks and did not dare raise his face. He had seen the duke from afar, and knew the stories, almost legends, of his bravery, but this was the first time Godfrey had ever spoken to him.

Godfrey gestured to Theo to rise, then rode on. He drew up before the largest of all the tents that dotted this end of the field. His men ranged themselves behind him, pennants snapping in the quickening wind. His trumpeter blew a long, sharp blast—the signal for the tournament to begin.

Theo snatched the reins from William's hands and mounted quickly. Count Garnier was already riding toward their allotted spot, the rest of his men following. The count would be among the early jousters, Theo knew. He turned his horse to follow him. At the kick of Theo's spurs, the charger rolled his eyes back to look at his new master, then strode majestically and unhurriedly forward, as if the decision had been his own.

"You do have a mind of your own, don't you?" Theo said. Ears set far apart on either side of the horse's broad head twitched back at the sound of his voice. "And a noble Roman nose. A noble Roman nose like that deserves a noble Roman name. I shall call you Centurion." The feel of the wide body between his knees was reassuring, and the strong horse smell enveloped him.

How will you fare in the lists, my friend? Theo wondered. His very life would depend on this horse. Then—how will *we* fare? The thought made him catch his breath. As the youngest and newest of all the knights, his turn would come late in the day, if it came at all, but suddenly there was a nervous sickness in his stomach and a sour taste in his mouth. In practice with the count's other knights, all well known to him, Theo had shown promise and done well, but today . . . Today he would be up against strangers, all formidable foes. He fought to breathe normally. He would be going into battle, real battle, very soon—a mere jousting tournament should not be cause for fright. But jousting tournaments were not to be taken lightly.

"A knight cannot shine in war if he has not prepared for battle in tournaments." The words of the count's old squire, Hugh, echoed in Theo's mind. Hugh had trained Theo well. "See your own blood flow, feel your own teeth crack with a well-aimed blow, that's what you need, my young friend." He had seen to it that Theo had experienced some of that pain, and Theo winced with the memory. Many of the tournaments Theo had taken part in had been, in fact, little more than undisciplined brawls. Men were injured frequently, and sometimes even killed. Godfrey, however, would have none of that. He had established rules and insisted on them being carried out strictly.

"We have many battles to come," he had said. "I will not have my men die needlessly beforehand."

Yet, as Theo watched, the very first bout brought death. Count Reginald, one of Godfrey's own noblemen, caught his opponent squarely on the shield with his long, blunt-nosed lance, and unhorsed him.

The warhorse bolted. With his foot caught in the stirrup, the knight was dragged the length of the field before grooms were able to run out and get the horse back under control. The knight lay still on the ground. His own two squires carried him off.

"One who will not be with us on our journey, I fear," Count Garnier said. His voice was tight. His own bout was next.

Theo willed his mind to go blank, to shut the fear out. He had seen death before. He dug his fingers into the thick, wiry gray mane of his warhorse. Centurion shuddered, and shifted nervously.

A superb horseman, the count defeated his opponent easily. The others of his house did equally well. By the time it finally came to Theo's turn, the nervousness in his stomach had turned into a knot of pain. He swallowed hard as he tightened up the reins. The sour taste was worse. He settled his shield into his left shoulder, and received his lance from his groom. Across the field from him, another knight was making his preparations. Sweat poured into Theo's eyes, but even with a free hand, he would not have been able to reach under the metal nose and forehead guard of his helmet. He blinked. The field in front of him blurred. A spot between his shoulder blades began to itch. Trumpets blared out. Centurion carved a deep half-moon into the green turf with one anxious stamp of a hoof. Theo clenched his right fist around the shaft of his lance, balanced the weight of it, and spurred the warhorse on.

"Now, Centurion!" he cried.

Centurion reacted with an explosion of movement unbelievable in an animal so immense. Theo found himself hurtling toward his opponent. The two horses crossed, careening within inches of each other. Great gobs of grass and earth flew into the air with the impact of the animals' hooves. Theo felt his lance strike the other's shield, then glance off. At the same instant, his opponent's lance struck Theo's shield with such force that, for a moment, Theo lost his balance. He tottered, almost lost his seat, then gripped desperately with his knees and managed to remain in the saddle. He was already past the other knight and galloping toward the far end of the field.

He pulled back hard on the reins, forcing Centurion into a tight turn. The charger snorted, flecks of foam flying from his mouth. Theo collected himself and quieted the horse. He settled his shield, renewed his grip on his lance. Across the field, his opponent was preparing himself again as well. They turned their chargers and faced each other. The warhorses, frantic with excitement now, tore at their bridles and ripped the ground with their hooves.

The signal sounded once more. Theo's training took over. Aim low, in at the side, under the shoulder. Get under the shield! The horses raced toward each other, sweat-soaked withers colliding. This time, his opponent's lance missed completely, but Theo's found its mark with a jar that sent splinters of pain up his arm and into his shoulder. He held fast. The other knight let out a cry and flew out of his saddle. Theo twisted to look, even as he pulled at Centurion's bridle to swing him around again. A clean fall. The other knight was already on his knees. A surge of triumph flooded through Theo. He had won!

As Theo checked Centurion and looked down at his fallen opponent, the other looked back up at him. Their eyes locked. The knight was young, probably not much older than Theo. What could be seen of his face was purple with rage and humiliation. Theo lifted his lance in a salute.

"Well fought," he began.

The other spat onto the ground.

The trumpets sounded for the last time, signaling the end of the tournament. Theo wheeled Centurion away. If the knight was so ill-mannered, that was his concern. He, Theo, would not have been so ungracious in defeat. Still, the triumph he had felt was lessened somewhat. He galloped back to the count's enclosure. When he reached it, he leaped from his horse and threw the reins to William. He tore off the confining helmet, tossed it to the ground and swept his short hair back out of his eyes. When dry, his hair was light, almost corn-colored, but now it clung to his scalp, dark with sweat. The count's men surrounded him. They thumped him on the back and pummeled him with affection until the breath was nearly knocked out of him. The squire, Hugh, shook his hand, dropped it, then reached to shake it again.

"A fine showing for your first joust as a knight, my young lord. A *fine* showing." His face shone ruddy with pleasure.

Theo glowed at the praise. My first victory, he thought. And there will be many others. So many others! Real victories against real enemies. The memory of his opponent's churlish behavior vanished from his mind. Of what importance was that? I've proven myself, Theo thought. And in front of my foster father and the duke himself.

"Come, Theo," Count Garnier called from outside the circle of men. "You have earned the right to your feast." He waved Theo forward and led the way across the field back toward the castle.

Around Theo, the whole meadow was a mass of moving color, converging in a noisy, babbling horde upon the castle grounds. Long trestle tables had been set up in the fields, and servants were heaping them high with food. Theo had passed through the great stone-floored kitchens early that morning and had seen the maids already hard at work, cauldrons boiling over the fires. Small boys had been turning spits on which whole carcasses of deer and boar roasted; pigeons and other birds by the hundreds had been tipped out of gamebags in sticky, bleeding heaps onto the floors. The heavy, oily smell of roasting and boiling meat had been overwhelming, almost nauseating then. Now, however, the smells awakened a voracious appetite within him. He had not eaten since the evening before. He strode eagerly to the feast, congratulating and receiving congratulations from everyone he met.

An arm suddenly landed on his shoulders. Startled, he looked up.

"That was bravely done!" A young knight fell into step beside him. He was dark of complexion, and thick curling brown hair obscured his eyes. "Guy will not soon forgive you for that embarrassment."

"Guy?" Theo stammered, taken by surprise.

"My cousin. He rides with me, but has no fondness for me. He has no fondness for any man, I think. He never forgives a slight. I am Amalric," he added. "Foster son to Godfrey, Duke of Lorraine."

"I am Theobald—"

"Foster son of Count Garnier. We go together on this grand adventure." Amalric's eyes shone and he tossed his head, almost in the manner of Theo's charger. "We are blessed, are we not? Surely this will be the greatest quest known to man."

"So it will," Theo answered eagerly. There was an enthusiasm and openness about the young knight that attracted him immediately. He matched his stride to Amalric's.

"Feast at our table. I would like to know you better." Amalric urged Theo toward several trestles set up at the very head of the field. Godfrey was already seated at the topmost table, surrounded by

13

knights and ladies. The women's flowing, colorful gowns fluttered in the wind like butterflies in a meadow of wildflowers. Children were there, too.

"Gladly," Theo assented. He raised his voice and called out to Count Garnier. "My lord?"

The count stopped and looked back.

"Will you excuse me? I would go with Amalric."

The count recognized the young knight. He bowed to Amalric, and smiled at Theo. "Certainly. Come to me later, son," he answered.

Theo followed Amalric.

"Gentlemen, meet Theobald, who disported himself with such glory today!" Amalric cried, as they took their places at a table groaning with food.

At these words, a tall man at the far end leaped to his feet.

"Can he not sup with his own kind, then?" he growled, the words already slurred with wine. "I fancy a better sort to share my food with." With that, he turned his back and headed for another table. In the instant the man had glared at him, Theo had recognized his adversary.

Amalric laughed. "Guy is his usual self, I see. By my life, it was sweet to see you unhorse him today. There are not many who can. And to be bested by such a young, untried boy!" He threw back his head and his laughter turned into a bellow of joy.

The others at the table joined in and made room for Theo. Theo hesitated. Boy he might be, and the worn

14

look of Amalric's mail and tunic showed him to be a more seasoned warrior, but Amalric was not that much older than Theo and his words grated. He almost decided to return to Count Garnier's men, but the warmth of the welcome from all sides overcame his misgivings. And to be singled out by the foster son of Godfrey himself was an honor. Jokes flew as the platters of meat were handed around. Theo's cup was filled with wine; the strong liquid warmed and relaxed him. He was soon laughing with the rest and comfortably at ease in his place beside Amalric.

When the first pangs of his hunger had been assuaged, he pushed back from the table, threw a bone to the hounds fighting in the grass beneath their feet, and looked around. His gaze was drawn to Godfrey's table. This was the first time he had had a chance to observe the famous Duke of Lower Lorraine closely. Godfrey lounged carelessly in his seat, laughing across at another knight. He was tall and massively built, his head and shoulders towering over the others around him. His hair was fair and cut longer than most. Disheveled now after the activity of the day, it hung almost to his shoulders. He had an air of complete confidence. Theo could believe that the tales told of his courage and nobility had not been exaggerated.

He let his glance travel to the others at the table. On one side of the duke sat a lady, and beside her two children. His family, Theo surmised. They would be accompanying the duke on this crusade. On the other side was a dark, wolfish-looking man, with a proud and haughty air. His black eyes stood out from a pale, almost startlingly white face. They moved ceaselessly, suspiciously, even as he held himself taut and almost immobile.

"Baldwin, younger brother to Godfrey," Amalric said beside Theo, following his gaze. "Not a bit like the duke, though. Destined for the church he was, and not allotted any of the family estates. Seems he didn't have the temperament for a churchman, however. Whether he left the church, or the church left him, no one really knows, but here he is now, taking his brother's charity. You'd never know it by his manner, though. You'd think *he* was the great lord, the way he carries himself. They say he's more interested in making his fortune in the east than in the holy quest."

A minstrel group struck up a few notes, and Amalric turned away, instantly distracted.

"Music! Now we shall have some fun!"

Theo remained staring at Baldwin. At his side sat a stout, rather homely woman, eating steadily. Baldwin seemed to pay her no attention at all. His wife, Theo guessed. Beside her sat a line of three children, and beyond them a girl—a girl with thick black hair that streamed down her back and over her shoulders in a mass of undisciplined curls. Unlike the other women at the table, she was dressed in rough, plain-colored homespun. As Theo watched, one of the boys pinched the other and an angry cry rang out. Their mother, her attention focused on the dripping joint she held in her grease-covered hand, gave them barely a glance, but the girl was quick to administer a sharp slap to the aggressor, who then set up a wail of his own.

The girl glanced up and caught Theo's eyes. She stared back at him for one long moment, defiant. Then she turned away.

"Theo!"

With a start, Theo realized Amalric was elbowing him in the ribs. The others were laughing at something he had missed.

"Your pardon?" Theo said quickly. The conversation swirled around him again, but he did not hear. His mind was full of the most wondrous dark, bright eyes he had ever seen in his life.

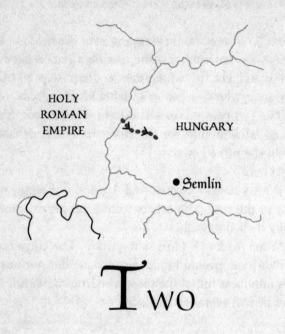

HOLY
ROMAN
EMPIRE

HUNGARY

• Semlin

Two

"**K**ing Coloman keeps us waiting still! It is eight days now since Lord Godfrey sent to him for permission to cross his lands!" Amalric's face was flushed and dark, his eyes angry.

"Perhaps he has had a stomach-full of crusaders," Theo answered. In the two months since the crusade had set out from the Frankish lands, Theo had come to know Amalric well.

He's in one of his moods, Theo thought. Almaric was as quick to anger as he was to enthusiasm.

Sometimes it was hard to keep up with him.

Nonetheless, Theo could understand Amalric's impatience. He remembered how they had set out, with such glory, pomp and fanfare. Hundreds of knights had assembled and ridden forth through the dim and leafy forest of the Ardennes in the early morning mists, chain mail gleaming, pennants flying, chargers bedecked in glowing color. Theo had never seen such an assemblage. They had been followed by all their retinue: wives and children in gaily painted wagons and litters, squires and grooms. Behind them, the archers and the foot soldiers, straight-backed, with their long-handled, spear-pointed halberds massed in unswerving, gleaming lines. Behind them, the pilgrims, on foot, on donkeys, in carts—all yearning to make their vows at the Church of the Holy Sepulchre in Jerusalem. A never-ending river of people, it seemed to Theo. Dogs barked and ran to and fro, cattle lowed and bellowed. Chickens and geese added their cackles and shrieks to the cacophony. It was a festive, almost delirious procession, and no one could resist being caught up in the spirit of it. This gathering had much more the look of celebration than of war. But now, it had been brought to a halt here at the frontiers of Hungary.

"He *must* help us. We are God's army." Amalric was vehement in his indignation.

"So is Peter the Hermit's band, and look what they did."

"Pah! Rabble! That's all his followers are. Criminals and murderers. The dregs of the prisons. Hardly a nobleman among the lot."

"Not so—there are noblemen, and honest pilgrims, as well. Yet they sacked Semlin—a Christian city! I can understand the king's reluctance to admit us. He has heard the tales, too, of the murder of the Jews along the Rhine. I wonder not that he fears us." Theo's voice was heavy. At first, he had not believed the stories of the massacres of the Jews by bands of crusaders in Trier and Mainz and other cities along the German rivers. And then had come news that Count Gottschalk's army had been massacred in its turn by the Hungarians, after the count's men had looted several villages and killed many of the peasants. A young Hungarian boy had been impaled by the crusaders, it was said, and left as a challenge to the Hungarian army. Theo could not bear to think of it. This was not the way the holiest of all wars was to be carried out.

"The villagers refused them food. The crusaders were in need . . ." Amalric's voice trailed off. The tales had been too full of horror. Even he, with all his enthusiasm, could find no excuses.

They were camped on wide fields beside the Danube River. When they had arrived, the fields had been rich with the late fall harvest. After eight days, however, any crops not pulled up by the crusaders had been trampled into garbage. Theo looked around. It was a dispiriting sight. As far as he could see were tents and makeshift shelters. People gathered by small fires, beginning to prepare their evening meal. Pennants flew as usual in the brisk October breeze, but somehow they did not impart any air of gaiety. The camp was unusually quiet. Here and there children's voices broke the stillness, and dogs barked defiance at one another and the world in general, but over all hung an air of listlessness and waiting. The weather had been warm for this time of year; the stink of the camp permeated everything.

At first, curious villagers had ventured out to see this incredible army, some even carrying gifts of food and clothing, but none had appeared for the last two days. Food was running short, tempers were rising. Fights broke out.

Suddenly, Theo could bear it no longer. "I must return to the count," he said.

"Will you meet me here tomorrow morning?" Amalric asked. "I would try my hand at hunting for a few birds in the woods. We're not overly short of food yet, but anything extra for the pot is welcome."

"Gladly." Theo felt a twinge of guilt as he spoke. Count Garnier had laid in wagonloads of supplies, and his people, like Godfrey's, were suffering no want of food as yet; but every evening, as Theo wandered through the camp, he could not help but realize that the mass of common people were beginning to suffer. Now, as he turned back toward his tent, he deliberately chose a path away from the river's edge where most were settled.

Baldwin's tents also lay in this direction. There was, perhaps, a chance he might see the girl who was nursemaid to Baldwin's children—the girl who had intrigued him so the day of the tournament. He had found out from Amalric that her name was Emma, but when Amalric realized how curious Theo was about her and began to tease him, Theo had not mentioned her again. Amalric could be merciless when he had the bit between his teeth, and, friend or not, was not above humiliating Theo completely before the other knights. He had done it before to other luckless young men.

Theo had seen Emma two or three times in the distance, but always with the children or with Baldwin's lady, Godvere. Now, as he drew near to their camp, he heard Godvere's angry voice. The sound of a slap followed. The bushes in front of him parted, and a figure pushed through. As if his thoughts had suddenly taken shape, Emma appeared.

The girl was wiping her eyes as she emerged, but at the sight of Theo her hand dropped. She swung her heavy hair away from her face with a toss of her head and faced Theo warily. A welt was rising on one cheek.

"Is anything amiss?" The words sprang from Theo's lips before he had time to think.

"Amiss? No more than usual." The girl's voice shook. Theo could see the effort she was making to steady it. She eyed him with distrust and took a step back toward her encampment.

22

"No—stay!" Again, Theo spoke impulsively. "I . . . I saw you at the feast," he added. To his chagrin, he realized he was stuttering.

"And I saw you looking at me," Emma replied. There was a hint of scorn now in her tone, as if she were well used to being stared at by rude young knights.

With her black hair billowing around her face, her dark eyes and her flushed cheeks, Theo thought her quite the most beautiful woman he had ever seen. He could well imagine men staring at her.

"Your pardon. I did not mean to discomfort you."

"You did not. I am not that easily discomforted."

Theo could well imagine that, also.

"You are nursemaid to Lady Godvere's children?" he asked, trying desperately for some way to reassure her, to keep her from leaving. He was careful to make no move toward her.

"I am. And you—you are foster son to Count Garnier, are you not?"

Theo looked at her in surprise. How did she know that? Had she, by any chance, been making enquiries about him?

"Amalric said so," she added, squelching his hope that she might be as interested in him as he was in her. "He is much about our camp and has spoken of you. I could not help but overhear."

"Oh," was all that Theo could manage.

Emma reached out to break a twig off a bush. She started to peel the bark from it with long, slender fingers. In the gathering dusk, Theo could see that her hands were work-hardened, but fine. She looked at him for a long moment, and bit her lip. Then she tossed the twig away with a decisive movement, as if she had made up her mind about him and concluded there was nothing to fear from this young knight after all. Her face brightened.

"This is a truly wonderful crusade we're on, isn't it?"

"It is," Theo agreed, still treading carefully.

"I wish I were a man. I wish I could fight. I do so envy you!"

"Women cannot fight." The words came out more stiffly than he had intended.

"Oh, I know women can't fight," she said, tossing her hair back again in a movement that completely bewitched him. "Still," she went on, "I can wish for anything I want, can't I? What about you? What will you do after we free Jerusalem?"

The question brought Theo up short. He had never given the matter any thought at all. The crusade alone had filled his mind—the reconquering of Jerusalem. "I shall serve my lord, Count Garnier," he said finally, stuttering again. "What else? He is my father now, and he has no other family but me."

"But will you stay in the Holy Land? They say you will all be given land, houses, riches. They say there are treasures beyond compare to be had there. But perhaps you have even more waiting for you back home?"

"No. No, that I certainly do not have. There is nothing waiting for me back home."

"No girl mooning at the stars and praying at night high upon the battlements of her castle for your safe return?"

Theo bristled. He liked it not that she should take that tone with him. He was not such a callow youth. There had been many girls. He was not that inexperienced. He scowled.

"There is nothing for me to return to," he repeated.

Emma ignored the scowl and smiled. "Then you'll probably stay as well." She looked as if the thought pleased her. Theo's fur settled back down. "It will be exciting, living in a new land, won't it? They say it is very different from our old countries. No poverty, no disease. Wealth and good living for all. I can hardly wait."

"It is probably not all of that," Theo said. "And we must fight for it first." He tried to sound cautious, but her words had chased away his misgivings and reawoken his enthusiasm. How fortunate he was that he was a man and not a mere woman, that he would be able to fight. And had he not shown his mettle in the tournaments? He was ready to go to battle for the glory of God—wealth meant nothing to him. Fighting God's war was what was important—doing God's will. And the battle would be magnificent, he had no doubt of it.

A voice clamored.

"Emma! Emma! Come here at once. Where are you?"

Emma grimaced. "My lady Godvere's gentle summons. I must go." She gave an irritated toss of her head, then smiled before turning to make her way back through the bushes.

Theo stood, looking at the spot where she had disappeared. He could almost believe he had imagined the whole encounter.

† † †

Amalric was striding back and forth when Theo arrived at their meeting place the next morning, just as the first birds began to sing. The rising sun had melted the early morning mists over the fields where the crusaders were encamped, but here, at the edge of the forest, the haze still swirled heavily around them. The air smelled damp, redolent with earth and decaying vegetation. The shadows were deep.

"We are leaving!" Amalric burst out as soon as Theo was within hearing distance. "Coloman has given his permission! We leave tomorrow at sunrise."

"How do you know? When did you hear?" Half asleep still and missing the warmth of his pallet, Theo was slow to react.

"The duke has just come back from King Coloman's court. It seems he made a good impression and managed to convince the king that we are different from the rabble that has preceded us. The word is being passed around the camp now," Amalric said. "We have no time for hunting, we must get ready to move. Besides, the king has agreed to give us all the supplies and provisions we need."

"That is wonderful news indeed," Theo answered. Wide awake now, his excitement rose to match Amalric's. "I wonder what swayed his mind?"

"Well, we are to accept a guard of the king's soldiers while we are crossing his lands. The duke had to give his pledge that there would be no lawlessness. He will call a gathering this afternoon, before the evening mass. He has threatened to kill any man who so much as steals a chicken."

"Then we are on our way!"

"On our way, and nothing can stop us now. We are to march to Constantinople, to the city of the Byzantine Emperor Alexius, and there wait for the other great princes and their entourages to join us. And then . . . Jerusalem!"

"Jerusalem." Theo almost whispered the word. He tried to picture the holy city, but could not. The name itself filled him with awe. He would walk in the footsteps of Christ. He would climb the very hills, follow the very paths His feet had trod . . .

"There is one other condition for our free passage, however."

At first, the words did not even register.

"We must leave hostages with the king."

27

Finally, Theo heard.

"Hostages? Who?"

"Baldwin and all his family. They are to remain with King Coloman until we are beyond the far borders of Hungary to ensure that we do no harm."

"All his family? Children, too?"

"Yes. There is no cause to fear for them, though. Our men will behave, Godfrey will see to that. No one would dare go against his will. Not that Baldwin would be any great loss, I warrant."

Emma! She would be left here as hostage while they marched on. Theo whirled around.

"Theo! Where are you going?"

He ignored Amalric's cry and dashed back. Early though it was, the camp was in turmoil when he reached it; word had spread that they were to move out the next day. He fought his way through a crowd of people. A dog nipped at his heels; he kicked at it, almost ran into a dying campfire, skirted it and ran on, heading for the outskirts where Baldwin's tents had been. They were already gone. Trampled grass and crumpled refuse were the only signs of where they had stood.

Theo stared at the abandoned camp. There was nothing he could do—nothing but hope that Godfrey could keep his knights and people in order as they marched through Hungary.

Three

Theo rode with his foster father, or with Amalric, as they followed the river down through Coloman's kingdom. He marveled at the wide fields along the banks of the Danube River. Most of the crops had been harvested, and the level land made the traveling easier than it had been in the narrow defiles and hills along the Rhine and Neckar rivers in Germany. It was still far into the night, however, before he saw the last pilgrims straggle in to make camp at the end of each day.

29

One morning, Amalric caught up to him, breathless, just shortly after they had set out.

"Peter the Hermit's band of crusaders has been trapped and massacred by the Turks!" he called out, reigning his horse in beside Theo's.

"Where?" Theo asked. "What has happened?"

"At a place called Civetot on the southern shore of the Sea of Marmora, past Constantinople," Amalric answered. He paused to gulp a mouthful of air, then went on. "No one knows for certain, but one tale has it that everyone who followed him has been killed!"

The news spread fast. Fear began to seep through the camp. At night, the mutterings that Theo heard around the fires grew louder and angrier with each passing day. Resentment at the presence of King Coloman's troops surrounding them every step of the way only made things worse.

Theo worried for Emma's safety. It was irrational, he barely knew the girl. She was nothing to him. But if the crusaders' anger boiled over . . . If trouble broke out, he was certain King Coloman would use his hostages in any way necessary to ensure the safety of his people. A small knot of unease sat in the back of his mind and accompanied him wherever he went, whatever he did. Emma was the first thing he thought of in the morning, the last thing in his mind at night before he sank into restless sleep. It amazed him, this preoccupation with her.

In the evenings, after they had made camp, Theo

often met Amalric to hunt. He enjoyed it, and it helped to keep his mind occupied. The Hungarian forests teemed with deer, wild boar and birds of all description. One evening, Amalric met him with further news.

"Peter survived," he said. "My lord Godfrey has just received word. The Hermit was in Constantinople at the time of the attack. A few of his leaders escaped as well, but it seems most of his followers died."

Theo jabbed at the ground with his spear. All appetite for hunting had suddenly deserted him. This news would only make matters worse. At that moment, a shout rang out from the trees ahead of them, and a boar burst into the open, foam flying from its snout, eyes wild and red. It was headed straight for Amalric, who had his back to it.

"Watch out!" Theo realized that Amalric could not possibly turn and defend himself. He braced his feet, raised and threw his spear all in one quick, instinctive movement. The weapon took the animal cleanly behind the shoulder. The force of the boar's charge was checked, but not stopped.

Amalric whirled around. The boar buried one razor-sharp tusk in Amalric's thigh, jerked it out with a tearing, sideways movement of its head, then faltered. Theo pulled his killing dagger from his belt and leaped forward. He was aware of more shouts, but all his attention was on the crazed beast in front of him. Its musky stink filled his nostrils. He yelled. The boar turned and fixed its eyes on Theo. It swerved away from Amalric toward him. Theo raised the dagger high, side-stepped at the last possible moment and plunged the dagger deep into the animal's throat. The boar gave a choking, gurgling snort and dropped to its knees. Its head fell to one side.

"That was *my* animal!"

Theo jerked his gaze away from the dying boar, startled by the shout. The knight he had defeated in the lists, Guy, was standing in front of him, spear held ready as if to throw at him.

"You had no right!"

"No right to defend myself? To defend my friend, your own cousin? Look what *your* animal did to him." Theo shot the words back. The blood-thirst excitement of the danger they had been in, of the killing, roared through him still. He tore the dagger from the boar's body and faced Guy with it. He almost wished the knight would take just one more step toward him.

Guy checked himself. He looked for the first time at Amalric, then turned back to Theo. His face contorted and he threw down his spear.

"You," he snarled, ignoring Amalric. "I might have known it would be you." He spun around and strode back into the woods. His groom, a nervous, bent little man, scurried out and snatched up the spear, eyes averted from Theo and Amalric. Apologies spilled out of him in incoherent fragments.

Theo took a deep breath, willing the storm within him to subside. "Your cousin certainly does not bear you much love," he said finally.

"And less for you, I think," Amalric answered. His words caught in his throat; his mouth twisted in pain.

Theo knelt quickly at his side. Blood was flowing from Amalric's thigh. Theo ripped a piece from the sacking they had been carrying to hold the game, and bound it firmly in place over the wound. Their own grooms, who had been holding their horses in the clearing behind them, came to their aid. Theo helped Amalric to mount.

"We'll get you back to camp," he said. Then, with a sudden mischievous look on his face, he turned to his groom.

"William," he said, "see that the boar is dressed and send it to Guy of Lorraine with my compliments."

Amalric snorted, almost laughing in spite of the pain. "Not a wise thing to do, my friend," he said.

Theo grinned.

†   †   †

By the end of November, they had reached Semlin. Godfrey had kept order; there had been no trouble. The knights and men of Godfrey's army knew very well that his were not empty threats. Thanks to King Coloman, food and supplies were plentiful, and this generosity helped to offset the resentment his troops caused. Still, Theo and Amalric, whose wound had healed well, hunted in the evenings—for the sport and companionship as well as for the food. Amalric had never actually brought himself to thank Theo for saving his life, but there was a respect in his manner now that made Theo feel he was safe from further teasing or humiliation. He still did not speak of Emma, though. The feelings he had for her were too private to share, even with Amalric. Besides, he had not yet figured out exactly what those feelings were. There would be time enough when he saw her again to try to make sense of them. Amalric, for his part, seemed to have forgotten Baldwin and his entourage entirely.

Theo made a point of keeping out of Guy's way. Guy, in turn, seemed no more inclined to meet Theo. He had never acknowledged the gift of the boar, but Theo doubted that he had eaten it. Thrown it to the dogs, more likely.

They were on the Byzantine frontier now. As soon as they crossed the Save River, they would be out of Hungary, and the hostages would be returned. News had it that Baldwin and all his family were well taken care of, but the knot of unease in Theo's mind still did not loosen. It would only unravel when Emma was free and he could see her again.

Late in the afternoon of their last day in Hungary, Amalric suddenly appeared at Theo's tent. William had just set flint to tinder to start the cookfire to boil the evening stew.

"Don't bother with that," Amalric cried out to Theo as he strode onto the campsite. "I've heard there's a tavern in town that serves a wondrous ale and stew. I shall treat you to a feast."

Theo hesitated for only a moment. The turnips and bit of meat in his pot suddenly looked much less appetizing. Besides, he had not yet had a chance to go into the town, although men had been allowed in, in small groups.

"Done," he agreed. "This stew is all yours, William." He sprang to his feet to accompany Amalric.

As they approached the town of Semlin, Theo looked up at the walls. Here, the arms and clothing of sixteen of Walter Sans-Avoir's men, who had robbed a bazaar, had been hung as a warning to Peter the Hermit's troops. The men had been driven out of the city, naked. It had been a futile warning. The story had been told all over camp before the crusaders had even reached Hungary: how it had only inflamed Peter's followers, and how a dispute over a pair of shoes had escalated into a riot. Peter's men had pillaged the city, leaving four thousand dead. Peter had only managed to save his army by beating a hasty retreat over the Save River, out of the Hungarian kingdom. It was no puzzle why King Coloman had been hesitant to let this new wave of crusaders through.

"I wonder that we would be welcome anywhere within those walls," Theo said.

"A man with money to spend is welcome anywhere," Amalric answered. "The widow who runs the tavern is a friendly sort, they say, and harbors no grudge as long as her customers pay their bills and keep the peace. Besides, she suffered no harm from the crusaders before us. She will make us welcome, be assured of it."

The tavern was overflowing with customers, many of them knights such as themselves, dressed in the rough homespuns of the north. For the most part, these knights were hearty men with simple tastes. They were relaxing after their long march, reveling in the good food and drink, and the warmth. As Theo and Amalric thrust their way among the crowd, a solid wall of smoke and smells hit them. A huge fire at one end of the timbered room blazed, welcome after the early winter chill outside, but contributing its own share to the thick fug within. The room was drowned in noise and loud, raucous laughter. A harried and slightly distraught young maid appeared soon after they had settled themselves at a long trestle table as near the fire as possible. She tucked a few strands of hair behind an ear with one hand, and wiped at the sweat on her forehead with the back of the other. She gave them a wary glance, but smiled nonetheless.

"Your pleasure, my lords?" she asked, her words barely discernible above the clamor.

"Ale, my maid!" Amalric cried. "And food. We hunger for your good victuals." She disappeared, with another smile and a more flirtatious glance at Amalric, and reappeared with tankards of ale. Platters of food soon followed, and within minutes Amalric and Theo were attacking a joint of venison and dipping chunks of coarse, hearty brown bread into a savory-smelling stew. Theo hadn't realized just how hungry he was.

It wasn't until he had filled his belly that he sat back and took a look around. A group in one corner caught his attention. A young woman—a girl, really, probably not even as old as he—was sitting slumped against the wall. A child was sleeping on her lap. The child's long, silver-fair hair was matted and dirty, and hung across her face. The girl's head rested against the timbers behind her; her eyes were closed. Beside her, stretched out on the same bench, with limbs flung out in the loose abandonment of exhaustion, a young man also slept. A dog lay at their feet. They seemed to exist on a silent island of their own, separate from all the hubbub surrounding them.

The landlady bustled up at that moment to enquire if all was well with them.

"Who are those people?" Theo asked.

Her eyes followed his. Her smile dimmed and her brows drew together.

"Those poor young things," she said. "With Peter the Hermit, they were—he that did such terrible things here last summer. There's many who will have nothing to do with them because of it, but I say it was none of their doing, what those soldiers did. They're just poor innocents who got caught up in the whole thing. They say nearly every soul who followed that mad monk was massacred, out there in the heathen lands. They're the first ones we've seen back, and it's a sorry state they're in. If they did do any harm, they've certainly suffered for it." She wiped her hands on her apron. "The wee one will not talk at all, just stares as if her wits are gone completely, and the boy . . . Well, he looks as if he's walking with the devil himself." She quickly made a sign to ward off evil. "The poor girl's done in completely, but she's determined to get them all back to her own land in Germany."

The girl's eyes suddenly opened. She looked straight at Theo, but her gaze was unfocused. Whatever she was seeing was not in that room. She sighed deeply, pulled the ragged cloak she wore more tightly around herself and the child on her lap, and then her lids fell shut again. One hand stroked the child's brow, brushing the hair back out of the little girl's eyes.

"Gave them some soup, I did." The woman's voice broke back in. "They didn't have a copper to pay for it, of course, but they have been on the crusade. It was only Christian charity. The crusade's a wondrous thing, the pope has said so himself—despite some evil men." She crossed herself and bustled off.

"The crusade's a wondrous thing." It did not look as if it had been so wondrous for that small group. Theo stared at them until a nudge from Amalric nearly knocked him off the bench.

"This young wench has a friend who has taken a fancy to you, Theo," he was saying. "Buy her a glass of mead. Show her a Christian knight's courtesy, for mercy's sake."

Theo looked up. The maid who had served them was sitting beside Amalric, who had his arm comfortably around her, and another dark-haired girl was squeezing onto the bench beside them. She laughed and raised her eyes coquettishly to Theo. Their dark brightness gave him a momentary jolt, but they were not the dark eyes that he remembered so well. Suddenly, the miasma of the dark, crowded room sickened him. He couldn't breathe.

"I must get back," he said, rising to his feet so brusquely that his mug of ale almost tipped.

Amalric looked at him in surprise. "So ungracious, my friend? I would not have thought it of you." The ale and the heat in the tavern had brought a flush to his cheeks.

"I'm sorry," Theo blurted out. The others stared at him as he turned and stumbled out.

†   †   †

The closer they got to the Save River, the more impatient Theo became, but finally, to his relief, they reached its banks. They crossed in all manner of boats and makeshift rafts, amid a chaos of wails and screams from frightened people, and lowing, bleating and neighing from even more terrified animals. The river was calm and not too wide, however, and despite the confusion no lives were lost, not even of livestock.

They reassembled on the other side and made camp outside Belgrade. The town lay silent and deserted. Peter's men had sacked it in celebration of their escape from the Hungarians; the townsfolk had fled and had not returned. Permission was granted to go into the abandoned town, but few took advantage of it. There was nothing left, and the streets had an eerie, desolate appearance. Theo couldn't shake the feeling that they were following in murderous footsteps, rather than progressing in triumph. As soon as they were camped, he hastened to find out if Emma had been released.

"Not yet," his foster father told him when he asked. "Baldwin and his entourage are still with King Coloman. They are being well treated, I hear, and Baldwin is not overly anxious to leave. I expect they'll be with us again soon, though. In the meantime, we will wait." The count gave Theo a curious look, but before he could question him about this sudden interest in Baldwin's affairs, Theo made a hasty excuse and left.

As the days went on and there was still no word of Baldwin's release, Theo's temper became shorter. William learned to avoid him except when absolutely necessary. Theo chafed against the enforced idleness in the camp. He was torn between a desire to get on with the journey, and the need to see Emma and make certain she was all right before they left. Meanwhile, Centurion had discovered the windfalls from the abandoned fruit trees in the orchards near where they were camped. He developed an insatiable appetite for them, plums in particular, and when he had eaten all the ones available on the ground, he devised his own unique way of procuring more of the late-season fruit that still hung on the branches. He ambled heavily up to a tree, leaned his massive weight against it and then bumped it. He was usually rewarded by a rain of fruit that he devoured, pits and all.

It was early in December, and winter was setting in, when they finally left, well rested and reprovisioned. Their way lay along the old Roman road; Centurion's hooves slipped on the ancient stones. Theo rode looking back over his shoulder; Baldwin had not yet rejoined the crusade.

From Belgrade, they would head straight through the Serbian forest to Nish, where the governor, Nicetas, awaited them. He would further replenish their provisions, and provide an escort through the mountains to Sophia and then on to Constantinople. Within a month's time they should be in the fabled city. Stories of its magnificence and grandeur ran the length and breadth of the camp.

"Streets paved with gold," Amalric asserted confidently. "The churches are roofed with it. Every man and woman in the city walks loaded down with jewels."

Theo did not believe half of it, but he knew for certain there were many wonders to be seen. The Hagia Sophia itself was one of the greatest churches in Christendom.

Finally, word came that the hostages had been released. Theo found himself in a frenzy of impatience to see Emma, but it was impossible to seek her out. They were no longer following the great river valley of the Danube, and their way now lay through forest-covered mountains. The marching during the day was difficult and dangerous; at night, the camp was strung out over long stretches of the trail. Halfway to Nish, Governor Nicetas's army met them and gave what aid it could; this time, the crusaders welcomed the escort. Even with the army's help, however, accidents happened daily. Sometimes the slippery paths they followed seemed little better than goat tracks, hanging perilously onto the sides of the mountains. Ponies and horses lost their footing constantly. At one point, the palfrey Theo rode on the trail slipped and almost toppled with him into a chasm so deep that Theo could see only the tops of trees when he looked down into it. Icy streams tumbled from the snow-covered peaks above—higher than any Theo had ever seen before. The travelers were often soaked crossing them. Each day at morning mass, the priest recited prayers for those who had been lost the day before.

At night, Theo bundled himself into his tent, exhausted, usually wet, and always cold, despite his campfire. But the air here in the mountains was so pure that sometimes on clear, dry nights, in spite of the bitter cold, he rolled himself into his cloak and slept out in the open next to his fire. He liked to lie and look heavenward. Never before had he paid any attention to the stars, but here he spent hours studying them. He could lose himself in the vastness of the vault above him. The occasional lonely howl of a wolf hunting in the forests around him inspired only awe, not fear.

It wasn't until they had crossed the mountains and encamped at Selymbria, on the Sea of Marmora, a day's march from Constantinople, that he saw Emma again.

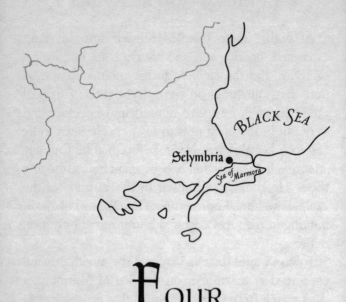

Four

The sea fascinated Theo. Never had he seen such an expanse of water. He had thought the rivers mighty, and had been in awe of their rushing, turbulent currents, but the sea was something quite different. In the cold December light, the far side of the Sea of Marmora disappeared over the horizon, its waters lay flat and dull. They gave an impression of immeasurable depth and secrecy. What lay beneath that opaque surface? Now and then, ships would cross— small wooden sailing ships such as those he had often seen in the great ports along the Rhine. Occasionally, far out at the edge of his vision, larger vessels loomed out of the winter mists, then disappeared.

The morning after they made camp, he rose with the dawn, finally free to seek Emma. Baldwin's camp was down by the shore of the sea, he had learned that much. Before he could leave, however, Hugh appeared outside his tent.

"Count Garnier would have you attend morning mass and break fast with him, young sir," he said.

Theo's heart sank, but a summons from the count could not be ignored. He followed Hugh over to his foster father's tent.

"What ails you this morning?" the count asked as Theo squirmed beside him at his campfire. The priests had finished saying mass; he and the count had returned to Garnier's tent. The first meal of the day was spread out on trestle tables: joints of meat, game birds, slabs of thick bread and overflowing flagons of ale. "You are wiggling around like a dog with fleas, and you haven't eaten a thing. Are you not well?"

"I'm fine, my lord. Fine," Theo answered. He grabbed a rib of venison and chewed at it. Normally he would have wolfed it down, but today the meat was dry in his mouth. He couldn't swallow. In his hurry to finish the meal and seek out Emma, he quaffed an overlarge mouthful of ale and choked on it.

When he was finally released, he had to restrain himself from running. He skirted the main tents and headed for the shore, almost frantic with impatience. The camp was noisy with the usual morning bustle. Children ran screaming underfoot, mothers called, men swore. A donkey brayed and was answered by another far in the distance. The smoke from innumerable fires mingled to cast a pall over the whole vast encampment. The smells of roasting meat, animal dung and unwashed bodies were so thick, they were almost visible. Theo kicked through the refuse that was already beginning to pile up, and hurried even more.

He came up to a tent, and heard a whining, bickering argument break out on the other side of it. A few sharp words stilled it; Theo's heart jumped as he recognized Emma's voice. He moved cautiously around the tent. Lord Baldwin's three children were sitting around the fire, finishing up their morning meal; Emma was with them.

Godvere's voice called from another, larger tent nearby.

"Emma, bring them to me now. I wish them to stay with me for a while. You may see to the washing."

Emma rose, looked up and saw Theo. She started, then put a finger to her lips and gestured toward the children.

Wait, she mouthed silently.

Theo backed into the bushes. A few minutes later, he heard a rustle, and Emma emerged, looking slightly disheveled and flushed.

"How good it is to see you!" she exclaimed. "I've been thinking of you all these miles since Hungary." The words burst out, and then she clapped a hand to her mouth. "I mean—" she added hastily, drawing herself up and making a quick attempt to recover her dignity. "I wondered how you were."

"I would have sought you out sooner," Theo answered, "but I could not." He, too, made an effort to keep his words light, his manner dignified. He would have liked to appear aloof, but that was impossible. There was no way under heaven he could suppress the smile that spread almost from ear to ear. She had been thinking about him!

"I have the most enormous load of washing to do. Down by the lake . . ."

"I'll go with you," Theo said.

"Not very fitting for a knight," Emma replied, "to keep company with a nursemaid and her laundry!" She had herself back under control and the teasing note had returned to her voice. This time, Theo didn't mind at all.

"I can help you carry it," he began.

"Now, that would be a sight, wouldn't it? A knight *carrying laundry*. No, that would never do. I know a spot where no one will see us. We'll meet there." She pointed to the woods behind Theo. "Go by that path, the one that leads off through the trees. Wait for me at the bottom, by the water's edge. I'll follow as soon as I can."

Theo followed her directions and found himself on a rocky shore nestled into a small, deserted cove. He looked out over the water—sparkling and deep blue today, with small flecks of waves roughening up the surface—and breathed deeply of the tingling air. He felt light and buoyant and unbelievably happy.

Emma appeared almost immediately, her arms full of linens. She dumped them all into the water, wet them, rubbed them with handfuls of greasy soap, then set to rinsing them and beating them on the rocks. All the while, she kept up a stream of chatter, as if she were feeling self-conscious, afraid perhaps of having seemed too bold. Theo let the words flow over him, only half listening. He was much more concerned with just watching her. Suddenly, she stopped the idle talk and sat back. Her face became serious.

"I think there may be trouble coming, Theo," she said. "It might be well for you to be prepared."

"How so?" Theo asked. It was amazing how the wind coming in off the sea tangled her hair into a forest of black curls, he thought.

"I heard my lord Baldwin talking to the duke last night at supper. It seems that Hugh of Vermandois has already arrived at Constantinople. They say he received wondrous gifts from the emperor Alexius himself, and indeed the reports are so lush that my lord is thinking of going on ahead to get his own share before the rest of you pile in. But there are other rumors as well, and they're more troubling."

"Other rumors?" Theo asked. "Of what sort?" His mind was not really on what she was saying. On a splendid day such as this, he did not want to hear rumors of trouble. It was still hard to believe that Emma was actually here. It was hard to believe how happy her presence made him, too, and that was giving him pause for thought.

"Well, some say that, gifts or no gifts, Hugh and all his men are being held prisoner."

"Do Baldwin and the duke give any substance to that talk?" Reluctantly, Theo began to pay attention to what Emma was saying, but he knew very well how easily rumors spread around the camp, and knew also that most of them were sheer inventions.

Emma paused and pushed a wet strand of hair out of her eyes. Washing the clothes had brought the color to her cheeks, and Theo thought she looked exceedingly fair.

"They do," she said.

"It's probably just nonsense."

"Probably. But I know the duke and Lord Baldwin are worried that when the men hear the rumors they will be angry. The common soldiers and the archers and others are expecting a great deal when we reach Constantinople, you know. They have been told they can rest there until all the great lords and princes have assembled with their armies, and they will be given all they need for their comfort. The way has been hard so far, Theo—they feel they deserve a reward, not punishment. At least, that is what the good duke says. My lord Baldwin cares not a whit about his men's feelings or comfort. He worries only about his own interests."

"Nonsense, surely," Theo said. "The men are much too afraid of the duke to disobey him. We are not the rabble that Peter the Hermit's army was," he added, echoing Amalric's words. Surely Emma exaggerated. After all, women loved to gossip. This army would remain disciplined, Theo was certain of it.

"Still," Emma said, "perhaps you should keep alert." She bent back to her laundry and picked up a garment. As she beat it against a rock, Theo saw that her fingers were red and swollen. The December wind off the Sea of Marmora that was tousling her hair so delightfully was cold, and the water, he realized, must be frigid.

"You must let me help," he said, and bent to pick up another piece of clothing. He flung it against the rock with vigor, but most of it slapped into the water. Spray dashed up and drenched Emma.

"My thanks, Theo! You are indeed of great assistance!"

Theo crimsoned. "I'm sorry," he began. What a fool he must look! Then he sputtered as a spray of water, aimed expertly by Emma, hit him.

Emma let out a peal of laughter and fell back against the bank.

"Your face! If only you could see your face! You

look like a rabbit that's just seen the biggest hound of its life!"

Theo leaped back to his feet, humiliated.

"Oh, Theo, I'm sorry. I'm not laughing at you. It's just . . . It's just, your face was so funny!" Her mouth twitched and she burst into another gale of laughter.

A wave of anger surged through Theo. He scowled. He was not used to being laughed at by a maid.

Emma sobered immediately. "Please," she said. "Stay with me. Do not go away angry because I am such a nitwit. I will not laugh anymore, I promise!" She fastened her eyes upon him, pleading, all trace of mockery gone.

The anger and humiliation melted away. Theo heaved a huge sigh. There was no way he could refuse that look.

By the time he returned to his own camp, he had forgotten all about her warning. It came back to him with a jolt, however, as soon as he arrived.

† † †

"The count wishes to see you immediately," William said. The groom's face was tense, his brow furrowed.

"What is it?" Theo asked.

"I know not, sir," William answered.

Theo knew at once the man was lying. He debated for a moment whether to press him further, then decided against it. The count would tell him soon enough if anything was afoot. He shrugged, and made for Garnier's tent.

The sound of loud, furious voices carried over to the edge of the clearing. Theo could make out the count's voice and, to his surprise, Godfrey's as well. Something must have happened indeed if the duke was that angry. He pushed through the tent flap warily. Once inside, he stood waiting to be noticed.

"There is no excuse," the duke stormed. "How many men are missing?"

"At least five knights and squires, with all their foot soldiers and archers. They must have slipped away before dawn." The count's voice was low and trembled with tightly controlled anger. He passed a hand over his brow and turned his eyes away from Godfrey's, catching sight of Theo as he did so.

"Ah, Theo." He gave a sigh of relief. "You are well come, my son. I have need of you here." He turned toward a group of men standing behind him. Theo recognized them as the most loyal of the count's knights—friends all, and known to him since boyhood. "You will ride with Aimery and these others. Some of our knights have gone berserk and have ridden off with all their men. We discovered their absence just after you left this morning. Already tales have reached us that they have attacked a village nearby and pillaged it. This insanity must be stopped. Alexius will not tolerate it. He will send his forces—" Garnier's control over his words slipped and his voice broke. Theo could imagine only too well what the count was thinking. This army was not to follow in the footsteps of Peter the Hermit's band. They were to be a true crusader army, fighting only for God and for the liberation of Jerusalem.

"You must go after them and stop them." He turned back to the other knights and addressed their leader, Aimery. "Take as many of the men as you need and leave now. At once!"

Theo bowed to his foster father, and bowed again to the duke. He backed out of the tent.

So, Emma had been right, he thought as he ran for his campsite. He must not take her words so lightly in future.

"William!" he called as he reached his tent. "Saddle Centurion. Make him ready for battle." He pushed into the tent and began to dress himself in his metal-ringed leather tunic. Of course, it wouldn't really be a battle, he told himself. They wouldn't be fighting their own men. Still . . .

His blood pounded in his ears as he raced back out. William held Centurion ready. Theo's hands, as he took the reins, shook slightly. He grasped the pommel of his saddle to steady them. He must not look like an excitable, untried boy in front of his groom. When he had got himself under control, he turned back to William.

"You knew, didn't you," he said. "You knew they were going to leave the camp."

"One of the grooms . . ."

"Why didn't you say something, or warn me?" Even as he asked the question, Theo knew it was useless. There was a brotherhood among the grooms that excluded even the most beloved masters, and he was certainly not one of those. "Never mind," he said. He put his foot in the stirrup and swung himself up into the saddle. "Is there food enough in my saddlebags?"

"Yes, master. For several days at least. And two skins each of water and wine." The groom looked relieved.

Theo hesitated. I should discipline him, he thought. He should have told me what he had learned. If I can't count on his loyalty . . . But there was nothing he could do at the moment. When I return, he told himself. William cannot go unpunished. He frowned. This business of being a master was difficult.

A shout called him to attention.

"Theo! Are you ready?" It was Amalric. "Godfrey has given me permission to ride with you. What fun! At last we will see some excitement!" He galloped heavily over to Theo, then reined in his charger with a yank that caused the animal to shake its head angrily and foam at the bit.

"You do your beast damage," Theo said. Amalric's exuberance grated on him. Did he not realize the enormity of the situation? The whole crusade was in danger.

Amalric reached over to throw an arm around Theo's shoulders. His eyes were bright, his cheeks flushed. His enthusiasm was contagious, and in spite of himself, Theo felt his own heart begin to race.

† † †

It was not until morning of the next day that they reached the village the crusaders had raided. They saw smoke rising from the site long before the houses themselves could be seen. Theo and Amalric rode side by side, as usual. Amalric kept up a constant stream of talk as they drew near, but Theo gradually fell silent. He looked around him with growing dread. No birds sang in the trees. He listened in vain for barking dogs. They rounded a bend in the path and the village itself came into view. Nearly every house was burned to the ground; some were still smoldering. There was no sign of life anywhere. A few sacks of grain lay spilt in the middle of the road. The body of a cat lay beside them under a seething blanket of flies. Theo felt his gorge rise. He and Amalric reined in their horses and stared. Finally, Amalric spoke.

"The townsfolk have taken to the hills, I warrant," he said. "Those who were left . . ." The words came out halting and uncertain, unlike his usual breezy manner. He shrugged his shoulders and tried to force the enthusiasm back into his voice. "We'll catch up with the scoundrels who did this, never fear, and take them back to face the duke. That will teach them a lesson!"

"Our own men." Theo's voice was heavy with disbelief. "Our own men destroyed this village, Amalric, and it was a Christian village."

"We'll catch them. They'll be punished." Amalric's face was blank. He didn't meet Theo's eyes. "These things happen in war. It can't be helped."

"We're not at war here." Theo stopped as Amalric dug spurs into his horse with a vicious kick and forged away. He stared after his friend. Amalric might be able to find excuses, to make some sense out of this, but he, Theo, could not.

It took eight days to find the renegade knights and soldiers—eight days of following behind and traveling through ruined villages and ravaged countryside. It seemed the soldiers had, indeed, gone mad. Here and there, Theo caught sight of survivors, but any who saw them ran quickly for the shelter of the woods.

"Should we not stay and help them?" he asked. It seemed to him that they must do *something* to atone for the terrible harm their own men had done. But Aimery just shook his head.

"We can help them best by leaving them alone. They want no more of us." His face was grim, etched with lines Theo had not noticed before.

By the time they did catch up to the marauding army, the renegades had had their fill of violence and looting, and were on their way back. Count Garnier's men took them under immediate arrest, but they seemed little chastened. Their saddlebags bulged, and they were red-eyed from carousing. Theo was sickened by the sight of them. Not so Amalric, however, who seemed to have recovered all of his original excitement. He pointed to a soldier who wore a stained rag tied around his head.

"Look, Theo, blood! That one has seen battle!"

"Battle? Cutting down unarmed villagers? Do you call that battle?" Theo's words were heavy with disgust. For the moment, Amalric sickened him as much as the soldiers did. This time, it was Theo who turned and rode away.

Five

By Yuletide, they were encamped on the stony, sparsely grassed hills outside the walls of Constantinople. The weather was raw and cold, although as yet there was no snow. The priests celebrated the Christmas masses with the domes and spires of all the churches of the great city looming behind them. Theo had never seen such a city before; he was in a frenzy of excitement to explore it. The emperor Alexius was cautious, however. It wasn't until the Christmas celebrations were over that he began to

58

allow small groups in. Amalric was quick to invite Theo to investigate the pleasures of the town's taverns with him, but Theo demurred. His friendship with Amalric was back on its sound footing, and he had managed to convince himself that his judgment of his friend was too harsh, but there was so much else he wanted to see in the city. Then Emma appeared at his campsite early one morning before he had even eaten.

"Theo!" She stood before him, breathless, and a little uncertain. "I have the day to myself and permission to visit the city. Will you go with me?"

He didn't hesitate. Emma would be the ideal person to explore Constantinople with. Besides, he had had little opportunity to seek her out in the past few days, and he had missed her.

"Most certainly, I will," he answered. "I have no duties today—I will ask permission of the count."

Within the hour, they presented themselves at the massive, metal-studded gate at the western edge of the city. Emma pressed through it eagerly and pulled Theo with her. Before them, tree-lined streets and alleys beckoned. Enormous houses of stone, unlike any Theo had seen before, sat surrounded by gardens, beautiful even in the cold of winter.

"I thought the churches of Cologne magnificent," he murmured in awe, "but these surpass even them."

"Truly," Emma agreed. "I could never have imagined such places. They are not covered in gold, though, as was said."

"And the streets are not laden with jewels," Theo added with a laugh.

"But they are wonderful, are they not?"

"They are," Theo said. There was something about the grace and the symmetry of the city that pleased him to the depths of his soul. A man could be happy living in such a place, he thought. The glory and the thrill of war seemed remote and unreal in such a setting.

The marketplace, where they had been told they could find all manner of foods and merchandise, was their main destination, but they lost themselves repeatedly in the maze of streets. Only after stumbling upon the old Roman aqueduct did they find it. The immense stone columns of the waterway towered over them, dwarfing all the buildings around. These pillars supported the gigantic open stone pipeline, built so efficiently by the Romans, that still brought the city's supply of water coursing down from the hills. Theo and Emma stood for a moment, heads tilted back, gawking at the spillway far above them; then they moved on into the market.

As soon as they entered, Theo was overwhelmed with the sights, sounds and smells of it. As he sniffed in the smoky, spice-scented air, the smells wafted around him. Some he could identify—vanilla, cloves, herbs of many kinds—and others were strange to him. Color and confusion reigned. The owners of the stalls called out ceaselessly, hawking their wares, until their voices blended into one loud jumble. The sound of thousands of tiny tapping hammers led him, with Emma in tow, to an area where men battered out platters of silver and copper. Looms thumped and clattered as women wove brightly hued wool into shawls and blankets.

"Oh, look, Theo—shoes! My lady gave me a few coppers and I mean to have a pair." Emma darted over to a stall and began to sort through the assembled footwear. The stall owner, a large, florid, black-haired woman with snapping dark eyes, unleashed a torrent of words at her.

"Greek, I expect," Emma said in an aside to Theo. "I know not a word of it." Undaunted, she held up the pair of soft leather shoes she had chosen and began to bargain with wild, expressive sweeps of her hands. The woman answered with gestures of her own, and an even greater flood of language. To Theo's astonishment, they seemed to understand each other completely. A deal was struck and Emma handed over her few coppers. Then there was nothing for it but to put her new shoes on immediately. She plomped herself down on the cobblestones beside the stall, ripped off her old worn shoes and bound the new ones on. She leaped to her feet and took Theo's arm.

"Are they not fine?" she asked at least ten times as they moved on, stopping each time to stick out a foot and admire it.

Next, they made their way to the food stalls. The aromas were irresistible, the foodstuffs exotic and enticing. They bought sizzling hot, fragrantly spiced meat pies that tasted strongly of mutton and garlic, and washed them down with a light, warm, pleasant-tasting mead. They tried the small black fruit called olives. When Emma made a face at the sour, flat taste, Theo mocked her, then persevered until he began to like them. They tried a strong goat cheese wrapped in grape leaves and drizzled with oil from the olives. Finally, they pushed on through the throngs of people to the other side of the market, and found themselves on a wide, spacious avenue adorned with statues and columns, and dotted with tree-filled plazas that gave shelter from the nipping wind.

"Look!" Theo exclaimed suddenly. "The Hippodrome!" He had heard so much of this stadium—famous for the public games and spectacles that had taken place there ever since the time of the Romans.

"Let's peek in," Emma said. "There's a gate. It's closed, but we can see through." She ran over to it. Theo caught up to her and peered through the iron railings. He could see a vast oval enclosure, ringed with stone tiers. He had heard that over a hundred thousand people could be seated in the Hippodrome. Several tall columns ran in a straight line lengthwise down the center of it. Today, it stood vast and empty, but in Theo's mind it was crowded with spectators. Their roar filled his head. Chariots pulled by crazed, frantic horses careened around the track.

One obelisk was sheathed in gleaming bronze; another column was topped with three serpents' heads holding aloft a tripod that shone golden in the weak winter sun. This was a pagan monument, Theo knew, dedicated to the old Roman god Apollo. The western Christian church disapproved of such things as these and the many other heathen icons that the Byzantine Christians kept by them, but the beauty of the monument entranced him nonetheless.

Emma was eager to go on. Beyond the Hippodrome was Saint Sophia, the Hagia Sophia— one of the oldest and most revered churches in Christendom. Theo could see its dome towering over all the other buildings, even over the Great Palace of the emperor Alexius himself.

"There, Emma. That is where I want to go." Of all the holy churches, the Hagia Sophia was the one Theo most wanted to see. There, he could kneel and pray.

I will pray for the success of our crusade, he thought. Here, it can really begin. The memory of the destroyed Christian villages flickered through his mind, but he pushed it firmly aside. That is not how it will be, he resolved. From here, we go on renewed. From here, the crusade will be a glory to God, and nothing else.

They entered the courtyard, then directed their steps to the small door at the side. Only the emperor himself, Theo had been told, could use the main entrance. Once inside the church, they passed through a low, arched doorway surmounted by a glowing mosaic of the Virgin Mary holding the child Jesus on her lap, with the great emperors Justinian and Constantine paying homage on either side of her. Theo stopped so suddenly that Emma bumped into him, and he heard her gasp, echoing his own sudden intake of breath. Never could he have imagined what now lay before him. Above, the shining dome stretched up higher than the tower of any church Theo had ever seen. The circular vastness was so great that Theo felt almost dizzy with the sense of space. All the columns and arches were intricately carved; the walls and ceiling glowed with the rich colors of the mosaics and paintings that covered every surface. The figures of Jesus and his disciples looked down on them from paintings illuminated with gold. Countless windows let in streams of light. Around the top ran a gallery enriched with a filigree of ironwork and colonnaded with smaller arches that duplicated the taller arches below. A magnificent cross blazed out from behind the altar, dominating all with a golden splendor of its own.

Theo brought his gaze back to look at the people around him. The church was crowded, filled with ordinary people as well as with men and women who were obviously of the nobility, but of a nobility very different from what Theo knew. On the whole, the knights of the German and Frankish lands were a rough lot. Their ladies dressed colorfully but modestly in woollens during the winter months, and in linen shifts when the weather was warm. The knights themselves worried little about their attire other than to ensure it was warm enough in the cold weather. The clothing of these nobles, however, dazzled Theo's eyes. The ladies' dresses shimmered and whispered with the softness of silk. Their hair was ornately styled and dripping with jewels. More jewels sparkled on their necks, arms and fingers. Shawls of gossamer wool were draped over their shoulders. If anything, the men outshone the women: they, too, were brilliantly dressed and flashing with gems. They knelt to pray on tiny, many-hued carpets.

Suddenly, Theo was uncomfortably aware of his dirty, travel-stained tunic and the coarseness of his drab, heavy cloak. He slid one leg in front of the other to cover a rip in his hose, but no one was paying the slightest attention to him. He tore his eyes away from the lords and ladies and dropped to his knees, fixing his eyes on the cross. Emma sank down beside him.

They remained praying for a long time. At last, Theo stood. When he glanced down at Emma, she was still staring at the altar; there were tears on her cheeks. She looked suddenly small and vulnerable, and he felt a wave of protectiveness surge through him as he reached down to help her to her feet.

"It is God's work we do, is it not?" Her words came out in the barest, but fiercest, of whispers.

"Of course it is. It has to be." Theo turned his back

on the brilliant personages, who seemed to be gossiping with each other as much as praying, and put them out of his mind. It was the crusade that mattered. Nothing else.

On the way out, Theo spied an old woman in the courtyard. She sat hunched under a woollen shawl, warmed only by a small fire. In front of her, spread out on a carpet, were bunches of sweetly scented dried herbs and roses. On an impulse, he stopped. He bent over her offerings and chose one. Gravely, he turned to Emma and gave it to her.

Emma took it with a startled, sideways glance at him. Then she lowered her eyes and buried her nose in the bouquet. "No one has ever . . ." The words came out muffled. "Thank you." It was so quiet, he barely heard.

"You should have come with us!" Amalric exclaimed the next morning. "We found a lively tavern, with men who made music and wenches who danced to it. The wine they make here is so strong my head is still spinning! You would have had a far better time with me than you had traipsing around churches with a servant maid!"

Theo smiled, but didn't answer. He thought not.

† † †

At first, Theo welcomed the pause at Constantinople, but as the weeks passed, he became restless again.

Some remnants of Peter the Hermit's forces arrived in the camp. Theo was present when Duke Godfrey interviewed them.

"Treason," they maintained. "Nothing less than treachery on the part of the imperial forces of Alexius led to our defeat."

"The duke does not believe them," Amalric said, "and nor do I. They just seek excuses for their own failure."

Theo was inclined to agree, but he heard the soldiers around him grumbling. They, too, were becoming impatient with the delay.

"If we could only go on!" Amalric was indignant. "Alexius has no right to hold us up here."

"But we must wait for the other lords who are coming to meet us," Theo answered.

"We could wait on the other side of Constantinople. He could let us pass. The only reason he keeps us cooling our heels here is because Godfrey will not swear allegiance to him."

Theo knew Amalric was right.

"My lord has only one master, Henry, the emperor of the Holy Roman Empire. He cannot swear loyalty to another," Amalric growled.

Again, Theo agreed.

Time dragged. Theo took to walking the camp from end to end, usually finishing up at the city walls. They towered above him, blank and forbidding.

It snowed, lightly at first, then more heavily. Theo found it hard to keep himself warm at night in his small tent. He slept wrapped in his woollen cloak and covered with a bearskin, but still woke stiff and cold in the frosty early mornings. Centurion, on the other hand, delighted in the winter weather. His coat grew rough and thick, and he downed the rations of four normal horses.

"Hugh of Vermandois has sworn the oath," Amalric reported with a sneer as he sought Theo out one morning. "Alexius's lapdog, that's all he is. The emperor thought Hugh would persuade the duke to give in and sign as well, but my lord Godfrey sent him back with a flea in his ear, I tell you."

Perhaps not a wise move, Theo thought. He was proven right when the supplies coming from the emperor suddenly ceased.

Angered by the short rations, the men erupted. Led by Godfrey's brother Baldwin, they began to raid the suburbs of Constantinople. Alexius reacted quickly.

"We are to move to Pera," Count Garnier told Theo as they ate together one morning. "The emperor has been most tactful. Pera is only a short distance away, and he suggests that we will be more sheltered from the winter winds there, but I think his real reason is that his imperial police will be able to watch and control us more closely there. I must say I cannot blame him. If Lord Godfrey cannot keep even his own brother in check . . ."

Theo looked at his foster father in surprise. It was the closest he had ever heard the count come to criticizing the duke. Garnier must be troubled, indeed.

Amalric, of course, was mightily offended. "They think us nothing but barbarians," he raged. "They treat us like thieves!"

"With good reason," Theo replied, but the behavior of the Byzantines had angered him as well. He had accompanied Count Garnier to a feast given by some of the nobles in the city, and although the visitors had dressed in their finest, Theo had been painfully aware of the disparaging glances cast their way. More than one elegant eyebrow had been raised at the rude manners of the Frankish knights. The Franks, on their part, spent the next few days mocking the effete manners of the Byzantines, but underlying their jokes was a bitter resentment.

More time passed. Still the other lords did not appear; still the emperor and Godfrey quarreled. Life in the camp around Pera settled into a routine that soon turned to boredom. Godfrey and his men were lodged within the city, but their families and all the others, including Count Garnier and his men, were encamped just outside.

Theo had fallen into the habit of meeting with Emma in the evenings to talk. He knew a few tongues wagged at this, but life in the camp was informal, and he cared little about the opinions of others. The count saw no harm in their friendship, and that was what mattered most to him. Emma always had the latest camp gossip, and she had a way of exaggerating the most trifling of stories until they became so ridiculous that the two of them usually ended up in gales of laughter. It was a relief to Theo to spend time with her after the tension of daily life in the camp. Amalric grew so frenzied with hatred against the Byzantine emperor that he could speak or think of nothing else. He was not alone in his feelings—indeed, most of the camp felt the way he did—but Theo could take only so much of his ranting.

Amalric had also angered Theo by teasing him about Emma, and had made a coarse, insinuating jest. Theo had reacted with an explosion of anger, and they would have come to blows if Amalric had not backed down. After his anger had cooled, however, Theo was shocked at his reaction. He had not thought that he could get so irate over such a thing. Just what did this girl mean to him? She seemed to be on his mind constantly. Somehow, Emma was different from the other girls he had dallied with, and he dared not behave with her as he had with the others. Friendly as she was, she held herself aloof from everyone. He had once seen another young knight throw an arm carelessly around her, only to find himself flat on his back in the mud. Emma was definitely not to be trifled with.

The end of March arrived. Winter was over and the weather began to grow warm; Holy Week was fast approaching. News spread that the other crusading armies were near. The tension in the camp reached an unbearable peak. Surely now, Theo thought, Alexius would let them move on. Instead, feeling perhaps that the other leaders would support him in his demand for oaths of allegiance, Alexius began to restrict the crusaders' supplies further. First, he withheld fodder for the horses; then, as Holy Week drew nearer, he cut off supplies of fish and bread. This was the final insult. How could they not have fish during Holy Week?

The crusaders exploded. Several of the knights led their men in raids on neighboring villages. Count Garnier kept his own knights and troops in order, but even the most loyal of them, Theo included, began to chafe at the bit.

"Things cannot go on like this," he told Emma one evening.

"No, they cannot," she agreed. "I fear for what is going to happen. It cannot be good."

Theo fell silent beside her.

On the Wednesday evening of Holy Week itself, Godfrey called a conference in his tent.

"Come with me," the count said to Theo. "I like not the sound of this."

They arrived to find the other nobles already assembled, Baldwin foremost among them. Godfrey was speaking. Theo had never seen him so inflamed.

"The emperor persists in his impossible demands. He has denied us passage across the Bosphorus, and he insists on my oath. That I will not give. The time has come for force. We attack Constantinople tomorrow."

Theo could not believe what he was hearing. Attack Constantinople? Constantinople was one of Christendom's most holy cities, second only to Jerusalem! Attack the emperor Alexius himself?

†   †   †

The next morning as he prepared for battle in the darkness before dawn, Theo moved as if he were weighted down with chains of iron. Again they were to wage war against Christians! The Byzantines were hateful, but they were the crusaders' own people. *They* were not the enemy he had sworn to conquer!

Centurion's breath steamed into the cool air. In the darkness around him, Theo could hear the clink of metal, the squeak of leather being adjusted, tightened. The occasional oath broke the stillness, but there was an unusual quiet. No one, it seemed, was going into this attack with bravado. Theo did not speak to William. He had disciplined his groom for not reporting what he had known about the planned outbreak of the count's and Godfrey's men, and William had been sullen and resentful ever since.

When all was ready, Theo accepted William's hand up and swung into the saddle. He reined Centurion in and guided him toward the gathering of Count Garnier's knights and squires. The count greeted him soberly as Theo fell in between his foster father and

Aimery. In silence, they walked their horses to the edge of Pera to wait for Duke Godfrey.

As they drew near to Pera's walls, pandemonium erupted. Cries broke out from within. Flames shot into the air. Men shouted; women screamed. The town gates were flung open, and Godfrey galloped out, closely followed by his knights and their squires. They had taken their revenge: the houses they had been lodged in were burning to the ground.

In an instant, all was mad confusion. Trumpets blared, war cries echoed across the hillside. When Count Garnier gave the signal, his trumpeters added to the cacophony, and he charged to join the duke. Belatedly, Theo urged Centurion to follow, and the warhorse burst into a gallop. All around Theo, men and horses jostled and jockeyed for position. The thunder of hooves and the cries of the knights filled the air. Dust rose in choking waves. The men in the crusading army fell in behind their leaders and galloped toward Constantinople.

Theo found himself riding so close to the count that their knees brushed. The crush of other animals and riders beside and around him blotted out all else. Blindly, he gave Centurion his head and concentrated on keeping up with his foster father. His heart was beating so loudly that his ears rang with the force of it, and he thought it would tear through the very walls of his chest. There was no time now to think about what they were doing, no time to think about who they were about to attack. He gasped for breath in the thick, suffocating air.

The army strung out as it thundered across the bridge at the headwaters of the Golden Horn, then reassembled outside the walls of Constantinople itself. For a moment, there was a pause. Theo struggled to calm himself. In front of him the great city slept, seemingly unprepared for attack.

Trumpets split the early morning. Godfrey shouted an order. Chaos erupted around Theo again. Yelling their battle cries, the duke's men charged the gate that led to the palace. Theo glimpsed Amalric among the foremost. Then, suddenly, as his own group rallied to follow Godfrey, Theo saw archers appear on the walls. Again, he spurred Centurion on and charged forward beside Count Garnier, but this time he held his breath. They were driving straight into the archers. He shrank in his saddle, and his stomach tightened into a ball as he braced himself against the onslaught of arrows that was sure to come. Incredibly, the first volley passed harmlessly over their heads.

When the gate did not give way under the foot soldiers' assault, Godfrey's men drew back in confusion. At that moment, all the other gates opened and Alexius's troops poured out. Again, Theo braced himself, but again, incredibly, the troops did not attack. They halted outside the walls, facing the now flustered duke and his army. Foot soldiers with halberds glinting in the first pale rays of the sun arrayed themselves deliberately in front of their mounted knights. The archers high on the top of the wall above them let loose another volley of arrows. Once more, the missiles flew over the crusaders' heads.

Godfrey's army froze, every man in his place, waiting for the duke's signal. For what seemed like an eternity, Theo watched as the two opposing forces faced each other. Then, instead of crying out the expected command to attack, Godfrey wheeled his mount around and galloped off the field. After an instant of silent disbelief, his men turned their horses and followed him. Aghast, Theo looked at the count. The count returned his stare with his mouth set in a hard, grim line.

As they retreated, Theo looked back over his shoulder. The domes and spires of Constantinople gleamed in the sunlight, unconquered, inviolable. He could make no sense of his feelings. Relief because they had not fought fellow Christians, and because he was alive. But his heart still thudded and his ears still rang. Gradually, the terror of the charge drained away, but in its place rose a vast emptiness.

He felt—cheated.

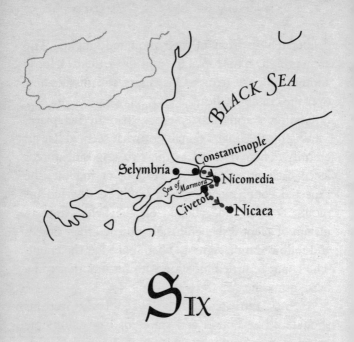

S_{IX}

In the aftermath of this debacle, Godfrey finally consented to take the oath of allegiance to Alexius. The ceremony was held on Easter Sunday. Godfrey, Baldwin and their leading lords swore to acknowledge the emperor as overlord of the campaign, and to hand over to the Byzantine officials any reconquered land that had previously belonged to the emperor. Theo saw Baldwin's mouth twist at that pledge, and remembered Emma telling him of Baldwin's greed. No land would be relinquished by the duke's brother if he could help it, oath or no oath, Theo thought.

Following the ceremony, the emperor organized a mammoth celebration. Even though Alexius had been horrified by Godfrey's attack during Holy Week itself, he showered gifts and money upon the assembled knights, and ended the festivities with a banquet of huge proportions. Then Godfrey and all his troops were transported across the Bosphorus, the narrow stretch of water that separated Constantinople from the lands to the east. They marched on to an encampment at Pelecanum, on the road to Nicomedia. There they would wait for the other crusading armies to catch up with them.

The weather melted into spring. One fine morning, Amalric and Theo stood together on a rise that danced with scarlet poppies and white and yellow daisies. The long grasses whispered around their legs. In the distance, toward Constantinople, a cloud of dust arose.

"That will be Bohemond of Taranto," Amalric announced with satisfaction. "Finally. They say he did not hesitate to give his oath to Alexius, but demanded to be named commander-in-chief of all the imperial forces in Asia."

"And did he get his wish?"

Amalric made a face. "Alexius waffled, what else? Gave him some vague assurances. Bohemond's brother, Tancred, was more clever. He slipped by

Constantinople at night and avoided Alexius altogether. But wait until Raymond arrives. Then we'll see the fur fly."

"Why?" Theo asked. These political wranglings irked him more and more. The crusaders were all sworn to the same cause; why did there need to be so much dissention?

"Raymond is the count of Toulouse. Connected to the royal houses of Spain, and very full of himself, he is. Lord Godfrey says Raymond is immensely jealous of Bohemond and feels he should be the leader."

Theo shrugged his shoulders irritably.

The powerful Bishop Adhemar of Le Puy was next to arrive with all his forces. Theo had heard many stories about this man. A holy cleric he was, but also a formidable soldier. Theo watched with interest as the bishop rode into the encampment. He sat tall in his saddle at the forefront of his army, helmetless, his iron gray hair flowing to his shoulders. An impressive man, even from this distance. He radiated strength and assurance.

Raymond sent word that he would join the crusading armies later, as did Robert, duke of Normandy, the final lord for whom they waited.

"Now," Amalric exulted, "now we can go!"

They left by the end of April on a bright and golden day. Loaded down with supplies and equipment, they put all resentments behind them. Nearly a hundred thousand strong now, scarlet crosses of Christ vivid on their chests and shoulders, the crusaders felt their spirits rise, and the mood throughout the ranks was again one of optimism and wild excitement. The heavy, bone-shaking gait of the warhorses was too uncomfortable to bear for long periods of time, so Theo and the other knights rode lighter palfreys. Their grooms and squires, mounted on nags or mules, led the more formidable, heavier animals. Behind them was a special detachment of engineers provided by the emperor Alexius.

Pennants flew in the brisk spring breezes. There was a smell of fresh earth and a newness to the air. The jangling, clanging sounds of an immense army on the march and all its followers echoed back from the hills on the one side, and over the shining blue of the long arm of the Sea of Marmora on the other.

It was an incredible, impossible, unbelievably unwieldy procession. The last of the pilgrims did not even set out until far into the day—long after the glittering head of the army had passed out of sight and was well on its way. Theo often turned in his saddle to look back at the people behind him. The line stretched out as far as he could see.

He could not bring himself to be as jubilant as the others. Eight months, he thought. We have been on the road for eight long months. He knew that many in the crusade had assumed they would have been in Jerusalem by now, that the Holy City would have been long conquered. Instead . . . Memories of the hardships they had already endured crowded into his head. The atrocities . . .

Eight months. And they had only just begun.

† † †

They camped that night at Nicomedia, on the way to their first objective, Nicaea, a Turkish city on the shores of the Ascanian Lake. There the battle to liberate the Holy Lands would truly begin.

Theo was called to a conference in Godfrey's tent almost as soon as he had finished making his camp. Leaving William to see to the fire and boil up a stew for their dinner, he made his way quickly to Count Garnier, and they went on together. Godfrey was speaking as they pushed aside the flap to his tent and entered. He had recovered from the disaster at Constantinople and, now that they were actually on their way, he was back to his old self. Looking at him, Theo told himself for perhaps the hundredth time that the duke had made the wisest decision at Constantinople—indeed, the only decision. It would have been a catastrophe if he had pressed the attack. The crusaders could not have won, and hundreds of Christians would have been killed.

But Theo was still troubled by the feeling he had had when the duke had turned away. He *had* felt cheated. He had been revolted at the thought of fighting fellow Christians, but sometime during that mad charge his emotions had taken over. All thoughts of God and the crusade's noble purpose had fled his mind, and he had been filled with a wild exultation. He had been ready to fight, fellow Christians or not. Worse, he had been ready—even eager—to kill.

He had not seen Amalric for days after the aborted attack. When they finally did speak together, Amalric had been quick to defend the duke's action. It was obvious to Theo that Amalric was bitterly disappointed at not having done battle, and shared none of Theo's misgivings about these feelings. But Amalric would not hear any criticism of the duke. In any case, Theo could not bring himself to speak about that day, and when Amalric realized this he changed the subject with obvious relief.

"We are in luck," Duke Godfrey was saying as Theo followed his foster father into the tent. "The Seljuk sultan, Kilij Arslan, is away fighting on the eastern frontier. It was he who defeated Peter's army so easily, and perhaps because of that victory he does not take us seriously. If he thinks we will be as easy to conquer, he will soon learn his mistake. Foolishly, he has even left his wife and children in Nicaea."

"And all his treasure," Baldwin put in. His eyes gleamed. Theo could have sworn he was restraining himself with difficulty from licking his lips.

A disturbance at the tent's entrance interrupted them. A man pushed his way in, brushing past protesting guards. He was dirty and ragged, with limp, greasy hair hanging down around his shoulders, but in spite of his appearance, he held himself with the bearing of a king. His eyes shone with a peculiar sort of light. Theo stared at him.

"I am Peter. I have come to join you and bring those of my followers who are still with me to you. You will have need of me." His voice rang out within the tent.

Peter the Hermit himself!

Godfrey rose. He gestured to the guards to leave. "You are welcome," he said. "Your knowledge of this area will be invaluable to us." There was a long silence. No one would speak of Peter's defeat, or the reasons for it, but thoughts of it hung heavily in the air.

"Continue. I would hear your plans." Peter spoke regally, as if graciously giving permission to one of his underlings.

A faint flush colored Godfrey's cheeks. He sat down abruptly.

"We will march cautiously to Nicaea," he said. "I will send engineers ahead to widen the track, which I understand is narrow in places, and scouts to warn us of any possible ambush." He looked meaningfully at Peter. It had been a lack of just this kind of planning that had led to the hermit's downfall.

Amalric stood behind Godfrey. When Theo caught his eye, Amalric raised an eyebrow. His easy-going good humor seemed to be restored. He looked as if he were enjoying himself.

† † †

They waited at Nicomedia for three days until all the troops were assembled and ready. There were fields here where the armies could spread out and camp. Peter and the remains of his army made their own camp somewhat apart from the others. Theo had heard that the monk was a great preacher, but Peter held no congregation here. He spoke little to anyone and seemed to seethe with a bitterness that escaped only through his burning eyes.

The morning chosen for their departure dawned bright and clear; the sun now gave a hint of the heat that was to come in the months ahead. They rounded the eastern end of the Sea of Marmora and headed for Civetot. The poppy-strewn fields at Civetot pushed out in a triangle into the southern shore of the sea. It was here that Peter's followers had camped, and here where the Turkish army had flooded in after ambushing and destroying Peter's army in the narrow defile to the south. The sultan's men had massacred almost everyone: women, children, old men, priests. Theo gazed at the scene and his mind went back to the three wanderers he had seen in the tavern in Semlin. They must have been here, the girl and the child, camped somewhere on this very plain. The boy—he would have been among the soldiers, fighting. Near the shoreline, a tall tree lent some shade to the field, a cairn of stones on the ground under its branches. What had happened here? What was war really like? The waves of the sea lapped at the shore with deceptive peacefulness. The blood-red poppies swayed in the breeze.

They turned south, through the pass where Peter's men had been ambushed. The engineers had done their work well; the way had been widened, but bones still lay strewn around the entrance and among the rocks at the sides. Human bones—with shreds of skin still stretched over them here and there, and remnants of moldering cloth among them. A series of wooden crosses marked the cleared track. A hush fell over the column of knights as their mounts picked their way through.

"Did you see the huts on the hillsides with roofs thatched with sticks and twigs?" Amalric asked that night when he sought Theo out after his evening meal. "I saw goats on top of one of them, prancing around! One was even eating leaves that were still growing from it." His voice was hard and brittle, full of careless laughter, but there was a new look in his eyes.

It could almost have been fear, Theo thought, but dismissed the idea immediately. Amalric afraid? Impossible. He laughed with him. Yes, he had seen the goats. But in his mind, all he could see were the bones.

† † †

A week's steady marching brought them to Nicaea. As they drew near the city, Theo could see massive walls rising straight out of the water on the western side. The same walls ran around the other three sides; there were towers at regular intervals.

"That will be a tough nut to crack," Amalric said as they drew nearer and the walls loomed high before them. "Now at last I wager we will see real fighting." His face was flushed and eager. Any doubts or fears he might have been harboring had obviously been cast out. He fingered the pommel of his sword nervously; the palfrey he rode danced a few skittish steps as if sensing his excitement. Theo felt his own heart quicken.

The excitement was contagious and traveled quickly throughout the army. Godfrey camped outside the northern wall, while Tancred and Bohemond took the eastern side. Raymond arrived and closed the circle to the south. Men set about entrenching themselves with an almost feverish haste.

The Turkish garrison sent messengers to open negotiations with the armies, but when news came that the sultan and his army had turned back and were now hastening to Nicaea from the south, the crusaders were quick to bring all talks to a halt. Preparations for war began.

Theo sharpened his sword and dagger and polished his shield, then did so all over again. He checked Centurion's bridle, saddle and girthstraps himself, to the annoyance of William, who took it as an insult to his competence. He was keyed up to a fever pitch and jumped to his feet, heart suddenly racing, when Amalric appeared at his fireside late one evening. Amalric had been at the nightly conference in Godfrey's tent, and would bring news of when the attack would come. His friend was scowling, however, all traces of excitement gone.

"The sultan will attack from the south," he said, his voice sullen. "Raymond's army and the Bishop of Le Puy will see all the action. We are to remain here, and not fight at all! The walls must be guarded, the duke says, so that there will be no possibility of forces coming out of the city and attacking our rear." He paced back and forth beside the fire, kicking angrily at the smoldering embers.

Theo felt a wrench of disappointment. Was he never to see battle?

"Perhaps the sultan will not return that way," he said. "Perhaps he will trick us."

"He must come back that way." Amalric glared as if Theo were being deliberately stupid, aimed another kick at the fire, then turned and strode away into the darkness.

He was right. Theo awakened with the dawn to the sound of trumpets and wailing horns on the far side of the city. The camp was up in an instant, everyone desperate to know what was happening, the men in a frenzy at not being allowed to leave their posts.

The battle raged all day. Theo could only hear vague echoes. Now and then, scouts brought news.

The crusaders were beating back the Turks . . . The Turks were massacring the crusaders . . . Theo felt he would go mad at the enforced inaction, and he was not alone. The men were enraged at their helplessness. The walls of the city seemed unmanned, almost deserted, but a cautious foray toward them by several crusaders frantic for battle drew a skyful of arrows. The knights were sent to ride up and down among the foot soldiers and archers, to keep them in their ranks and alert. Theo welcomed the opportunity to do something—anything—but Centurion, who knew that a battle was underway, fought the slow pace his master insisted on. The warhorse was soon covered in sweat and foaming at the mouth as he champed at his bit. Theo needed all his strength and skill to hold the charger in.

It wasn't until night fell that the battle was over. Scouts arrived after dark with the news that the sultan's forces had retreated. Immediately, a delirious, almost insane joy swept away the paralyzing frustration of the previous hours. Shouts and cheers filled the air, and rose even louder when a detachment of Raymond's knights rode triumphantly into the camp, bearing the heads of their vanquished foes on pikes. The knights paraded their trophies before the gates of the city by torchlight, then hurled them into the enclosure within.

"That will show the Turks who they are up against," Amalric gloated, his eyes shining. Then his voice turned heavy with jealousy. "Next time, we must be the ones who fight! They cannot keep us from them now!"

Theo could not answer. Although he was as disappointed as Amalric at not having been part of the battle, he could not get the image of the bloody, impaled heads out of his mind. The taste of bile rose sour in his mouth and he swallowed it down. What was the matter with him, anyway? Did he, after all, have too weak a stomach for a man?

"We suffered many losses," he said finally, but there was a quiver in his voice. "The count of Ghent was killed, I heard."

Only the night before, Theo had seen the count, a slight, quiet man, sitting alone in front of his tent, pensive in the light from his fire. Emma had told him that the count was a great storyteller. Godvere's children would listen to him, entranced, for hours.

"Losses!" Amalric sneered. "Of course there were losses. There is no battle without them." He looked at Theo, his eyes piercing, almost suspicious. "You speak weakly for a knight, my friend."

Theo bristled. His thoughts of the moment before made his voice suddenly harsh. "Do you question my courage?" he snapped. "I am no more afraid of battle than you."

"Of course not," Amalric replied, taken aback. A conciliatory smile immediately replaced the sneer. "Of course not. And we shall see great battles together, you and I. It is our destiny." He threw his arm around Theo's shoulders. "We are going to be heroes, you and I, Theo. We will fight nobly, for fame and glory."

"What about for God?" Theo asked.

"Of course," Amalric replied quickly. "And for God."

† † †

Robert of Normandy finally arrived with his brother-in-law, Stephen, count of Blois, and his cousin Robert, count of Flanders.

"Stephen did not want to come at all," Emma informed Theo, "but his wife forced him to."

With their arrival, the great crusading armies were now all assembled. They dug in, and the siege of Nicaea began in earnest.

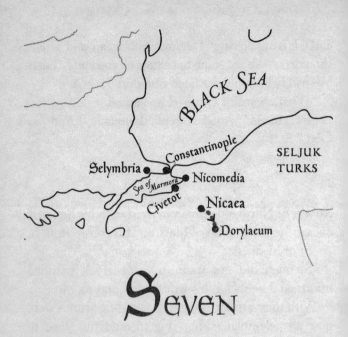

Seven

Theo sat in on the plans for the taking of Nicaea. He soon realized the difficulties facing them.

"The fortifications of the city are formidable," Duke Godfrey told them. "We have sent some of Alexius's engineers in to dig under the walls during the day to undermine them. We've even lit a huge fire under the southern tower. But at night the Turks just repair whatever damage we manage to inflict." He paced back and forth within the narrow confines of his tent. "Worst of all," he continued, "the city is still open to the lake on its western side. They can receive all the supplies they want that way."

"We need boats," Count Garnier said.

"The emperor Alexius has promised to send them. When he does, we can close off the city from the lake," Godfrey replied. "Until then, we can do nothing."

When the boats finally arrived, under the command of the emperor's most trusted engineer, Butumites, Amalric was first with the news to Theo.

"Now," Amalric gloated, "now we can attack, and this time, there will be no denying us. This time, we will fight!"

But when the morning of the planned attack dawned, the crusaders awoke to see the flag of the imperial emperor Alexius flying over the city. The Turks had surrendered to Butumites! His forces had entered the city through the lakeside gates during the night, and the city had been handed over to them.

"It is treachery, pure and simple!" Godfrey exploded, as his knights assembled around him in a hastily called meeting. "Butumites dealt directly with the city; he told us nothing of his dealings. And now he has taken the city for himself!"

Beside him, his brother Baldwin glowered. There was treasure beyond compare in that city—all of it now out of reach of the crusaders.

Tempers were not assuaged by the sight of Turkish

nobles being escorted out of the city to safety by the emperor's troops.

"They've been allowed to buy their freedom—all the nobles and the court officials," Amalric told Theo. "The sultana and her children were escorted to Constantinople and received by the emperor with full honors. All the ransom money has gone to fill *his* coffers. Baldwin is almost inside-out with fury."

Gifts of food arrived from the emperor for every soldier on the crusade. All the leaders received gold and jewels from the sultan's treasury, but these presents were not enough.

"Treason!" The word resounded throughout the camp. "We were the ones who set up the siege. We were the ones who fought the sultan and defeated him. The city should have been ours. The emperor has betrayed us!" Nevertheless, with the capture of Nicaea, word went out that the crusade was a success, and recruits poured into the camps.

They left Nicaea and took the old Byzantine main road across Asia Minor to the Sangarius River, then left the river to climb up a tributary valley to the south. The way was easy and, as they climbed into the hills, the early summer's heat was tempered by a constant breeze. Numerous springs gushed out of the hillsides to quench the thirst of beasts and humans alike. They feared no attack along this stretch, and although scouts were still sent out, discipline relaxed somewhat. Theo rode often with Amalric, but he also managed to find excuses to fall back and ride with Emma as well. Emma caused something of a scandal by choosing to ride horseback, rather than in the wagon with Godvere and her children. Godvere objected furiously, but for some reason Baldwin found the situation amusing and overrode his wife's objections.

"She is, after all, a distant kinswoman of mine," Baldwin announced. "She is entitled to her own will." This was the first time he had ever acknowledged that Emma was more than a servant. When Theo heard this news, he was taken aback.

"Why did you not tell me you were kin to Lord Baldwin?" he demanded as they rode together one day.

"I am very distantly related," Emma replied. "Our family fell on hard times back in the days of my father's father. We have never begged a thing of Lord Baldwin, and he had never seen fit to offer anything— until he sent word that he needed a nursemaid for his children on this crusade."

"But it is not fitting. The whole world thinks you are a servant."

"And a servant I am. I am quite content with it. I'm grateful, in fact, for the opportunity to earn my own way in the world and not be a burden to my poor parents, who have a swarm of other mouths to feed." The words were tart. Emma's face took on an irritated expression that warned Theo off.

"I think, too, my lord may have his own reasons for

humoring me," Emma continued. The irritation vanished and her lips twisted into a wry smile.

"And what would they be?" Theo asked.

"He has been very friendly toward me lately," Emma replied. "More so when we are out of sight of Godvere's wagon. When he rides beside me, his hand will sometimes stray to settle upon my leg."

Theo scowled. "You allow such impertinence?" he asked.

"Impertinence? I am, in fact, his servant, distant relation or not. I owe him a debt. No behavior of his toward me could possibly be considered impertinence."

At this, Theo straightened in his saddle and turned to glare at her. "He has no right."

Emma, however, seemed much less concerned. She laughed. "Don't puff yourself up so, you're worrying your horse. I am well able to take care of myself, thank you, and always have been, but I do it in my own way. It does not serve me to make an enemy of him."

"But still . . ." Theo protested.

"I have perfected a trick of tickling my dear mare with the toe of my shoe in just the right spot to make her shy suddenly," Emma replied calmly. "It invariably takes me out of reach. My lord cannot understand why such a gentle creature is the victim of such nerves. He has even offered to procure me a steadier nag but I, of course, would not dream of allowing him to go to the trouble."

Theo looked at her. He had been thinking of casually reaching for her hand sometime as they rode together, but he reconsidered. He decided it was a risk better not taken.

† † †

The army wound its way slowly through a pass in the hills. The crusaders reached the Blue River and paused there to reassemble. A small Byzantine detachment under one of the emperor's most experienced generals, Taticius, joined them. The detachment, war-blooded soldiers all, was welcome, but many muttered that Taticius was no more than the emperor's spy. By the bridge at Leuce, on the Blue River, the leaders decided to divide the army into two sections to facilitate travel, the first to precede the second by a day's interval. The French and the Lorrainers were to be in the second.

Amalric and Theo lounged together by the remains of Theo's morning campfire and watched the vanguard leave with a shared resentment. Although it meant only a day's delay, they chafed at it. It was the first truly hot day of summer and the heat was bothersome. Small insects flew around their heads incessantly, tormenting them.

"If there is any action, they will be the first to see it," Amalric grumbled, swatting at a fly. "They will take all the spoils before we even arrive."

"Spoils!" Theo retorted. "Is that all you think of? You are as bad as Baldwin." The heat and the delay had irritated him so much that he spoke without thinking. He scratched furiously at an itch that was just out of reach below the neck of his leather jerkin. Although the hour was early, sweat was already pouring into his eyes.

"You think yourself such a noble crusader," Amalric shot back, "yet I did not see you refusing your share of the rewards the emperor passed out to us at Nicaea."

Theo jumped to his feet. "A bit of food and a ring! Not so much to accuse me for."

"If there had been more for you, you would have taken it," Amalric said.

"I do not fight for spoils." Theo's anger blazed. "And in this most holy of all wars, all I have heard so far is bickering about what there is to be gained! I want to fight, not loot."

"You rarely have one without the other, and more thanks for that, I say." Amalric rose to his feet as well, and faced Theo. "You'll see. You'll take your fair share when the time comes and bargain for as much more as you can get. You're no different from the rest of us. Except, of course, for your taste in riding companions." He cast a sly glance at Theo, then went on. "For a quick snuggle at night, that I could understand, but to ride with a servant girl during the day, as if she were your equal . . . You make yourself ridiculous there, my friend."

Theo felt the blood rush to his head. There was a quick pressure, a pounding in his ears. His dagger was suddenly in his hand, the point at Amalric's throat.

Amalric took a step backward. His hand went for his own dagger, and then he stopped. His eyes were suddenly as black as stones.

"You would be wise to sheath that, my friend."

Reason returned to Theo like a douse of cold water. He thrust the dagger back into his belt. Pride, however, would not let him apologize.

"You are too free with your opinions, *my* friend," he said.

For a moment, they glared at each other. A voice from the path beyond the campsite startled them both.

"What's this? My two pups snarling at each other? Good, I say. You'll be in fine fettle for the battles to come." A tall figure strode across the clearing toward them. It was Godfrey himself. "And there will be battles, my bloodthirsty young men, trust me. You will have more opportunities than you can count to bloody your swords in the service of Christ. Keep your mettle up, but do not go too far. I will not have fighting within my ranks, remember that." The words were light, but underlaid with iron. In two easy strides, he was across the campsite and heading up the path to his own tent.

He left a silence behind him. Then Amalric spoke.

"I take back my words," he said, his voice carefully controlled. "Your preferences are your own business.

Still . . . ," he threw his arm around Theo's shoulders in his old familiar way and his face relaxed into a smile, "if it's servant girls you like, come with me after we sup tonight. There is a certain wench in the duke's party . . ."

Theo forced himself not to stiffen under Amalric's touch.

Amalric prattled on. "The duke was right," he said. "We need a battle! That is the trouble with us. We are, after all, friends, are we not?"

Theo detached himself. "Yes, of course," he said. If he hesitated, Amalric did not seem to notice it.

It crossed Theo's mind to blurt out that Emma was no mere serving girl, that she was kin, even if distant, to Baldwin, but he kept silent. Emma did not need him to defend her. In fact, he felt certain she would flay him alive for trying it.

† † †

They forged on steadily for the next two days. On the evening of the second, their half of the army had gained on the first contingent, and was within a half day's march from where it was camped, near a town called Dorylaeum. The mood in Godfrey's camp was easier now. The next morning, however, the priests' prayers and the bustle of making ready for departure were interrupted by the arrival of a scout. The horse he was riding was covered in foam and staggering. It foundered even as the man rode up beside Godfrey's tent. He threw the reins to a nearby groom and dashed in, unannounced. Theo and Amalric, waiting nearby, were astounded at the man's impudence, but within seconds the duke was outside, roaring for the other leaders to assemble.

"The first section has been attacked!" The word spread like wildfire. "The sultan laid an ambush for them and attacked this morning at sunrise!"

Count Garnier burst out of his tent and ran for his horse.

"To me, Theo!" he cried.

All over the camp, the morning routine was broken by shouts and roared commands. The knights and their mounted soldiers galloped off, leaving the foot soldiers and archers to follow at a double-march behind. The rest of the camp was in total confusion.

Theo rode at Count Garnier's right hand. Gritting his teeth against the bone-shattering pounding of Centurion's hooves, he checked that his sword was holstered securely, readjusted his dagger and settled his shield more firmly into his left shoulder. At last! The blood sang through his veins.

Godfrey and Hugh of Vermandois led. When they slowed down to give the chargers a rest, the horses, as frenzied as the knights themselves, tossed their manes, rolled their eyes wildly and tore at their bits.

It seemed to take forever to negotiate the last pass through the hills above Dorylaeum, but finally they burst out onto the plain above the city. Below them, they could see the embattled crusaders. They had formed a circle, with the non-combatant pilgrims in the center. Women were carrying water from springs to where the wounded were lying. The camp was surrounded by the Turks. As Godfrey drew his army up into position, Theo could see Turkish archers run in a line to the front of their soldiers, discharge their arrows into the ring of defending crusaders and then quickly retreat behind their own men to reload. Another line rushed to take their place. A ceaseless rain of arrows shot into the crusaders, making it impossible for them to advance and fight the Turks hand to hand.

"A cowardly way to wage war," Aimery raged, beside Theo.

"Cowardly perhaps, but very effective," Theo replied grimly.

Even as they watched, knights fell and horses crashed to the ground. Earsplitting battlecries from the triumphant Turks reached Theo's ears. Then Godfrey's own trumpets sounded out.

"Charge!" The cry rang out all along the lines. Bohemond, Robert of Normandy and Stephen of Blois led their men on the left flank. Raymond of Toulouse and Robert of Flanders took the center. Count Garnier, with Theo close beside him, followed Godfrey and Hugh on the right. There was no time for fear; Theo drew his sword, and they were upon the enemy.

In an instant, Theo's world became a howling hell of clashing weapons. A blow landed on his shield, almost knocking him from his saddle. Before he could recover, a scimitar from the side caught his helmet with a crack that sent a ringing right through his brain. Everything went red before him. He reeled in the saddle.

So soon? he thought, desperate. Am I to die so soon? Before I have even struck a blow? Anger swept his mind and his vision cleared. The noise around him disappeared. He was alone in his own silence. A figure loomed up before him, turban flaming in the sun, scimitar raised. Theo slashed with his sword and felt the sudden shock as the blade sank deep into flesh. He yanked it out, even as he was wheeling Centurion to meet another figure on his right. He thrust back-handed at the man, and caught him in the side. The man fell, but Theo was already past him and joined with another. Thrust, cut, parry. Thrust again. Theo fought in a frenzy. When trumpets sounded again, they seemed to belong to another world. It wasn't until he found himself charging after a horseman and realized the Turks were retreating, that he came back to the reality of where he was.

† † †

"It was Adhemar, Bishop of Le Puy, who saved us," Amalric gasped, grunting with pain as a servant doused his leg with water. A scimitar had ripped open his old boar wound. "He's a clever tactician for a churchman. Bribed guides to take him over the hills behind the Turks and fell on them from the rear. They broke as soon as he attacked."

The crusaders had regrouped to tend to their injuries. Theo had found Amalric, although he couldn't, at the moment, remember how. Amalric's words came to him as though from a vast distance. He stared at blood flowing down his own right arm, and wondered stupidly where it was coming from.

Eight

The army rested at Dorylaeum for two days to recover from the battle. It had been an enormous victory, and the sultan was in full retreat, but there had been many losses and the crusaders felt a new respect for the Turks as soldiers. Tancred and Bohemond's own brother William had been slain. Fortunately, Theo's wound was slight.

The general mood within the camp, however, was one of elation. In their flight, the Turks had left behind their tents to be overrun by the crusaders. At last, the

103

booty they had wished for so eagerly was theirs. The
sultan had carried a good part of his treasure with him,
and the crusaders were quick to plunder it. They captured many fine horses, too, and some other animals
that Theo had never seen before. Tall, gangling,
sandy-colored beasts, they had long, ugly faces with a
decidedly insolent look to them. What amazed Theo
most of all, however, were the humps on their rough-
coated backs that swayed when they moved. They
walked with a lolling, lumbering gait, on splayed
hooves at the end of thin, ungainly legs. Theo could
never have imagined more unlikely animals.

When Godfrey called a general conference of his
leaders and their knights to plan the next stages of the
march, Theo accompanied Count Garnier. The count
had praised him for his conduct during the battle, and
Theo's heart was light as he strode beside his foster
father to the duke's tent. He had fought, finally, and he
had fought well. He had a right to feel proud. But, deep
inside, something lurked. He could not forget the
feeling of his sword sinking into flesh for the first time,
and the flash of the eyes beneath the crimson turban
as the man attacking him realized he had been mor-
tally wounded. The memory made Theo uneasy, and
he did not want to examine it. Each time it recurred,
he thrust it back down and thought of other things.

"We keep together from now on. There will be no
repeat of the ambush at Dorylaeum." Duke Godfrey's
voice rang out as they entered.

"We will march along the edge of the mountains. The going will be hard, but Taticius has assured me that there are Christian villages along the way, fertile fields and many good wells. Provisions should not be a problem."

A murmur arose, an undercurrent of suspicion, at the name of the emperor's engineer.

"Taticius knows the route. He will guide us." Godfrey's tone of voice quelled any argument; the murmuring ceased.

The sun was high and the early July heat already almost unbearable when the crusading army set out yet again. The mountains to the south of them looked coolly inviting and green, but the winds that blew off the wide, seemingly endless salt marshes to the north were arid and dry. Never had Theo seen such a bleak land. They were well provisioned, however, and carried a more than ample supply of water that easily lasted until they reached Pisidian Antioch. The town was peaceful, its leaders eager to provide the crusaders with supplies. Spirits rose in spite of the heat, which was increasing daily.

Once they had left the town's shelter, however, conditions deteriorated quickly. The heavily armed knights and foot soldiers began to suffer in the heat, and they drank recklessly, heedless of the need to ration. Water quickly became scarce. At Philomelium, they were able to take on a little more, but not nearly enough, and the country beyond this city became more and more desolate.

On the third day out of Philomelium, the vanguard of the army spotted a village. Word spread back quickly. They would be able to reprovision here, and supply themselves with badly needed water. The knights spurred their horses forward eagerly. Theo rode with Amalric at the very front. His mouth was dry and parched; the horse he rode wheezed and heaved with thirst beneath him. He saw the trees waving above the low village walls and licked his cracked lips in anticipation. He could almost taste the cool velvet of the water.

"It is very quiet," Amalric said.

The knights around them, who had been calling out in their excitement, fell silent, one by one.

None of the noise and bustle of a normal village welcomed them. No dog barked at their approach, no chickens scrabbled in the dust, no goats nibbled at the stunted bushes by the roadside. The surrounding fields, which should have been heavy with grain, were overgrown and wild. And nowhere was there any sign of human life. Not an adult, not a child.

The gates of the village hung wide open, askew. As they filed through, a sight of complete destruction met their eyes. Houses were burned, walls tumbled down. The streets were strewn with refuse. In the center of the village, a bridge over a dried-up stream had fallen, or been destroyed. The wind soughed between the abandoned buildings. It looked as if all life here had ceased years ago.

Godfrey drew up beside the large cistern at the town center. He stared down into it, then raised his eyes to the men watching him.

"Sand. It is filled with sand."

† † †

So it was with every village they came to and every well they found. The men suspected treason and were quick to blame Taticius and the Greek guides, but Alexius's men were suffering equally. They had had no way of knowing that drought, years of warfare and Turkish invasions had reduced the countryside to a wasteland since they had last traveled this way. The army trudged on. The horses' hooves turned up stones from the rocky beds of parched streams. There was no water anywhere. Every cistern they found along the way was dry. Theo saw men, in their desperation, ripping off branches of thorn bushes and chewing them in a vain attempt to find moisture. Theo rationed the pitiful amount of water he had left carefully, using it only to wet his lips and tongue whenever the thirst became unbearable. Then, even that was gone. He tore off a thorn branch himself to chew, but threw it away in disgust when the dryness of it made his torment worse. His tongue swelled within his mouth until he could hardly speak. And always, the sun beat down upon them mercilessly, causing them to sweat and lose even more precious moisture from their bodies.

Horses were the first to perish. Theo worried about Centurion, who was in great distress. He set William to gathering the prickly plants that grew along the way, and rubbed them between his hands to provide fodder for the horse. By the time they made camp at night, Centurion was covered in sweat and would hardly eat. He grew weak, and faltered during the long daily marches. Knights whose horses died were forced to go on foot. Poorly shod for walking on such stony roads, their feet soon became sore and inflamed. Sheep, goats and dogs were used to pull the baggage trains. The camels, the strange beasts captured from the Turks, fared the best. They seemed to be able to trudge on, unmindful of the heat, and not bothered in the least by the lack of water. They were useful as beasts of burden, but cursed with ugly tempers and liable to bite. They could also spit a slimy, noxious stream a surprising distance, as more than one groom found out.

"How are you?" Theo asked Emma as she appeared on her mare beside him early one morning. Her face was gaunt, her eyes enormous in her face.

"I am well enough," she said. She, too, seemed to have trouble speaking. "But the children are suffering." She brushed a tangled strand of greasy hair out of her eyes. "How much longer will this go on, do you think?"

"Iconium is two days' march from here," Theo answered. His brow furrowed. In spite of what she said, she did not look well. "It is a large town," he went on, trying to sound reassuring, but a note of bitterness crept into his voice. "Well provisioned, Taticius says. There are streams in the valley of Meran behind the city that cannot run dry, he tells us. But he has been wrong every step of the way up until now. And we do not know whether the Turks have taken the city. I do not think we have the strength to fight for it if they have." He turned to look at the column strung out behind them. He could not see the pilgrims that followed at the very end, but he knew they straggled farther and farther behind every day; every night fewer of them made it into camp.

"What is to become of us, then?"

There was a quaver in Emma's voice that Theo had not heard before. It shocked him into looking at her more carefully. He saw then how thin her wrists were, and how bony the slender fingers had become. He looked at his own hands and realized for the first time that they, too, were lean and sinewy, roped with veins like an old man's. Without thinking, he reached out to her.

Her fingers tightened around his as he grasped her hand. She met his eyes and drew a deep breath. She straightened in her saddle. Then she gave a small nod, as if to reassure him, or herself. Or perhaps both of them.

Two days later, toward the middle of August, almost a year to the day since Godfrey's crusade had left the Ardennes, they reached Iconium. The city lay in a now familiar, deserted silence as they rode toward it. The heat rose in shimmering waves. There were signs that the Turks had, indeed, occupied it, but they must have fled at the coming of the crusaders.

Theo's heart sank. Then a joyous shout from the knights in the lead sent a thrill of hope through him, and he spurred his horse forward eagerly. A well lay just within the gates. Knights were kneeling beside it, scooping clear, sparkling water out in great handfuls. Theo raised his eyes to the hills beyond. Streams glinted and tumbled down the slopes between rows and rows of carefully tended orchards. Taticius had finally been right.

† † †

Count Garnier set up his camp across a swiftly flowing stream from Duke Godfrey's. Theo's tent lay under a grove of trees whose leaves filtered out the harsh sun. Within a day, he had forgotten what thirst was like. Centurion spent the first twenty-four hours planted in the river, then began to graze without stopping. The news that they would rest there for several more days restored the spirits of all the crusaders. When Amalric burst in upon Theo to invite him on a bear hunt in the foothills, Theo accepted with alacrity.

The duke himself led the party, but Theo's enthusiasm was checked when he saw Guy. During the past few months, while they had been on the road, it had been easy to avoid him. Now, however, there was no escaping the confrontation. Guy drew his horse up sharply when he saw Theo.

"So." The word was a sneer. "You will have better luck keeping to your own game today, I hope."

A sharp answer rose to Theo's lips, but he bit it back. The day was too fine and the relief from the harshness of the road too great to spoil with arguments. He forced a nod and determined to keep out of Guy's way.

Beyond the shelter of the valley, the land became more densely wooded and rose gently toward the mountains. A pack of dogs had been let loose and were loping ahead of the knights, casting about for the scent of game. All of a sudden, one caught it. A nose was thrust skyward and the hound howled to the heavens above. Another animal took up the scent, and then another. Howls turned into frenzied barking, and the pack headed into the forest. Theo spurred his horse on. The animal, startled, gave a great leap forward and they were off at a gallop.

As soon as they entered the trees, they were forced to rein their mounts in. Soon the bush became too thick for riding, even at a walk. Tossing their horses' reins to their grooms, the knights dismounted and began to thread their way through, the hounds' belling drawing them on.

"There! Do you hear it? They have caught up to their prey!" Amalric shouted, at Theo's shoulder.

The dogs' crying had changed in note and tone; the barks had become frantic.

"On!" Godfrey cried, and drew his sword. Footmen fanned out as best they could on either side, their halberds and spears hampering them in the dense underbrush. The dogs' noise grew closer.

Sweat poured into Theo's eyes, but he was hardly aware of it. He drew his sword and beat back the low-hanging branches of the trees. Without warning, he stumbled into a clearing. The dogs were circling a tree, leaping and snarling. Theo looked up. There, in its branches, dark against the dark background of the forest, was a bear. Theo caught his breath at the size of it. Even from where he stood, it looked larger than any animal he had ever seen. A rank smell hit his nostrils. The bear did not seem frightened. Its eyes, small in the enormous head, were fixed on the mad animals beneath it with what seemed to be contempt.

"Call off the dogs!" The duke's order rang out, but the dogs were beyond hearing, let alone obeying. Two of the animal trainers stepped forward with whips and began laying about them in the pack. Godfrey moved forward impatiently, hitting at the nearest hound with the flat of his sword. At that instant, the bear jumped.

As the huge animal hurtled out of the branches above him, Godfrey threw himself to one side. The bear landed a sword's length away from him. It hesitated for a moment, as if confused, turned toward the prostrate duke and raised itself up on its hind legs to its full height. Godfrey was on his feet in an instant. His sword flashed. At the same moment, every man in the party surged forward. The closest to the duke was Guy. He slashed at the bear with his sword and hit it on the shoulder, drawing blood. The bear whirled, unbelievably graceful for a creature of its size. Godfrey took advantage of its movement to thrust with his sword, and the blade sank deep into its side. The bear whirled back and, with one swipe of its forepaw, sent Godfrey spinning. Guy struck again. Theo and Amalric closed in beside him, adding their blows to his. The bear roared and lashed out with first one, and then the other of its massive paws. Theo had an overwhelming impression of teeth, the flying froth of saliva and a red, cavernous mouth. The bear's roar paralyzed him for an instant, and then he struck again. Another blow from the bear's paw felled Guy. He lay, stunned, as the bear turned toward him. Theo took a step forward and straddled the fallen knight, protecting him. With his sword, he struck the bear just above its eyes. The animal lunged for him. At that moment, a spear hurled by one of Godfrey's men whistled past Theo's shoulder and buried itself deep in the animal's chest. For a moment, everything seemed to stop. The bear stood, immobile. As Theo drew back his arm to strike again, the animal crumpled to the ground.

Blood was everywhere. Guy groaned, then raised himself to his knees and shook his head as Theo stepped back from him. Duke Godfrey lay ominously still. His men ran to him. It was impossible to tell how much of the blood on him and around him was his, and how much was the bear's. Amalric and the rest of his party slid a cloak under the duke and raised him carefully. Guy stood for a second, still trying to clear his head. He looked at Theo. For a minute, Theo thought he was going to say something, but then he shook his head again and joined the party of men carrying the duke.

† † †

There was feasting that night in Godfrey's camp. Great chunks of bear roasted over every fire. Godfrey was not seriously injured, although his wounds were substantial. The bear's claws had raked his chest in deep grooves. A healer had bound the gashes as well as he could, but the duke was too weak and in too much pain to participate in the celebration. Theo and Amalric, however, wolfed down their share of the hot, greasy meat. When he had stuffed himself to the point of nausea, Theo tossed his last bone to the hounds that skulked around their feet, and sank back beside the fire with a sigh of contentment. As he did so, he caught sight of Guy sitting on the other side, glaring at him through the firelight.

"Guy does not look overly grateful for the favor I did him today," Theo said to Amalric, trying to make his voice light.

"It was the worst thing you could have done," Amalric replied. He wiped the grease from his chin. "He is a twisted sort. I truly think he would rather have died than have you save him."

Nine

They took water with them when they left Iconium, well rested and eager once again, but the valley through which they now traveled was fertile and flowing with streams. Almost at once, they ran into a Turkish army led by the Emir Hassan. Bohemond led the attack and the outnumbered Turks retreated without resistance. The crusaders fired off a comet that night in celebration. Theo and Amalric watched it streak through the blackness, shedding sparks.

"An omen," Amalric said. "We shall have nothing but victories from now on."

And so it seemed. As the summer wore on, the crusaders forged ahead, defeating the Turkish troops wherever they encountered them. They followed the road through Caesarea, but Baldwin, with some of the Flemish knights and the Lorrainers, split from the main party and crossed into Cilicia.

"He's after more gains for himself, of course," was Emma's scornful comment. "It galls him to share his spoils with all the rest of the crusaders."

"How do you and Lady Godvere manage without him?" Theo asked.

"Perfectly well," Emma retorted. "We have the servants to help us, and a groom. It is a relief not to have him around."

By the end of September, with the summer heat abating somewhat, they reached Caesarea to find it deserted by the Turks.

"Our good fortune holds," Theo remarked one evening, sitting by the campfire with Amalric.

"Good fortune has nothing to do with it," Amalric responded. "We are invincible. Nothing can stand in our way."

Theo laughed. The battles they had fought together had forged their friendship fast. There was, however, one great difference between them. After each battle, the blood lust lived on in Amalric until he had worked it out with riotous celebration. In this, he was like most of the other men. With Theo, it was different. In the wildness of battle, he was one with Amalric, but when the fighting was over, there was always a time of sickness. A time during which he had to be alone. Amalric could not understand. He had teased, cajoled and even tried to shame Theo into joining the carousing that followed each battle, but to no avail. Finally, he had shrugged his shoulders and given up.

"I know you are among the bravest of us all," he said. "You should be one of the most eager to make merry."

"I cannot explain it," was Theo's only response, and Amalric was finally forced to relent. To Theo himself, his sickness after battles was a gnawing, secret worry.

In October, the rains began. The mountains they had been following now loomed ahead of them, their towering peaks already snow-capped. They rose to heights higher than many had seen before.

"We are to cross *those*?" For once, Amalric seemed taken aback as Theo drew up beside him and they paused to contemplate what lay before them.

"So it would seem," Theo answered.

The way they followed could not really be called a road. It quickly turned into no more than a muddy path that led up steep inclines and skirted terrifying precipices. As they climbed higher, the mud became icy. The pilgrims shivered and slipped on the treacherous slopes. No one dared to ride. First one horse slipped and fell over the edge, then another, and yet another. A whole line of baggage animals, roped together, fell and dragged each other down into the abyss that yawned at their side. Heavily armored knights began to unburden themselves. At first, they offered their arms and equipment for sale to any who would buy. Then, in desperation, as the way grew ever steeper, some merely threw them away. Men following behind could pick up whatever they wished, but few did. It was only too apparent that the more lightly they traveled, the better were their chances.

"These mountains are cursed!" The words were muttered up and down the line, and indeed the crusaders were losing more men through accidents than they had in all the battles so far. The pilgrims at the end of the procession fared even worse. Carts and wagons were either abandoned or lost to the depths below; people kept only what they could carry on their backs. There was no stopping, not even for a rest; the rain was fast turning to sleet, and snow was on the way. They had to make the crossing before it came.

Theo led Centurion, leaving William to deal with the palfrey and the groom's own nag. He had fastened his weapons and his chain mail onto the charger's saddle. If Centurion slipped and was lost, lost as well would be all that Theo owned; but Centurion was proving to be amazingly sure-footed in his own heavy, plodding way. Suddenly, Theo heard a cry behind him. He turned just in time to see the hindquarters of

William's nag sag beneath him and slide over the edge of the path. To his horror, Theo saw that William had, against all advice, mounted the horse. The groom had complained unendingly about the need to walk ever since the climb had begun and, it would seem, had at last given in to the temptation to ride. Before Theo could move, the horse tumbled off the edge of the precipice. William uttered one short scream, and then there was silence. Appalled, Theo looked over the edge, but thick trees below masked any sign of horse or rider. Theo's palfrey, reins trailing, stood listlessly at the spot where William had gone over. Theo had no time to try to see any farther. The horse was blocking the trail; men and animals on the path below were beginning to back up.

"Move on up there!" a rough voice shouted. "No stopping on the trail!"

Theo reached over, grabbed the palfrey's reins and moved forward, leading the two animals. It had all happened so suddenly. He bowed his head into the driving sleet and urged the horses on. He had not liked William very much, but they had marched together, shared meals together for over a year now. It was unthinkable that he could be gone—that from one moment to the next, he could just cease to exist.

Theo stumbled and caught himself just as one foot slipped toward the edge of the path. Centurion snorted as if indignant at his clumsiness. Theo shook the rain out of his eyes and focused all his senses on the task of leading the two horses safely. Finally, the path evened out and they began to descend.

On a wet, cold afternoon, just before darkness overtook them, the leading knights and their entourages emerged from the pass into the valley that surrounded Marash. The Armenian population there, under their prince, Thatoul, came out to meet them in a joyous welcome. As he tethered the horses and unpacked his tent, Theo looked back at the mountains. Streams of exhausted pilgrims still trickled down to the plain below where tents were starting to rise and fires starting to flicker. Hundreds more were on the crossing behind them. Night was falling fast, and the sleet had turned to snow. He could see it driving whitely across the dark trees on the mountainside. Theo's breath steamed into the wintry air. He rubbed his chilled hands together to warm them. How many more would perish before they reached this side of the mountains?

As soon as he could, Theo searched out Baldwin's camp. He was worried about Emma. How had she and the Lady Godvere survived the crossing? As he approached their tents, he heard the sounds of a child wailing, a high-pitched, keening noise that seemed to go on and on. He was surprised to see no sign of a fire.

"Emma?" he called out. When there was no answer, he made for the tent where the child was crying.

As he pulled open the flap, he gasped, and drew back at the smell. Then he took a deep breath and pushed his way in. The two boys lay on blankets. Beside them, the girl sat, hair tangled over her face and down her shoulders, wailing. Godvere lay on another blanket, breathing heavily; her wide, flat face shone with sweat. Emma knelt, bathing her forehead with a rag soaked in water. She looked up as Theo came in.

"What has happened?" Theo asked.

"They are all ill. Godvere is the sickest right now, although the children are worsening quickly. They took a chill during the crossing and are now all burning with fever."

"And you?"

"I am well, thanks be to God. But the crossing was terrible. We lost our wagon."

"Why do you not have a fire? Where are the servants?"

Emma shrugged. "I know not. One perished when the wagon went over. The others disappeared as soon as my lady and the children took ill. Our groom helped to raise the tents, and then he also left. I think they fear the fever."

"Have you eaten?"

"There has not been time."

"I'll make a fire for you. Do you have food for a broth?"

"Yes. A woman was here from the village. A kind woman. She brought vegetables and bread, but she wouldn't stay. She, too, was afraid." Emma gestured toward a basket by the door flap.

"I'll make a soup for you, then."

"You cannot . . ."

"I most certainly can. I am an excellent cook. It was necessary to learn rather than eat the messes William prepared—" He stopped. William's cry echoed again in his mind.

Within the hour, he had made a nourishing soup, supplementing it with meat from his own stores. He brought a bowl in to Emma and helped her feed it to the children. The boys were too weak to take more than a few sips. The girl drank greedily, then fell into a heavy sleep that was more like a stupor. They could not raise Godvere sufficiently to get her to taste even a mouthful. Her breathing was rapidly getting more labored, and her breath was foul. Each snoring breath was followed by a lull that threatened to be her last.

"They have sent to Cilicia for Lord Baldwin," Emma said when they had done what they could for Godvere and the children, and were sitting together beside the fire. Emma held a bowl thick with vegetables and meat in her hands. As she ate, color began to come back to her pale, drawn face. "But he is busy conquering territory to lay up for himself, I hear, and I would not be surprised if he did not bother to come." She looked at the bowl of soup in her hands, then back up at Theo. "I thank you, Theo," she said. "You are a good friend to me. My only friend here, I fear."

Friend. As Theo looked at Emma, he knew that what he felt for her was much more than friendship.

Baldwin did come, but only in time to watch his wife die. The children followed soon after. Theo saw him standing, tall and sombre, beside their gravesides as the priests said mass over them. Emma stood slightly behind him. As Theo watched, Baldwin turned to her and said something. They were too far away for Theo to make out the words, but he saw a quick flush rise to Emma's cheeks.

The next morning, he hurried over to Baldwin's camp, determined to talk to Emma. Now that Godvere and the children were gone, he feared for her safety alone with that man. When he walked into the clearing where the tents had been, however, they were gone. He stopped, shocked and uncomprehending for a moment, then raced to Godfrey's encampment.

"My Lord Baldwin," he gasped out to the first sentry he came upon. "Know you where he is?"

"He and all his entourage left with the first light," the man replied. "Stricken with grief over the death of his lady and children, no doubt." Sarcasm lay heavy over the words.

"Where did they go?"

The guard looked at Theo, surprised at the intensity of his questioning.

"To the east, where there is more to be gained, rumors say. He is more anxious to carve out his own kingdom, I am told, than to remain with the crusade." As if suddenly aware that he was speaking unwisely, the guard snapped his mouth shut and would say no more.

Theo turned away, a sickness in his stomach. What about Emma? For a moment, he thought wildly about saddling Centurion and riding after them, but even as the thought formed itself, he heard the trumpets sounding and the bugles calling. They were to march today—on to Antioch.

✝   ✝   ✝

Theo saddled his palfrey and made Centurion ready for the trip without any awareness of what he was doing. His mind was reeling. It was inconceivable that Emma should disappear from his life in such a manner. It was impossible! And with Baldwin . . . He hadn't the slightest doubt about the treatment she would receive at his hands. Why had she gone? Why hadn't she at least contrived to tell him she was going and to say farewell? Didn't she care for him at all? She had called him friend—even if she felt no more than that, how could she have left him in such a way?

He finished his preparations, swung into the saddle and rode to join his foster father. To the east, the guard had said. He scanned the horizon. Where in the east? Where had she gone?

"Why so glum, my son?" the count asked as he rode up. "Are you not excited? Once we liberate Antioch, the way southward to the Holy Land will be open to us. Our journey goes well!"

Theo didn't answer. He swung his horse alongside

the count as they took their places in the train. Centurion stomped behind on a lead rope that Theo held loosely in one hand.

"We must see about finding you another groom," the count said as Centurion edged forward and irritably tried to shoulder Garnier's horse out of the way. The slight nudge was powerful enough to cause the animal to stagger off the path. The count gathered his reins and brought his horse back to Theo's side with difficulty. It eyed Centurion nervously. Centurion bared his teeth and tried to nip the unfortunate animal's flank. Theo only just managed to haul on the lead rope and forestall him.

"I'm sorry for poor William, but he must be replaced," the count said. "That warhorse of yours is a menace."

"He dislikes sharing the path," Theo said, but his mind was not on the horse. He rode in silence for a while, but finally could keep quiet no longer.

"Know you where went Baldwin, my lord?" he asked.

Count Garnier's mouth twisted and his normally open face closed. "Tarsus, the rumor is. He wants the city for himself. Bohemond has sent a troop of Normans after him to keep control in crusader hands." He paused for a moment. "It seems sometimes there is more fighting and jealousy among ourselves than between us and the enemy. It is disheartening."

When they camped that night, Theo refused Amalric's offer to drink and make merry at his campsite.

"There are wenches galore who will make you forget that little servant girl of Godvere's instantly," Amalric teased.

Theo flushed. "I had not given her a thought," he snapped. "I was hardly even aware she had gone."

"And is that why you have been so intent on discovering Baldwin's whereabouts?"

Theo turned abruptly and left.

He boiled water for soup, threw in a few turnips and a bone with meat on it, and then just sat, staring into the flames. He had no appetite for food. A rustle in the bushes startled him into awareness.

"Who goes there?" he demanded, springing to his feet.

A figure emerged, leading a decrepit nag. It was a young boy, hair chopped off short in the Norman fashion. In the gathering darkness, Theo had difficulty making out his features.

"You are in need of a groom, my lord?" the boy said.

At the sound of the words, Theo's heart took a great leap. For a moment, he couldn't speak. Then he found his tongue.

"Emma?" It was barely a whisper. "Come closer to the fire!"

The figure emerged into the flame's light. Theo looked at him incredulously. The boy bore a slight resemblance to the girl, but the short hair changed the look of the face completely. He was dressed in a belted tunic and leggings; a small dagger such as the servants carried was tucked in at his waist.

"Emma?" Theo repeated, not daring to breathe.

The boy smiled, and in that instant became recognizable.

"Emma! What are you doing here? And in that garb?"

"You need a groom, do you not? Then, I am here to be your groom."

Ten

"Impossible!"

"Why?" Emma was defiant.

"Because . . . because you'll be recognized."

"Not now that my lord Baldwin's gone. No one else in the camp except you knows me well, and even you didn't recognize me until I spoke. I'll just not talk when others are around."

"It can't possibly work. Besides, you can't be a groom!"

"It *can* work. I've given it thought. And why could

I not be a groom? I know much about horses. At home, I helped my father many a time. What I don't know, you can teach me."

"But why, Emma? Why do you want to do this?"

Her brows drew together. Her mouth set. "I do not want to be with Baldwin now that my lady is no longer alive. I am not really his servant. You said so yourself. I have the right to do as I wish."

"But to travel with me as my groom—it is impossible!" Theo repeated. He realized he was blustering.

"Do you not want me here?" Emma's chin tilted. "Would you rather that I traveled with Lord Baldwin?"

"No, of course not! I trust the man not at all and I am very glad you are not with him." Theo stopped short. The fact that Emma had *not* gone with Baldwin finally sank in, and a singing lightness began to bubble up through his veins.

"I got the clothes from a groom who was anxious to rid himself of extra weight on the trek over the mountains. I thought they might be useful, although at the time I wasn't really certain what for. It was good I did so, though, wasn't it?"

The situation was impossible. What would the count say if he found out? He would send her back to Baldwin, of course. One thought after another tumbled into Theo's mind. But over all the joy within him rose, and in spite of himself he broke into a broad smile.

"You make a comely lad, I must say," he said.

Emma answered his smile with one of her own.

"The night before my lord Baldwin left, I stole the least of his horses, snuck out of his camp and have been trailing you ever since." She sounded extremely pleased with herself.

"So, a horse thief as well."

"I brought a mule with me when I joined Lady Godvere," Emma answered quickly. "Baldwin has the better bargain, for it was a far better animal than this nag, but I dared not steal the mule back, nor take the sweet mare I usually rode, which belonged to my lord. This half-dead beast will not even be missed." She looked full at Theo. The smile died and her face became serious once more. "I cannot come back to this crusade if you do not take me in, Theo. A woman alone . . . It is not possible. I would have to return to Baldwin." Her hands clenched into fists at her sides. She took a deep breath. "May I stay? May I be your groom?"

"I know not how . . . If anyone should find out—"

"I have thought that out, too," she broke in. "Say I am an Armenian, from one of the villages we passed through. That I wished to join the crusade. And say that I am a mute. Then I need not speak at all. My voice is most likely to give me away." She stopped.

"I have a small tent that William used," Theo said slowly, getting used to the idea. "You could have that. It would be best if you always set it up close to mine. You would have to avoid the other grooms—they will think you strange for doing so, but you must not let them get too close to you."

"Strange they may think me, and strange I will be." She bit her lip and looked down at the fire, then raised her eyes back to Theo. "You understand, Theo, that I will be your groom. Nothing else."

Theo felt the blood rising to his cheeks. "Of course." The words came out more brusquely than he had intended.

"I did not mean to insult you," Emma said. "It was just . . . I had to make it clear."

"Of course," Theo repeated stiffly. "I would never have thought of anything else." But the racing of his blood belied his words.

She had been facing Theo rigidly, her whole body immobile and tense. Now, suddenly, she relaxed.

"So," she said, "I will go to war after all." Her lips curled in a smile of pure satisfaction. "And as a man, not a mewling maid."

"Grooms do not make war any more than women do," Theo said. The words came out even more stiffly.

"Perhaps not," Emma replied. "But I will be at the front, not the back. And I will be helping you prepare for your battles. It will be almost as good. Now, where is that tent?"

† † †

"You have a new groom, I see," Amalric said as he rode up beside Theo a few days later. He was munching on one of the small, purplish fruits that the people in these parts loved.

The way was along level plains and the riding was easy. Once through the mountains, the rains had ceased and the cool autumn weather was a relief to them all. Amalric held out one of the figs, as they were called, to Theo. Theo took it, and used the opportunity of splitting it and squeezing the soft, sweet, seed-filled pulp into his mouth to marshal his thoughts. Emma rode discreetly behind, leading Centurion. She had found a loosely woven hood somewhere and wore it constantly, far down over her eyes. No one tried to ride near her. The other grooms had learned to give Centurion plenty of space and their horses knew well enough not to get within his reach. Centurion, however, was behaving himself admirably. He had taken to Emma immediately, and followed wherever she led him as docilely as a pup.

"My groom says he is none too sociable. Keeps to himself."

"He is mute," Theo answered quickly.

"How came you by him, then?" Amalric asked. He seemed only moderately curious, making conversation merely to help ease his impatience. His eyes searched the road ahead of them as if willing the walls of Antioch to come into view.

"He appeared in my camp one evening," Theo answered, casting a quick, nervous glance at his friend. He had considered telling Amalric about Emma, but had decided against it. He was not altogether sure how Amalric would react. At the very least, he would laugh, and he would certainly think Theo was mad. "He is from one of the Armenian villages. He understands a little of our language and managed to make me know that he wanted to join the crusade. I thought he might do as my groom."

Amalric was only half listening.

"Good fortune for you," he answered, but clearly his thoughts were elsewhere. "We should arrive at the gates of Antioch in a few days' time." He threw the fig skin to one side. "What shall we find there, I wonder?"

† † †

What they found were fortifications that exceeded all imagining. They had a skirmish at the Iron Bridge that crossed the Orontes River but, after a sharp struggle, the army of Bishop Adhemar defeated the Turks who were defending it, and led the way across. Once past that barrier, the crusaders followed the river until, after a sharp bend, the walls of Antioch suddenly appeared ahead. Theo, riding with Amalric, drew in his breath.

On their right-hand side, to the north, the wall rose out of the low, marshy ground along the river, solid and formidable. Directly ahead, the massive fortifications towered above them. On their left, to the south, the wall followed steeply up the slopes of a mountain, then over the summit and out of sight on the far side.

All along, at regular intervals, towers were built so that every meter of wall was within bowshot of one of them. At the very peak of the mountain, within the southern wall, a stone citadel stood guard, with the flag of the Turkish governor of the city, Yaghi-Siyan, flying defiantly above it. The crusaders could see that the citadel, walls and towers were heavily manned, but there was no sign of soldiers.

"He knows we are here," Amalric muttered. "Does he have such contempt for us that he does not even bother to put his army on display?"

The city of Antioch spread itself out within these fortifications. From where he was, Theo could see houses, villas and palaces dotting the hillsides above him. Gardens stretched out luxuriously. The climate was so much milder here than in the north that they were still filled with flowers and trees in full leaf. Smoke rose from innumerable cooking fires, and the heavy scent of spices wafted down to them.

With a flourish of trumpets, the crusading army advanced. Theo could not tear his eyes away from the sight of the magnificent city sprawled out behind its walls on the mountainside before him. But something was wrong. It took him several moments to realize that, beyond the noise that surrounded him—the blaring of horns and trumpets, the neighing of horses, the shouting of men and the usual crash of arms as the foot soldiers followed—there was no sound. The city was silent. He could see no one on the streets, in the gardens or around the houses. The people were keeping themselves out of sight. Waiting.

Godfrey signaled to his followers to halt, as Bohemond and the other leaders spread out along the wall toward the mountain. It was immediately obvious that they could not surround the city as they had Nicaea. It was also immediately obvious that taking Nicaea had been child's play compared to the battle ahead. And yet, Antioch had to be defeated; take it they must. If they left it as a Turkish bastion, they were leaving themselves open to attack from behind as they continued on to Jerusalem.

Besides, Antioch was one of the most important Christian cities. St. Peter had preached here, and the followers of Christ had been proclaimed "Christians" for the first time within these walls. There was still a large Christian community in the city, led by a patriarch of the church. It was imperative that they reclaim Antioch. But, looking at those massive, silent fortifications, Theo felt a creeping doubt within him. How was this to be done? He settled himself deeper into his saddle and stared at the city before him. Even Amalric had fallen silent.

Godfrey's army was deployed around the northern gate, on level ground with the Orontes River behind it. Bohemond took up a key position facing the eastern gate on the road they had taken from the Iron Bridge. They guessed that reinforcements for the city, if any were needed, would come this way. Robert of Flanders and Stephen of Blois watched over the remaining gate on this side, flanked by Raymond of Toulouse and Bishop Adhemar. There were two other gates, one that faced west, and the main river gate where a stone bridge crossed the Orontes; but the crusaders did not have enough men to guard them as well. This meant that the Turks within the city still had access to the western road that led to the sea.

"This siege will be a long one, my son," Count Garnier said, as they set up their tents.

† † †

At first, the footsore crusaders settled down with relief. As October passed into November and the weather became even cooler, they were grateful for the rest. The surroundings of Antioch were fertile and the vegetation abundant. There were fields of grain, grape vines everywhere, and trees bent down with the weight of oranges, lemons, figs and other fruit. Herds of cattle roamed freely; the soldiers killed them indiscriminately and ate only the choicest cuts of meat, throwing away the rest to the dogs. Horses grazed on what seemed to be limitless fodder. Every morning, the priests gave thanks for God's abundance and mercy. But within weeks, the thousands of hungry mouths had taken their toll, and detachments of the army had to be sent out to scavenge in the surrounding countryside. Still, no plans were made for storming the city.

"This cannot go on." Theo strode furiously into his campsite late one evening. "Our leaders wrangle among themselves and come to no decisions. And while we sit and do nothing, the Turks are brazenly going back and forth through the river gate and the western gate whenever they please." He paused. "What are you doing to that horse?"

Emma looked up from the shadows at the edge of the fire where she was tending Centurion. "Scratching his stomach," she answered complacently. "He loves a good belly tickle now and then." The hulking charger was standing with his head down, snuffling with contentment.

"He is a warhorse, not a puppy dog," Theo said irritably.

Emma quirked an eyebrow. She was about to make a sharp retort when a rustle in the bushes silenced her. Quickly, she lowered her head and drew her hood down over her eyes. She began to brush Centurion.

A figure stumbled out of the bushes.

"To me, Otto," he mumbled, voice sodden and blurry with drink. He staggered toward Emma.

"You are mistaken, sir," Theo said, advancing to ward him off. "This is not your camp."

"You! What are you doing here?" The figure straightened and glared at Theo.

With a shock, Theo recognized Guy.

"This is not your campsite," he repeated, his voice cold. "You are mistaken."

Guy stumbled over a root and fell flat. He reached out and grasped Emma's foot.

"You, boy, help me up," he commanded.

Emma wrested her foot from his grasp and stepped back.

"I said, help me!" Guy commanded. He got to his knees. Emma still made no move toward him.

"Is this how you train your minions?" Guy demanded, pulling himself up by Centurion's halter. The horse snorted, as if insulted, and side-stepped away from him. Guy swayed and caught Emma by the shoulder. She wrenched herself out of his grasp, sending him stumbling forward into Centurion's hindquarters. Centurion kicked out angrily, grazing Guy's shin. If the blow had landed squarely, it would have broken his leg.

With an oath, Guy swung out and hit Emma full across the side of the head. He raised his hand to strike again, but she was too quick for him. She dodged out of his reach, but in that second her hood fell back. For a moment, he stared at her, her face illuminated by the flickering firelight.

"You're pretty for a boy," he began, and then his brow furrowed. He shook his head as if trying to clear it. "Familiar," he muttered. "You look . . ."

Emma darted off into the darkness. Guy stood, still swaying, looking after her. He turned to Theo.

"Your groom has a familiar look to him. Where did you get him?" His speech was less slurred; the effort of thinking seemed to be clearing his head.

"He is Armenian, from Marash. There are many lads there who have his looks," Theo said quickly. He made a move toward Guy. "May I help you?" he asked, controlling his voice with an effort. It had taken all of his will not to lash out at Guy when he had struck Emma.

"I need no help from you," Guy retorted, drawing himself up. He took a step away from the campfire, and halted. He looked into the darkness where Emma had disappeared, then back at Theo. "There is something amiss here," he began. But the thickness was back in his voice. He shook his head again, passed his hand across his eyes and staggered away.

•Antioch

MEDITERRANEAN SEA

ELEVEN

"**S**iege engines, that's what we need. Good strong catapults to lob stones at the walls. You should advise Duke Godfrey to start building them at once. Ouch!"

"Hold still." Theo was bathing Emma's forehead where an angry, purple bruise was forming. "I do not *advise* the duke on anything. He does not listen to anyone as unimportant as I." Theo was fuming at Guy's cruelty, but knew there was nothing he could do. Knights cuffed grooms regularly. If he made any kind

141

of protest, he would only draw attention to Emma, and that he dared not do—especially since Guy had already sensed something unusual about her. Emma herself seemed to have taken the matter in her stride.

"And how does it come to pass that you consider yourself such an expert on war?" he asked, trying to keep his voice light.

"I have good ears. I listen."

"Perhaps the emperor will send us siege engines. He knows how things stand here and he is pledged to help us."

Emma snorted and tossed her head. The sodden cloth that Theo was using to bathe her forehead went flying.

"I wouldn't waste time waiting for his help," she said. "He hasn't done much for us so far. I think he is glad to see us gain back his lands for him, but he is not about to put himself in peril. That's what the talk around the campfires is, anyway. Perhaps my lord Raymond is right. He advocates attacking at once. God has protected us so far; surely he would give us victory over these heathen. It must gall Him immensely to see this holy city of His so desecrated."

"So now you speak for our Father Himself?" Theo cast a cautious glance around as he bent to retrieve the cloth. The talk verged on blasphemy. He quickly changed the subject. "You should not skulk around campfires. You might be discovered." Emma seemed to be getting more and more independent since transforming herself into a man, and worry made him sound like an over-anxious parent.

"How else should I know what is going on? I cannot converse with anyone or ask questions."

"I will tell you what you need to know." A mistake, and Theo realized it at once.

Emma arched an eyebrow, then winced. "It may be that you do not always know what *I* need to know."

Theo let out a grunt of exasperation. Living with Emma as his groom was presenting him with more complications than he had imagined. He was about to reply when yet another rustle in the bushes silenced him. He signaled to Emma and she quickly drew her hood back over her eyes. Theo turned toward the noise.

A man emerged. Theo reached for the dagger at his waist.

"Stay! Do not fear me! I am a Christian!" The man spoke the Frankish language of Godfrey and his people with difficulty.

"Who are you? Where are you from?" Theo's hand stayed on the haft of his weapon.

"From Antioch. Many of us have slipped out of the city this night. I have come with my wife and babe." He nodded to the shadows behind him, where Theo could just make out the figure of a woman holding a child in her arms.

"Take me to your lord, I pray you. I would speak with him."

"Your name?"

"Arnulf, my lord. Arnulf of Antioch."

Theo hesitated, then made his decision. "Come then. I will take you to my father, Count Garnier. But I warn you, if you mean any ill, he is well protected. You will not escape."

Not taking his eyes off the man, Theo reached out his right arm. Emma hastened to retrieve his sword from the tent and handed it to him. He buckled it on. As far as he could see, the man from Antioch was not armed, but Theo would take no chances.

He directed the way to the count's tent, keeping close behind Arnulf and his family. At the flap of the tent, he spoke to the halberdier on guard, a man Theo had known since his youth.

"I would speak with the count, Reynald. This man has something to say to him." He motioned to Arnulf to wait, then eased himself inside.

Count Garnier sat on a chest, a plank drawn up before him, supported by two other chests. He was peering at a crudely drawn map of the city of Antioch and its surroundings. He sat in a flickering pool of light given off by a burning wick floating in a dish of oil. The rest of the tent was in darkness. The smell of the lamp filled the tent, and smoke pricked at Theo's eyes. The count looked up as Theo came in.

"We must have a bridge of our own over this river if we are to receive any supplies from the coast," the count said. "What do you think, son, of building a bridge of boats?"

"Of boats?" Theo echoed, startled. "How could such a thing be done?" A bridge was necessary, he knew. The Orontes River ran from east to west at this point, and they were camped on the southern side of it, between it and the city walls. The only bridge across the river was at the western end of the city, where the Turks had control. The sea lay to the west, and the road to it was across the river. If the emperor did send supplies—*when* the emperor did send supplies, Theo corrected his thoughts immediately—there had to be a way across the river to the crusaders' encampments. But a bridge of boats? With a shake of his head, he brought his mind back to why he had come.

"There is a man outside, my lord. His name is Arnulf. He says he is a Christian from the city. He would like to speak with you."

Count Garnier looked up quickly. "Good!" he exclaimed. "News from within the walls would be invaluable. Bring him in, Theo, I would hear what he has to say, although I do not harbor much trust for these Byzantine Christians. They are a tricky lot. I have been warned."

Theo leaned out and signaled to the man. Arnulf slipped through the tent flap and stood before the count, head bowed. Even so, his hair brushed the ceiling. He was a big man; his shoulders were heavily muscled, and muscles rippled down his arms as well. His hands were large and splayed, worn and hardened by work.

"I am a blacksmith," he said. "Would you have use for me in your camp? My family and I do not want to stay longer in the city, although it has been my home since birth."

"By all means," Count Garnier replied. "We would welcome your services. But tell me, what are conditions like in the city, and why do you want to leave it?"

"Yaghi-Siyan has been a good governor, and fair to the Christian community within his walls, up to now. Since their conquest of this city, the Turks have been just rulers, but with your arrival, things have changed. I fear for what is to come, and I would like to help you. The thought of returning Antioch to the fold of God gives me great delight."

"In what way have things changed since our arrival?" Count Garnier asked. "From our vantage point here, nothing has occurred at all."

"From here, perhaps, it looks peaceful and quiet, but within there are stirrings."

"Tell us," the count commanded. "I would know what is going on inside the walls."

"We Christians have been well treated by the governor up to now," Arnulf repeated. His accent was heavy and he searched for words with difficulty. The dialect spoken by the Christians in Antioch was far different from the Frankish tongue. "Our patriarch, John, was permitted to reside with us and tend to our spiritual needs; our churches were allowed to remain Christian and not converted to Muslim. But, since your arrival, Yaghi-Siyan grows angry. The patriarch has been thrown into prison. Many of our leading Christian citizens have been banished, others such as myself have fled. The churches . . ." His voice roughened. "The Cathedral of St. Peter has been desecrated. The emir is using it as a stable for his horses!"

"And the governor," the count asked, "does he seem to be preparing for a long siege?"

"He is, my lord. And is well able to do so. There is abundant water within the walls, market gardens and pasture for any number of flocks. And the troops pass in and out at their pleasure through the western gates to reprovision the city as it needs."

"The mood, then?"

"The mood is one of triumph. The governor is confident he will defeat you."

"I thank you," Count Garnier said. "Theo, see that this man and his family receive food and shelter. I must report to my lord Godfrey on this."

In the days following, more and more Christian refugees slipped out of the city into the encampment. Some, however, came out only to spy, and then slipped back in. By no means were all the Christians within the walls discontented with their lot. Many feared any change. Their life had been peaceful and secure under the Turkish governor. In fact, they paid lower taxes than when the city had been under Byzantine rule. They wanted nothing more than to keep things the way they were and avoid conflict. Some were eager to take any information about the crusaders' plans to the governor, and so curry favor with him.

In this way, Yaghi-Siyan learned of the crusaders' reluctance to attack until reinforcements came, and he began to organize sorties against them. Turkish soldiers crept out from the western gate to cut off any small bands of foraging knights. The governor was clever enough, as well, to plant rumors among the Byzantine Christians that massive Turkish reinforcements were on the way. As the autumn weather turned to winter, and their second Yuletide season found them still so far from Jerusalem, the crusaders' initial optimism died and many began to lose heart.

✝   ✝   ✝

"I did not become a man in order to sit and stare at city walls," Emma grumbled as she and Theo sat beside their dying fire one evening.

"You have not become a man at all," Theo answered. His words were short. The wait was hard on him as well. He had celebrated Yuletide in the camp with the priests, but he had not celebrated it in his heart. "And you will have no part in the fighting when it comes," he added.

"That's another thing I want to know about. Why won't you talk about the battles? You have fought now, you've even been wounded. What was it like? Was it glorious?"

"Glorious?" Theo considered the word. "Not glorious. No."

"But to wield a sword! To charge into battle! What could be more spendid?"

"It's what comes after that is not so splendid." Theo paused. "I have killed men, Emma."

"Of course you have. But only your enemies. Only those who would kill you. That is what war is all about, surely."

"You speak more truth than you know. That *is* what war is all about." Theo stirred the embers of the dying fire with the toe of his boot. "I did not know what it would be like when we left Ardennes. My head was full of pomp and glory. We were doing God's bidding . . ."

"And so we are!"

"The first man I killed looked at me as I struck him, Emma, and he knew he was dying. I saw it in his eyes. He was not the enemy then. He was just a man, like me. And there have been so many others—so many."

"I do not understand. I would give anything to be a man and wield a sword for the glory of God." Emma leaped to her feet. "We are fighting God's war, and you—you will be one of the privileged ones to restore Jerusalem to the true faith. How can you speak so gloomily? How can you look so torn?"

In the heat of the moment, she had forgotten all caution. She stood, hood thrown back, face aglow in the light of the fire. A startled voice called out from the edge of their campsite.

"By all that's holy—Emma!"

Emma gave a cry and turned away. She pulled the hood over her head. Too late. Amalric stood across the fire from her, eyes wide with shock.

†   †   †

"This is madness. Madness." Amalric had repeated the words a dozen times. "You cannot do this, Theo. A servant girl!"

Theo's patience snapped. "She is no mere serving wench. She is kin to Baldwin himself."

"Even worse! Dressed as a man, living with the troops. What if Lord Baldwin finds out? She should be with him, safe under his care. You have lost your wits, Theo."

"She was not safe with him." Theo glared at Amalric. "It is far safer for her to be with me."

"Far more convenient for you, you mean," Amalric said with a sneer, "to have your little wench nearby at night."

Theo reached for his dagger, but Emma forestalled him. So far she had not spoken, but now she put herself between Amalric and Theo, eyes blazing.

"Things are not what you think! Not at all! I cast myself on Theo's mercy because I knew very well what Lord Baldwin's designs on me were. Theo has protected me and cared for me well."

"I'll wager he has."

Emma's hand flashed out. The sound of the slap was echoed by a sudden cracking from a log on the fire. Amalric put a hand to his cheek, eyes wide with astonishment. For a second, there was absolute silence. The three stood frozen. Then Amalric reacted. He raised his own hand and would have struck Emma back if Theo had not leaped forward and grabbed it.

"You would stop me from slapping this insolent slut as she deserves?"

"She is no slut. She is well born and virtuous. You will not touch her."

"The count will hear of this. I promise you that."

Amalric wheeled as if to leave.

"Stay!" Theo called out. "Amalric! We are friends—you cannot leave like this!"

"You ask me to overlook this insult?" Amalric was breathing so hard the words came with difficulty.

"I do, for the sake of our friendship. I would not lose that. She will apologize."

"I will not." Emma's voice cut through theirs.

"I do not accept apologies from servants," Amalric growled.

"I do not apologize to those who insult me!"

"Amalric. Emma. We have all lost our tempers. Pray, let us cool down and talk about this." Theo grasped Amalric's arm. "We will drink a little of the wondrous wine they make here, and think about what we must do." His mind was in a fever, trying to find a way out. Emma *will* apologize, he was about to add, but the look on her face silenced him.

"Emma," he said instead. "Please. Fetch us wine. And for yourself as well."

Amalric's eyes followed Emma as she whirled away. They were still hot and angry.

"You are laying up trouble for yourself, my friend."

"Possibly," Theo agreed. "But I knew not what else to do. She appeared at my campsite attired as a groom and determined to accompany me." He had mastered his temper now, and was determined to settle the argument. "I could not send her back to Baldwin, Amalric. Without the lady Godvere there, he would have used her as he wished and then cast her off. I had to protect her."

"She will be discovered. What will you do then?"

"We will be more careful. As long as you say nothing . . ."

Emma returned with skins of wine for Theo and Amalric.

"Join us," Theo said to her.

"No," she replied. She fastened her eyes on Amalric. "I will not apologize," she said. "If I do not defend my own honor, who will? But I will beg of you not to give me away. You were probably within your rights to assume things, but it is not as you think. I serve Theo as his groom, nothing more. And I am a good groom, am I not, Theo?"

Theo managed a nod.

"I beg of you not to give me away," she repeated. The words were humble, but her stance was not. Her eyes were still locked onto Amalric's.

He was the first to look away. He shrugged and laughed.

"I do not make war with maids," he said. "I think you both mad, but I will not interfere. I forgive you." He tossed the last words out as he raised the skin of wine and drank it down.

"I did not ask for forgive—" Emma caught Theo's eye and stopped. "Thank you," she said instead. She turned to go back into her own tent. "And I forgive you," she threw back over her shoulder.

Amalric stiffened. He glared after her. Theo held his breath.

"Truth, that is no ordinary maid," Amalric said finally. His face lightened. "And this is no ordinary wine. Do you have more?"

Twelve

It did not snow in Antioch, but the rains set in just after Christmas. Every day, every night, it poured down incessantly. Every piece of clothing Theo and Emma owned was wet; it was impossible to dry anything. The damp cold seeped into their bones. Emma developed a cough that caused her to double over in pain, gasping for breath, until it was over. Duke Godfrey was seriously ill. His healers were at his bedside continuously but, despite all their efforts, he seemed not to improve. Bohemond and Raymond sent out a foraging army, but it ran into a Turkish contingent coming to relieve the troops in the city. Weak from hunger and taken by surprise, the crusaders were badly beaten. They suffered enormous losses; the survivors were too weak to continue foraging. Theo and Amalric watched as the remnants of the army straggled back into camp. Emma, hood low over her face, hovered in the background.

"The news?" Theo called to a passing knight.

"Not good," the knight replied. He passed a hand over a forehead caked with dry blood. He was horseless, walking awkwardly with pain or exhaustion, or both.

Amalric strode away without a word.

As Theo, followed closely by Emma, made his way back to his tent, he felt a sudden shifting of the ground under his feet. A curious, rumbling noise began, low at first, then increasing in volume.

"Theo!" Emma cried. The tent in front of them began to sway as if a wind were inside it, then collapsed. Theo reached for a tree to steady himself, but the tree itself was shuddering! He had a moment of complete disorientation. The world was tilting, slipping away from underneath him.

As suddenly as it began, it was over. The rumbling died away, leaving an unnatural silence. For a moment, the camp was completely without sound; not even a bird sang. Then the screaming began. Theo and Emma rushed for their tents. The whole camp was in chaos. Cooking pots had fallen into fires; tents had collapsed, trapping those inside. People were running to and fro in a frenzy, screaming. Miraculously, Theo saw no one who had sustained any injuries. Indeed, there seemed to be more danger to the people in this panic now than there had been during the upheaval.

When Theo and Emma reached their campsite, they found it intact. Centurion grazed imperturbably on the few scrabbly weeds that remained. If the earthquake had bothered him, he showed no signs of it now. Emma's nag side-stepped nervously away from them as they approached, jerking against its tether. It rolled its eyes wildly.

"Stay here, Emma," Theo said. "I must go and see if my foster father is all right."

The count's campsite was adjacent to Theo's. He reached it in a few steps, and was relieved to see that there, too, all seemed in order. Aimery and some of the other men were calming down horses and hysterical servants.

"Theo! Is all well with you?" Aimery called out as he caught sight of him.

"All well, thanks be to God," Theo replied. "Where is my father?"

"He has just left to see the duke and ensure that his camp, also, suffered no harm."

Theo looked around. Aside from one tent that lay in a heap, all was in order. Two of the servants were busy setting it to rights.

"An earthquake, they're calling it. Have you ever seen the like before?" Aimery asked. "Truly, I thought it was the end of the world."

"I've heard of such things," Theo replied, "but never felt one before." He was making an effort to appear calm, but his knees still shook and he had trouble keeping his balance. It was as if his body no longer trusted the stability of the earth.

Around him, the screaming had stopped, and the shouts were gradually dying down. The camp was beginning to return to its normal level of noise and bustle.

But that was not the end of it. That night, as Theo and Emma sat by their campfire, scraping the dregs of a watery stew from their bowls and talking of the incredible thing that had happened, Theo became aware of a crackling intensity in the air. He stopped speaking and looked up, beyond the trees. The rain had ended and the sky was clear.

"Emma," he breathed. "Look!"

Emma raised her head. Above them, the heavens shimmered and shivered with curtains of color. Sheets of green and blue stretched from the horizon to the sky above them. As they watched, the bands dimmed, narrowed, faded to yellow and silver, then blossomed again into vibrant color.

"What does it mean?" Emma asked in a whisper. "First the earth moves, and now this. Is it a portent from God?"

"I know not," Theo answered.

"The earthquake—it was as if God was displeased with us. But this—this is such beauty!"

†   †   †

The next morning, Theo was awakened by a clamor of voices.

"They can't do this!"

"Sacrilege!"

He thrust his head out of his tent to see men, women and children running toward the edge of the camp nearest the city walls. He pulled on his tunic and ran to join them.

"What's happening?" Emma materialized out of the morning mist beside him.

"Pull down your hood," Theo barked. "Do not speak!" He glanced around quickly to make certain no one had seen or heard her, but the people were too fevered to notice.

"It is the patriarch of Antioch himself!" a woman cried as she rushed by them.

In the general confusion and pandemonium, it was impossible to determine what was happening, but as they reached the walls, the situation became all too clear. Hanging over the wall, suspended in midair, was a cage constructed of rough planks bound together with rope. It swayed in the morning breeze. Inside, a man crouched, clad in a long, brown mantle, clasping a golden cross. As Theo and Emma drew near, they could hear him chanting. One horrified look was enough.

"It *is* the patriarch!" Theo gasped. "How could they inflict this indignity on him! How could they insult God Himself in this manner!"

The patriarch of Antioch, one of the holiest of God's priests—Theo could not believe his eyes. People were dropping to their knees all around; Theo and Emma followed their example.

"God is displeased with us," Bishop Adhemar declared at that morning's mass. "He has set the earth itself to shaking, and the heavens to display His warning. Now He allows the holiest of His servants to be punished for our sins. We are living in sin here. Our soldiers are pillaging and stealing instead of working toward the completion of God's will. There is sloth and laziness instead of planning for the conquering of Antioch and the liberation of Jerusalem. We will fast for three days and pray for His mercy."

Fast they did, but with famine already stalking the campsites, their self-denial made little difference. By February, the crusaders were starving. The countryside all around had been stripped of food, and the peasants' and villagers' winter supplies were exhausted, despite Adhemar's injunctions against thievery. Some began to eat their horses. Sorties from the camp were met with continual ambushes set by the Turks. The loss of knights and troops mounted daily.

"The monk Peter tried to flee," Theo reported to Emma one evening after he had returned from the daily meeting in Godfrey's tent. "Bohemond's brother, Tancred, brought him back."

"Why bother?" Emma answered. "He has been nothing but trouble since he joined us."

"There are many who regard him as a symbol. He was one of the first to follow the pope's call for a crusade."

"And a fine mess he made of it," Emma replied. She was sitting slumped in front of her tent, hood low over her eyes, wiping dust off Centurion's bridle. Her words were low and dispirited.

"We could not have allowed him to leave. It would have caused widespread disillusionment. Too many people are deserting us as it is." But privately, Theo agreed with Emma. The monk raged and disagreed with every decision the crusaders made. He was more of a nuisance than anything else.

† † †

The crusaders could not think of attacking the city until siege engines and mangonels had been constructed, and supplies for those machines had to come from the emperor Alexius. But the bridge of boats was built. Theo and Amalric watched the procedure with amazement. First, the boats themselves were constructed. Flat-bottomed and sturdy, they were lashed together, side by side, from one bank of the river to the other. Then planks were laid across them. When that was completed, a steady, floating bridge spanned the river, strong enough to support knights on horseback.

"Perhaps we have underestimated Taticius and his engineers," Theo remarked to Amalric, as the bridge took shape under their eyes.

As soon as it was completed, the first sortie across was planned.

"It is just what we need," Bohemond told the assembled princes and knights. "A battle to restore our flagging spirits! We will slip out tomorrow before daybreak."

The meeting was being held in Bishop Adhemar's tent. Theo sat at his foster father's side. Godfrey was present as well, but lounged to one side, supported by cushions. He was finally recovering from his illness, but was still weak.

"My scouts tell me that more Turks, under Ridwan of Aleppo, are massing to come to the aid of Antioch," Bohemond said. "They will travel along the road from Aleppo and try to cross the Iron Bridge to the east of us. We will be waiting for them. The infantry will remain in camp to contain any sortie from the city," he continued. "We will take up our position on the other side of the river. Ridwan knows not that we have the means of crossing it now. When he arrives, he will meet a surprise!"

In the darkest hour before dawn, the crusaders snuck out of their camp. Some of the horses balked at stepping onto the floating bridge, but Theo had no trouble with Centurion. The warhorse tested it with one massive forefoot, snuffed at it, then gave his wiry gray mane a shake and moved forward without further hesitation.

The need for absolute silence was paramount. If the Turkish sentries on the walls realized what the crusaders were doing, they would send scouts to warn Ridwan. In front of him and behind him, Theo could hear muffled curses in the black, early morning drizzle. The horses' hooves thudded dully on the wet wood. All metal pieces on bridles and reins had been swathed in cloth to prevent jingling. It was as if an army of ghosts was making its way in the mist across the floating bridge.

Once across, they guided their horses along the northern bank of the river until they reached a hilly outcrop just before the Iron Bridge, out of sight of any Turkish scouts. They took up their position between the river and the Lake of Antioch. In complete silence, they closed up their ranks and waited. It was still the blackest of nights. The cold, unrelenting rain drummed down upon them.

"Why in God's name were we ever cautioned against the sun in Syria?" a voice muttered at Theo's side. He looked over to see Stephen of Blois hunched down into the saddle of his charger. Water streamed down his helmet and made a steady waterfall off the iron nosepiece.

The first traces of dawn began to lighten the sky to the east. Just as the blackness changed to gray, the noise of an approaching army could be heard. Careless and confident, Ridwan's troops made no attempt to be silent.

Trumpets shattered the air. Knights and warhorses were galvanized into action. Theo felt Centurion charge forward before he gave the command. He raised his shield, settled his lance and braced himself for the heavy, bone-shaking lurch of Centurion's gallop. His stomach knotted, but an almost overwhelming joy flooded over him and blotted out everything else. At last, after months of inaction, starvation and bickering. At last!

The crusaders hit the mass of Turkish soldiers before the advancing army realized what was happening. They gave the Turkish archers no chance to form into lines; they had learned only too well how fearsomely effective the rain of arrows from those archers was. The charge did not break the Turks, however. The trumpets blew for a retreat and the knights withdrew. The Turks, sensing victory, raced after them—and fell straight into a trap that the leaders had cleverly conceived in Adhemar's tent the night before. The crusaders had now lured the Turks onto the very terrain where they wanted them. The lake on the left and the river on the right prevented the great numbers of Turks from surging around the crusaders and outflanking them. With the Turks pressed together in the narrow tract facing them, the crusaders charged.

Theo thrust and thrust again. In the heat of battle, there was no time for thought. It was strike and kill, or be struck and killed. He swung his sword, felt it sink into flesh. At the same time, he felt a blow to his shoulder that almost made him drop his shield. A spray of blood blinded him. He did not know whether it was his adversary's or his own, but in the frenzy of battle he felt no pain. The familiar silence enveloped him. He thrust and cut in a world without noise, a world without screams. He did not even hear the wild, barbaric cries that burst from his own throat.

The Turks broke. They turned and fled.

There was wild celebration in the camp that night. Theo submitted impatiently to Emma's bandaging of his shoulder wound, and then, for the first time, he allowed Amalric to lead him off to the festivities. There, he listened to the boasting and telling of tales of the deeds of the day that grew more and more grand with each horn of wine quaffed. There, the battle as it had really been gradually ascended into the realm of myth and glory; became battle as it was supposed to be. For the first time, the sickness that always attacked Theo after fighting did not overwhelm him. He lost himself in the firelight, the comradeship of fellow warriors, the wine. For the first time, he could forget the feel of his sword sinking into flesh, and the sight of dying eyes staring into his own.

He returned to his tent just before daybreak the next day, befuddled by the wine and the chaos of the celebration. Unseen, in the shadows of the tent where she had been waiting, Emma watched him stagger in.

† † †

With the construction of the bridge, the road to St. Symeon, the Christian port on the sea, was now open to the crusaders. They began to receive supplies sent by ship by the emperor Alexius. A fleet manned by Englishmen and led by Edgar Atheling, the exiled claimant to the English throne, sailed into the port, loaded with siege materials and mechanics sent by the emperor. At last, they could begin to build the machines necessary for the taking of the city.

Hunger was still prevalent, but the famine had been relieved somewhat by the emperor's supplies. Skirmishes between the Turks and the crusaders occurred daily, with great losses on both sides, but gradually the crusaders were able to build towers to guard all the bridges into Antioch. When the final one was completed, the Turks in the city were finally cut off. No convoys of food could reach them now, and the inhabitants could no longer send their flocks to pasture outside the walls. No further sorties could be mounted against the crusaders. The tide began to turn.

Spring came. Almost two years had passed since Godfrey and his crusaders had left their homes in the Ardennes. Theo wondered briefly how his father and brother fared, but he gave them little thought. They seemed part of another, distant world, one that he would probably never see again. His world now was the world of the crusaders. His family was Count Garnier, Amalric and the other men he rode beside every day and stormed into battle with. And Emma. But his feelings about her were so mixed—it was easier just to put them out of his mind. Besides, there was so much else to think about. The rains ceased. Food became plentiful.

"We can do it now," Theo exulted. "We can starve them into submission." There was a hardness in his voice that was new.

Emma stared back at him without answering. Her cough had gone and color was beginning to return to her face, but she was still thin and weak. If she had been quieter and somewhat distant since the night of the battle with Ridwan's army, Theo hadn't noticed.

Thirteen

h e did, however, notice with a mounting irritation Emma's frequent absences from the campsite. Spring burned into summer. No longer did Stephen of Blois complain about the lack of sun. The June heat was intense, more searing than Theo could have imagined. It bounced and shimmered off the walls. The knights were forced to wear linen coverings over their mail and helmets because the metal became too hot to touch.

As always, the camp was alive with rumors. One was

that the Turk Kerbogha was advancing. But this news was more fact than rumor, Theo believed, as did a great number of crusaders. The stories of Kerbogha's might and cruelty spread throughout the camp, creating panic. He would fall on them from the rear. The garrison would emerge and cut them down from the city. No one would escape. They would all be massacred.

More and more deserters began to slip away during the concealing hours of darkness. The lords and their knights issued commands and posted guards, only to find each morning that the guards had deserted as well. Clearly, the time had come when they must either attack or retreat.

Amalric slipped into Theo's campsite early one morning.

"Bohemond has a plan," he said. He looked around cautiously. "It is a secret; no one must hear of it. Where is Emma?"

"She is not here," Theo answered. He cast an annoyed glance at Centurion, who had not yet been groomed. Where was Emma, anyway?

As if to echo his irritation, Centurion blasted out a snort that sent Emma's nag skittering.

Theo thrust Emma out of his mind. "What kind of plan?"

"There is a man," Amalric said, his voice low. "He is an Armenian, a Christian now converted to Islam. He is a captain inside the city. His name is Firouz. He has a high position in Yaghi-Siyan's government, or so he claims. He has been loyal so far, but now he is angry. His master fined him for hoarding grain, and he is beginning to regret his conversion. He wishes to come back to the true faith. He has got in touch with Bohemond through a Christian in our camp—Arnulf, a blacksmith."

Theo looked up, surprised.

"What?" Amalric asked.

"Nothing," Theo answered. "I know the man, that is all. He is to be trusted, I think. Go on."

"Well," Amalric continued, "Firouz will sell the city to us. To Bohemond, anyway. I have some suspicions about this need for secrecy. It smells to me as if Bohemond is plotting to be in command when the fighting is all over."

"I have no doubt of it," Theo answered. "And I could not care less. Someone will have to govern."

"Why should it be Bohemond? My lord is equally fit to govern."

"Bohemond and the other lords have never stopped arguing about who is in command of this crusade since we left Constantinople. I, for one, am sick of the squabbling. What does it matter?" Theo jumped to his feet and strode over to Centurion. He began to groom the horse with quick, angry strokes. When Centurion turned his great head and glowered at him, Theo moderated his touch.

"It matters—" Amalric began, but at that moment Emma appeared.

Startled, she stopped and pulled her hood farther down over her face, then relaxed as she recognized Amalric. The two of them had come to a truce that was beginning to develop into actual friendship. She would have greeted him, but Theo interrupted.

"Where have you been? Centurion has not been groomed. The morning fire has not been kindled."

Emma shrugged. "I had business of my own."

"You are my groom. Your only business is my business," Theo snapped back. In the morning light, he saw a flush rise to her cheeks. "I'm sorry," he said. "I spoke hastily. I meant not . . ."

"You are quite right," Emma replied. Her voice was cold. "I must not forget that I am the servant of such a great warrior." She bent to the fire and made a show of arranging sticks and kindling.

Amalric looked from one to the other and raised his eyebrows. "A lovers' spat?" He laughed.

Both Theo and Emma whipped around to glare at him.

"Mercy! It was said in jest. I give you my apologies!" He turned to go, then half turned back. "Come to Godfrey's tent this evening, Theo. There will be news by then, I am certain of it."

† † †

They did not have to wait that long. Shortly after the noon meal and prayers, a herald galloped around the camp, trumpet blaring. They were to prepare for a raid into enemy territory at sunset. Even as Theo and Emma began organizing his equipment, Theo puzzled over the summons. Why a raid just now, when they should be preparing to attack the city itself?

"It may be a bluff," Emma said, polishing Centurion's bridle and testing a suspected weak spot in the leather.

She seemed to be right. Or perhaps the secret had not been kept as well as Bohemond had wished. Secret or not, the news had probably traveled, as news was wont to do, throughout the web of servants and grooms. Somehow Emma had learned how to tap into that web, despite her pretended muteness.

Another messenger followed more quietly, bidding the nobles and their knights to assemble in Bohemond's tent.

"Firouz is in command of one of the wall towers—the Tower of the Two Sisters, they call it," Bohemond announced when they had all gathered. "He is ready to betray the city. He urges us to mount our attack on the walls at that spot. He will give over the tower to us, and then we can seize the others."

Theo's blood began to beat more loudly in his ears and he felt the now familiar excitement rising within him. His fingers opened and closed on the hilt of his sword as Bohemond outlined the plan for the next day. The urge to withdraw the weapon was almost overpowering.

At sunset, with great fanfare and amid a cacophony of preparations, the army set out eastward as if to intercept Kerbogha. Theo mounted Centurion and gathered up the bridle.

"Go with God," Emma said. She gave Centurion a last stroke on his broad, stone-hard forehead, then stepped back.

"Thank you," Theo said. He reached to grasp her shoulder, but she had already moved away; his hand closed on empty air. He hesitated a moment, then urged Centurion on. There was something about Emma—something strange in her manner. He turned back one last time before he was out of sight of the campfire, but she was no longer there. He stared at the empty site. It was odd that she had not waited until he had ridden out of sight. Odd...

"Theo! Make haste!" Amalric's voice rang out over the general noise and confusion.

Theo set spurs to Centurion and fell in beside him.

† † †

The cavalry led, as usual; the infantry and the archers toiled over the hill paths behind it. Bohemond kept the pace slow so the different parts of the army would not be separated. They marched until night was well upon them; only then did the trumpets signal a halt. As the vast army came to a stop, orders were shouted down along the ranks, from the knights to the infantry and the archers. The army turned and began to march back, this time in silence. Bridles and reins were muffled; no man spoke.

Just before dawn, Theo saw the Tower of the Two Sisters loom up out of the darkness before them. All was quiet. There was no sign of a guard. The vast army materialized out of the surrounding hills almost without a sound.

A small detachment of about sixty knights, led by Bohemond, dismounted and crept forward. Theo was annoyed to find that Emma was not there, as they had agreed, to take Centurion, so he left the horse instead with Amalric's groom. He was puzzled at her failure to appear, but there was no time to dwell on it because Count Garnier was signaling to him. The count and Duke Godfrey were at Bohemond's side. Amalric and Theo followed closely. Some of the knights carried a long, wooden ladder. Still in the utmost silence, they placed it against the tower. One by one, the knights climbed up it and through a window high on the wall. Theo found himself behind Amalric. The ladder shook under the weight of the knights climbing above him. The rungs felt rough under his leather-shod feet. He climbed awkwardly, his chain mail heavy and impeding.

Amalric disappeared through the opening. Theo held his breath, waiting for an outcry, but the night was still. He reached for the last rung, then grasped the stone sill. With one mighty effort, he heaved himself over and inside. His linen shift muffled the jingling of his mail somewhat, but the slight noise still sounded loud to his ears. He struggled to his feet. Around him in the pitch dark he could sense, more than see, the assembled knights.

"This way," a voice hissed. Theo turned toward it and saw a figure silhouetted by torchlight in the open doorway. This must be the Armenian, Firouz, Theo thought. Following his silent directions, the knights slipped out of the room and made their way, some to the left and some to the right, to the other two towers that were under Firouz's control. Then they signaled to the rest of the waiting army below. Ladders were raised; the army poured up them.

At this, Bohemond gave the order to attack. The walls and battlements suddenly rang with the clash of weapons, and shouts shattered the dark stillness of the night. Theo drew his sword and rushed forward, Amalric at his side. Men tried to block them but together, shields protecting each other, they cut the Turks down and stormed along the wall and into the city. Their first objective was to open the city gates to the rest of the crusading army. To Theo's surprise, a horde of people surged to their aid: the Christians of Antioch were roused and ready to fight. Within minutes, the two main gates of the city were opened, and the mass of infantrymen and archers poured through.

Under this onslaught, the Turks were soon in full rout. Yaghi-Siyan and his bodyguard fled from the city and up the gorge that led to the Iron Gate. No one bothered to pursue him. His son, Shams ad-Daula, did not follow him, but instead led his followers up to the citadel at the mountain peak.

"After them!" The cry went up. Theo and Amalric, behind Bohemond, raced to follow, but were checked at the entrance. The citadel was solid stone and well fortified. Once inside, the Turks were safe. Frustrated, Bohemond nonetheless planted his purple banner on the highest point he could reach.

"We cannot get in, but they cannot get out. Let them stay in there like the trapped rats they are!" Amalric shouted. As the sun rose and touched Bohemond's banner with glints of gold, a great cheer arose from the crusaders. The knights turned and forged their way back down into the city.

The fight was over; the looting and sacking began. At first, the morning echoed and re-echoed with screams, but by nightfall they had ceased. Not a Turk was left alive in Antioch. The head of Yaghi-Siyan was brought to Bohemond by a peasant and impaled beside the purple banner so that his son might look out upon it from his refuge in the citadel. The houses of the citizens of Antioch were pillaged. In the chaos, not even the houses of the Christians were spared. Treasures were scattered or wantonly destroyed. Corpses lay in the streets, already beginning to rot in the summer heat.

Count Garnier and his men were assigned houses in the center of the city. Theo helped to clear them of bodies. The corpses were piled in the streets to be burned. It was late at night by the time the job was done.

"Go, Theo, rest. You deserve it. You have fought well today," his foster father told him finally. Theo was too exhausted to argue. He retrieved Centurion from Amalric's groom, then stumbled to the house the count had designated his. Of Emma, there was not a trace.

The house he had been given was built of white stone, and had a garden that someone had tended lovingly. The heavy scent of many flowers filled the air and mingled with the stench of blood and bodies. Theo unsaddled Centurion, found water for him, and tethered him to graze. He sank down on the front steps of the house. His mind teemed with the memory of streets filled with bodies, and of soldiers running amok and slicing down every person they saw. He had not taken part in that madness, but he had not been able to stop it, either. He dropped his head into his hands and retched. This sickness was worse, far worse, than any he had ever suffered before. It was not just a sickness of the body. It was a sickness of his very soul.

A commotion at the gate startled him.

"Your boy! It seems he decided to become a fighting man." It was Guy. A body was slung over his shoulder. "A womanly chap like this—you should whip some sense into him. I told you, did I not, that you spoil him?"

Theo leaped to his feet. Guy dumped the body on the ground.

"We are even now. A favor for a favor. A life for a life." Incredibly, he smiled. His face was covered in blood. His eyes glittered in the torchlight from the street. "Although I warrant this life is of very little value. Nevertheless, I pay my debts." He turned and left.

Theo stared down at the body. Blood had seeped into the heavy, woollen tunic of the boy lying there. His short hair was matted and covered his face. An empty archer's quiver was slung across his back; his left hand still clutched a bow.

It wasn't possible. Theo's eyes refused to see what lay before him. Only when the body moved and a moan escaped the bloodless lips did he allow himself to recognize Emma.

Antioch

MEDITERRANEAN SEA

Fourteen

Theo knelt to examine her. In the dim, smoldering light, it was impossible to tell how
badly she was injured. He ran out into the
street and wrested one of the torches from the ground,
then set it into the earth beside her. He knelt again.
Blood had soaked into her tunic around the left
shoulder. He pulled his knife from his belt and cut the
tunic away. An ugly gash ran from the bone under her
neck halfway to the shoulder. It did not seem too deep,
and was no longer bleeding, but Theo knew she must

have lost a lot of blood already. He picked her up and made his way into the house with her, shocked at how light her body felt in his arms.

In the unfamiliar darkness inside the house, he tripped and then realized he had stumbled into a low bed of some kind. He laid Emma down on it and went back outside for the torch. By its light, he managed to locate a dish of oil with a wick floating in it, and made a light. He leaned over Emma again. Her hand still gripped the bow. He loosened her fingers and took the weapon from her, then slipped the quiver off her back so she could lie more comfortably. Now, he had to clean the wound. He had found a well in the yard when he had tended to Centurion. He could get water there.

He was trying to think calmly, to do the things that had to be done, one at a time. He was trying not to think beyond that—not to think that Emma might be dying. He *wouldn't* think that. He straightened and went out to the well. An earthen bowl lay on the ground where it had probably been dropped that morning by whoever lived here. Used to live here . . . He filled it with water and went back to Emma.

She had not moved. Nor had she made a sound since that single moan.

Theo tore a strip of cloth from the bed covering, wet it and began to bathe the gash. When he was finished, he tore more strips and bound the wound as tightly as he could. He fought down the urge to run and try to find one of the healers that accompanied the crusaders. He dared not leave Emma for so long. If she awoke, alone and confused, there was no telling what she might do. The flow of blood was stanched; all he could do now was wait.

He sank down onto the floor beside the low bed and drew his knees up to his chest. He wrapped his arms around them, but kept his head upright, eyes fixed on Emma.

Whatever had possessed her? How had she managed to take part in the battle? The bow, the quiver— who had taught her archery? He began to think back to all her unexplained absences. Finally, he could not stave off the thought any longer: what if she died? No Emma? In an instant, the future turned bleak.

Toward morning, he slept. He was awakened by the first rays of the sun striking in through a window. The wick had burned out. Heat already hung heavy around him, and the smell from the streets outside permeated the room. Today would be spent disposing of bodies before they rotted even more. He couldn't face the thought.

"Theo?"

Emma's eyes were open and fixed upon him. Her face was flushed and covered in sweat. Theo dipped a clean rag in the bowl of water and knelt beside her to bathe her forehead.

"Where are we, Theo? How did I come here? I remember a sword . . . a sword flashing down upon me. I thought I would die. What happened?"

"Guy saved you. He found you lying wounded and brought you here."

"Guy? I thought he hated you. I know he disliked me. Why would he help me?"

"God alone knows. He is a strange person."

"Did he realize . . . that I am not . . ."

"No. By the grace of God, he did not."

"Just as well I am so scrawny." She attempted a smile and tried to raise her head, then dropped it back. "Where are we?"

"In a house. It has been given to me."

"Given to you? By whom? Whose house is it?"

These were questions Theo did not want to answer. He evaded them by going for clean water. When he came back, he knelt beside her once more.

"Why did you do this, Emma?" he asked.

"I wanted to fight, to be a part of it." She turned her head away, but not before Theo saw her eyes fill with tears.

He reached to bathe her forehead again.

"Rest then, Emma," he said. "We will talk later. I'm going to make a soup now—you need nourishment. Then I'll find a healer to tend to you."

"No!"

"Why not? You need a healer. Your wound is grave, it must be seen to."

"No!" She made a feverish effort to rise, then let out a cry of pain and sank back onto the bed. "You must not bring a healer, Theo. He will see that I am not a boy. I will be discovered!"

"But, Emma, you might die!"

"I will not die." Weak as she was, she dashed the tears away and managed to glare at him. "I'm not ready to die. Make me some soup and cleanse my wound and we'll see this through together—just you and I."

"You *must* see a healer."

"I will not. If you bring one to me, I will scream and carry on so much that it will probably do me even more harm."

Theo looked at her. Her face was set in a way he knew only too well.

"Soup, Theo. That's what I need. I pray you, good, hot broth. I will not die, I promise you."

Nor did she. Theo nursed her every moment he could steal away from his duties to the count, and gradually she began to mend.

"Truly, that maid has a will of iron," Amalric said one evening a fortnight later. He had come to share the evening meal with Theo, and Emma had insisted on sitting up with them. He looked at her and shook his head. "I would not have you for an enemy, Emma."

"And why should you?" Emma retorted. "As long as you keep my secret, we should be the best of friends."

"The best of friends," Amalric repeated. "The best of friends with a groom, who is really a nursemaid, who is really kin to a nobleman, and who decided to become an archer and go to war. An odd turn to my life, indeed."

Emma raised an eyebrow. "An adjustment that a clever young knight such as yourself can make, I vow."

"Emma . . ." Theo began warningly. Why did she always go too far? Why could she not at least pretend to maidenly modesty?

"I tire," Emma said. "I would sleep now. I'll leave you two to settle the affairs of the land by yourselves."

"A mercy," Amalric replied.

† † †

When the triumphant celebrations attending their victory died down, the crusaders took stock. They were inside Antioch now, and had the walls and towers of the city to protect them from Kerbogha when he attacked. All their civilian followers were sheltered as well within the walls, and were no longer the liability they had been outside. They could now be defended with ease. But there were problems.

"We do not have enough men to defend all the walls," Duke Godfrey said. "The walls are too long. And we must build another barrier between us and the citadel, or we will be attacked from there one night. Shams ad-Daula is in an enviable position to keep watch on us and report all of our movements to Kerbogha, while we can do nothing about it."

"Can we not mount another attack on the citadel?" Amalric strode back and forth in front of his foster father. "Surely, we must not just let Shams ad-Daula abide there."

"There is nothing else we can do for the moment," the duke replied. "Lord Bohemond has said that we must begin readying ourselves for the arrival of Kerbogha. We must find provisions, too. The city was much more in need than I had realized. There are practically no stores of food left." He did not add that the crusaders themselves, in their madness, had destroyed most of the city's wealth.

Little by little, order was restored. The patriarch John was released from prison and put back on the patriarchal throne. The Bishop of Le Puy had the Cathedral of St. Peter and the other desecrated churches cleaned and restored to Christian worship.

Early one morning, Theo awoke to a stirring in the city. He dressed quickly and sought out his foster father.

"Kerbogha and his army have arrived," the count said. He led Theo to one of the wall towers. Looking out from between the battlements, Theo could see the Turkish army encamped in the very positions the crusaders had occupied. He stared in awe at the sheer number of men. Tents stretched out along the walls for as far as he could see in either direction. The encampment teemed with soldiers, archers and horses—a moving, seething mass of brilliant color. The noise was indescribable. Men shouted, horses neighed and whinnied. Dozens of camels added their outlandish brays to the din.

Before the week was out, Kerbogha had reinforced the citadel above his troops and encircled the city completely. Cut off from any hope of foraging or replenishing their supplies, the crusaders were now the besieged, and the Turks the besiegers.

"Only the emperor can help us now," Theo said to Emma. "He must send troops to help us."

Emma was grooming Centurion. Her own nag had been lost or stolen during the battle. She came every day to Theo's house to perform her duties for him, but she refused to live there, preferring instead to pitch her tent in a nearby field.

"There are bloodstains on the floors," she said when Theo offered her one of the rooms. "Bloodstains from innocent people—a family, perhaps. I could not possibly live here."

Theo tried to persuade her, but his arguments were weak. In truth, he himself felt uncomfortable in the house and spent as little time there as possible. The knowledge that its former owners had undoubtedly been killed in the slaughter was just one more thing he did not wish to think about.

Emma paused to take a rest. She was still weak, but insisted on carrying out her groom's duties in spite of any protests Theo might make.

"If we are to depend on the emperor, then we are finished for certain," she said.

Theo shook his head. "We must have faith. We are here at his bidding, after all, to help regain Jerusalem and his lost empire."

"To fight his battles for him and reconquer the cities his Byzantine Empire has lost—that I am certain he desires us to do. But I doubt he wishes to help us much to do it—not if he has to put his own men in peril. And as for our quest to liberate Jerusalem, that is of no consequence to him whatsoever, I fear."

That evening, news came that Stephen of Blois and a company of other noblemen and knights had slipped out of Antioch and were on their way to the port of St. Symeon.

"Deserting rats," Emma said.

"Not so," Theo argued. "They will tell the emperor of our plight. They will make him send help."

"You are innocent as a babe, Theo. They will save their own skins, that is all."

Rumor was quick to prove her right.

"The traitor!" Amalric burst into his friend's house the next night as Theo was preparing for sleep.

"Who? What has happened?"

"Stephen of Blois. A scout just came back. The emperor did send the imperial army. The men were on their way to help us, but they met Stephen and he told them we were lost. He told them there was no hope for us. The army turned back!"

"And the emperor believed him?" Theo asked.

"Why should he not?" Amalric answered.

"Why should he not, indeed." Emma's voice came out of the shadows of the garden. "It gives him reason for abandoning us—for not risking the lives of his soldiers."

"So, this is how the Greeks repay us," Theo said.

"This is how," Amalric replied.

† † †

Two days later, Kerbogha attacked. Before the crusaders could mount an effective defense, his soldiers took possession of one of the towers on the southwestern wall. Bohemond responded by ordering the whole section of the city around that tower to be burned. Streets, houses, all went up in flames. When the fires died down, troops of halberdiers and archers were sent to fill the area and mount guard against the Turkish troops in the tower.

"And the people who were living there—what of them?" Emma asked.

"They will have to find other dwellings," Amalric answered.

"How grateful these Christians must be to us for liberating them from the Turks," Emma said.

"It is war," Amalric answered shortly. "These things cannot be helped."

"I am beginning to understand more and more what this thing called war really is," Emma said. "Not at all what they had us believe when we first started out on this venture, is it?"

Theo looked away from her. Amalric was right. Of course, he was. How could Emma be expected to understand?

Fifteen

We are starving. No help is forthcoming. We must fight."

Bohemond drew up the battle plans with all the leaders in a tent that was ominously quiet. There were no arguments, no suggestions. Theo and Amalric stood by the door and listened.

"We are vastly outnumbered," Bohemond said, "but we will make the best use of what we have. I will divide our troops into six armies. Two hundred men will be left in the city to keep watch on the citadel."

189

Theo and Amalric exchanged a tense look, but their worry was short-lived. They were to be among the attacking force.

"You will not sneak out with the army this time, Emma," Theo said when he returned to his house. He was about to say, "I forbid it," but stopped himself in time. Those words might be all she needed to decide to go. To his surprise, she gave him no argument.

"I have had my war," she answered. "I begin to think war is men's work after all. I want nothing further to do with it."

"It is God's work," Theo replied. "How else could we liberate His holy city?"

"God's work? Killing innocent people? Torching their homes and destroying everything they own? You yourself tried to tell me what it was like. *You* were shocked by the killing. I didn't understand then, but I have learned. I, too, saw men killed." Her voice faltered. "I, too, have killed."

"You can't be certain of that. An archer never knows where his arrows go in the fury of battle. It is not the same as striking a man down with a sword."

"I *am* certain. I saw the man fall, pierced by an arrow from my bow. It was at that moment, when I stood frozen, realizing what I had done, that I was struck down. The feeling is the same, Theo. Killing is killing."

"Killing is necessary." The words came out of Theo's mouth in a harsh voice that didn't sound like his. He rubbed a hand over his eyes. He was suddenly tired. He did not want to debate this with Emma. His duty was clear: he would follow his foster father and their leaders to war, to do God's work.

"Even the bishop himself makes war, Emma. Tomorrow, many of the priests will march into battle with us. Surely, they understand God's will. It is not for us to question."

"But I do," Emma replied. She turned away. "Anyway, you need not fear for me in the battle tomorrow. I will not be there."

† † †

Theo rode out with the knights at dawn. Each contingent was under its own banner, but he could not help seeing that the banners were tarnished, the panoply of war no longer as glistening and glorious as it had been. There was a worn and weary air to the men who marched and rode with him. Many knights were horseless. They marched on foot or rode donkeys and mules. Theo felt a sense of desperation in the air. This was a battle they *had* to win.

They filed out through the gates and over the fortified bridge that protected the city. Massed on the horizon, frozen in silence, Kerbogha's mighty army waited.

"Look!" Amalric hissed. He was riding behind Godfrey at Theo's side, as usual.

A herald detached himself from the Turkish army and rode across the field toward them. Theo waited for Bohemond to give the signal to pause. The signal was not given. Instead, the crusaders spread out into their appointed positions as soon as they had made the crossing. There were to be no negotiations.

The herald wheeled his horse around and galloped back to the Turkish ranks. As if nervous at this show of confidence by the crusaders, Kerbogha's army fell back.

A great shout arose from the crusaders and they surged forward. Trumpets blared, but if the command to halt was given, the eager knights heeded it not. Fooled by the very same trick they had used with the Turks, they galloped across the level field chosen by Bohemond as a good fighting ground, and were lured into the hills. Several of the horses stumbled in the rougher terrain. A few went down, carrying their riders, cursing, with them.

"It is a trap!" Theo shouted, as Kerbogha wheeled his army back to face the crusaders, archers at the ready. A hail of arrows shot into the crusaders' ranks. Theo felt one whistle by his cheek. More horses went down, their screams mingling with the cries of the surprised knights. A section of Kerbogha's army detached itself from the main body and galloped to outflank the crusaders on their left.

"Stop them!" Bohemond cried. Theo and Amalric charged, side by side.

Theo saw Bishop Adhemar's standard-bearer fall. The flag was instantly trampled into shreds, but the bishop himself was fighting still. Theo's sword flashed in the morning sunlight. Over and over it rose and fell, rose and fell. Theo lost count of the number of men he struck. The familiar, wild lust took over. The familiar, welcome silence descended upon him, wrapping him in a cocoon of invulnerability.

Only gradually did he realize the Turks were falling back. He was shocked to discover they were retreating. Beside him, Amalric let out a whoop of victory and spurred his warhorse on. Centurion, half-crazed, surged after him. Together with their comrades, they chased the fleeing army as far as the Iron Bridge, killing all they caught up to. Some of the Turks sought shelter in the keep that Tancred had constructed near the bridge. Theo only had time to see a group of crusaders surround them before he hurtled past. Their screams followed him, and then were lost behind him.

Finally, the fields before them were empty. There was no one left to kill. The crusaders reined in their warhorses and turned back, triumphant, to the city. At the gates, Bohemond turned to face his army.

"Send a message to the emperor!" he cried. "Antioch is ours!"

"Our victory is complete," Godfrey announced with satisfaction when he had gathered his knights together the following day. "The Syrians and the Armenians in

the surrounding countryside have finished our work
for us. Reports tell me they have killed all the remnants of Kerbogha's army they could find, and the
citadel has surrendered to us."

"Now, to celebrate," Amalric gloated.

"Our leaders are quarreling already over who is to
command the city," Theo said.

"What matters that to us?" Amalric responded.

† † †

"There is much sickness in the camp," Emma
reported as she groomed Centurion a few days later.

"There is always sickness," Theo answered.

"Not like this. I fear it is a plague, Theo."

Theo felt a stab of fear, quickly followed by a rising
anger. Were they never to be spared?

"Bishop Adhemar is sick."

The priests offered prayers daily for his recovery,
but to no avail. The whole crusading army was
stunned when they finally announced his death. The
bishop had been a true hero of the crusade, one of the
few people whom everyone followed and trusted.

The summer heat mounted; more and more victims succumbed to sickness. Aimery, Count
Garnier's beloved squire, took sick when the plague
was at its height. The count himself nursed him,
but he died. Theo mourned with his foster father.
Aimery had been Theo's friend from childhood. To

194

Theo, it seemed as if the last vestige of his boyhood was now gone.

Most of the crusaders thought the plague was carried in the air and that nothing could be done to avoid it, but Emma believed otherwise. She was convinced the disease lay in dirt, and she scrubbed Theo's house with a determined fury every day. She boiled all their woollen clothes over the fire until they were shrunken and stiff, and Theo forbade her to touch another of his garments. Then, from somewhere, she procured tunics and shifts of linen for them that were far cooler to wear, and could be washed as often as she pleased.

"All this washing and cleaning is not groom's work, Emma," Theo remonstrated. "People will think you odd."

"They already think so." Emma shrugged. "That is of no importance."

Thanks either to her industry or plain good fortune, Theo and Emma survived. Amalric also made it through the epidemic unscathed—and without Emma's obsessive cleanliness, he was quick to point out.

"The devil takes care of his own, they say," Emma replied with a sniff.

But the nobles still delayed their departure to Jerusalem. Summer ended and the cooler winds of winter began to blow.

"Our leaders fight constantly among themselves," Theo told Emma bitterly. "The emperor has sent word that now, after we have secured the city without any help from him, *now* he will come to Antioch. And our princes will not budge until he arrives."

"Why do they so wish to see him?" Emma asked. "I thought the only thing they could agree on was their hatred of him."

"Oh, they hate him well enough," Theo replied. "But he will undoubtedly bring rich gifts and rewards, and none of them wish to be done out of their share of that."

"Have you heard?" Amalric asked one morning as he joined Theo and the count for their first meal. "Jerusalem has been taken from the Turks by the Egyptians—the Fatimids!"

"What does this mean?" Theo asked.

"Nothing to us, as far as Bohemond is concerned," Amalric answered. "The Fatimids are Muslims, the same as the Turks they conquered. We will simply fight them instead of the Turks when we get there."

"*If* we get there," Theo muttered. "Our leaders would rather sit here and rot than get on with it."

"We will go soon, my son," the count assured him. "I have heard that the soldiers and the common folk have had enough of all this haggling, and I, for one, agree with them. They have threatened to march on their own and tear down the walls of Antioch as they leave if we do not come to some decision."

Amalric frowned. He would tolerate no talk that even remotely sounded like criticism of Duke

Godfrey, but he could not argue with Count Garnier.

"Three Yuletides, now, since we left our homes," Emma said, when Count Garnier had left and she had joined Theo and Amalric. She was always careful to stay far away when the count was present. "Who would have thought the journey would take so long?"

"Much has happened," Theo said. He scraped the last of the gruel from his bowl.

"Much," Emma agreed. She rubbed her finger around the rim of her bowl and then licked it. "We were so young when we left, were we not?"

Theo looked at her in surprise. In the privacy of the house, with only Amalric there, she had thrown back her hood, and Theo saw her clearly for the first time in months. There were lines around her eyes. Her mouth had a firmness and determination that had not been there before. In truth, she was a young, carefree girl no more. He supposed that he, too, had changed just as much.

"Well, I, for one, am still young, and I intend to remain so for the rest of my life. I will never grow old," Amalric announced.

"How will you accomplish that, my friend?" Theo asked.

"Live well, die young. In battle, preferably. That is the life I choose."

Theo searched his friend's face carefully. Amalric had not changed very much. His eyes were still bright and eager, his brow was unlined. There was, perhaps, a hardness that had not been there before, but that was all.

"The warrior's life suits you," Theo said.

"It does," Amalric agreed. "Most admirably."

It was true, Theo thought. Amalric fought when he had to fight, and enjoyed life to the hilt whenever he could. He was plagued by none of the doubts, the fears, the waves of sick desperation that overwhelmed Theo.

† † †

Finally, in January, they left. The weather was pleasantly cool as they made their way through the hills south of the city toward the coast. Theo's palfrey had died in the summer heat at Antioch, so he often walked with Emma, leading Centurion. He had a small Turkish pony that had been captured during the battle, but used it to carry their possessions, as he did not want to load Centurion even lightly. The long journey was taking its toll on the warhorse. He had been able to rest in Antioch most of the time, but now he was forced to cover many kilometers each day. Theo worried about him. He had not been bred to do this kind of work. The horse sweated profusely and some evenings refused to graze, just stood, head hanging with exhaustion and dejection. Emma tempted him with the sweetest grass and leaves she could find but, more often than not, he rejected them.

It was only when they had crossed the mountains and began to near the sea that he seemed to revive.

Theo could feel a difference in the air now. There was a salty tang to the breezes that sprang up in the early mornings. Tales began to be told among the crusaders of the immensity of the sea toward which they traveled.

"It stretches to the very end of the world," Amalric reported with authority.

In the end, however, nothing could have prepared Theo for the sight of it when they finally reached its rocky shores. An endless, moving, shining expanse. The waves murmured in, one after another. Wet, shiny seaweed festooned the rocks. When he bent to touch it, the water was warm, welcoming.

The first evening, after camp had been set up, Emma and Theo stole away to a secluded cove near their campsite. Out of sight of any of the other crusaders, Emma shed, for a few moments, her groom's disguise. She dropped onto a rock, tore off her worn, stiff leather shoes, and dangled her bare feet in the water with a sigh of absolute bliss. Theo could not bring himself to enjoy quite such a liberty, but he sank down beside her. At first, afraid someone would come upon them, he sat tense and alert, but gradually the quietness and beauty of the evening soothed and settled him.

They didn't speak. A few seabirds swooped out over the waves. Their cries sounded strangely mournful and lost. Behind them, the noise and bustle of the army and the pilgrims making camp were muted, as if they came from another world.

Suddenly, Emma stood and waded out into the softly plashing surf. Theo watched as she bent to run her fingers lightly through the water, as if caressing the small waves. She straightened up again, and then ventured a few steps farther out. A wave, larger than the others, caught her by surprise. She staggered with the force of it, then found her balance and turned back to face Theo, laughing.

"Come in, Theo," she cried. "Join me!"

He shook his head.

"But it's wonderful!"

When he still did not move to follow her, she made a face at him, shrugged her shoulders and splashed back to sit beside him. Her toes curled around the rocks. He felt the warmth of her body against him, smelled the musky, earthy smell of her . . . He stiffened and forced himself to draw away.

Emma had made it very clear what their bargain was.

Sixteen

"An envoy arrived last evening from the Fatimid Eyptians," Amalric announced one morning.

It was early April and the army had halted once again after traveling south, following the shores of the great sea. The heat increased daily, but there were always sea breezes to offset it, and the country-side was green and fertile. Orchards were in blossom. Beyond them, farther inland, snow-topped crests of mountains gleamed in the sun.

The crusaders were quarreling again. Raymond of

Toulouse had led his troops inland to lay siege to the town of Arga. Even though the town was of little importance to the crusade and the other princes refused to support him, he would not desist. Word had come from the emperor Alexius that he would join them by June, and once again Raymond intended to wait for him.

"We are nearing the Fatimids' territory, are we not?" Emma looked up from where she was trimming the long hair around Centurion's hooves. It collected mud and dirt and made the going harder for him. When she didn't immediately resume the work, the horse gave her a nudge that knocked her back on her heels. She righted herself and gave him a good-natured cuff on the ear. The warhorse was suffering now with the heat as well, and she was inclined to humor him.

Not that she ever did otherwise, Theo thought.

"We are," Amalric answered. "The Fatimids have driven the Turks out as far as the Dog River, a scant week's travel from here."

"And what did the messenger have to say?" Theo asked.

"He brought an offer from the Egyptian vizier, al-Adfal. He promised that if we abandon any attempt to force our way into their territory, they will allow us free access to all the holy places in Jerusalem."

"And Bohemond's answer?"

"He rejected it. Jerusalem must be Christian again—nothing less will do. The envoy went away furious. He said we will all be killed like dogs."

They celebrated Easter amid palm trees that Christ Himself must have looked upon. A month later, the count told Theo that the princes had convinced Raymond to abandon his siege of Arga.

"The fighting has cost the lives of many of his men," he told Theo, his voice weighted with sadness.

When the remainder of Raymond's men rode, sagging and defeated, back into the crusader camp, Theo saw rivulets of tears staining channels down Raymond's dirt-encrusted cheeks.

"Not a prince who accepts failure easily," Amalric muttered.

† † †

"Finally, we move again," Theo announced to Emma early the next day. They struck camp and the army continued its progress down the coast, through the small seaport of Jabala, where the emir surrendered to them with hardly any resistance, and on to the port of Tortosa, where the inhabitants made no resistance at all.

"I see that our army is behaving with its usual gratitude and respect for those who do not oppose us," Emma remarked, as she stood by Theo and watched soldiers march into camp with animals that they had captured on raids into the surrounding countryside. Ponies, goats and even more of the curious camels were led in. The camels could go for the most amazing periods of time without water, but they were not suited for riding, Theo discovered. He had tried it, and found that the rolling lurch of the beast made Centurion seem a model of comfort and ease in comparison.

They reached Tripoli, where the emir greeted them effusively.

"He has not only released three hundred Christians that he has been holding captive, but he's given them fifteen thousand bezants in compensation and fifteen fine horses," Amalric reported. "He's provided us with pack animals and provender for the entire army as well."

"Only too glad to see us on our way out of his city and supplied well enough to tackle the Fatimids for him," Emma remarked.

"She is probably right," Amalric admitted. "The Egyptians press ever closer. It will make the emir feel much better to have us as a buffer between him and them."

The army warily approached the Fatimid frontier at the Dog River. Although shallow here, the river was a fast-flowing stream that cut its way down through boulders and rocks from the wooded mountains above to hurl itself into the sea. Both Theo and Emma rode Turkish ponies now, and carried their supplies on one of the emir's pack animals. Centurion plodded beside them, head down and sweating profusely. He waded into the cool water and stood there, letting the current swirl around and past him as if he were one of the great boulders themselves.

"Move him out of there," Theo ordered Emma. "He is in the way."

"He will not move," Emma replied.

"Make him," Theo insisted.

"I cannot," she said.

"You cannot?" Theo echoed. He scowled.

"No," Emma answered, "I cannot. He will move when he wishes."

Theo's scowl deepened. "You spoil that animal entirely too much," he said. "I will not have this." He strode into the water and took hold of Centurion's reins.

Emma relinquished them and made her way to the river's edge. There she stood, hands behind her back, and watched. Her hood covered most of her face, but Theo could see a small smile twitching at the corners of her mouth. He tugged on Centurion's bridle. It was like tugging on a stone wall. He tugged again. "Move!" he commanded. Centurion snorted and bent his head to drink.

Theo suddenly became aware of amused looks as the soldiers forded the river on either side of him. He dropped Centurion's reins and waded to shore.

"Stay here with the stubborn beast, then, and catch up to me when he chooses." He gathered up the reins of their ponies and stormed off down the path.

He had expected that they would make camp after crossing the river, but the signal came back to forge on.

"We must conserve our supplies," the count told him. "All the ports from here on are in Fatimid hands and we can expect no further reprovisioning. Bohemond is anxious to press on with as little delay as possible."

Emma and Centurion did not rejoin him until evening.

"He refused to move until the entire army finished crossing," Emma said, with a rueful shake of her head. "But he is much refreshed now."

They drew near to Beirut. Theo marveled at the lavish city, and the luxuriousness of the gardens and orchards surrounding it. Instead of rocky shoreline, he saw vast beaches of sand. Truly, Beirut seemed like a paradise, set on the shores of the gleaming sea. The citizens of the city, at first fearful, began tentatively to come out of their houses as the army passed. Bearing gifts of fruit and all kinds of food, they pressed the offerings onto the crusaders.

"We are guaranteed safe passage through the city if we do no harm to the fruit trees, crops or vines," Godfrey told them. The order was passed down through the ranks. The troops obeyed, and the passage became a kind of celebration. The townsfolk came out laughing, carrying armfuls and baskets of food; the crusaders accepted it all with delight.

The next town on the coast was Sidon. Here, the

garrison made a sortie against the crusaders. The army repulsed it easily and, in retaliation, the troops were let loose to plunder and ravage the gardens of the suburbs. Then they moved quickly on to Tyre.

"We will rest here," Bohemond finally decreed. So they made camp outside the high walls of the city.

Theo could see soldiers from the town's garrison spying on them from behind the safety of the walls, but none came out.

† † †

If Beirut had seemed a paradise, Tyre was even more beautiful. Emma tethered Centurion in the shade of a wide-branching tree where the breeze from the sea could help cool him. Although it was still only May, the weather was already hot. Theo was entranced by the sandstone houses of the city that glistened pink and amber in the sun. The town was set comfortably among fields and groves, with the sea on one side and thickly wooded mountains rising on the other, some still snow-capped. Rivers of blossoms from countless orchards cascaded down through the valley that cleft the hills above them.

"I must go exploring," Emma declared the morning after they had made camp. "Will you go with me?"

"Exploring," Theo questioned. "Where?"

"Up there." She pointed to the trees rising up the hillside above them.

"But the camp—the beasts—we cannot leave them unattended for so long."

"I know a boy who will watch them for us and make certain Centurion stays in the shade and has plenty of water. He's the son of a friend of mine."

"You seem to have made a lot of strange friends," Theo answered. "Is this the friend who taught you how to use the bow and arrow?"

Emma flushed. "Yes," she said. "He is one of the archers. You do not know him."

"Does this friend know you are not really mute? That you are not a boy?"

"He does not."

"How did you manage that?"

Emma shrugged. "I managed." She would say no more.

Theo looked up at the cool darkness of the woods, the inviting flash of small streams among the fruit blossoms. He gave up the questioning. It did not matter. "Get your boy, then, and we'll go," he said. "It's a good idea."

They made their way out of the camp, Emma following behind Theo with her hood pulled low over her face as if she were a dutiful groom attending to his master. As they reached the outskirts, they were hailed by a shout. Theo looked back to see Amalric coming after them.

"Where are you going?" he called.

"Exploring. Up in the hills," Emma answered. "Will you come with us?"

Amalric hesitated. He looked at Theo.

Theo grinned. "I echo my groom's invitation," he said.

Amalric shrugged, and made up his mind. "All right," he said, "I'll come." He fell into step beside Theo. Emma followed.

They climbed toward the wood through fields bright with purple asters, sweet-smelling clover, daisies and scarlet-petaled anemones. In the distance, they could hear bleating and the occasional tinny ring of goat bells. Past orchards heavy with the scent of oranges and lemons, past silver-leaved olive trees, higher and higher they clambered. The air was cooler here, crisp and clean.

Once out of sight of the camp, Emma could control her eagerness no longer and raced to lead the way. She climbed at such a pace that Theo and Amalric, although they would never admit it, began to find it hard to catch their breath. Finally, she stopped at the mouth of what seemed to be a small cave. She dropped down to sit on a rocky outcropping, and faced back the way they had come.

"Look!" she exclaimed.

Theo and Amalric threw themselves on the ground at her feet, and looked where she was pointing. Below them, behind its walls, the city of Tyre lay spread out to their view. Gray marble streets, as ancient as history, dissected it neatly and formally. Flat-topped houses, minarets, domes slumbered among the fronds of palm trees as if stunned by the heat of the sun that beat down upon them. At the shoreline, rows of pure white columns, their original purpose lost in the memory of time, stretched from the city out into the sea itself. From here, they could see, through the crystal-clear turquoise water, more columns broken and scattered in the sand on the bottom, as if cast there by a giant hand. Fishing boats sailed over and among them. In the eastern part of the city was a ruin piled high with Roman bricks; in the west, strange to their eyes, a vast circular amphitheater, ringed with rows of seats.

"I've heard tales of those places," Theo said. "In olden times, the Romans forced Christians to fight within them—with each other, with other men and with fearsome beasts."

A stream cascaded in a foam of white off the edge of a cliff far above them. Too far away for them to hear, the water fell into a silver ribbon that wound its way past them and on into the valley below.

They sat for a long while in companionable silence. Amalric, ever restless, busied his hands with the making of a wreath out of the meadow flowers around him.

When Theo finally turned to look back at Emma, he saw that the stones she sat on were part of a terrace built by human hands. The cave behind her was flanked with more stones. From where he sat, he could see markings on them. He got to his feet and walked over to examine them more closely.

"What is it?" Emma asked. "What have you found?"

"These marks," Theo answered, "they look like writing, but of a sort I have never seen before."

Emma was on her feet in an instant to join him. "They are on either side of the cave," she said, tracing them with her fingertips. "I wonder if there are more inside?" She made as if to go in.

"Wait," Amalric called. He leaped to his feet as well and caught up to her, the wreath in his hand. He lifted it up and placed it upon her head. "A crown, my lady."

Emma smiled. She had thrown her hood back. Her hair had grown out somewhat, and the flowers glowed crimson against the black curls that framed her face.

"I thank you, my lord," she answered, dropping him a curtsy.

He responded with a deep bow of his own and an answering smile.

"At your service, madam."

Emma turned back to the cave with a flourish worthy of a queen, and walked into it.

"Take care—" Theo began, but his words were drowned out by a cry.

"Oh, Theo!"

He ran in, then skidded to a halt. The sun struck the far wall, lighting up a throne carved into the rock. Two monstrous beasts, heavily maned and baring their teeth, flanked either side of it. Their long, tufted tails curled around them to meet at the base.

"This must be a temple," Emma cried. "An ancient, pagan temple!" Queenly dignity forgotten, she ran across to the throne, pulled herself up and sat on it, one hand on each of the beasts' heads. She lifted her flower-crowned head high. A shaft of sunlight limned her with brightness.

"Emma!" Theo was appalled. Heathen though the temple was, Emma's brazenness seemed like sacrilege.

"A goddess. A goddess summoning her slaves to do her bidding."

Amalric's voice came mocking from the opening of the grotto.

Seventeen

At that moment, the sun dimmed, and the cave was plunged into gloom. "I like this not at all," Theo said. He made the sign of the cross. "Let us get out of here."

Emma laughed. "For shame, a Christian knight afraid of the old gods."

"I am not afraid," Theo said. "But this place has an evil feel to it. We should get back into the clean air."

When they emerged, they found that dark clouds were fast covering the sun. The rumble of thunder rolled out. In the distance, lightning flashed; they watched it strike first one hilltop, then another. The sudden change from the bright, sunlit day was so dramatic that they stood watching the approaching storm as if mesmerized.

"We are going to be drenched," Theo said finally, wrenching his gaze away from the spectacle. "We must hurry."

They started down, but the rain caught them on the outskirts of the camp. Emma led the way, laughing and excited by the storm. The sudden onslaught of the downpour only seemed to exhilarate her all the more. Her crown of flowers shredded; wet petals glued themselves to her forehead. Her cheeks were flushed, her eyes bright. She had flung back her cloak and her tunic clung wetly to her body.

At that moment, Guy emerged from the trees. He stopped when he saw them, eyes fixed, wide with astonishment, on Emma.

Emma grabbed the folds of her cloak and wrapped them around her. Her hands searched desperately for the hood to cover her face, but it was too late.

Guy recovered his voice. He began to laugh.

"So this is your groom! And I suspected it not when I saved her life. Baldwin's wench! Truly, Theo, I would not have thought you capable of such a trick."

"You don't understand—" Theo began.

"Oh, but of course I do. I only wonder that you allowed such a delightful toy to play at war. You might well have lost her."

"She is not—"

Guy interrupted Theo. "What an interesting situation," he said. "I wonder what I should do with it."

Before Theo could answer, he turned and left. His laughter rang out behind him, loud and scornful.

✝   ✝   ✝

Theo lay sleepless in his tent that night. He had heard rumors that Baldwin, who had established his own little kingdom in Edessa, was thinking of riding down to rejoin the crusade, now that the army was so close to Jerusalem. If he did, and Guy spoke out—and why would he not?—Baldwin was certain to demand Emma's return. What would they do? Theo was certain of one thing only: he would not let Baldwin get his hands on Emma again. But how could Theo oppose him? His own foster father would be shocked at what he had done. The count would be certain to side with Baldwin.

Theo tossed restlessly on his pallet, turning the questions over and over in his mind. He had barely dozed off into a fitful sleep when a sudden, muffled cry awoke him. He leaped up and dashed outside. The cry had come from Emma's tent. As he ran toward it, he saw the small shelter wobble. The sides seemed to bulge for a moment, and then a figure scrambled out through the opening, on his hands and knees. Guy was backing out as quickly as he could, followed by Emma, who was wielding a stick of firewood and beating him on the head and shoulders. She was swearing in almost every dialect to be heard in the camp.

Theo began to go to her aid, then stopped. His help wasn't needed. Guy managed to get to his feet, and for a moment it seemed as if he would attack Emma, but she stood her ground, brandishing her weapon.

Theo could hold back no longer. This time, it was he who laughed.

Guy whipped around.

"I think you will keep our secret now," Theo chortled, "or the entire camp will be delighted to hear the story of how a maid beat you off with a stick of firewood. It would cause many an hour of merriment, I vow."

"You!" Guy's eyes darkened. "You have made one mistake too many, my friend."

Theo sobered immediately. His hand went to the dagger at his belt.

"Take care that *you* do not make a mistake," he said, his voice suddenly ice-cold. Emma stared at him in surprise. "The maid is under my care. When the crusade is over, we are to be wed. You will not harm her in any way."

"I do not take orders from you," Guy spat. He whipped out his dagger and lunged toward Theo.

Not quickly enough. Theo met the other knight's charge with a slashing blow that slit open the sleeve of Guy's tunic and drew blood. Guy's dagger dropped to the ground. Theo placed a foot on it and faced him.

"One word from you about her true identity, and I will inform Duke Godfrey of your assault upon her. The duke punishes most harshly those who commit the crime of rape, as you know. Punishment and ridicule will be your reward if you do not keep quiet about this. Not only will the story be told of how you could not master a mere maid, but I will be glad to inform anyone who asks how you came by that wound on your arm." Theo bent to retrieve Guy's dagger. He tossed it carelessly from one hand to the other. "And I will take delight in showing them your dagger as proof."

Guy faced Theo, his face contorted with rage, his fists clenched as if he would attack Theo barehanded. Then he spat again.

"You will pay for this!" Guy whirled around and strode off.

"We are to wed?" The words were spoken in a light, mocking tone, but Emma's voice shook slightly. "May I ask when you intended to inform me of this decision?"

Theo looked at her across the campfire, at a loss now for words. "I did not know myself," he brought out, finally. "It seems my tongue has spoken of its own accord and told what my heart is feeling."

"You would marry me?"

"I would." And then he knew, suddenly and completely, that marrying Emma was all he wanted in the world. He was at her side in two quick steps. "When you were wounded . . . When I thought you might die . . . I truly did not know how I could go on living without you. Will you—when the crusade is done—will you wed me?"

He reached out, almost fearfully, and took her face between his hands. He rubbed gently at a smudge of dirt on her cheek. One strand of hair curled down over her eyes, and he brushed it back. She looked up at him, then dropped her head to his chest. He encircled her with his arms and drew her close. Her body relaxed into his embrace. For a moment, he could feel the soft warmth of her, and then she stiffened. She raised her eyes to his once more.

"Ask me again, Theo," she whispered. "When all this is over . . . if it is ever over . . . if we two are still alive . . . ask me again, then." She reached up to touch his cheek, then slipped back into her tent and pulled the door flap closed behind her.

Theo built the fire up. He sat beside it until the first pale streaks of dawn began to lighten the sky.

†   †   †

After that, Theo insisted that Emma set her tent up at night immediately beside his. He would have had her move her pallet right into his tent, but she refused. During the day, he kept close by her as much as possible. He could not forget the look in Guy's eyes. The man was poisoned with hate; Theo knew he would take his revenge somehow.

They left Tyre and marched on down the coast to Acre. There, the governor pressed more gifts of fruits and food upon them, ensuring the safety of the fertile farms in his territory. They proceeded to Haifa and on, under the shadow of Mount Carmel, until they finally reached southern Caesarea.

"We are to stay here for four days in order to celebrate Whitsun properly," he told Emma, as he returned to camp after breaking his fast with the count. There had been a shyness between them since Guy's attack, but neither of them had been able to speak of it. Nor did they speak of Theo's declaration. Jerusalem was only a week's travel away. The final battle loomed. Time enough, then, to think of themselves.

At the end of the celebration, they set out again, inland this time, following an old road that led away from the coast and wound upwards into the Judean hills. As they traveled, it grew even hotter. The sun blazed down upon them out of cloudless skies. The land was changing; there were fewer and fewer trees to provide shade. Emma trailed behind Theo, both walking to save their horses' strength. The Turkish ponies managed well enough, but Centurion was in trouble.

"Theo," Emma called, low, so that no one else should hear. It was noon of the second day after they had begun the climb inland.

Theo turned to her, wiping sweat out of his eyes. His tunic stuck to his back, and small flying insects tormented him.

"It is Centurion. He can go no farther. We must rest."

"Ramleh is close before us," Theo called back. "We can rest there. There will be shade and water for him."

"I know not whether he will make it," Emma answered. There was a note of desperation in her voice.

Theo stopped and came back to look more closely at the huge warhorse. He pulled their ponies and pack animals to one side to let those behind pass them by. Centurion took two more steps, as if unaware that his masters had halted. His eyes were glazed and unseeing. His breathing came in ragged, sucking gasps. Emma tugged gently on his halter to stop him. He came to a halt and stood, his immense body swaying slightly, head hanging down. Sweat foamed on his neck and withers and ran in streams to drip off his belly onto the ground. Flies clustered around his eyes, but he seemed oblivious to them. As they watched, he gave a convulsive shudder. Emma reached for a skin of water and held it out to him. He ignored it. She brushed the flies away.

"We cannot go on, Theo. He is going to die if he does not rest. This heat is too much for him."

Theo did not answer. Of the huge warhorses that had left the Ardennes, Centurion was the last one left. The others had succumbed to the rigors of the journey long ago, or had been left in the towns they had passed through when the horses had become too exhausted to go farther. Theo had clung to the possibility that Centurion's enormous strength and force of will would carry him through. Now, it seemed, he had reached the end.

"We will rest awhile," Theo said.

No matter how much she coaxed, however, Emma could not get Centurion to drink. He had stopped eating days ago. She picked up a coarse piece of sacking and began to rub him down. She scratched his belly thoroughly with a brush made of twigs. He shivered from time to time, but otherwise seemed insensible to her ministrations. His breathing became even more labored. Finally, Emma stopped and just leaned her head lightly against his neck. With one hand, she caressed the woolly gray hair of his mane; with the other, she rubbed his forehead on the spot where she knew he liked it best.

Theo watched. He rebuked her not for spoiling the horse, nor for treating him in an undignified manner.

Suddenly, Centurion tossed his head, knocking Emma aside. For one moment, his eyes cleared and he looked full at her, and then they dulled. One last convulsive shudder shook the massive frame and, with a ground-jarring thud, he fell. His breathing stopped.

Emma threw herself upon him. Tears streamed down her face, mingling with sweat and dirt. Theo knelt beside her. He would have put an arm around her, to comfort her, but the steady stream of curious crusaders and pilgrims passing by precluded any show of tenderness toward one who was supposed to be his groom. He laid a hand on the warhorse's head.

"So, after all, you will not be there to carry me into Jerusalem," he said. His voice broke. "I shall miss you, my old friend."

† † †

They left Centurion by the roadside. There was nothing else they could do. The birds of prey began to circle high above almost before they had traveled out of sight.

It was night before Theo and Emma reached the town of Ramleh. There they found the crusaders already comfortably installed. The inhabitants had fled the town in terror at the news of their coming, but only after destroying the great Church of St. George that had stood in the ruined village of Lydda on Ramleh's outskirts.

They rested there for three days, the crusaders exulted by the taking of a Muslim town in the heart of the Holy Land. Only Theo and Emma took no part in the celebrations. The death of Centurion was too much with them. On the fourth day, the army resumed its march on Jerusalem.

The crusaders traveled all day and on through the night. The wooded hillside gradually gave way to stony, red-earthed slopes, shaded only by stunted trees and bushes. The alien nature of this new land began to exert a strange kind of hold on the crusaders.

"It is so barren," Emma whispered. "It chills my soul."

There was an eclipse of the moon that night. While the crusaders marched, they watched in awe as the moon dwindled to a crescent, and then was blacked out completely.

"It is an omen," the priests told them as they halted briefly for mass the next morning. "It portends the eclipse of the Crescent of Islam itself."

But their words brought no reassurance to the crusaders. They pressed on in an ever-increasing silence.

Theo turned once to look back at the procession. How few we are compared to the vast army that set out from Constantinople, he thought. Hardly more than a thousand knights were left, and fewer than half the foot soldiers remained. How many pilgrims had died, Theo could only guess. Certainly, there were not nearly as many straggling in at night as there had been. It was a sad and dispirited army that trailed behind him now—a ghost of the glorious crusade that had set out so triumphantly to do God's will almost three long years ago.

Before noon on the seventh day of June, the vanguard of the army—Theo, Emma and Amalric included—reached the summit of the road at the mosque of the prophet Samuel, on the hilltop that the pilgrims called Montjoie, the Hill of Joy.

There, before them, stood Jerusalem. Theo dropped to his knees. All around him, nobles and soldiers alike were doing the same.

Jerusalem! God's own city. At last!

MEDITERRANEAN SEA

Jerusalem

EGYPT

Eighteen

Theo sat beside his campfire, staring at the city. God's own city—but it was also one of the greatest fortresses in the world, secure behind its formidable walls and towers. The crusaders had been deployed and were ready to begin the siege. Godfrey's troops had been assigned the northwest side of the city as far down as the Jaffa Gate. Beside the gate, directly in front of Theo, was the citadel, the Tower of David. Its bulk loomed against the dying light of the day. Cicadas shrilled in the scraggly cypress trees behind him. Small, swift birds darted in the twilight. Smells of cooking wafted out to the crusaders' camp from the other side of the walls, amid the sounds of a city settling itself for the night. Calls, cries, the wail of thin, strange-sounding music. Firelight flickered through the slit-holes of the citadel and the other towers, where Theo knew the Egyptian Fatimid soldiers stood guard—staring at the crusaders, even as the crusaders stared at them.

"The governor is Iftikhar ad-Dawla," Godfrey told his troops. "An experienced and well-seasoned soldier. He has had ample warning of our coming and has used the time to strengthen his walls. He has driven all the flocks and herds into the city, and the city is well supplied with cisterns for water. He is prepared for a long siege."

Theo had wondered at the absence of animals and herders in the hills as they had approached. The duke's words explained it.

The next morning, he was worried to find Emma gone from the campsite when he stumbled out of his tent. He became uneasy now whenever she was out of his sight. The sun was just beginning to send streaks of color through the sky, and a mist lay heavy in the valleys around them.

"Please God she doesn't get into any more trouble," he muttered, as he gathered sticks and twigs for a fire. Very little on this bare hillside could be used for fuel. That is going to be a problem very soon, Theo thought. He rationed out oats for the horses, but there was no water. Another problem. Perhaps that was where Emma was—fetching water from the nearest well.

The sun rose. A pitiless, blazing orb, it burned off the mists below and drained the blue out of the sky above with the intensity of its heat. Theo moved the horses into what little shade the sparse trees provided, but they stamped their feet restlessly and tossed their heads back and forth. They ate only half the food Theo had given them, even though he had skimped on their usual portion. It was obvious they were thirsty. Where was Emma?

He had almost decided to go and look for her when she reappeared. She staggered under the weight of two buckets of water, one dangling on either end of a stick she had slung across her shoulders. Her face was bright red under her hood and running with sweat. Theo hastened to take the buckets from her.

"Iftikhar . . . He has poisoned or filled in all the wells outside the walls," she panted. "The dog! Mind you, I would have done so myself if I'd been in his position, but it's annoying just the same." She dropped to the ground beside the tiny fire. "There is only one good well left and it's away around by the south wall. I managed to fill our buckets, but the soldiers on the walls jeered at me the whole time I was doing it. Could just as well have been arrows rather than words, though, so I think myself rather fortunate."

"Our only source of water is within bow range of the walls?" Theo asked incredulously.

"I'm afraid so," Emma answered.

"We will have to find a river . . . a stream . . ." Theo looked around him. The few trees that grew on these stony hills did not provide nearly enough shade. Even this early in the morning, the heat was intense. A breeze had sprung up, but it gave no relief. If possible, it was hotter than the still air, and only made their discomfort worse.

"We will not be able to hold out here for long," Theo said. "This siege must be short. We must take Jerusalem quickly, or we will die."

✝   ✝   ✝

Godfrey planned an attack the next week. As usual, Theo fought side by side with Amalric. Together, as the mangonels and catapults bombarded the walls with boulders and stones, they swarmed up the ladders behind the duke and Count Garnier. They charged the soldiers at the top, overrunning them with the ferocity and desperation of their attack. For a time, Theo thought they might have a chance of success. Then he heard Godfrey call for a retreat.

Back down the ladders they scrambled, in a frenzy of panic and humiliation. The Egyptian soldiers poured liquid fire down upon them as they fled. Theo had heard of Greek fire, as it was called, but had never seen it and had not really believed in it. But as the rivers of oily flame cascaded down onto the soldiers still on the ladders, the screams of the burned men proved its existence only too well.

"We had too few ladders and too few engines of war. Too few of our men were able to storm the walls," Godfrey told them at their council that night. "If we are to take Jerusalem, we must wage an all-out attack. We need more siege machines, more mangonels, battering rams and ladders, many, many more. We must attack from as many positions as possible. All of us—all at once!"

There was a general murmur of agreement, then one dissenting voice.

"Where are we to get the wood to build these machines, my lord? There is barely enough here to feed our fires. And what of the nails and bolts for fitting them together?"

"There are forests around Samaria. Tancred, you and Robert of Flanders, take your men and cut down trees. Take the camels—they are by far the best beasts of burden in this heat and need next to no water. As for the rest of us—we will pray that supplies come from the coast. In the meantime, we build. All of us."

Theo and Amalric worked with the rest. Emma did her share as well. Princes worked side by side with pilgrims. Women and children worked from sun-up to nightfall. Tancred and Robert came back laden with rough-hewn logs and planks. Theo helped to tear wagons apart for the nails and bolts, and then the army burned the wagons for fuel. The lack of water was deadly, however. Pack animals and herds they had captured along the way began to die of thirst in large numbers.

"At least they provide food," Amalric remarked cynically.

Godfrey sent out detachments from the camp every day to find streams and wells. They were guided by native Christians who had been turned out of the city and had joined the crusaders. Some even went as far as the Jordan River to find water. The well Emma had found the first day—the Pool of Siloam, the Jerusalem Christians called it—was deep and brimming with cool, clear water, but the sentries on the walls had left off taunting and had settled down to killing all who came near it.

The hot breeze Theo had felt the first day outside the walls of Jerusalem became a steady wind. Dry and burning, it laid a fine film of sand and dust on everything and everyone in the camp. It never ceased, and it drove men and women crazy.

"Many of the crusaders are undergoing baptism in the river Jordan, gathering palm branches from the riverbank and deserting," Theo told Emma.

"I know," she answered. "This is not what they expected. They feel we will never conquer Jerusalem." She looked at the walls towering above them. "They think we will die here."

They might be right, Theo thought, and thrust the unbidden idea out of his mind immediately.

A few days later, Amalric barged into their camp with news.

"Six Christian ships have put into Jaffa. Their scouts arrived at the camp last night. They have supplies! Food, ropes, nails, bolts—everything we need!"

"Now, we can really build," Godfrey announced at their evening conference. "And as well as everything else, I will build a siege castle, as high as the walls themselves. Higher! A tower set on wheels that we can roll right up to the walls. Then we can attack from within the tower without the need of ladders. We'll fit it out with catapults as well." He strode back and forth, his tall figure seeming to fill the tent.

"We can fight with fire, too," he added. His eyes blazed and he flung his long, fair hair back with an impatient toss of his head. "I have Christians here who escaped the city and have brought the secret of the Greek fire with them. We can hurl it down upon the Egyptians from the tower and the mangonels can send it flying over the walls." He turned to Gaston of Béarn. "Build the castle well out of sight of the fort. It will be a surprise to the garrison, and not a very welcome one, I warrant." He laughed, a sound that had not been heard in his tent for many months. His eagerness and enthusiasm were infectious. Amalric thumped Theo on the back with such gleeful force as they left the meeting that it knocked the breath out of him.

But the work went slowly, and they suffered terribly from the heat. In spite of their leaders' assurances, more and more people deserted every day. Then Theo heard news that a great army had set out from Egypt to relieve Jerusalem.

"The mood in the camp is desperate," he told Emma. "The priest, Peter Desiderius, says we must do something. He is calling for three holy days of fasting. He says Bishop Adhemar himself appeared to him, and told him we must hold a fast and then walk barefoot around Jerusalem. Only then will we be able to gather our forces and attack."

"Once again, when we are starving, they call for a fast," Emma muttered. "These priests do have a sense of humor."

✝   ✝   ✝

They fasted for three days, but did not cease to work. On the Friday of that week, the procession formed. Theo and Amalric lined themselves up with their lords behind the bishops and the priests, who carried the crosses and holy relics they had brought all this way with them. The foot soldiers and pilgrims followed; Emma, in her groom's garb, chose to walk with them.

Theo was lightheaded from the heat and the lack of food. He was barely aware of the soldiers and towns-folk who gathered on the walls to mock them. He kept his eyes on the ground, concentrating only on putting one foot ahead of the other. He tried to follow the prayers of the priests, but a buzzing in his head drowned out their chanting. They circled the city, then climbed the Mount of Olives. There, the priests began to preach.

"We are here!" Arnulf of Rhohes proclaimed. "We are outside the walls of Jerusalem itself!" He was widely acknowledged to be the finest preacher in the army, and a silence fell on the vast crowd as they listened intently to him. "We have followed God's will and done His bidding, and now we are at the gates of the holiest of His cities. Will you not rejoice? Will you not look within your hearts and find the strength for one last battle? One last battle, and then our glorious crusade will be ended. God's will *will* have been done!"

As the priest spoke, Theo saw heads around him begin to lift. The dullness began to clear from people's eyes.

Peter the Hermit rose next. Forgotten by all was his inglorious defeat at Civetot, his attempt to desert the crusade at Antioch. As he preached, his eyes blazed with their old intensity. His voice rolled over the hilltop. After so many months, he spoke most of the dialects heard around the camp—translators were quick to interpret his words into the others. The people began to murmur, and then to shout. They raised their fists to the sky and shook them at the very walls of Jerusalem itself.

"We *will* conquer. God wills it! God wills it!"

The old battle cry of the crusade rang out, and echoed back and back again from the surrounding hills.

Theo found himself shouting with the rest. Gone was the lightheadedness, gone the weakness. The clamor of the multitude surrounded him and filled him with strength.

"God wills it!" he cried. "God wills it!"

† † †

During the next two days, Theo and the crusaders returned to their work with renewed fervor. Even the oldest of men and women did their part, sewing ox-hide and camel-hide onto the exposed woodwork on the siege machines to protect it from the Greek fire.

"Raymond of Toulouse is building a second siege castle," the count announced. "It is also being built out of sight of the city walls. We will have some surprises for our enemy, never fear."

By the second week in July, the siege castles were ready.

"Now," Godfrey commanded. "Let us wheel them out of hiding!"

Theo and Amalric pulled on their castle, shoulder to shoulder with the count and Godfrey himself, along with dozens of their men. It was an enormous tower. At first, the wheels refused to turn. The struggle to get the castle into motion seemed impossible. Theo felt the veins in his forehead swell with the effort. Beside him, Amalric swore as his foot slipped and he almost fell. Then, slowly, cumbersomely, the tower began to move, up the hillside, and down the slight decline on the other side. Then up to face the northern wall, where startled faces were beginning to show themselves over the tops of the battlements. To the south, Theo knew that Raymond and his men were setting his castle into position. A third, smaller one would be set against the northwest corner.

Theo wiped the sweat from his eyes. He straightened. The battle for Jerusalem was about to begin.

Nineteen

Their first task was to fill in the ditch that prevented the siege castles from being placed right up against the city walls, but the work was dangerous. As soon as the Egyptians saw the castles approaching, they began to bombard them. Theo worked side by side with Amalric and Emma. It seemed to him that everyone in the crusade had turned out to help, in spite of the deadly rain of stones and liquid fire. The sun burned down upon them out of a cloudless sky.

Theo stopped briefly to rest around midday. He looked up and was amazed to see the heat-shimmering air alive with color. He passed a hand over his eyes, certain his brain was crazed by the sun, and then realized he was surrounded by brilliant, multi-hued butterflies. He reached out to touch Emma's arm.

"Look," he croaked. His throat was parched and dry, his head pounding with pain. The butterflies darted and swooped in a sun-mad, dizzy-making dance all their own.

Emma straightened up and leaned on her shovel. A butterfly alighted on the handle. She stared at it, dazed, as if unable to make sense of it. Then she raised her eyes. For several long minutes the butterflies danced; then, obeying some mysterious signal obvious only to them, all flew off. A boulder crashed to the ground beside Theo and Emma. They flinched, ducked, and began to dig again.

On the morning of the next day, they pulled Godfrey's tower over the filled-in ditch. Theo had time only to grasp Emma's hand for a brief second.

"Stay safe, Theo," she whispered, and then she and the other pilgrims ran back out of range of the missiles being hurled from atop the walls.

Theo saw Godfrey himself, oblivious to the lethal hail all around him, standing tall and proud on the top story as they pushed the castle the last few meters. Immediately, crusader soldiers began to bombard the wall with boulders and clay pots filled with Greek fire.

The assault was returned in full force by the Fatimid soldiers manning the walls. As soon as the castle touched, a swarm of engineers set about making a bridge between it and the top of the wall, while a steady stream of arrows from Godfrey's archers held off the Egyptians.

While the bridge was being finished, Theo waited with Amalric and the other knights in the enclosed bottom half of the tower. The press of men in the gloom was great; the smell of sweat and fear almost overpowering. They could not see what was happening outside, but all around them the battle raged. The tower shook with the shock of the catapults every time they fired on the top stage. It shuddered every time it took a hit from the opposing army. The smell of burning hide began to seep into where the knights waited. Several men cried out; panic was not far away. Theo felt Amalric's shoulder press against his own and he took comfort from it. Both were wearing their mail-ringed leather armor, necessary for the fighting to come, but its heaviness added to the heat and discomfort. The waiting was almost unbearable. Theo felt stomach-churning, almost overwhelming fear. Far better was the crashing, chaotic charge on horseback, with trumpets blaring and war-cries echoing all around. In battle, there was no time to think—no time to imagine your own death waiting for you.

A roar from above was followed by a sudden wave of movement. Theo found himself scrambling for the ladder that led to the upper story. Men behind him shouted and pushed forward. When he reached the upper level, sunlight blinded him for a moment. Then he saw Godfrey standing on the wall on the other side of the bridge, waving them on. He pulled his sword from its scabbard and raced across.

"The gate, Theo!" Count Garnier was at his side. "We must open the gate for the rest of the army!"

Theo followed him, bounding down steps carved into the stone wall. At the bottom, the gate stood, barred and bolted. The Fatimid guards drew their swords. Theo charged the nearest one and their weapons crossed with a jarring clang. His opponent drew back and struck again, but his sword glanced off Theo's shield. At the same moment, Theo struck at the man's unguarded side and felt his sword sink deep. He pulled back and the man fell off it. A froth of blood spewed from his mouth and he lay still at Theo's feet. Theo whirled to face the others, but they lay sprawled around him in slowly widening pools of blood. The count and two of his men were already tugging at the heavy crossbar that sealed the gate. Theo leaped over the body of the soldier he had slain and raced to help. They slid the crossbar free, but before they could open the gate, it was pushed wide by the press of people on the other side. Theo jumped aside to avoid the foot soldiers, who were the first to burst through, and then, to his amazement, he saw a horde of pilgrims—men, women, even children—

come rushing through after them. Armed with cudgels, sticks and shovels, they poured through, screaming hate and defiance, maddened beyond belief after weeks of starvation and heat, years of pain and sacrifice. The defenders of the city fell back before them.

All of a sudden, Amalric was at his side again.

"Theo!" he shouted, and pointed.

Theo looked. A group of Egyptian soldiers was running for a mosque.

"After them!" Amalric cried, and set off in pursuit.

They caught up with them at the mosque door. Theo saw the gleam of a scimitar flash down toward him. He parried, but the scimitar faltered and the soldier screamed as Amalric's sword struck first.

This battle was short. A crowd of crusaders rushed to join them; the Muslims were soon slain. For a moment, there was chaos as pilgrims poured in as well, wielding their makeshift weapons. Then another band of Fatimid defenders was sighted.

"Kill them!" a voice screamed, and the crowd swarmed in their direction.

Suddenly, Theo heard a cry from behind him.

"Theo!"

He felt a searing pain streak down his back. He whirled around. Guy stood there, sword raised, dripping blood, poised to strike again. Theo raised his own sword to defend himself, but Guy's eyes were wide with shock. His arm fell, and the sword dropped from his hand. He stared at Theo a second longer with a puzzled, uncomprehending look, then slowly toppled forward. A dagger was embedded in his back.

Only then did Theo see Emma. Her eyes were fixed on the dying man. She looked up to meet Theo's stare. Her hands were at her sides, held out in an oddly imploring gesture.

"He was going to kill you," she whispered. "I had to kill him first."

Then the world turned black, and Theo fell across Guy's body.

† † †

He regained consciousness slowly. First, he became aware that he was lying on cold stone, on his stomach. His back was afire with pain. It was dark, but he seemed to be in a protected place. There were walls all around him. From somewhere outside, he could hear noises. Screams. He turned his head. Now he could see a rectangle that must be a window, lit by flames from without. More screams. As he came back to full consciousness, they became louder. A figure moved past the rectangle of light. Theo tensed and tried to sit up. Pain roared through his body and he whirlpooled back down into dizziness.

"Theo? Are you awake? Oh, thanks be to God. I thought you were dying." It was Emma's voice, but thin, on the verge of hysteria.

He fought to speak. "What's happening? How goes the battle?"

"The battle is over."

"But those screams . . ."

"They are people—people being murdered. Oh, Theo, it is like a vision of hell itself out there! I dragged you here, and then I tried to go and find help for you, but the crusaders . . ." She dropped to her knees on the stone beside him. In the flickering light, he saw her bury her face in her hands. "They have gone mad, Theo. All of them. They are killing everyone they can catch. Men, women . . . I saw a knight strike down a child, Theo! A child!" Her voice broke. Sobs racked her body.

Theo clenched his teeth and rolled onto his side. He reached out and managed to touch her.

"Lie beside me, Emma."

She burrowed into him; he wrapped his arms around her.

He held her all through the rest of that terrible night. Emma could not stop shaking. She shuddered with every scream from the street outside.

By the time the dawn sent tentative fingers of light through the window, the screams had stopped and Emma finally lay quiet in Theo's arms. He thought she slept and dared not move in case he wakened her, but his back was torturing him. Then Emma spoke.

"I must go and find help for you, Theo."

"You cannot go out there alone."

Emma sat up. In the early morning dimness, he could see only the dead-white oval of her face. Theo sat, too, but could not suppress a moan of pain.

"It is quiet. It is all over. I will be safe."

Before Theo could make a move to stop her, she had risen to her feet and disappeared. He made a futile attempt to get up and follow her, then sank back into unconsciousness.

He woke again to the sound of two voices: Emma's and another's. The alcove where he lay was light now; he recognized the man who followed her in as one of the crusaders' healers, a man well known for his skill and compassion. He carried bandages and a skin of water. With Emma's help, he cleansed and bound Theo's wound. By the time he had finished and left to tend to the many others who awaited him, Theo's head had cleared and he felt steadier. He sat up. Emma was standing by the window, staring out.

"They killed them all." Her voice was so low at first he thought he had misunderstood her.

"All?"

"All," Emma repeated. "All afternoon, all through the night, they killed. They spared no one. A band of Muslims took shelter in one of the mosques after surrendering to Tancred. His banner flew above them, to protect them, but our glorious crusaders broke in and slew every one of them."

Theo started to say something. She silenced him with an abrupt motion.

"The Jews, Theo. All the Jews in the city fled to their synagogue. The crusaders set it on fire and burned everyone within. There is not a Muslim or Jewish man, woman or child left alive. The streets are piled with their bodies." Her voice was toneless with the horror of what she had seen and what she had heard. "The victory is complete, Theo. Jerusalem is once again a Christian city. They will say mass this morning in this very church."

Theo struggled to his feet. Ignoring the pain that shot down into his legs and threatened to collapse them beneath him, he walked over to Emma and stood beside her. She turned to him. Her eyes were dark. Dead.

"What have we done, Theo?" she whispered. "What have we done?"

† † †

Theo and Emma attended the mass. The nave of the church was filled to capacity. Some of the nobles and the leaders had managed to find time to cleanse themselves of the blood of battle, and were dressed with as much pomp and finery as they could assemble, but most were still as blood-stained and filthy as Theo and Emma. Emma had protested at Theo's going, fearing he was too weak, but he had insisted. The walk from the alcove to the nave where the service took place was only a short one, but he was sweating and weak by the time they arrived. They found a stone for him to sit on at the back of the church.

Duke Godfrey sat at the right hand of the priest, Peter Desiderius. Count Garnier stood behind him. The count caught sight of Theo and his face lightened with relief.

"God's will has been done. We gather here victorious in His sight." The priest's words rolled out around the gathering. There was no wild exultation, however, only a heavy silence. The heads of all in the congregation bowed as the priest blessed them. From outside, the sound of the streets being cleared filtered into the silent assembly. Huge pyres of bodies were being piled up in every vacant lot and set on fire. An oath rang out, shocking the silence with its vulgarity. Theo moved slightly, then flinched. His back felt as if it were being torn apart. The wound inflicted by Guy's sword was superficial and would heal well, the healer had said. But inside Theo, as the smell of the burning bodies seeped into the church, a far deeper wound festered.

✝   ✝   ✝

Theo sat in the garden of a small house on the outskirts of Jerusalem. It was a house he had purchased from a Christian of the city who had wanted to journey to Antioch. He knew very well that Emma would not live in any dwelling where blood might have been spilled. He and Emma had gone to the count after the service in the Church of the Holy Sepulchre. They had confessed their deception to him and received his forgiveness and blessing. They had been wed not long afterward.

This day, Emma was digging in a small plot of earth outside the front door. She was planting vegetables. A scarf covered her hair, and she reached up now and then to push a stray lock out of her eyes.

Theo had just returned from the morning council. Jerusalem had been restored to order, but there was still much to do. He had been given the task of clearing the sand-filled wells outside the city. It was hard, hot, tedious labor, and his wound still gave him trouble, but the work suited him well. He toiled beside the men assigned to help him from sun-up to sundown, grateful for the opportunity to tire himself to the point where he could not think. There were many things he did not want to think about. After the battle, he and Emma had turned to each other in desperation. Neither of them could sleep. Nor could they talk; there were no words for the guilt and horror that haunted them. Each night, they had held each other wordlessly during the long black hours until the dawn.

At first, Emma had dug in the garden soil with a kind of frenzied fury. Gradually, however, as she created order and beauty out of the wild bramble that had been there before, she calmed. Her hands shaped the earth with more tenderness. Theo brought water every evening and they rationed it out carefully onto the long, straight rows she had created, nourishing the life that lay hidden in the buried seeds. Finally, she and Theo could sleep. They found words to say to each other. They could comfort each other with their love. As the days went by, life slowly became bearable again.

Now, as he watched her, Theo felt a hollowness within him being filled. Flowers bloomed in their garden, as if in defiance of the red-earthed desolation of the hills around them. Thick-leaved trees gave shade. In one of them, the song of a solitary bird trilled out clear and pure. Emma looked up just then and met his gaze. She smiled—a small, tentative smile. Theo's heart leaped. It was the first time she had smiled since the taking of Jerusalem.

A hail from the gate startled them. Amalric leaped over the low stone wall and loped over to sit beside Theo.

"Good morrow, Emma," he called. "Your garden does marvelously well."

Emma straightened up and brushed off her skirt.

"And a good morrow to you, Amalric," she called back. She disappeared into the house, but reappeared almost immediately carrying a bowl of oranges the color of sunshine itself and a flagon of wine. She brought them over and placed them on a low table beside Theo and Amalric, then seated herself.

"You heard, Theo, this morning—Duke Godfrey steadfastly refuses to allow himself to be crowned king of Jerusalem," Amalric said, picking up one of the golden fruits and tossing it from hand to hand. "He will allow himself only the title 'Defender of the Holy Sepulchre.'"

"Duke Godfrey is an honorable man," Theo replied. "He is as honorable in peace as he was in war."

"*Was* in war?" Amalric exclaimed. "So you believe our fighting days are over now?"

"We have won Jerusalem," Emma said. "We have given the Holy Lands back to the Church. What more is there to do?"

"What more, indeed?" Amalric asked. "So we will grow old and fat in peaceful governing of this land and city?"

Theo looked at him. "What more do you want, my friend?" he asked.

Amalric jumped to his feet. "Something! I know not what, but something!" He began to stride back and forth across the narrow garden. "This suits you, Theo, I can see that. You are growing brown and contented. I am pleased for you. But this peace that you enjoy so much is suffocating me. I am dying here!"

"Peace bores you?" Emma asked.

"It does. I need the excitement of battle, the sound of trumpets to send the blood coursing through my veins."

"And the killing? It bothers you not?" Emma asked.

"Killing is part of war. I accept it."

"Perhaps you need it."

Amalric looked at Theo sharply. "What do you mean by that?" he demanded, his voice suddenly harsh.

"Nothing. I am sorry. Please, forget my words, I spoke nonsense." Theo rose and placed his hand on Amalric's arm.

"What will you do?" Emma asked.

Amalric turned to her, and his eyes brightened again. "I have asked my lord Godfrey if I can return to Bouillon. There are still battles to be fought. I could be useful there."

"You would leave us? You would leave Jerusalem?" Theo stared at him.

"I would, my friend. And I would tempt you to come with me if I could, but I fear that would be impossible." He looked over at Emma and laughed, then tossed her the orange.

She caught it and held it carefully, as if it were something very precious.

† † †

"Would you go with him?" Emma asked that night as they lay entwined on their cot, the room lit only by the lambent glow of the last embers of their fire. "If it were not for me, would you go with him?"

"No," Theo answered, "I would not. I will miss Amalric when he goes. He has been my constant companion and true friend for the last three years. We have fought together and saved each other's life more times than I can count, but I would not go with him."

"Why not?"

The clash of weapons echoed in Theo's memory. The noises and the smells of war. The eyes of every man he had ever killed. He held Emma even more tightly.

"I could not," he said. "I am not like Amalric. If that means I am less of a man, then so be it. But I, too, have had my war. All I pray for now is that this peace that torments Amalric so should continue. I want not my children to know war."

He looked beyond Emma to where his sword stood propped in the shadows. The iron blade was twisted and notched. He had not yet asked the blacksmith to repair it.

He knew then he never would.

KARLEEN BRADFORD is one of Canada's most respected young adult authors. She is the author of several historical and contemporary stories, including *Windward Island*, which won the 1990 Max and Greta Ebel Award, *There Will Be Wolves*, winner of the 1993 Canadian Library Association Young Adult Book Award, and the recently published *Thirteenth Child*.

Having lived in cities all over the world, Karleen Bradford now lives in Owen Sound, Ontario.

Maybe it ... *his tie tugged off and the first few buttons of his white shirt opened.*

Maybe it was her reaction to the black chest hair peeking out. Maybe she thought about all he'd done for her.

Maybe, for just a short time, she gave in to the thought that she might *need* a protector. She only knew thoughts weren't running through her brain as fast as heat was flashing through her body.

Lily wasn't thinking at all when she leaned forward.

Rather, she was feeling and wishing and hoping and remembering what it had felt like to be held in a man's arms.

Dear Reader,

Veterans are close to my heart. My father-in-law served
in World War II. My dad was a soldier then, too. These
men were honorable, brave and quiet about what they'd
experienced.

My hero, Mitch Cortega, an Iraq War veteran, has scars
that are deeper than the physical. Only opening his heart
to my heroine, Lily Wescott, can begin the real healing
process. A widow from the Afghanistan War, Lily wants
to stand on her own with her newborn twins. Yet she
needs Mitch's inherent strength. Together Lily and Mitch
realize that love truly can conquer all.

I hope you become as deeply involved in this romance as
I did writing it. I hope you are uplifted by the power of
love.

All my best,

Karen Rose Smith

TWINS UNDER HIS TREE

KAREN ROSE SMITH

SPECIAL EDITION

Published by Silhouette Books

America's Publisher of Contemporary Romance

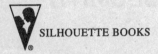

SILHOUETTE BOOKS

ISBN-13: 978-0-373-65569-4

Recycling programs
for this product may
not exist in your area.

TWINS UNDER HIS TREE

Copyright © 2010 by Karen Rose Smith

All rights reserved. Except for use in any review, the reproduction
or utilization of this work in whole or in part in any form by any
electronic, mechanical or other means, now known or hereafter
invented, including xerography, photocopying and recording, or in
any information storage or retrieval system, is forbidden without
the written permission of the editorial office, Silhouette Books,
233 Broadway, New York, NY 10279 U.S.A.

This is a work of fiction. Names, characters, places and incidents are
either the product of the author's imagination or are used fictitiously, and
any resemblance to actual persons, living or dead, business establishments,
events or locales is entirely coincidental.

This edition published by arrangement with Harlequin Books S.A.

For questions and comments about the quality of this book please contact us
at Customer_eCare@Harlequin.ca.

® and TM are trademarks of Harlequin Books S.A., used under license.
Trademarks indicated with ® are registered in the United States Patent
and Trademark Office, the Canadian Trade Marks Office and in other
countries.

Visit Silhouette Books at www.eHarlequin.com

Printed in U.S.A.

Books by Karen Rose Smith

KAREN ROSE SMITH

Award-winning and bestselling author Karen Rose Smith has seen more than seventy novels published since 1992. She grew up in Pennsylvania's Susquehanna Valley and still lives a stone's throw away with her husband—who was her college sweetheart—and their two cats. She especially enjoys researching and visiting the West and Southwest where her latest series of books is set. Readers can receive updates on Karen's releases and write to her through her website at www.karenrosesmith.com or at P.O. Box 1545, Hanover, PA 17331. Readers can also visit her fan page on Facebook.

To my father-in-law, Edgar S. Smith, who served in
World War II in Patton's army. We miss you.

For all servicemen who strive to keep us safe.

Thanks to Captain Jay Ostrich,
Pennsylvania National Guard,
who so readily and patiently answered my questions.
I couldn't have developed my hero's character
so deeply without his input.

Chapter One

Late February

Dr. Lily Wescott stood at the podium, peering through the spotlight into the sea of faces in the hotel ballroom. Many grinned and waved as she prepared to accept the Medical Professional Woman of the Year Award.

She brushed tears away, stunned and totally overwhelmed. These days, she blamed the rise and fall of her emotions on her pregnancy, though memories of the husband she'd lost in Afghanistan were never far from her heart.

Suddenly an odd sensation gripped her back and a cramp rippled through her stomach. As best she could, she fought to keep her shoulders back and a smile on her face. She couldn't go into labor now! She was only at thirty-three weeks.

But she was an ob/gyn—and she knew all too well that her twins would come when *they* were ready. Lily could only hope for the best....

"Thank you," she said into the microphone. "I never imagined I'd win this award." She'd really expected one of her friends at the table to win. After all, they were all baby experts at the Family Tree Health Center in Lubbock, Texas. She went on, "At the Family Tree Fertility Center, we strive to help women who—"

A second cramp squeezed Lily's side and she caught the wooden podium for support. Out of the corner of her eye, she saw her friend and colleague, Dr. Mitch Catega, jump to his feet, concern on his face. He rushed to the stage and up the steps.

As she managed to suck in a gulp of air, hot liquid washed down her leg. *Oh, God—I am in labor!*

She was *not* going to panic. She was *not* going to crumple to the floor. She was *not* going to be embarrassed.

At her side now, Mitch's arm curled around her waist...his injured arm. *The one he never let anyone see,* she thought, needing something other than the pain to concentrate on. His arm was always covered, tonight by a well-cut black tuxedo that made his shoulders seem even broader than usual. She'd noticed that tonight... and it wasn't the first time...

"Can you walk?" he asked, his breath warm at her ear.

A murmur swept through the audience.

She turned, the side of her cheek brushing his chin. "I'm not sure."

Mitch's angular jaw tightened, his almost-black gaze held hers with...something she couldn't define. But then it was replaced by the empathy and compassion she'd felt from him many times before. "The twins are our main priority. Hold on to me if you can't stand on your own."

She really thought she could. The cramp faded away. If it weren't for the wetness between her legs, she could deny what was happening.

With Mitch's arm still around her, she took a couple of steps. Maybe she could even give the rest of her acceptance speech—

The lance of pain that pierced her back stole her breath and weakened her knees. She exhaled, "Mitch…"

And he was there…lifting her into his arms…carrying her down the dais steps.

"I'm driving her to the hospital myself," Mitch said, as Lily's friends and colleagues rushed toward him. "It will be quicker than waiting for an ambulance."

"And more economical," Lily realized aloud, trying to think practically. But that was difficult with Mitch's cologne reminding her of the last time he'd held her so close on the day she'd discovered she was having twins. His grip felt safe now as it had then…as if no harm could come to her while she was in his arms.

She must be delusional.

"I'll ride with you," Jared Madison offered as he jogged alongside Mitch and pushed open the ballroom door. "I'll be handy if the twins won't wait, since Lily's doctor is at a conference."

Jared had his own obstetrical practice at Family Tree but took turns covering with the doctors in *her* practice. Lily knew and liked Jared and felt comfortable with him. Still, she murmured, "They'd darn well better wait. It's too early. They'll be too small!" Her last words almost caught in her throat and her bravado deflated.

In the middle of the hotel lobby, Mitch stopped. Looking her directly in the eye, he said, "If you panic, Lily, you won't help the babies. Take calming breaths. You can do this."

Her heart felt lighter, as if Mitch was really part of this pregnancy, too. Not just because her husband had asked him to watch over her but because he *cared*. "If I'd taken the childbirth classes this month instead of next—" She'd been putting them off, maybe trying to deny the inevitable—that yet again, her life would be altered in an earth-shattering way.

"The twins would still come early," he reminded her. "They apparently want to meet their mom *now*."

Yes, they did. And she wanted to meet *them*. She couldn't wait to hold them and tell them how much she loved them. How much their daddy would have loved them...

Mitch's expression was gentle, as if he could read her thoughts, but his gaze didn't waver. His arms were so strong. For a moment, she felt a little trill of excitement in her chest. But that was because of the babies—wasn't it?

"Let's go," she whispered, shaken by the emotions she didn't understand.

Mitch paced the maternity floor waiting room and stopped when he saw Lily's friends watching him peculiarly. He didn't like the worried expressions on their faces. Raina, Gina and Tessa were all baby experts. Along with them, he knew premature babies often had problems—thirty-three weeks was iffy.

Trying to loosen up the tight feeling in his shoulder, arm and hand—injuries that reminded him all too often of his service in Iraq—Mitch flexed them, then sank down on one of the vinyl chairs.

Moving forward on the sofa, Tessa said gently, "It really hasn't been that long."

What was worrying Mitch was that they hadn't heard anything in the hour they'd been here. Closing his eyes, he remembered the day Lily had learned she was having twins. It had been the week before Thanksgiving. One of the techs in the office had performed the ultrasound. Mitch had just finished discussing fertility procedure options with a couple. As his clients had headed for the reception area, he'd noticed Lily exit the exam room, her complexion almost sheet-white, her blue eyes very bright.

"The ultrasound go okay?" he'd asked.

"Oh, Mitch, I'm having *twins!*"

He hadn't been able to tell if she was totally elated or totally terrified.

Clasping her hand, he'd pulled her into the office he'd just vacated. "What's going through your head?"

She'd stood at the chair in front of his desk, holding on to it for support. "The obvious. I'll be a single mom. My friends all say they'll help, but these babies will be *my* responsibility."

"Twins will always have each other," he pointed out. "They won't grow up lonely. They'll be able to play together." He hoped Lily could see the upside of this monumental news. "Girls or boys?"

"They're girls."

"Our techs are pretty good at distinguishing the difference."

Lily had actually blushed a little. Until he'd met her, he didn't think women blushed anymore. But she was blonde with fair skin and all of her emotions seemed to show in her complexion. Major ones had played over her face over the past few months—grief, fear, determination and the sheer loss of her husband.

"Troy would be so proud," she'd said, tears beginning to run down her face.

That's when Mitch had done something he *never* should have done. He'd taken her into his arms. She'd laid her head on his shoulder, crying. And he'd felt desire that had no place in that room.

Mitch had met Troy—at that time Troy and Lily had been engaged—when the Family Tree staff had planned a dinner to welcome Mitch into the practice. Since he'd once served in the Army National Guard and Troy still had, they'd developed an immediate rapport, becoming friends. After Troy and Lily married, Troy had even asked Mitch to watch over Lily while he'd served overseas.

But then Troy had been killed in action, leaving Lily pregnant and alone.

When Lily had finally looked up at him, Mitch hadn't been sure *what* he'd seen there. Yet he'd known damn well it hadn't been interest. Gratitude, maybe?

She'd pulled away, wiped her eyes and mumbled an awkward apology, and they'd gone their separate ways. They'd gone back to being colleagues. She hadn't really confided in him again.

That was okay. Being merely colleagues was safer for both of them.

Now, however, it was the last week in February and

she was in labor. When he'd seen her double over on that dais, he'd felt panic twist his gut.

"Mitch!" A male voice called his name.

When he opened his eyes, he saw Jared, gesturing from the hall.

He stood immediately. "What's going on?"

"She wants you."

"What do you mean, she wants me?"

"She's in labor, and she wants you to coach her."

Her friends all glanced his way. He knew they were wondering why and so was he. But he wasn't going to ask Jared his questions. He was going to ask Lily.

"Suit up," Jared advised him. "When you're ready, she's in delivery room two."

Five minutes later, Mitch had pulled sterile garb over his clothes. It would feel strange being back in an operating-room setting, even though he had to admit a delivery room wasn't *exactly* that. When he'd rushed through the ER with Lily, one of the nurses had waved at him. Years ago, she'd worked with him in trauma surgery.

Sometimes he itched to be doing that kind of work again. Reflexively, he bent his fingers, most of them not responding well. But he'd gotten used to limited use of his right hand, as well as insomnia and nightmares. At least the stiffness in his shoulder and leg could be relieved with the right amount of exercise. He was damn lucky he'd left Iraq with his life. There was no point in complaining about what might have been. Changing his specialty to endocrinology had saved his sanity.

When he pushed open the door of the delivery room, he forgot about whether he should or shouldn't be there. Seeing Lily on the table, her face flushed, her hands clenched tight on the sheet, a protective urge took over. She was hooked up to monitors that measured the frequency and intensity of contractions as well as the babies' heart rates. She looked small and frightened…and fragile. Yet he knew she was the strongest woman he'd ever known. She'd proved that since her husband had died.

He strode to the bed, hooked a stool with his foot and positioned it beside her. Glancing at Emily Madison, Jared's wife and a professional midwife, he asked, "Don't you want Emily to coach you?"

Lily pushed damp hair behind her ear. "She's assisting Jared."

He knew why he was fighting being here. Witnessing a woman in labor, watching a birth, was an intimate experience. Right now, bonding with Lily would be foolish.

He could see a contraction gearing up in intensity. Maybe she just wanted him here instead of one of her friends because he might be more detached yet professional about the births.

With a mental kick that he hoped would push him toward that detachment, he took hold of her hand, felt the softness and warmth of it.

Suddenly she squeezed his fingers so hard he lost any feeling he *did* have left. But the pressure reminded him he had a job to do. If he concentrated on coaching, maybe he wouldn't notice how her chin quivered or how her eyes grew shiny with emotion.

When the contraction eased, he admitted, "I'm not sure how best to help you."

"You worked with men in the field. You helped

them. Help me the same way. Just help me *focus* on something."

She was right. He had helped men before and after surgeries, with mortar blasts exploding, with rocket-propelled grenades shattering the air. Finally he really did understand why she wanted him here.

Realizing what he had to do, he smoothed his thumb over the top of her hand, telling himself his need to touch her was simply for her comfort. "Watch my nose," Mitch ordered Lily.

She looked at him as if he was crazy. "You're kidding, right?"

"I'm not. Use it as your focal point and listen to the sound of my voice."

She focused on his eyes instead of his nose. He saw so many emotions there—worry, hope and grief…the resoluteness he'd admired as she'd exhibited it each day, ready to go on with her life and care for her twins.

Mitch saw her tense and turned to the monitor. With another contraction coming, he squeezed her hand. "You can do this."

She was still looking into his eyes instead of at his nose. He felt as if his heart was going to jump out of his chest. He felt as if…he *shouldn't* be here. Again, he warned himself that he couldn't make such an intimate connection. He should just be watching over her.

But how could he watch over her without getting involved?

At this moment, he wished he'd never made that promise to Troy.

At the foot of the bed, Emily said, "Lily, you can start pushing now."

At that moment, neonatologist Francesca Fitzgerald came into the room with two nurses behind her.

Lily gasped, "Francesca."

The doctor patted Lily's arm and summed up the situation with a quick assessment. "My team's here. You do your part and we'll take care of the rest."

Lily's contraction peaked and her cry of pain sliced through Mitch.

Jared encouraged her. "Good one, Lily. Come on. I want this baby out."

"You can do this," Mitch reminded her. He held her hand as the tension built in her body again. Her face reddened and she gave another fantastically effort-filled push.

All at once he heard Jared say, "I've got one!"

"Is she all right?" Lily asked. "Please tell me she's all right."

A light infant cry came from the area where Francesca was standing. It was very soft, but it *was* a cry.

"She's a beauty," Jared told her. "We might have a few minutes now. I want to get her sister out, as quickly as I can."

"I don't think I have a few minutes," Lily gasped. "It's starting again." She practically sat up with the strength and pain of the contraction.

"Use it," Mitch said. "Go with it."

"Just one more push," Emily encouraged her. "She's your youngest. You're going to have to coax her a little harder."

Mitch realized Lily wasn't focusing on him anymore. She was breathing when she had to, breathing any way she could. She needed a different type of support, physical as well as emotional. Knowing exactly what he had to do, Mitch stood, went to the head of the birthing table and wrapped his arm around her shoulders. He warned himself he was only a substitute for Troy. But he didn't feel like a substitute. His arms around Lily, he knew he was doing this for himself as well as his friend.

Tears swept down her cheeks. Her bangs were plastered to her forehead. She pushed her shoulder-length hair away from her face and stared straight ahead.

As her contraction built, her body curved into it, curved around it. Mitch held her as she delivered a second little girl.

Jared announced, "And here's princess number two."

Again he passed the infant to Francesca who worked at clearing her airway, cleaning her eyes, checking her lungs, hooking her up to the ventilator to help her breathe. When Mitch saw that, a lump rose in his throat.

"I've got them," Francesca reassured Lily. "I'll be around to give you a report as soon as I can." Then she pushed the babies away, out another door before Lily even glimpsed them.

Reluctantly, Mitch released Lily as she collapsed onto the bed, murmuring, "Maybe I should have quit work sooner and stayed in bed. It's often recommended with twins. But I rested the past two weeks. I kept my feet up as much as I could."

Mitch knew he had to keep Lily calm after her ordeal. "You did everything you thought was best. That's all you could do."

Lily surprised him when she caught his hand again and held it tight. "Troy should have been here. He should have seen his girls born. He should have helped me name them. He should have…he should have…"

"He should have never died," Mitch filled in.

Lily bowed her head and finally let the tears fall unchecked. Mitch did the only thing he could—he held her in his arms until she simply couldn't cry anymore.

Lily had been settled in her hospital room for at least two hours and was growing anxious. Why hadn't Francesca come yet? Wouldn't they have told her if something had happened to either of the babies?

Her gaze landed on Mitch, who was standing at the window. He was as calm as she was agitated. Where did that calm come from after what he'd been through? He'd been presented a Combat Medical Badge, awarded a Silver Star and a Purple Heart, though he never spoke of them. All Troy had told her was that Mitch had been involved in an IED explosion.

"How do you do it?" she asked, following the train of thoughts in her head.

Minus his jacket and tie, his tuxedo shirt was rumpled. He turned to look at her. "Do what?"

"Stay calm under any circumstances."

He shot her a wry half smile. "It's a learned technique."

Interested in anything that would keep her mind off what was going on down the hall, she asked, "Like meditation?"

Even though she'd worked with Mitch for more than two and a half years, she didn't know much about him. Just the little Troy had told her. She knew he was forty-five, had been born in Sagebrush—the small town where they both lived about fifteen minutes outside

Lubbock—but he had no family there. He'd been deployed to Iraq, injured and changed specialties—from trauma surgery to endocrinology—because he'd lost the fine motor coordination in his hand that he needed to perform surgery. But that was about the extent of her knowledge of his background.

"I learned several techniques," he replied, running his hand through his jet-black hair. "Meditation was one. Guided imagery was another."

Her gaze went to his hand and the ragged scars there. She wanted to ask if he'd learned the techniques when he'd been hurt. Had they been his method of recovering? But that was such personal territory. If he didn't mention Iraq himself, she knew better than to jump into it.

In spite of herself, she still remembered gazing into his eyes rather than looking at his nose while he'd coached her. Every time since the day she'd told him she was having twins, she'd felt such an intense...

She wasn't sure what it was she felt. Mitch knew things. He'd *felt* things. She could just instinctively sense that. The compassion he showed her seemed personal, but maybe he was that way with everyone.

"You know, your friends wanted to stay," he said.

Yes, they did. But they all had children and husbands and practices to see to. "I told them there was nothing they could do here. I'm going to call them as soon as we find out about the babies. Oh, Mitch, what's taking so long?"

Leaving his pensive position at the window, he crossed to her bed. He was so tall...confident...strong.

She remembered being held in his arms—in the exam room at the practice, on the dais, in the delivery room. His cologne had wrapped around her as he'd given her his strength. That's why she'd needed him with her through the delivery—because he was so strong. Now when she looked at him she could hardly swallow.

With one push of his booted foot, the comfortable chair by the nightstand now sat beside her bed. He sank down into the chair. It was well after 1:00 a.m. and she knew he had to be tired after a full day of work. She should tell him to go home, too. But he seemed willing to see her through this and she felt she needed him here.

Though she realized her body was ready for a good long rest, she couldn't relax. Adrenaline was still rushing through her because she was so concerned about her twins.

In the labor room, Mitch had taken her hand. Now he didn't.

Why should it matter? she wondered. She quickly decided it didn't. After all, she was still in love with Troy. At times, she thought she heard him in the next room. Other times, she expected his booming voice to announce that he was home. She fought back sudden emotion.

Mitch's deep, even voice reassured her. "I have a feeling Francesca will only come to you after the babies are stabilized...after she can tell you something for certain."

"You're so honest," Lily blurted out. "I wanted you to say she probably had another emergency and that's why it was taking her so long."

"Do you believe that?"

His expression wasn't stern. His lean cheeks and high cheekbones just made him appear that way sometimes.

As his black brows drew together just a little, he looked expectant...as if he knew she couldn't lie to herself.

"It's possible," she murmured.

"Yes, it's possible," he agreed.

"Talk to me about something," she pleaded. "Anything."

She knew she might be asking for a lot. Mitch communicated, but only when he had something to say. Chit-chat didn't seem to be in his nature. But now she would be glad for anything her mind could latch on to.

"When is Raina McGraw's baby due?"

Lily smiled, picturing her friend with her rounding stomach. "June fifth. Talk about having a lot on your plate."

"I understand Shep adopted three children before she married him."

"They're still in the process with Manuel, their two-and-a-half-year-old. Shep had started adoption proceedings, but then he and Raina married. It was almost like starting over. Their housekeeper, Eva, is wonderful, but Raina could be running from morning to night once the baby's born. I think she's going to take a leave from her practice."

"Have you decided yet how long you're going to stay out?"

"I'll make up my mind soon. Everything about my life is in flux right now."

"You don't have to decide right away. You might have to consider getting help with the twins."

"No, I won't need it. My roommate Angie—Gina's sister—says she'll help me. She's a nurse, away right now on the disaster relief team. But she should be back soon. Besides, there are lots of moms who take care of two babies."

"Not necessarily at the same time." His tone held a warning note that maybe she was being a little too Pollyanna-ish.

"I can handle it, Mitch. You'll see."

She was contemplating the idea of breast-feeding both babies when the door pushed open and Francesca walked in. She seemed surprised to see Mitch there, but didn't comment.

Lily hadn't known Francesca very long. But one evening, the women who'd lived in the Victorian house on a quiet street in Sagebrush had gathered there and just enjoyed a ladies' night of chatting and sharing backgrounds. All of them were connected in so many ways—through their professions, friendships or family ties.

Lily had felt so alone after Troy had died, but that night all of the women had made her feel as if she had a support network.

"Tell me," Lily said to Francesca.

"Your older daughter weighs four point two pounds, is seventeen inches long, and needs a little time to put on weight. We're giving her CPAP treatment. She's breathing on her own and is definitely a crier when she's unhappy."

The continuous positive airway pressure would help the infant breathe but not breathe for her. Lily's heart swelled with love for this tiny baby although she hadn't even laid eyes on her yet. "And my youngest?" Lily's voice shook a little bit when she asked.

"She weighs four pounds, is sixteen and a half inches and had trouble breathing." Francesca immediately held up both hands. "Now, don't panic. We have her stabilized. She's on a ventilator for now—"

"Oh my God!" Lily's chest felt so tight she could hardly breathe.

"I mean it, Lily. Don't panic. We'll wean her off it. Her lungs need to develop and, of course, she needs to gain weight, too, before she can go home."

"When can I see them?"

Francesca sighed. "I shouldn't allow it, but I know you're not going to rest or get any sleep until I let you visit them."

Lily nodded. She was happy, afraid and plain exhausted. But she had to see them.

"All right. I'll find a wheelchair. But you can only have a few minutes with them, and then I need to tuck you in. Childbirth is natural, but it's traumatic, too, and you need time to recover."

"I know," Lily said. "When do you think I'll be discharged?"

"You'll have to ask Jared that, but my guess is you'll be here until Sunday morning."

At least she'd be here so she could visit her babies. *Her babies.* Everything about their birth came rushing back, especially Mitch's presence and support. "Can Mitch come, too?"

Francesca hesitated and looked from one of them to the other. "This is just for a few minutes. You both have to wear masks and sterile gowns. I'll be right back."

Mitch looked troubled. "Are you sure you want me there, Lily?"

"You helped me bring them into the world. Of course, I want you there."

Maybe it was because of the letter Troy had left for

her. In it, he'd told her he'd asked Mitch to look after her if anything happened to him. He'd trusted Mitch, and that made it easy for her to trust him, too. He'd certainly come through for her tonight.

Ten minutes later, Lily and Mitch were in the NIC unit, staring at her two precious little girls. The babies absolutely snatched Lily's breath away.

Mitch stood behind her, his hand on her shoulder. "Have you considered names?"

"Now that I see them, I can name them." She pointed to her firstborn, saying lightly, "Sophie, I'd like you to meet Mitch. He helped me bring you into this world."

Her baby opened her eyes, seemed to gaze at them both for a few seconds before she closed them again.

Lily's heart overflowed with love as her focus turned to her youngest, who needed help to breathe.

Mitch's fingers tightened on Lily's shoulder and she was so grateful for his quiet strength, his stalwart caring.

"And this tiny angel is—" Lily's voice caught. Finally she managed to say, "Her name is Grace."

Mitch crouched down beside Lily so he could see her children from her vantage point. The slant of his jaw almost grazed her cheek as he reassured her, "They're going to gain weight and strength each day."

When Mitch turned to her instead of the twins, Lily's heart beat faster. "Thank you," she said simply.

"You're welcome," Mitch returned with a crooked smile. Just for tonight she'd let Mitch Cortega be her rock. Just for tonight, she'd depend on him.

Then she'd stand on her own two feet and raise her babies alone.

Chapter Two

Mitch stood in Lily's hospital room on Sunday afternoon. She was ready to go home and be a mom, but her babies couldn't go home with her. At least, not for a few weeks, and only then if no further problems developed. She didn't want to leave them, but she had no choice. She also couldn't drive herself home. Gina was in Houston again. Angie was still away, helping flood victims. And Raina, six months pregnant with a new husband and three boys to think about, had enough on her plate.

So Mitch had offered to drive Lily home, and she'd accepted. In fact, the thought of being with him again had made her feel…less worried. But now that he was standing in the room, dressed in jeans and a dark-green V-neck sweater, her pulse was speeding faster. She told herself she was just excited about leaving the hospital.

However, she snuck another peek at him and felt her stomach flutter.

Maybe she should have just paid taxi fare from Lubbock to Sagebrush instead of accepting his assistance so readily.

He seemed to read some of her thoughts. "I know you want to be independent, Lily, but I'm only giving you a ride home. You'll be driving again soon."

She did have to put this in perspective. "I just never expected to be going home without my babies and without—" She abruptly stopped.

"And without Troy," he filled in, not afraid to say it.

Blinking very fast she zipped the overnight case that Raina had dropped off for her. "I'm ready to get out of here and finish decorating the nursery. Everything needs to be perfect when my girls come home."

Mitch came up behind her, gently took her by the shoulders and turned her around. "You don't have to hide what you're feeling."

"I have to get *over* what I'm feeling, Mitch. I have two babies to take care of, to support. I can't think about Troy not being here and do what I have to do."

"You can't deny it, either. That will only bring you more heartache in the end."

Gazing into his deep brown eyes, she felt that unsettled sensation in the pit of her stomach again.

"I'm ready to go," she said firmly. She'd cry at night when she was too tired to do anything else. In the meantime, she was going to put a life together for her children.

Mitch dropped his hands from her shoulders and

picked up her overnight case. "Then let's get you home."

Their fifteen-minute drive from Lubbock to the small Texas town of Sagebrush was quiet for the most part. Mitch didn't seem to feel the need to talk and stared straight ahead as he drove. She had too many thoughts buzzing through her mind to want to be involved in conversation—including her unsettling awareness of the black-haired, broad-shouldered, protective man sitting beside her. Before her labor, hadn't she looked at Mitch as the person he was? Had she just seen him merely as a colleague? Simply a friend of Troy's? A person on the outskirts of her life but not really *in* her life?

He pulled into the driveway in front of the detached garage at the large blue Victorian-style house with yellow shutters, then turned to her with questions in his eyes, voicing one of them. "Who's going to be staying with you?"

"No one's staying with me."

Silence fell over the SUV as wind buffeted it.

"Isn't Angie back yet?" Mitch asked.

"No. When she's called away on the disaster relief team, there's no knowing how long she'll be gone."

"What about Raina?"

"I can't expect her to come over here and sit with me with all her responsibilities. Besides, I don't need a babysitter."

"As soon as you walk into that house, you're going to be surprised by how tired you feel. You can't stay here alone tonight."

Lily suddenly felt panicked without knowing exactly why. "What are you suggesting?"

"I'm not suggesting anything. I'm going to give you

two options. One, I can take you home with me and you can stay there for the night."

She was shaking her head already.

"Or, two, I can sleep on your couch."

She was still shaking her head.

"Is your refrigerator stocked?"

"I don't know."

"Do you feel like cooking supper?"

Though she didn't want to admit it, she did feel really tired. "I can make myself an egg."

"I seem to remember Jared ordering you to go home and rest today, for what's left of it, and turn in early tonight."

"He's just being cautious."

Mitch unbuckled his seat belt and shifted behind the wheel to face her. "I know as doctors we make the worst patients, but you've got to be sensible. When those babies come home in a few weeks, you have to be ready *physically* as well as emotionally. So, at least for today, accept help without argument."

Was she being unreasonable? *Was* she trying to be too strong? Why was that? Because she didn't want anyone helping her…or she suddenly didn't want *Mitch* helping her? The thought of him sleeping on her couch tonight made her stomach do something more than flutter. She felt as if she'd gone over the top of a Ferris wheel.

But she certainly wasn't going to Mitch's place. The gossips in Sagebrush would have a field day.

"Let's go inside and you can curl up on the sofa," he suggested. "I'll get you something to drink and we'll go from there."

"Don't you have other things to do today?"

"Repairing winter's damage to the patio? Sweeping out my garage?" He gave her one of his rare smiles.

Ever since Mitch had started with the practice, she'd noticed the long hours he worked, longer than any of the other physicians. He even scheduled consultations on Saturdays. He had rarely taken off work in the time she'd known him. Didn't he have a life outside of the fertility lab? Did he have friends other than the service buddies Troy had once mentioned? Mitch was an enigma, a puzzle she couldn't solve—one she shouldn't be interested in at all.

She nibbled on her lower lip for a couple of seconds and then asked, "Do you know how to cook?"

When he chuckled, she liked the sound of it. "I do. My mother taught me the basics," he said with fond remembrance. "I do all right."

The air in his SUV seemed stifling. She was relieved they were separated in the bucket seats because being physically close to Mitch now seemed…dangerous.

She asked in a low voice, "Why are you doing this, Mitch?"

"I made a promise to Troy. I keep my promises."

That's what she thought. This was duty for Mitch. He was a man who knew duty and honor well.

She let out a long breath. "All right, you can sleep on my couch. But just tonight. That's it. Tomorrow I'm on my own again."

"Deal," he agreed.

Even though he said it, she saw a considering flicker in his eyes. How long would his promise to Troy hold?

Minutes later they were escaping the blustery weather outside and walking into the old house that Lily now thought of as home. Last September she'd moved out of the apartment she'd shared with Troy because the memories there had been too painful.

She breathed in the scent of cinnamon emanating from the potpourri dish beside the Tiffany lamp in the foyer. Angie had filled it before Christmas. Her housemate had understood how difficult the holidays would be for Lily and had included her in her family's celebrations. So had Gina and, of course, Raina. They'd kept Lily too busy to think if not feel. At night, alone in her room, she'd faced her loss and spoken to her unborn babies about their dad and about what their first Christmas the following year might bring. She had to look toward the future.

"Where would you like your overnight case?" Mitch asked, stepping in behind her.

"Upstairs on my bed would be great."

"The steps won't be a problem?"

"Not at all. But I'll only do them once today."

"Which room is yours?"

A jolt of reality hit when she realized Mitch would be standing in her bedroom in a few minutes. He'd see the baby catalogs and magazines splayed across the chest at the foot of the bed, as well as the photo of Troy on her dresser. What else would he notice?

And why was the idea of Mitch standing in her bedroom so unnerving?

"What's wrong?" he asked.

"Nothing. My bedroom's the second one on the right. It's the one with the yellow rose wallpaper."

"Got it," he said with the flash of a smile that made her breath hitch a little.

Confused, she decided she was just tired from the trip

He brought the bag to her and settled it in her lap. "What are you making?"

After opening the Velcro closure, she extracted a pink sweater that sported one sleeve. "I didn't know whether to make these both pink or not. You know, stereotypes and all. But then I thought, two baby girls. What could be cuter than matching pink sweaters?"

He laughed. "I'm sure Sophie and Grace will agree."

She turned the sweater over in her hands and then admitted, "I was an only child. I wanted a sister desperately. Sophie and Grace will always have each other." She looked up at him again. "Do you have brothers or sisters?" She really didn't know anything about Mitch's background or his childhood.

"Nope. No brothers or sisters."

"Troy and his sister Ellie were close," Lily said in a low voice.

"He talked about her often," Mitch responded, in the way he had ever since Troy had been killed. She was grateful he made it all right for her to speak about her husband and anything connected to him.

"She's in a tough situation right now," Lily said to Mitch. "She had a small store where she sold her own line of baby clothes. But her area of Oklahoma was hard hit by the economic downturn and she had to close the store."

"What's she doing now?"

"She's trying to take her business to the internet."

"Is she coming for a visit?"

"Ellie and Troy's mom, Darlene, both want to visit after the babies come home." She'd always gotten along well with Ellie and Darlene...with all of Troy's family.

She knew he'd moved to Texas because the construction market had been thriving around Lubbock, unlike Oklahoma. She'd often wished his family wasn't so far away.

An odd expression crossed Mitch's face, one she couldn't decipher. He said, "You'll have a lot of people to help with the babies. That's just what you need."

"*Is* that what I need, Mitch? I'm their mom. I want to take care of them myself."

"Sure you do. But twins are a lot of work. There was a kid in my neighborhood when I was growing up. His mother had twins. She was always run ragged. And when you go back to work, you're definitely going to need child care."

"I have to go back," she said. "Insurance money and savings will only go so far."

"You'll have Troy's benefits," Mitch reminded her.

"That money is going into a trust fund for the twins."

He didn't contradict her, or try to convince her otherwise. She wanted to give her girls the advantages she'd had growing up. Yet, most of all, she wanted them to appreciate the people around them who loved them. When she'd lost her parents, she'd realized how little material possessions actually meant, and she'd grown up quickly.

"Did you grow up here in Sagebrush?" she asked Mitch, curious about his childhood.

"Yes, I did."

Frustrated he wasn't more expansive, she prompted, "But you don't have family here."

"No, I don't."

"Mitch," she said, letting her frustration show.

"What do you want to know, Lily? Just ask."

Studying his collar-length black hair, his chiseled features, she let the question pop into her head. *Are you just here out of duty or do you care?* Instead she replied, "I *am* asking. But you're not telling me much."

"And why is this suddenly important?"

That was a good question. "I'm not sure. I guess talking about Ellie, thinking about how I'm going to raise the twins— It just made me wonder, that's all. At least give me something to think about while I rest and twiddle my thumbs."

"Crochet," he pointed out.

"Same difference."

The silence in the living room enveloped them for a few moments until Mitch said, "Your background and mine are very different."

"How do you know about mine?"

"Troy shared some of it when we played pool."

Lily's husband and Mitch had gone out and shared an evening of guy stuff now and then, the same way she shared time with her friends.

"Just what did he tell you?"

Mitch's shrug told her he was attempting to make the conversation casual. "That your father was a respected scientist and professor at Stanford. That your mother was a pharmacist who developed her own line of cosmetics and did quite well with them. Something about after your father died, she sold the formula to provide you with a college education."

"Yes, she did," Lily murmured, mind-traveling back to a time that was filled with bittersweet memories. "Daddy died of a massive coronary when I was in high school. My mom died of breast cancer when I was in

college. Losing them both made me want to find a pro-
fession that gave life."

"If your father taught at Stanford, how did you end
up *here?*"

"My mom had a friend who lived in Lubbock, so we
moved here. But she and my dad had always planned
I'd go to their alma mater. I was at Stanford when she
got sick. I flew home as often as I could, but then took
off a semester when we called in hospice."

"You've had a lot of loss."

"The people I love leave me." She stared at her hands
when she said it, but then she raised her gaze to his. "I
know. I know. I shouldn't believe that. If nothing else,
I should think positive to change the pattern. But this
negative pattern is awfully fresh again and it's hard not
to wonder."

"You have two little girls now to love."

"I do. And you can bet, I *will* be an overprotective
mom."

"I don't think there's anything wrong with that."

Somehow the conversation had rolled back to Lily
again. Mitch was so good at deflecting. Why had she
never realized that? But she was also determined to
delve below the surface.

Hiking herself up higher against the sofa arm, she
nodded toward the space at the end of the couch where
her feet had been. "Tell me how you grew up."

He looked as reluctant to sit on her couch as she
was to have him sleep there tonight. But in the end, he
decided she wouldn't rest until he gave her something.
So he sat on the sofa, his thigh brushing one of her
stockinged feet. He looked terrifically uncomfortable.
"There's not much to it."

She waited, her gaze on his rugged profile.

With a grimace, he finally said, "My father married my mother because she was pregnant when they were both eighteen."

She knew Mitch was probably going to need some prompting, so she asked, "Did it last?"

Mitch's brows drew together as he, obviously reluctant, answered, "He stuck around for a year, then took off on his motorcycle and bailed. She went to business school and became a medical transcriber, but she couldn't always find work. Other times she held two jobs, cleaned offices at night and saved for when times were thin again. I was determined to make life better for both of us."

"Did you always want to be a doctor?"

"Do you mean was it a lifelong wish from childhood? No. Actually, at first I thought I might become a stockbroker or an investment banker."

Lily couldn't help but smile. She couldn't imagine Mitch as either of those. She didn't know why. She just couldn't. "So why aren't you working on Wall Street?"

"I was good at sports...basketball. I won a scholarship to college. But during my sophomore year my mother got sick and didn't tell me. She didn't have insurance so she didn't go to the doctor. She developed pneumonia and died."

"Oh, Mitch. I'm sorry. That had to be awful for you."

Again he looked uncomfortable revealing this part of his past. "She'd been my motivator. After she died, I took a nosedive. I'd been a good student, but my grades tanked. Then one day, after a few months of drinking into the night and sleeping too late to get up for class, I looked out the dorm window and knew that campus wasn't *real* life. Guys hooking up with girls, frat parties, learning to play teachers for better grades. I thought about my mom's life, how hard it had been and how it ended, and I decided to make a difference. I wanted to help patients who didn't have much of a chance. I wanted to give life when it was hardly there any longer. So I juggled two jobs, got my B.S., and went on to med school. I decided on trauma surgery. In my last year of residency, September 11th happened."

Lily thought of Raina and her first husband, a firefighter, who had lost his life that day. Her knowledge of Mitch's character and her intuition where he was concerned urged her to ask, "And that's when you signed up for the Army National Guard?"

"Yes."

"When did you go to Iraq?"

"Two years later."

They were both quiet for a few moments.

Mitch flexed his hand and moved his fingers as she often saw him do, and she knew he was remembering something he never talked about…something that caused those deep fatigue lines around his eyes some mornings.

To break the heavy silence, she asked, "Are you happy being part of our fertility practice?" She and two other doctors had been in unanimous agreement, voting him into their partnership.

"You mean would I rather be performing surgery? Sure. But I like what I do. You and me, Jon and Hillary…we give the seeds of life a chance, as well as at-risk pregnancies. That's rewarding. What I miss is not being part of the Guard, no longer having that unique camaraderie and sense of spirit. Before deployment, it was tough trying to be a doctor as well as a guardsman. But it was what I wanted to be doing."

Abruptly he stood, his body language telling her that this conversation was over. He already knew Lily was the type who wanted to know more, who would ask questions until she got her answers. He was cutting that off before it could go any further. To her surprise, she already missed his presence at the end of the sofa.

"I checked your refrigerator and you have a couple of choices," he said with a forced smile. "Scrambled eggs, scrambled eggs with asparagus and bacon on the side, or… I think I saw sausage in there that I could turn into sausage and pasta of some kind, maybe with canned tomatoes."

"Are you kidding me?" Her eyes were open wide and she was staring at him as if she really didn't know him.

"I told you my mom taught me the basics. But in college I had an apartment with two other guys. I couldn't stomach pizza every night, so I cooked. I borrowed a cookbook or two from the library and they kept me going for the year."

"You're just full of surprises," Lily said, laying her head back against the arm of the sofa, suddenly tired and feeling weak.

"Is the adrenaline finally giving out?" he asked her.

"If you mean do I feel like a wet noodle, yes. Are you happy now?"

The corner of his mouth turned down. "Seeing you tired doesn't make me happy. But knowing that because of it you'll get some rest does." He took hold of the afghan and pulled it above her breasts. He made sure she was covered from there to her toes. Then he gave it a little tuck under her hip so it wouldn't fall away.

Mitch's fingers were strong and long. She felt heat from them with just that quick touch. He'd used his left hand. From what she'd heard, he didn't have much feeling in the fingers of his right hand.

She caught his arm before he moved away.

His gaze crashed into hers and they stared at each other for a few moments.

"Thank you for bringing me home."

"No problem," he responded, as if it was no big deal.

But it was a big deal to Lily. She'd never forget his friendship with Troy. She'd certainly never forget his kindness to her. But something about that kindness and her acceptance of it unsettled her. She had to figure out why it bothered her so much that Mitch would be sleeping on her couch tonight.

Chapter Three

Lily stared at the TV that evening, not really focused on the newsmagazine show that was airing. She was too aware of Mitch rattling the back screen door, fixing loose weather stripping.

Over supper they'd talked about the house and former tenants, needing dispassionate conversation. When they didn't stay on neutral territory, they seemed to wander into intensity...or awkwardness that came from being alone together. It was odd, really. For the past two and a half years while working with Mitch, she'd found him easy to be with. Now...

The phone rang and Lily picked up the cordless from the end table. When she saw Gina's number on caller ID, she breathed a sigh of relief.

"Hi," Gina said. "How are you and Sophie and Grace?"

"I called the hospital a little bit ago. They're doing okay. And I'm…good. I'm at home."

"So you said in your message. I'm sorry I just got it. My plane had a delay taking off. It was a whirlwind trip, leaving yesterday and coming back today. But I didn't want to be away from Daniel and Logan any longer than I had to be."

A baby development expert, Gina had received an offer from a Houston hospital to start her Baby Grows center there, too. Lily was sure Gina would someday not only have an additional Baby Grows center in Houston but many all around the country.

"So Mitch is keeping you company? How's that going?"

"It's okay. It's just…he's hovering. He insists I shouldn't be alone today. He gave me the option to sleep over at his place, or his sleeping on my couch. So he's sleeping here on my couch tonight."

"Are you okay with that?"

"Sure." But Lily knew her voice didn't sound sure. A man who wasn't her husband sleeping under her roof. Is that what was bothering her? Or was there more to it?

"Do you want me to come over?"

"No," Lily was quick to answer. "You need to be with your family."

"I was going to take off work tomorrow. Why don't I drive over first thing? Then Mitch can go to Family Tree."

"Are you sure you don't have other things you have to do?"

"I don't," Gina replied. "Tomorrow we can talk about Sophie and Grace, possibly visit them, and maybe I can get some things ready for you."

Seeing her twins. Baby talk. Girl talk. That sounded great to Lily. "I really appreciate this."

"No problem. Have you heard from Angie?"

Angie was Gina's sister, and Lily knew Gina worried about her when she worked on the team. "No. Have you?"

"No, not since she reached the Gulf. But the disaster relief team really doesn't have time for anything but helping the victims." After a short pause, she asked, "Why don't I stop at the bakery and pick up croissants on my way over?"

"I'm supposed to be losing weight, not gaining it."

"You don't have that much to lose. Besides, if you're going to pump milk and then breast-feed, you need some extra calories."

"The croissants sound good. That way I can convince Mitch he doesn't have to make breakfast."

"Did he make supper?"

"He did. And now he's doing some minor repairs on the house."

It must have been her tone of voice when she said it that made Gina ask, "That bothers you?"

"I don't want to be indebted to him. Do you know what I mean?"

"Oh, I know. But remember, Troy asked him to watch over you. That's what he's doing."

Last fall, Lily had shared Troy's letter with Gina, Angie and Raina. They also knew Mitch was simply fulfilling a promise. She should be grateful instead of uncomfortable.

Lily had just ended the call when Mitch strode into the living room. She told him, "Gina's coming over early tomorrow morning so you don't have to worry about me."

No change of expression crossed Mitch's face, but there was a flicker of reaction in his eyes that said he would worry anyway.

"I have a new client tomorrow who will be making decisions about in vitro fertilization and a few follow-up appointments after that. So if you need anything, I can try to rearrange my schedule."

She jumped in. "No need. I'll be sorting baby clothes with Gina and hanging decorations on the nursery walls. I wasn't prepared for an early delivery, which isn't like me at all!"

Mitch set the duct tape he'd carried in on an end table. "You wanted to stay in the pregnant zone as long as you could."

Although diplomatic, what he wasn't saying was obvious. She'd wanted to put off the idea of becoming a mother without Troy by her side for as long as possible. For once in her life, denial had definitely been more palatable than reality.

But now reality had smacked her in the face.

"You look lost," Mitch said, with a gentle edge to his voice.

That gentleness fell over her like a warm cloak. But then she had to ask herself, *did* she feel lost? Adrift? Alone? But she wasn't alone when she had good friends helping her. "No, not lost. Just off balance. I hate the unexpected. And my life has been one unexpected crisis after the other."

Rounding the coffee table, he approached her and she wished he'd sit beside her on the sofa. But he didn't.

"Sophie and Grace coming home will be grounding. You'll see."

His dark eyes didn't waver from hers and she felt sudden heat rising in her cheeks. Not from looking at Mitch! How many times had she looked at him in just that way?

No. Not just *this* way.

"The bedding for the sofa is upstairs," she said in a rush. "I'll get it."

"Are you staying up there?"

"I suppose." She produced a smile. "You'll have the downstairs to yourself if you want to watch TV or get a snack."

"I'll walk up with you."

There was no point in protesting. What would she do? Toss him the bedding over the banister?

When she swung her legs over the side of the sofa, Mitch was there, holding out his hand to help her up. She could be stubborn. Or she could accept a hand up when she needed it.

His strong fingers closed over hers, and her heart raced as her mind searched for something to say.

"Take it slowly," he reminded her as she rose to her feet.

Everything Mitch said today seemed to be full of deeper meaning. Although she longed to keep her hand in his, she slid it free and headed to the stairs.

A few minutes later in the hall on the second floor, Lily stopped by the linen closet and opened the door. Blankets lay folded on the shelf above her head. She reached up but she shouldn't have bothered. Mitch was there, behind her, easily pulling a blanket from the closet. His superior height and strength was obvious.

She could sense both, even though he wasn't touching her. Jittery, tired and anxious about what was going to happen next, she knew her hormones were out of whack. That was the best explanation she could think of to explain how she was feeling around Mitch.

He stepped away, bedding in hand. "This is great."

"Don't be silly. You need a sheet and pillow." And *she* needed something to do with her hands. She needed something to do with her mind. She needed something to *do*.

Choosing a pale blue sheet, she yanked a matching pillowcase from a stack. "The extra pillows are way up on the top shelf," she explained, moving away, letting him reach.

He easily removed one of those, too.

"I wish the sofa pulled out. You're going to be uncomfortable all scrunched up."

He laughed. "Believe me, I've slept on a lot worse. You worry too much, Lily. Did anyone ever tell you that?"

Her husband's name came to her lips, but she didn't say it. She didn't have to. Mitch knew.

He looked disconcerted for a second—just a second—but then he took the sheets from her arms. "Do you have a phone in your room?"

"My cell phone is in my purse. You brought that up with my suitcase. Why?"

"If you need something, call me. You might go to bed and an hour from now figure out you want a pack of crackers or a glass of milk."

There was only one way to answer with a man like Mitch. "I'll call you if I need you."

But somehow they both knew she wouldn't.

She went to the door to her room, which was only a few feet away. He didn't move until she stepped over the threshold and murmured, "Good night."

He gave her a slight nod, responded, "Good night, Lily," and headed for the stairs.

As she closed her door, she leaned against it and sighed. She wanted to make up the sofa for him so it would be comfortable.

How silly a notion was that?

"What do you mean you sent Gina home?" Mitch demanded as he stood in Lily's living room the following evening, a gift-wrapped box under one arm.

"She arrived before I was up this morning, as you know. She helped me ready the nursery. She took me to see the babies, and then I told her she should go home to her husband and son."

"And she just went?" He seemed astonished by that idea.

"She protested, but I plopped here on the sofa, told her I'd stay here, and she saw I meant it."

Lily was one exasperating woman! There was no doubt about that. But he had to admire her in spite of himself. "What did you do for dinner?"

"What is this, the third degree?"

He just arched a brow.

"Gina made a casserole for lunch and I had leftovers, with a salad and all that. What did *you* have?" she returned, almost cheekily.

All day he'd thought about eating dinner with her last night…saying good-night at the end of the day, spending the night on her couch in the strong grip of an insomnia he knew too well. Yet that was better than waking up in a sweat after too-real flashbacks or nightmares. Moments of sensual awareness when Lily had come downstairs this morning had been unsettling enough to push him on his way as soon as Gina had arrived.

Answering her, he said, "I went to the drive-through at my favorite burger joint." At her expression, he laughed. "Don't look so outraged. I have to do that once a week to keep fit."

Lily laughed then, even though she tried not to. That was the first real laugh he'd heard from her since be-fore—even he had trouble saying it sometimes—since before Troy had died. He wanted to keep her spirits up. "So…how are Sophie and Grace?"

"Sit down," Lily said, motioning to the sofa. "I hate it when you loom. What's under your arm?"

"We'll get to that." He considered her comment. "And I don't loom."

"Whatever you say," she said too quickly, with a little smile.

Shaking his head, he set the box on the coffee table and lowered himself to the sofa. Not too close to her. Before he'd driven over here, he'd warned himself about that.

"The babies are so small," she explained, worried. "I can touch them but I can't hold them, and I'm dying to hold them."

"You'll soon be able to hold Sophie, if not Grace. How's their weight?" he asked, digging for the bottom line like a doctor.

"They're holding their own. My milk should be in soon and I'm going to pump it—" She stopped as her cheeks turned more pink.

"Don't be embarrassed. I'm a doctor, Lily. We talk

about this all the time with our patients." Right now he had to think of her as a patient so other images didn't trip over each other in his head.

"I know. But it seems different with…us."

Yes, something *did* seem different. Her perception of him? His of her? The fact that they'd been friends and maybe now something more was going on?

Nothing should be going on. It was way too soon for her. Maybe way too late for him.

"Can you tell them apart?" he asked, knowing conversation about her little girls would be comforting for her.

"Of course. Sophie's nose is turned up a little bit more at the end than Grace's. Grace's chin is just a little daintier, a tad more refined. They both have Troy's forehead and probably his eyes. It's a little too soon to tell. Sophie's a half inch longer than Grace, but Grace could catch up if she gains weight."

"She'll gain weight. They both will."

"Grace is still on the ventilator." Lily's voice trembled a bit.

Needing to fortify her with the truth, he asked, "What does Francesca say?"

"Francesca insists they're doing as well as can be expected and I have to give them time. I just feel like I should be doing something. Do you know what I mean?"

"Oh, yeah. Sitting still isn't easy for either one of us." He patted the box. "That's why I brought this along. Doing is always better than worrying."

"A gift?" Lily tore the wrapping paper off and read the information on the outside of the box. "Oh, Mitch, this is one of those new baby monitors."

"It is. The screen is small, but there's a portable handset you can carry with you to another room. So I'm also going to hook up a larger monitor you won't need binoculars to see. It's in my car."

"I can't let you—"

He shook his finger at her. "Don't even say it. You're going to be running yourself ragged when those babies come home. Having cameras in their cribs and a monitor down here so you can see them will help save a little bit of your energy."

"It will save a lot of my energy. Thank you."

Her blue eyes seemed to try to look inside him, into his heart...into his soul. That unsettled him. His soul was tormented at times by everything that had happened in Iraq. He hadn't been able to save his friend, and that, along with the PTSD symptoms, clawed at his heart. He quickly replied, "You're welcome. Why don't I get this hooked up? That way it will be ready whenever you bring the babies home."

"The cribs were delivered this morning. Gina supervised so I didn't have to run up and down the steps. But I don't know if she put the bedding on."

"Don't worry about it. I can position the cameras with the bedding on or off."

"Do you need my help? I can come up—"

"No." If Lily came upstairs, she would definitely be a distraction. "I brought along a toolbox and everything I might need. You drink a glass of milk and crochet or something."

"Drink a glass of milk?" She was smiling and her question was filled with amusement.

That smile of hers packed a wallop. It turned up the corners of her very pretty mouth. It seemed to make the few freckles across her cheeks more evident, her face actually glow.

Had he been attracted to Lily before Troy's death? If he was honest with himself, he had to say he had been. But attraction was one thing, acting on it was another. He'd shut it down when he'd learned she and Troy were to be married. He and Troy had become good friends and he'd congratulated them both at their wedding, always keeping his distance from Lily.

Being colleagues at their practice had been difficult at times. But not impossible. He kept their dealings strictly professional. They'd been cohorts, interacting on an intellectual level. He and Troy had been close. He and Lily? They'd just existed in the same universe.

Until…after Troy had died. When Mitch had hugged Lily that day after her ultrasound, he'd experienced desire and felt like an SOB because of it. That day, Mitch had realized that if he was going to keep his promise to Troy, he couldn't deny his attraction any longer. At least to himself. *She* didn't have to know about it.

But now—

Now nothing had changed. He had baggage. She had a world of grief and loss and new responsibility to deal with.

Turning away from her smile, which could affect him more than he wanted to admit, he muttered, "Milk's good for you and the babies. You've got to keep your vitamin D level up, along with your calcium. I'll go get what I need from the SUV and be right back."

Sometimes retreat was the best part of valor. Remembering that might save them both from an awkward or embarrassing situation.

* * *

Lily was emptying the dishwasher when Mitch called her into the living room. She'd been aware of his footfalls upstairs, the old floors creaking as he moved about. She'd been even *more* attuned to his presence when he'd come downstairs and she'd heard him cross the living room. She'd stayed in the kitchen. Somehow that had just seemed safer...easier...less fraught with vibrations she didn't want to come to terms with.

Hearing her name on Mitch's lips was unsettling now, and she told herself she was just being silly. Yet, seconds later when she stepped into the living room and found him taking up space in his long-sleeved hoodie and jeans, she almost backed into the kitchen again.

Making herself move forward, shifting her eyes away from his, she spotted the twenty-inch monitor on a side table. One moment she glimpsed one white crib with pink trim and green bedding. The next he'd pressed a button and she spotted the other crib with its pink-and-yellow designs. She could watch both babies by changing the channel.

"The wonders of technology." A smile shone in his voice.

She knew Mitch was good with electronics and especially computers. He was the first at the office to understand a new system, to fix glitches, to teach someone else the intricacies of a program.

"Are systems like this a side hobby for you?"

"Always have been. I'm self-taught. The skills come in handy now and then."

As long as she'd known Mitch, he'd downplayed what he did and who he helped. "You're a good man, Mitch."

He looked surprised for a moment.

She added, "If you can do something for someone else, you do."

"Lily, don't make so much of setting up a monitoring system."

Telling herself she should stay right where she was, she didn't listen to her better judgment. She advanced closer to Mitch and this time didn't look away. "You're not just helping *me*. It's sort of an attitude with you. If someone has a problem, you take time to listen."

Maybe he could see she was serious about this topic. Maybe he could see that she was trying to determine exactly how much help she should accept from him. Maybe he could see that this conversation was important to her. Nevertheless, by his silence he seemed reluctant to give away even a little piece of himself.

"Does it have something to do with being in Iraq?" she asked softly.

The flicker of response in his eyes told her she'd hit the mark. She saw one of his hands curve into a fist and she thought he might simply tell her it was none of her business. Instead, however, he lifted his shoulders in a shrug, as if this wasn't important. As if he didn't mind her asking at all.

"I survived," he told her calmly. "I figured there was a reason for that. I returned home with a new understanding of patience, tolerance and simple kindness."

Although Mitch's expression gave away nothing, Lily knew he was holding back. He was giving her an edited version of what he felt and what he'd experienced.

"Have you ever talked about Iraq?"

"No."

"Not even with your buddies?"

"They know what it was like. I don't have to talk about it."

She supposed that was true. Yet from the tension she could sense in Mitch, she understood he had scars that were more than skin deep.

With a tap on the control sitting next to the monitor on the table, he suggested, "Let me show you the remote and what the lights mean."

Discussion over. No matter what she thought, Mitch was finished with that topic, and he was letting her know it. She could push. But she sensed that Mitch wasn't the type of man who *could* be pushed. He would just shut down. That wouldn't get her anywhere at all. Why was she so hell-bent on convincing him that the bad stuff would only damage him if he kept it inside?

She'd let the conversation roll his way for now. For the next few minutes she let him explain the lights on the remote and how she could carry it into the kitchen with her and upstairs to her bedroom. When he handed it to her, their fingers skidded against each other and she practically jumped. She was so startled by the jolt of adrenaline it gave her, she dropped the remote.

She stooped over to retrieve it at the same time he crouched down. Their faces were so close together… close enough to kiss…

They moved apart and Lily let him grasp the control.

After Mitch picked it up, he handed it to her and quickly stepped away. "I'd better get going," he said. "Do you want me to turn off the system?"

"I can do it."

He nodded, crossing to the door, picking up the toolbox he'd set there.

She followed him, feeling as if something had gone

wrong, yet not knowing what. "Thank you again for the monitoring system. I really appreciate it."

"Are you going to be alone tomorrow?"

"No. Raina's coming to visit. She's going to drive me to the hospital so I can spend time with the twins while she makes rounds."

"That sounds like a plan. I'm glad you have friends you can count on."

"I am, too."

As their gazes found each other, his dark brown eyes deeply calm, Lily felt shaken up.

"If you need help when you bring the babies home, you have my number."

Yes, she did. But the way she was feeling right now, she wasn't going to use it. She couldn't call on him again when she felt attracted to him. That's what it was, plain and simple—attraction she was trying to deny. Oh, no. She wouldn't be calling his number anytime soon. She would not feel guilty believing she was being unfaithful to her husband's memory.

Maybe Mitch realized some of that, because he left.

Even though a cold wind blew into the foyer, Lily stood there watching Mitch's charcoal SUV back out of the driveway. When his taillights finally faded into the black night, she closed the door, relieved she was alone with her memories...relieved she might not see Mitch for a while.

Then everything would go back to normal between them.

Over the next few weeks Mitch didn't see much of Lily, though he stopped in at the hospital NICU almost

every day. A few days ago, the twins had been moved to
the regular nursery. This morning he'd run into Angie,
who told him they'd gone home. Lily hadn't called him.
Because she was overwhelmed with bringing the twins
home and everything that entailed? Or because she
wanted to prove to herself she could be a single mom
and manage just fine?

He was going to find out.

When Mitch reached the Victorian, he scanned the
house and grounds. Everything *seemed* normal—until
he approached the front door. Although it was closed,
he could hear the cries of two babies inside. New mothers had enough trouble handling one, let alone two. But
where were Lily's friends?

With no response when he rang the doorbell, he
knocked. When Lily still didn't answer, he turned the
knob—no one in Sagebrush locked their doors—and
stepped inside.

Immediately he realized the wails were coming from
a room down the hall from the living room. Turning
that way, he found the room that had been the women's
exercise room. Now it looked like a makeshift nursery.
There were two bassinets, a card table he assumed Lily
used for changing the twins, and a scarred wooden rocking chair that looked as if it could be an antique. His
gaze was quickly drawn to her. He knew he should look
away from Lily's exposed breast as she tried to feed one
baby while holding the other. Respectful of her as a new
mom, he dropped his gaze to an odd-looking pillow on
her lap, one of those nursing pillows advertised in baby
magazines. But it didn't seem to be doing much good.
Lily looked about ready to scream herself.

When she raised her head and saw him, she practically

had to yell over the squalls. "I couldn't come to the door. I can't seem to satisfy them," she admitted, her voice catching.

Without hesitating, Mitch took Sophie from her mom's arms, trying valiantly to ignore Lily's partially disrobed condition. He had enough trouble with the visions dancing through his head at night. Concentrating for the moment on Sophie, he flipped a disposable diaper from a stack, tossed it onto his shoulder and held the infant against him. The feel of that warm little girl on his shoulder blanked out any other pictures. Taking in a whiff of her baby lotion scent, he knew nothing in the world could be as innocent and sweet as a newborn baby. His hand rubbed up and down her little back, and miraculously she began to quiet. In a few moments, her sobs subsided into hiccups.

Lily, a bit amazed, quickly composed herself and tossed a blanket over her shoulder to hide her breast. Then she helped Grace suckle once more. This time the baby seemed content.

"Did your friends desert you?" He couldn't imagine them doing that.

"No, of course not. Gina and Raina were here most of the day. When Angie got ready for work and left, Sophie and Grace were asleep."

Mitch watched as Lily took a deep breath and let it out slowly. "But they woke up, crying to be fed at the same time."

"Do you have milk in the fridge?"

"Yes, but—"

"Breast-feeding two babies is something that's going to take practice. In the meantime, I can give Sophie a bottle." He gestured to her lap. "Nursing pillows and experts' advice might work for some people, but you've got to be practical. There is no right way and wrong way to do this, Lily. You just have to do what works for you and the babies."

"How do you know so much about babies?" Lily asked in a small voice, looking down at her nursing child rather than at him.

His part in the practice was science-oriented and mostly behind the scenes. "Training," he said simply, remembering his rotation in obstetrics years ago.

That drew her eyes to his. He added, "And...sometimes in the field, you have to learn quickly." In Iraq, he'd helped a new mother who'd been injured, returning her and her newborn to her family.

Before Lily could ask another question, he gently laid Sophie in one of the bassinets and hurried to the kitchen to find her milk. A short time later he carried one of the kitchen chairs to the nursery and positioned it across from Lily. Then he picked up Sophie again and cradled her in his arm. They sat in silence for a few minutes as both twins took nourishment.

"What made you stop by today?" Lily finally asked.

Lily's blond hair was fixed atop her head with a wooden clip. Wavy strands floated around her face. She was dressed in a blue sweater and jeans and there was a slight flush to her cheeks. Because he was invading private moments between her and her babies?

"I was at the hospital and found out they were discharged today."

Lily's eyes grew wider. Did she think he was merely checking up on her so he could say he had? He wished! He was in this because she'd gotten under his skin.

"Feeding these two every three hours, or more often, could get complicated. What would you have done if I hadn't arrived?"

"I would have figured something out."

Her stubbornness almost convinced him to shock her by taking her into his arms and kissing her. Lord, where had that thought come from? "I'm sure Gina and Raina never would have left if they knew you were so overwhelmed."

"Raina and Gina have families."

"They also both have nannies," he reminded her.

"They also both have—"

Mitch knew Lily had been about to say that they both had husbands. Instead, she bit her lower lip and transferred Grace to her other breast, taking care to keep herself covered with the blanket.

"I'm sorry I just walked in on you like that." He might as well get what happened out in the open or they'd both have that moment between them for a while.

"I'm going to have to get over my privacy issues if I intend to breast-feed them for very long. I sat down with the accountant last week. I can take a leave for seven or eight months and be okay financially. My practice is important, but I really feel as if I need to be with them to give them a good start in life."

Since she was the only parent they had, he could certainly understand that.

"Do you think the practice can do without me for that long?"

"We can manage. You know our client list is down because of insurance issues. This could work out to everyone's advantage. We can always consult with you from home if we need your expertise."

Suddenly remembering the need to burp Sophie, he set the bottle on the floor and balanced the tiny baby on his knee. His hand was practically as large as *she* was. What would life be like taking care of them every day? Being able to watch their progress and all the firsts? Keeping his palm on her chest, he rubbed her back until she burped.

Smiling at Lily he said offhandedly, "She's easy."

Lily smiled back.

In that moment, he knew being here with Lily like this was dangerous.

What he was about to suggest was even *more* dangerous.

Chapter Four

"Do you want me to sleep on the couch again tonight?" Mitch asked as he cradled Sophie in his arm once more and offered her the bottle again. He couldn't help studying her perfect baby features. He was beginning to recognize a warm feeling that enveloped his heart when he was around Sophie and Grace.

After a lengthy pause, he cast a sideways glance at Lily to gauge her expression. As long as she was upstairs and he stayed downstairs, he wouldn't worry her with the restlessness that plagued him at night.

She looked somber as she debated with herself about what to say. He could almost hear her inner conversation because he'd already had the same one. If he stayed, they'd connect more. If he stayed, they might get to know each other better.

Quietly, she responded, "If you stay, I think I can

keep Sophie and Grace happier. The two of us are obviously handling them better than *I* was handling them alone. I have to learn what works and what doesn't. That will just take time. In the meantime, I want to stay calm. I want to enjoy both of them. I can't go into a panic just because Grace and Sophie are crying at the same moment."

"Why *did* you panic?" Extreme reactions weren't at all like Lily. But she'd never been a mom before. She bit her lower lip and he found himself focused on her mouth much too intensely.

"I have these two little beings depending on me twenty-four hours a day, seven days a week," she attempted to explain. "I don't want to let them down. I don't want either of them to feel neglected."

It was easy to see Lily had already bonded with her daughters and she wanted nothing to interfere with those bonds, not even another willing pair of hands giving her aid. He attempted to be reasonable, realizing he wanted to stay more than he wanted to go. "Right now, they need to have their basic needs met—feeding, changing and cuddling. They'll learn to know you," he reassured her quickly. "They won't mind if someone else gives them what they need. In a few months, they'll both be more particular. They'll want you when they want you. So for now, take advantage of the fact that someone else can help."

"You make it sound so simple," she said with a wry smile. "And we know it isn't."

No, nothing was simple. Besides the sheer enormity of the twins' birth, other feelings besides affection for Sophie and Grace were developing between him and Lily. However, neither of them were going to mention those. No. They wouldn't be having that discussion any-time soon…which left the door wide open for his desire to cause trouble. Yet he still wanted to be close to her.

As he set Sophie on his knee to burp her again, he asked, "Will you take the babies upstairs to sleep tonight?"

"Yes. I want them to get used to their cribs. I've got to get the hang of breast-feeding both of them, but that might be easier to juggle during the day. I thought I might put a small refrigerator upstairs for night feedings."

"That sounds like a good idea. Maybe I can go pick one up for you tomorrow."

"But I'm paying for it."

"Okay, you're paying for it." He knew better than to argue.

With her gaze locked on his, he felt a turning so deep inside of him that he had to stand with Sophie and walk her back and forth across the room. She'd drunk three ounces of the bottle and that was good. Taking her to the card table, he unsnapped her Onesies so he could change her.

"Mitch, you don't have to do that."

He glanced over his shoulder while he held Sophie with one hand and picked up a diaper with the other. "I don't mind changing her. But if you'd rather I didn't, I won't."

Mitch guessed Grace was still locked on Lily's breast. Just imagining that—

"As long as *you* don't mind," Lily finally said.

He seemed to be all thumbs with the small diaper, but he hoped Lily wasn't noticing. The tiny snaps on the Onesies were a challenge, too, but his left hand had almost become as proficient as his right hand had once been—before shrapnel had torn into it.

Finally Sophie was ready for bed. Her little eyes were practically closed and her angelic face was peaceful. "I'll carry her upstairs and lay her in her crib. You can come up when Grace finishes."

"I have receiving blankets up there on the side of each crib. Can you swaddle her in one? They're supposed to sleep better if I do that."

"I'll try it."

"And you have to lay her on her back."

"I know, Lily."

She flushed.

"After I put her to bed, I'll pull out a blanket and a pillow for the sofa. I remember where you got them."

Lily nodded, but dropped her eyes to Grace and didn't look at him. If they didn't admit to the intimacy developing between them, then the intimacy wouldn't exist, right?

Right.

They were tiptoeing along a line in the sand, hoping neither one of them fell onto the other side.

He let out a pent-up breath he didn't even know he was holding when he left the downstairs nursery and headed up the steps, Sophie sleeping against his shoulder. The hall light guided him into the babies' room, where he grabbed the blanket and carefully wrapped Sophie in it on the changing table, murmuring softly to her as he did. Then he gently laid her in her crib and switched on the monitoring system.

After turning on the castle night-light by the rocker, he went to the hall for his bedding. At the closet, he glanced back at the room, almost ready to return and wish the little girl a good night. But he knew he couldn't become attached, not to the babies any more than to Lily. Nothing was permanent. Everything ended. He had no right to even think about Lily in a romantic way. He had no intention of making life more complicated for either of them.

After Mitch went downstairs, he made up the sofa and sat on it, staring at the monitor. Sophie did look like a cherub with her wispy blond hair, her blue eyes, her little body that seemed more heavenly than earthly. Her tiny face turned from left to right and he wondered if she missed Grace already.

He was so engrossed in his reflections that he didn't hear Lily come into the living room until the floor squeaked. She was holding Grace in a sling that kept her nestled against her chest.

"Is Sophie asleep?" Lily asked.

"Come see."

"I have to put Grace down, too."

"A couple of minutes won't matter. Come here."

Lily just stared at Sophie, her sweet sleep as entrancing as her little nose, long eyelashes and broad brow. "The monitor is wonderful, Mitch," Lily said in a low voice. "But they're so small. I'll probably be going in every fifteen minutes to check on them."

"You need your sleep. I'll be watching from down here. How about if I stay awake until the first feeding?"

"You need your sleep, too."

"I'm used to not sleeping. I was a trauma surgeon, remember?"

She remembered and unintentionally her gaze went to his arm and his hand.

Self-consciously, he moved it and balled it into a fist. Though he expected her to move away, she didn't.

"Do you think about what you used to do very often?"

"Often enough. But that was then and this is now. Why don't I walk you upstairs? We'll make sure both babies are settled."

Lily took one last look at the image on the monitor and then crossed to the stairway. Mitch waited a beat or so and then followed her.

Upstairs, by the glow of the night-light, Lily took Grace from her carrier and wrapped her in a blanket as Mitch had done with Sophie. After Lily laid Grace in her crib, she stooped over the baby and kissed her forehead. "I love you, sweet girl. I'm glad you're home."

Then she moved to Sophie's crib and did the same.

Aware Mitch hadn't come far into the room, Lily glanced at him as he stood by the chair, his arms crossed over his chest—watchful and distant.

When he'd arrived at the house earlier and come into the downstairs nursery, she'd felt so many emotions that they'd tumbled over each other. Yes, she'd been embarrassed. But she'd also felt a little proud. Only a few moments had passed until she'd realized she *should* feel embarrassed. And then she had.

As they'd put the babies to bed, though, the situation had seemed right. Mitch handled them so well... so comfortably...so like a father. Sometimes she could see the affection he felt for them. But other times, he removed himself.

Like now.

He fell into step beside her as she left the nursery

and walked down the hall to her bedroom. At her door, she was ready to say good-night, ready to fall into bed, exhausted from the stress, the worry and the joy of bringing the babies home today. Yet a simple good-night didn't seem adequate and when she gazed into Mitch's eyes, she couldn't look away.

He seemed to have the same problem.

There was something about him standing there, perfectly still, his shoulders wide enough to block the doorway, his height filling the space. Maybe it was the sight of him without his tie and with the first few buttons of his white shirt open. Maybe it was her reaction to the black chest hair peeking out. Maybe she thought about all he'd done for her. Maybe, for just a short time, she gave in to the thought that she might *need* someone to watch out for her. She only knew that thoughts weren't running through her brain as fast as heat was flashing through her body. She wasn't thinking at all when she leaned forward. Rather, she was feeling and wishing and hoping and remembering what it had felt like to be held by a man.

Her babies were so little. Her life had been torn apart. In the midst of caring for her girls and forging ahead, her attraction to Mitch seemed to be a living, breathing entity that at that moment she couldn't deny.

When his strong arms enfolded her, she felt safe. As he murmured her name, she felt cared for. He lowered his head and she lifted her chin. Their lips met.

Lily's senses whirled and she couldn't deny a longing that came from deep within. As Mitch's mouth opened over hers, she lost all sense of time and place. All she cared about was now, the rush of wanting, the scent of

Mitch that was new and exciting, the thrill of feeling like a woman again.

Suddenly her womb tightened as it did when she nursed the babies. Troy's daughters.

What in God's name was she doing?

As suddenly as the kiss began, she tore away. The expression on Mitch's face told her he knew why. She clamped her hand over her lips and tears rushed to her eyes. She saw that determined look come over Mitch and she couldn't face it, not tonight.

"Talk to me, Lily," he coaxed gently.

She shook her head. "I can't. Not now. Maybe in the morning."

"Do you want to let us both stew all night when what you need is sleep?"

"It was a mistake."

He sighed. "Maybe that's one of the things we need to talk about."

When she remained silent, he stroked a tear from her cheek, finally agreeing. "All right. Go to bed. I'll be here if you need help with the babies during the night."

"Mitch, I'm sorry."

He put his finger gently over her lips.

Backing into her room, she closed the door. She heard his boots on the wooden floorboards, his tread as he walked down the stairs. Then she collapsed on her bed, not even taking her clothes off, shutting her eyes and praying sleep would come quickly.

The following morning, Mitch made scrambled eggs while Angie and Lily fed the twins in the upstairs nursery.

He'd crossed the line last night. He'd known physical

contact with Lily was taboo. But it hadn't been until his lips had touched hers that he'd realized how truly vulnerable she was.

He'd damaged their relationship and he didn't know if he could fix it. But he had to get the old one back—he'd made a promise to Troy.

When Angie had arrived home after midnight, the twins had been starting to stir. She said she'd help him feed them so Lily could sleep. But Lily had heard them, come in, taken Grace from Angie and told her to go to bed. She'd hardly glanced at him.

They'd fed Grace and Sophie in silence. When the twins woke again at four, they'd both fed them again. Mitch had never actually appreciated how complicated this was for women. They hadn't recovered completely from giving birth and they had to use reserves they didn't know they had to combat sleep deprivation, fatigue and chores that seemed to multiply with each hour.

And what had he done? Stirred up something that was better left alone. He didn't know if Lily was ever going to look him in the eyes again.

He'd just switched off the burner when she and Angie rolled in a double stroller. Grace and Sophie looked as if they were content and almost asleep.

Crossing to the refrigerator, Angie pulled out milk and orange juice, snagging the coffeepot and bringing it to the table. "You should go back to bed," Angie told Lily as they pulled out their chairs.

"I have laundry to do, and I want to make up a couple of casseroles and freeze them so we can just pull them out this week if we need them."

Although Mitch sat at the table with them, Lily

glanced down at her plate. She picked up a slice of toast, took a bite and set it down again.

For the next ten minutes, the lump in Mitch's chest grew as he and Angie made conversation.

Finally, his breakfast eaten, he asked Lily, "Can I talk to you for a minute before I go?"

Her attention automatically went to her daughters, but Angie reassured her quickly. "I'll watch them. Go ahead."

There were so many things he wanted to tell Lily as they stood in the foyer. But he couldn't think of one. She was wearing jeans and a pink sweater and looked as if she were going to face the new day with determination and courage, the way she always did.

He knew what she wanted to hear from him, so he said it. "You were right. Last night was a mistake. I was out of line."

"You weren't the one who started it," she admitted honestly. "I don't know what got into me."

"You were grateful for a little help," he said with a smile that didn't come from inside.

"A *lot* of help," she returned, gazing into his eyes like she used to.

"Are you going to be okay when Angie leaves for work?"

"I'll be fine. It's Raina's day off. She's coming over."

He nodded, sure her friends would give her any help she needed, at least for a while. But he also knew Lily wouldn't want to burden them and she'd soon be taking all of it on herself.

They couldn't get involved for so many reasons. What if Lily ever saw his scars, learned his fears? The last relationship he'd tried a few years ago hadn't worked because of all of it. Nothing had changed since then, and on Lily's part, her grief and her connection to Troy was sustaining her in some ways. Missing and longing for him meant loving him. She wasn't ready to let go of that. Still, Mitch didn't know how to walk away from her. He couldn't because he'd promised he wouldn't.

"I'll call you in a couple of days, just to see if Grace and Sophie are settling in. If you need anything, you have my number."

She reached out and touched his arm, probably feeling the same wall he did, a wall they were both standing behind so they wouldn't get hurt.

"Thank you," she said softly.

He left the Victorian again, realizing he didn't want her thanks. What he *did* want was still a mystery to him.

A few weeks later, Mitch was driving home from work when he decided to call Lily. They'd had a *brief* phone conversation last week because neither was comfortable with what had happened and they couldn't seem to get back on that "friend" footing. Now her cell phone rang and rang and rang until finally—a man picked up.

"Who is this?" Mitch asked, surprised by the male voice. A repairman, maybe? But why would he have Lily's cell phone?

"This is Craig Gillette. I'm the manager of Sagebrush Foods."

"Sagebrush Foods? I don't understand. Where's Lily Wescott?"

"Mrs. Wescott had an incident in our store. She's okay now but…"

An incident? What the hell was that? "Put her on," Mitch ordered.

Apparently speaking to the authority in Mitch's voice, the man said, "Sir, I can't right now. We've got two crying infants and she's feeling a little dizzy."

Dizzy? "You tell her not to move. I'll be there in five." Mitch didn't give the manager time to protest or approve. He stepped on the gas.

Minutes later Mitch rushed into the store, scanning the produce area. Rounding a corner, he spotted Lily in the canned goods aisle, holding a paper cup. There were cans of green beans all over the floor around the folding chair where she sat. The twins were ensconced in their stroller. Sophie's little face was screwed up in displeasure, but Grace seemed content for the moment to stare at the bright lights and rows of colorful cans.

Mitch let his training prevail rather than the fear that threatened his composure. In as calm a voice as he could muster, he asked, "What happened?" followed by, "Are you all right?"

Lily looked so pale, and all he wanted to do was lift her into his arms and carry her somewhere safe. But the twins were a concern, too, and he had to get to the bottom of what had happened.

"I just felt a little dizzy, that's all," she said in a soft voice, taking another sip of water. "I haven't gotten much sleep lately and I ran out of diapers…" Grace reached out a little hand to her and Lily reached back.

He got the picture much too well and he didn't like what he saw. His guess? She'd felt faint and she'd run the stroller into the corner of the green beans display.

"Did she pass out?" he asked Gillette.

"No, sir. We wanted to call an ambulance, but she said she just needed to put her head down between her knees for a while—" He stopped when Lily gave him a scolding look as if he were divulging too much information.

Mitch went to Lily and crouched down beside her, looking her over with a practiced doctor's eye. "Be honest with me. Do I need to call an ambulance?"

There were deep blue smudges under both of her eyes. Her hair was a disheveled ponytail and she wore a sweatsuit. This wasn't the Lily he was used to, with her composed attitude, neat hairdos and tailored clothing.

Looking up at him, she forced a smile. She was clearly exhausted.

With his fingertips to her neck, he felt her pulse beating fast.

"Mitch," she protested, turning her head.

His fingers stayed put. "Quiet for a few seconds," he suggested.

Her pulse was definitely racing.

"No ambulance," she said.

"Then tell me what's going on. But drink that water before you do." He guessed she was dehydrated.

"You're acting like a doctor."

"I'm also acting like a friend."

Their gazes met and Mitch could see she was remembering their kiss as vividly as he was, even in these circumstances. Just friends? Not likely.

She didn't argue with him, but rather drank the cup of water.

"Are you still dizzy? Should I call Hillary?" Their colleague was her OB/GYN.

"No. I'm seeing her in a few days for a follow-up. I know what's wrong, Mitch. Not enough sleep, not enough liquids, probably not enough food. I forget to eat when I'm busy. Please don't scold."

He would have, but he could see she realized what he'd known could happen all along—she was overwhelmed.

"Let's see if you can stand on your own."

He held her around the waist and helped her to her feet. She felt slight to him. She'd definitely lost weight. He should have been checking in with her daily, no matter how uncomfortable things were between them. So much for looking after her.

His body was responding in ways it shouldn't as he kept his arm around her waist and they walked a few steps down the aisle.

"Do you think you can walk to your car on your own steam? I'll drive yours then walk back here for mine."

"I drove over here for the diapers because I didn't want to bother anyone," she muttered, then added fiercely, "I'm capable of walking to the car."

At least she wasn't protesting him driving her home. He wanted her to understand the seriousness of what was happening to her. But that discussion would have to wait until she was on the sofa with her feet up and Sophie and Grace were fed and diapered.

In the house a while later, they sat on the sofa, hips practically touching, watching the babies in their cribs on the monitor. Mitch had found laundry in the washer and dryer, bottles in the sink, and had coaxed a little information from Lily. The babies now had a fussy spell that lasted from after Angie left in the evening until well after midnight. And they were nursing at least every three hours. She *was* exhausted and dehydrated and had to do more to take care of herself. But she couldn't do that unless the twins needs were met first.

Mitch began, "You need help, Lily, and you've got to get it before you can't take care of Sophie and Grace. Hire an au pair who will stay at the house for free rent."

He shifted so they weren't quite so close as he expected Lily to protest. She didn't. Rather, she just looked pensive. "I really hadn't thought about doing that. I don't know if Angie would like having a stranger move in."

"She can probably see you need help, too, but doesn't know what to do about it. Talk to her. Talk to Raina and Gina. Maybe they'll know of someone who needs a job and is good with children. But you can't go on like this."

"I know. Believe me, Mitch, I do. What just happened scared me. I just wish—" She swallowed hard. "If Troy were here—"

Mitch watched as she blinked fast and faced the cold splash of reality once more. He didn't know whether to cover her hand with his or move even farther away. Everything had become so complicated between them.

After a few moments of silence, Lily seemed to pull herself together. "Thinking about Troy…" She stopped. "His sister Ellie might be the perfect person to help me."

"Isn't she in Oklahoma?"

"Yes, but Troy's mom and Ellie have wanted to visit. Maybe they could come and help out and maybe…" A smile bloomed on Lily's lips. "Maybe Ellie could stay! She could set up her web business from here. I'm going to call Angie first. If she's agreeable, then I'll phone Ellie."

Lily picked up the handset from the end table.

As she dialed a number, Mitch realized he should be happy she was going to get the help she needed. Yet part of him knew that if Troy's sister came to assist her, Lily could stay entrenched in the past instead of moving on.

That shouldn't matter to him. But it did.

Chapter Five

Lily hung up the receiver and glanced at the glass of juice Mitch had brought her, now empty. She knew better than to let herself become dehydrated. She knew better about a lot of things. She should be grateful Mitch had called right when he had. Troy had always maintained, *There are no coincidences*. She'd always laughed when he'd said it, but maybe he was right.

She found Mitch in the laundry room, pulling baby clothes from the dryer. "You don't have to do that," she said.

He just arched one heavy brow at her and removed the last of the Onesies, settling them in the wash basket.

"I ordered takeout from the Yellow Rose." He glanced at his watch. "It should be here in about fifteen minutes."

"Takeout? But they don't deliver unless—"

"I ordered two dinners for tonight, and three more. You should have enough for a few days so you don't have to worry about cooking."

She knew better than to protest. She should have ordered food herself. She'd intended to cook, but with Angie on the late shift, it had seemed a bother when she had so many other things to do. Still, almost fainting had scared her. She had to eat, drink and get some rest.

"That was a long phone conversation," Mitch commented, carrying the laundry basket into the kitchen and then the living room.

"Just set it on the coffee table," she said. "I have to divide the clothes. I keep some down here, and the rest upstairs."

After he set it down, he asked, "So is the cavalry coming?"

She smiled. "Troy's mother is going to stay for a week. She doesn't want to leave his dad for longer than that. But Ellie will drive her here and stay as long as I need her. She said she could use a change of scene, and Texas seems like a good spot. She's going to bring her sewing machine and make baby clothes and get her website up and running while she's here. If the three of us get along well, she might stay indefinitely."

"I assume since she makes baby clothes, she likes babies."

"She worked at a day-care center for a while, so she's had more practical experience than *I* have."

"I'm glad that's settled. When are they coming?"

"Next week."

"And in the meantime?"

"In the meantime, I'll get by. But I'll take better care of myself."

"That's a promise?"

"It's a promise."

There was about six inches of space between them that seemed to be filled with all kinds of electricity. Lily couldn't understand why, when she was around Mitch now, every nerve in her body tingled a new message.

"Why don't you take out the clothes you want to keep down here, and I'll carry the rest upstairs."

She took a few outfits from the basket and laid them on the coffee table. As Mitch lifted it again, she found her hand going to his forearm.

He pulled away and she realized she'd clasped his scarred and injured arm. "I'm sorry," she said.

He put down the laundry and took a step closer to her. "There's nothing to be sorry about. I'm just not used to having anyone touch me there."

"Does it hurt?"

"No."

"Do you ever let anyone see it?" She didn't know why the personal question had rolled off her tongue so easily, but what had happened at the grocery store had solidified the bond between them.

"Do you?" she prodded. "You wear long sleeves, winter and summer."

"Why does it matter?"

"Because we're friends and I'd like to know."

His expression remained steady, his voice steely. "Most people can't handle seeing scars. They're fascinated by them, but they're afraid of them. They want to ask questions, but they turn away."

"Do you think I'd turn away?"

The two of them were breathing the same air, standing in the same space, but a shield went up in Mitch's eyes that sent him somewhere apart from her. Suddenly she suspected why.

"Have you been in a relationship since you returned from Iraq?"

He started to swivel away from her to go into the kitchen. She wouldn't let him evade her that easily. She didn't touch him this time, but just slipped in front of him so he couldn't take another step without running into her.

"Lily," he said with exasperation. "I don't want to talk about it."

"Have you ever talked about it...talked about *her?*"

"No."

"Just as you haven't talked about Iraq."

"That's right."

Men! Lily thought. Troy had been the same way. He hadn't spoken to her about his earlier deployments, and she hadn't pushed. She had imagined that he'd eventually confide in her. But they hadn't had time. And maybe if he had confided in her, she would have been more prepared—

"So don't talk about Iraq," she conceded.

"But tell you about my love life?" Mitch asked, almost amused.

She realized how ridiculous she was being, when Mitch was a private man who didn't reveal much at all! "I guess I just need something to think about besides my own life right now."

That shield was still in his eyes but his face took on a gentler look.

"Okay. I'll do this once." He jammed his hands into his trouser pockets. "I was back over a year. I'd gotten a fellowship in endocrinology in Dallas and met Charlene, who was a reporter for the local news. She wanted to do a story about my new specialty and why I was changing, but I told her no. After a few tries and a few conversations, we started going out. I wore long sleeves most of the time then, too. One night I took her out to dinner. Afterward, things progressed naturally but when we got to the bedroom and I took off my shirt— She couldn't bear to see my scars, let alone touch them. That's when I realized reality was just a little too difficult for most people to handle."

"Most *women*," Lily murmured, realizing how little emotion Mitch had put into that recital. "That's what you meant to say."

"Maybe I did."

"Not every woman is the same." She could see right away that he didn't believe that. "The scars are more extensive than on your arm and hand," she guessed.

"Yes. They're on my shoulder, back and side, too."

Lily thought about what he'd said but kept her gaze from falling to his shoulder, or to his flat stomach. She was feeling almost dizzy again. Could that be from imagining Mitch without his shirt? Was she different from that reporter? Would extensive scars make her want to turn away?

The doorbell rang.

Mitch took a step back, looking…relieved? Was *she* relieved that the personal conversation was over? Or did she *want* to delve deeper? Somehow she knew Mitch wouldn't let her do that. At least, not tonight.

"So what's for dinner?" she asked brightly, knowing the Yellow Rose delivery had arrived at the door.

Getting to know Mitch any better would mean ties

she might not want…problems she didn't need. Getting to know Mitch better could lead to another kiss.

Neither of them wanted that—right?

Lily's cavalry arrived and Mitch stayed away. He knew it was best for both of them.

Almost a month after the grocery store incident, he received a call as he sat at the desk in his spare bedroom, ready to check email and eat dinner—a slice of pizza and a beer. When he recognized the number on his cell phone, he quickly swallowed his mouthful of pizza and shut down his email program.

"Hey, Lily. How's it going?"

When he'd called to check on her a couple of weeks before, Troy's mother had just left Lily's home and Ellie was settling in. Mitch had known Lily didn't need him there, or even want him there. He knew what had probably gone on while Troy's family was with her—lots of remembering.

It was best that he stay on his side of town and not interfere.

"Darlene and Ellie have been wonderful. They gave me a chance to pull myself back together, get my diet straightened out and find a sleep schedule. And Ellie's definitely going to stay. Angie really likes her, and we all get along great."

After a long pause, she asked, "Why haven't you been over lately?"

"I really didn't think you needed another visitor. Besides, the practice is picking up. I've been working late many nights."

"The beginning of May is a time for growth and

thinking about the future. I can see why the practice picks up this time of year. I miss it."

"I thought you might."

"Don't get me wrong, I love taking care of Grace and Sophie. Doing that, even with Ellie here, is enough to keep me busy all day. But working with you and Hillary and Jon and the staff is part of my life, too."

"So you're coming back?"

"I have to, Mitch. I'm going to see how the summer goes with Ellie, then I'll give you all a definite date."

Lily sounded less frazzled, more peaceful, maybe even a bit happy. He guessed the babies were bringing her joy, not just work, and that was lifting her up, fulfilling her in a new way.

She went on, "They're both cooing. And they're fascinated by their mobiles. You've got to come see them, Mitch, and meet Ellie."

Ellie was Lily's family now, along with her friends. He would bet a week's pay that their first meeting was going to be...uncomfortable. He thought about what type of visit this should be, how much time he should spend with Ellie and Lily, how much time with the twins.

"Have you been out of the house much?"

"Nope. The twins keep me a prisoner," she said with a laugh. "Seriously. I went to the grocery store again last week. This time I made it without knocking anything over. But that's been about it."

"Would tomorrow night be convenient?" he asked. "I could meet Ellie, see how the babies have grown, then take you for a drive. In fact, we could drive to the lake to hear the outdoor concert. How does that sound?"

"That sounds wonderful! But you realize, don't you,

I'm going to have to call back here every fifteen minutes to see what the twins are doing."

"That's a mother's prerogative. Why don't you check with your housemates to see if they mind your leaving, then give me a call back. I think the concert will be a nice break for both of us."

"Your idea sounds perfect. I'll get back to you shortly."

"I'll talk to you soon," Mitch said and hung up.

He didn't know whether to hope for this idea to go through or not. It could become more than a casual outing. Then he grabbed hold of reality again. Not if they *wanted* only casual. After all, it would be easy to stay casual. Lily could tell him all about the memories she and Troy's mother and sister had stirred up during their visit.

Casual would be the theme of the evening.

"How long have you been working with Lily?" Ellie asked on Saturday evening.

He'd arrived a short time before and looked in on the twins, who'd been finishing their supper. They were asleep in their bassinets now and Lily had gone upstairs to change.

Studying Ellie, he noticed she wore her light brown hair in a short, glossy bob that swung against her cheek. The style accentuated her heart-shaped face. At twenty-six, she was ten years younger than the brother she obviously missed.

Mitch tried to answer her question without becoming defensive. After all, who could blame her for watching out for her sister-in-law. "We've worked together for two and a half years."

"Troy mentioned you," she admitted. "Something about playing pool at the Silver Spur Grill."

"We did."

"He said you were in Iraq and had to leave the Guard for medical reasons." She looked him over as if expecting to find his injury and her gaze settled on his hand. She quickly looked away.

"I did," he answered crisply, not intending to go into *that*, even for Troy's sister. The screws the doctor had put in his shoulder and leg, his missing spleen, never mind the damage to his arm and hand, had shut down his ability to serve. Most of the time, no one could tell he'd been injured.

It was time to go on the offensive with Ellie. "Lily tells me you worked in a day-care setting."

"For a while," she responded.

If he got her talking, she might relax. "But you like to sew?"

Looking surprised that he knew a detail like that, she responded, "I started making customized outfits for gifts for friends and relatives. They became so popular, I was getting orders. That's when I decided to open the store. At first I did pretty well, but then when harder times hit, even folks who had the money for those kind of clothes decided to spend it elsewhere."

"I hope your web-based business takes off for you."

"I hope so, too. But in the meantime, I'm going to enjoy taking care of Grace and Sophie. Did you spend much time with them when you brought Lily home from the hospital?"

She clearly wasn't giving up on turning over every leaf of his association with Lily. But he didn't have anything to hide—not really. "Two babies are a handful. That's why I think it's important Lily get away for a bit tonight."

Ellie's green eyes canvassed his face as if searching for motives. Finally, she admitted, "I'm glad the weather turned warm enough."

At that moment, Lily came down the stairs.

Automatically, Mitch turned her way. She was wearing blue jeans and a red blouse with a yellow windbreaker tossed over her arm. She'd fashioned her hair with a clip at the nape and she looked...fantastic. Her blue eyes seemed even bluer tonight as she gave him a tentative smile. He couldn't look away and she seemed to be as immobilized as he was...

...Until Ellie cleared her throat and asked, "How long do you think the concert will last?"

Lily burst into motion, as if in denial that the moment of awareness had ever happened. "Oh, we won't stay for the whole concert, and I'll call in to check with you. That's the nice thing about going to the lake. I don't have to worry about anybody being bothered if I make phone calls during the concert. Since this is the first concert of the season, the audience will be sparse. So call me if the least little thing is wrong, or you think I should come home."

Lily talked very fast when she was nervous, and that's what she was doing now. Her last comment led him to wonder if she was looking for an excuse not to go. Was it because she was still uncomfortable since their kiss? He'd find out shortly.

Lily gave Ellie a list of instructions along with phone numbers, then hiked the strap of her purse over her shoulder, took a last look at the monitor, blew a kiss to the image of her daughters and went out the door.

On the drive to the lake they didn't talk, but rather enjoyed the peaceful scenery—ranches and cotton fields that spread as far as the eye could see, tumbleweeds rolling by.

After he turned off the main road, down a gravel lane, and bumped over a dusty area used as the parking space for the concert, Lily finally said, "I think I'd forgotten how green everything is at this time of year, how spring smells, how the sky turns purple and orange at sunset. In some ways, I feel like I've been locked in a closet since last summer, not really seeing what was around me. Except the twins, of course."

"You've faced a lot of change in the past ten months."

She lowered her window and took a huge breath of outside air as the May breeze tossed her hair. "I don't want to go back into that closet again."

"Then don't. You have help now. While you're on leave, take some time for yourself, too. Figure out who you are again in your new life."

Turning to him, she reached for his arm, and he guessed she didn't even realize she'd done that. "You've been through this, haven't you?" she asked.

Her fingers on his forearm seemed to send fire through his body. Trying to smother it, he responded roughly, "You know I have. I'm not sure major life change is anything anyone welcomes, especially when it's borne from tragedy."

He gently tugged away from her touch. "Come on. Let's go to this concert."

His body still racing with adrenaline from their

contact, Mitch pulled a blanket from the backseat. They headed toward the people gathering in a large pavilion. They didn't see anyone they knew as Mitch dropped the blanket on one of the park benches facing the bandstand. The sides of the pavilion would block the wind and Lily could always wrap herself in the blanket if she got cold.

Their shoulders brushed. Mitch considered moving away, but didn't. Still, he was glad they hadn't recognized anyone. He didn't want Lily having second thoughts about coming. Something told him Ellie would be grilling her when she got back, and she'd have plenty of second thoughts then. He was just glad she'd accepted his invitation tonight, even if it was only to escape her figurative closet for a little while.

The quartet that performed with oboe, bass, clarinet and guitar played instrumental versions of popular songs. The crowd didn't grow much larger as Mitch was sure it would have if this had been a country-and-western or bluegrass band, or even an oldies night. But it suited his purpose to be here tonight with Lily, to listen to calm and easy music so she could relax. Even when she called home, no worry lines fanned her brow as Ellie reassured her that her girls were fine.

When Lily recognized a song, she hummed along. Her face was in profile as she gazed toward the lake, and he could study her without being afraid she'd catch him. Her hair waved in gentle curls under the barrette. Her turned-up nose was so recognizable on Sophie and Grace. Lily's bangs were long, brushed to one side, her brows a shade darker than her hair as they drew together when she concentrated on the music. She'd never worn much makeup, but tonight he noticed a sheen of gloss on her lips.

He could watch her all night and not tire of her expressions, the tilt of her head, the slant of her cheeks. He felt desire grip him again.

At that moment, she turned away from the music toward him…as if she wanted to sneak a peek at *his* expression. They both froze, their gazes locked, their bodies leaning just a little closer until the press of their shoulders was noticeable. Mitch reminded himself that there were so many reasons to keep away from Lily.

The music ended and the quartet announced a break.

Not moving away, Lily asked, "What do you think?"

About her? About the night? About the music? Which was the question to answer?

"My mother would have called them a dance band."

Lily blinked as if she hadn't expected that at all. But then she rallied. "Did she like to dance?"

Letting out a silent sigh of relief, Mitch leaned back so the pressure between their shoulders eased. "She didn't go out dancing, if that's what you mean. She didn't date. She always told me she didn't have time. She'd say, 'Who could work and have time for a man, too?'"

"A modern philosophy if I ever heard one," Lily joked.

Mitch chuckled. "Maybe so. But once in a while, she'd put on the radio and I'd catch her dancing around the kitchen. She always got embarrassed, but I could tell that if she'd had the time and a partner, she'd be good at it."

To his surprise, Mitch felt his phone vibrate against his hip. When he checked the caller ID, he recognized the number of a friend, Tony Russo. "I should take this," he said.

"Go ahead. We can go back to your SUV. I really should be getting home."

Because of that pulsating moment when he'd almost kissed her again? "You're sure?"

"Yes."

The certainty in her answer told him she didn't want to take the chance of staying longer, the chance that darkness and a starry sky might urge them to become more intimate.

A few minutes later, Lily stood beside Mitch at his SUV, wondering why she had agreed to come with him tonight. This seemed so much like a date and it just couldn't be! She'd known right away Ellie didn't approve when she'd told her where she was going.

She had to ask herself…would Troy approve of her being here with Mitch tonight? Troy's approval still mattered to her. She fingered her wedding ring, still feeling married.

Inhaling the scents of spring on the wind, she attempted to stay in the moment. She exhaled confusion and loss, in favor of life and music and the sliver of moon above. She was aware of Mitch's conversation, his deep laugh. He asked about someone named Jimmy and reported he'd gotten an email from Matt last week.

She was learning Mitch had more facets than she'd ever imagined. He had depth she'd never known about. He had a past he didn't want to talk about.

Now, however, when he ended his call, he smiled at

her. That smile both comforted her and made her breath hitch!

"An old friend?" she guessed, taking the safe route.

"Yes, Tony served with me in Iraq."

Surprised he was forthcoming about that, she asked, "Is he coming for a visit?"

"You heard me mention the bed-and-breakfast."

She nodded.

"Every year, the first weekend in December, I get together with servicemen I knew in Iraq. We alternate locations and their families come, too. This year it's my turn to host."

"What a wonderful idea!"

"We usually start planning this time of year to get the best airfares and accommodations. We have a money pool so if someone can't afford to come, the cash is there to draw on."

"How long does your reunion last?"

"Friday to Sunday. My house will be home base on Saturday. Do you have any ideas to occupy kids?"

"Besides enlisting someone to play Santa Claus?" she joked. "I used to do some face painting."

"You're kidding."

"No. I'm *not* just a doctor. I have an artistic bent."

He laughed. "That would be perfect."

A bit of moonlight drifted over them as they stood close. The look in Mitch's eyes was recognizable to her. He'd had that same look before he'd kissed her outside her bedroom.

When he reached out and stroked her cheek, she didn't pull away. She couldn't. There was something about Mitch that drew her to him, that made her want to forget her inhibitions, her idea of propriety, her sadness and loss.

"Lily," he murmured as the stars bore witness, as the moon seemed to tilt, as the ground trembled under her feet. The touch of his fingers on her face was filled with an aching longing.

But then he dropped his hand to his side and opened the passenger door. He didn't have to say anything and neither did she. They knew they couldn't kiss again. If they did, they might not stop there.

Ellie, Sophie and Grace were waiting for her. She didn't want to be any more confused when she walked in that door than she already was now.

Chapter Six

Time rolled by so fast, Lily could hardly count the days. She spent a lot of time thinking about Mitch, of how he'd touched her face at the lake. That night they'd silently but tacitly backed away from each other. Because of Ellie? Because they both feared their feelings were inappropriate?

The last week in May, Lily pushed Sophie and Grace's stroller into the office suite that was still familiar to her. Yet when she looked around at the sea-foam-green furniture, the rose carpeting and the green-and-mauve wallpaper, she didn't feel as if she *did* belong any more. She'd only been away three months, yet it seemed like a lifetime.

"This is where I work," she told Ellie, motioning to the reception area, the glass window behind which their receptionist Maryanne sat, the hall leading to exam rooms, office suites and the lab.

"It's really kind of…cozy," Ellie remarked as if she was surprised. "I think I expected white walls and tile and a sterile atmosphere."

"We try to keep it relaxed," Lily explained. "The couples and women who come to us are stressed enough. The more relaxed we can keep the process, the better."

"How many doctors work here?"

"Four, as well as two nurse-practitioners, two techs and our receptionist."

Lily rolled the stroller up to the receptionist's window.

Maryanne slid the glass open and grinned at her. "We miss you, Dr. Wescott," she said to Lily.

"I miss all of you, too," Lily returned, meaning it. Helping other women have babies was important to her, and even more so now, since she knew the joy of her twins.

She introduced Ellie.

Maryanne came out of her cubicle to coo over the babies. "They're adorable. I'm so glad you brought them in. And at just the right time. Everybody's on their lunch break. Go on back to the lounge."

Ellie took a peek down the hall. "Maybe I shouldn't go with you. I don't want to interrupt anything."

"Don't be silly," Lily said. "The practice is usually closed from twelve to one every day. That's why I was glad when we finished with Tessa right on time. I know Hillary will want to meet you. When I had a checkup with her, I told her about your baby store and your customized outfits. She has a one-year-old. She could be your first paying customer in Sagebrush."

Although Lily had attempted to prepare herself to see Mitch again, she didn't feel ready. Not after their awkward parting the evening of the concert.

As soon as she pushed open the door to the lounge and saw Mitch sitting at the table with Hillary and Jon, she was tossed back to that night, standing close to him by his SUV, the heat of his fingers a scalding impression on her cheek.

Mitch stood as soon as he spotted her and Ellie, the white lab coat he wore giving him the professional appearance that had been so familiar to her before the night of the banquet, before Grace and Sophie had been born.

The twins were the center of attention now as everyone crowded around. Lily was glad for that, relieved to be able to introduce Ellie to her colleagues, grateful that no one could see how being in the same room with Mitch affected her. Lily couldn't believe it herself. Maybe she just didn't want to believe it.

What kind of woman was she? She'd loved her husband, loved him to the moon and back. He'd only been gone for ten months. Many nights she still cried herself to sleep, missing him, needing him, longing for him. Her reaction to Mitch didn't make sense. Not at all. Before the twins were born, she'd never looked at him as anything but a colleague. But now, as everyone babbled to the babies and chatted politely with Ellie, Mitch's gaze passed over Lily's lilac top and slacks then swiftly returned to her face. His appraisal left her a little short of breath.

Hurriedly, she ducked her head and bent to scoop

Sophie from the stroller. "I don't know what I'd do without Ellie," she told everyone. "I seem to need six hands when these two are crying at the same time."

"So when are you coming back?" Hillary asked, her short chestnut hair fringing her face.

"Probably in November," she answered, not knowing what the next months would bring.

"You take your time deciding," Jon said. He was tall and lean with narrow black glasses that made him look scholarly.

Hillary asked, "May I hold Sophie?"

"Sure."

Hillary took the baby and settled her in the crook of her arm, looking down on her with the affection moms feel for kids. "I believe these little girls are going to be petite."

"Maybe. Or they could eventually grow as tall as Troy." Lily felt the need to mention his name, to bring him into the conversation.

Jon leaned a little closer to her. "How are you doing, really?"

"I'm okay. It's just the world's very different without Troy in it. Some days I expect that. Other days I expect him to come walking through the door, pick up Grace and Sophie, to figure out which one will look for his approval and which one won't."

Hillary had obviously overheard. She said, "I'll always remember Troy, Lily. I really cherish the table he made for me. It's absolutely beautiful craftsmanship."

Lily vividly remembered the piece of Troy's unfinished furniture still in storage. In fact, he'd been in the last stages of completing the plant stand she'd asked him to make when he was deployed. So much was unfinished and Lily didn't know how to complete the tapestry of the life that had been hers and Troy's.

Mitch had heard their conversation, too, and turned away, crossing to the refrigerator, closing the top on a juice bottle and setting it inside. His actions were slow and deliberate. She knew she'd brought up Troy to put a boundary around herself again, a boundary that would keep Mitch out. Why had she dropped in today? To catch up with old friends? Or to see *him?*

As Hillary moved away, rocking Sophie and cooing to her, Lily's gaze landed on Ellie, who was glancing toward her and then Mitch. No one else seemed to notice the vibes between Lily and Mitch, but apparently Ellie did.

Lily hung out with her colleagues in the lounge for a while. They all wanted to take turns holding the twins and see if they could distinguish between the two. As Lily had suspected, Hillary asked Ellie to tell her all about the clothes she created.

Stepping away from the group with Grace in her arms, Lily went in search of Mitch. He was her friend, and they would be working together when she returned. She had to keep communication open between them. She had to know what was going on in his mind. Maybe it had nothing to do with her. If it didn't, she'd be relieved. At least that's what she told herself.

She found him in his office, at his computer. She stood there for a few moments, listening to Grace's little soughing sounds, studying Mitch's profile. Her gaze went to his hands as his fingers depressed keys. His left hand was faster than his right and she wondered if the fingers on his right hand hurt to use. What kind of pain did he experience on a daily basis? With what he'd told her, she guessed his injuries had left repercussions. On the other hand, were the memories in his head more painful than anything physical injuries could cause? She wished he could talk to her about all of it. She wished—

Moving into the room, she said, "You should still be on your lunch break."

"A fertility specialist never sleeps," he joked. "I have a couple coming in this afternoon because the time is right."

"They're going the artificial insemination route?"

"For now. In vitro doesn't fit into their budget." His gaze went from Lily to Grace. "She seems content."

Lily checked her watch. "Probably for about fifteen more minutes."

Rolling his chair back, Mitch stood and approached her. His large hand gently passed over Grace's little head, his thumb brushing her strands of cotton-soft blond hair. "So you just decided to stop in or did you and Ellie have errands in the area?"

"Sophie and Grace had appointments with Tessa. Since we were in the building…" She trailed off.

"You wanted to stay in touch."

"I think it will be easier for me to come back to work in the fall if I do."

He nodded.

"Mitch…" She didn't know what she wanted to say, or how to say it. "I need to talk about Troy."

"I know you do. That was another good reason for Ellie coming to stay with you."

"You left the lounge and I thought—"

"I told you I have clients coming."

"I know." She felt so stymied for the right words to

say. She could say, *I want to be around you, but when I am, I feel guilty.* Yet that couldn't come out because she and Mitch were both fighting becoming any closer.

She bowed her head, placing a tiny kiss on Grace's forehead, trying to figure out what she was doing in this room with Mitch and why she had actually stopped in today.

Yet Mitch wouldn't let her stand there, stewing in her own confusion. He slipped one knuckle under her chin and lifted it. "I think we're both feeling things we don't believe we should be feeling. You don't know whether to run in the other direction or pretend we're just friends."

"I don't want to pretend!"

His brows arched as he gave her a crooked smile. "That *is* the crux of it."

"Lily." Ellie was standing in the doorway with Sophie, studying the two of them standing close, Mitch's finger under her chin.

He quickly dropped his hand to his side while Lily turned to face her sister-in-law. "I know. They're both going to start crying for lunch soon."

"If you'd like to use my office, you can," Mitch offered. "I have work to do in the lab."

Crossing to his desk and reaching for a file folder, he picked it up, then stopped in the doorway. "It's good to see you again, Ellie."

"You, too," she said politely.

Mitch stood there for a few moments as if waiting to see if Troy's sister had something else to say. But she didn't. After a last glance at Lily and the twins, he strode down the hall.

Lily waited, not knowing if Ellie might have something to say to *her*. But her sister-in-law just moved toward the door. "I'll get the diaper bag." Then she was gone, too, leaving Lily with Grace in Mitch's office with very chaotic thoughts and feelings.

"They sure like those swings," Angie observed a week later as Lily came into the kitchen and watched her putting together a casserole for lunch.

Lily stirred the white sauce she was cooking and glanced over at her content daughters. "They're settling into a real schedule."

"Where's Ellie?"

"She went shopping to get material she needed."

Angie poured herself a cup of coffee and took a seat at the kitchen counter. "Mitch hasn't been around for a while. Did you two have a fight or something?"

Or something, Lily thought. "I saw him when I visited everyone at the practice."

"That was a week ago. He stopped in to see Sophie and Grace every day when they were in the hospital and he worried about you. It seems odd he hasn't called or dropped by more."

"I think he's giving me space."

Angie studied Lily over her mug. "Do you want space?"

"We're just friends." If she repeated those words often enough, she might believe them.

"I know that. And I know he's watching over you because Troy asked him to."

Lily found herself wanting to protest, to say that wasn't the only reason. Yet she wasn't sure she should. She didn't know what was in Mitch's mind. "I feel I owe him so much for everything."

"So why not call him and ask him to dinner?"

Angie made it sound so simple. On the one hand, Lily would love to do that. But on the other, she wished she and Mitch could have a little time alone, maybe straighten out everything between them.

"I could go to his place to cook dinner," she said aloud, testing the idea.

From the doorway, several bags in her arms, Ellie asked, "You want to cook dinner for Mitch?" There was wariness in her tone and an element of disapproval.

"He did so much for me, including encouraging me to call you. I'd like to thank him."

Ellie came into the kitchen and dropped her bags on the table. Then she went to the twins and crouched down, greeting both of them.

"I'm off for the weekend," Angie offered. "I could watch Sophie and Grace if Ellie has plans."

"No plans tomorrow. Just the concert with you in Amarillo on Saturday," Ellie said to Angie, without looking up. "I can watch them."

"Are you sure?" Lily asked. "Because I could invite Mitch here instead."

"No," Ellie responded, standing. "It's fine. Angie and I and Sophie and Grace will have a girls' night together. It will be a blast, even if the babies can't eat popcorn yet."

"Before we make too many plans, I'd better find out if Mitch wants me to cook for him. I'll leave a message on his cell phone." She picked up the cordless phone in the kitchen before she lost her nerve.

An hour and a half later, when Mitch returned her call, Lily had just finished breast-feeding both babies.

It was much easier now than when she'd first tried to juggle their needs.

"I got your message," Mitch said. "Is everything all right?"

Lily looked down at her sleeping daughters. "Everything's fine. I..." She cleared her throat. "If you're going to be home tomorrow evening, I'd like to cook you dinner."

"Home? As in at my house?"

She laughed. "Yes. Angie and Ellie offered to watch Sophie and Grace, and this would be my way to thank you for everything you've done."

He didn't say, "You don't have to thank me," because they'd gone through that routine before and he probably knew it would fall on deaf ears. "A home-cooked meal would be a nice change," he agreed noncommittally.

"What's your favorite meal?"

"Why don't you surprise me."

"You're not going to give me a hint?"

"Nope. I like everything."

"Okay, I'll stop at the market and then come over."

"I'm taking off tomorrow afternoon to meet with the couple who own the bed-and-breakfast around three. But I should be home by four. I can tape a spare key under the garage spout in case I'm tied up longer."

Lily was surprised Mitch was taking off, but she knew planning the reunion was important to him. "That's perfect. I can get started and then when you arrive, we can really catch up."

"Catching up sounds good," he responded, as if he meant it.

Lily's heart seemed to flutter but she told herself it was just her imagination.

After she ended the call, she wondered if she was doing the right thing. But showing her appreciation was important to her. No matter what Mitch said, she believed it was important to him, too.

She'd find out tomorrow night.

Lily found the key behind the spout on Friday and let herself into Mitch's brick ranch-style house situated on the outskirts of Sagebrush. She liked the looks of the outside with its neat plantings and tall fencing, and the protected entrance where she'd set the grocery bags on a wooden bench that perfectly fit the space. Slipping the key into the lock, she pushed open the door and stepped inside.

To the right of the small foyer, a door led into the garage. Beyond that lay a rambling living room. It was huge, with a fireplace, tall windows and a cathedral ceiling with a fan. The comfortable-looking furniture was upholstered in masculine colors, navy and burgundy. Distressed-pine tables and black wrought-iron lamps sat in practical positions around the furniture. She was surprised to see only a small flat-screen TV in the entertainment center rather than a larger model. But then maybe Mitch didn't spend much time watching TV.

The kitchen was straight ahead and she eagerly picked up the bags, took them in and set them on the counter. Stainless steel appliances looked shiny and new. An archway opened into a sunroom where French doors led outside to a large rustic brick patio. A round table and four chairs nestled in a corner of the dining area of the kitchen under a black wrought-iron chandelier. She liked the clean lines of the house, its spaciousness, its practical floor plan.

She was unpacking the groceries when her cell phone rang. She thought it might be Mitch telling her he was on his way. Instead, she recognized Raina's number and happily answered. "How are you?"

Her friend said, "I'm in labor!"

"You're not due till next week," Lily said practically.

Raina laughed. "Tell that to our son or daughter."

"Where are you?"

"At the hospital. Emily is with me."

Lily knew Raina was comfortable using a midwife, but her husband hadn't been so sure. "How is Shep handling this?"

"Let's just say he drove here under the speed limit but that was a struggle. Now he's pacing while Emily's trying to keep the mood relaxed."

Raina had wanted to have a home birth, but she'd compromised with Shep. Since Emily and Jared had managed to bring about changes at the hospital to include a midwife in the birthing process, there were two suites there now that were supposed to simulate the comforts of home. The birthing suites provided the advantages of delivering a baby in a more natural setting while having a doctor nearby should any complications arise.

"How are *you* handling labor?"

"I can't wait for this baby to be born. Wow," she suddenly exclaimed, "I'm starting another contraction and it's stronger than the last one. Either Shep or I will let you know when the baby's born. Talk to you later."

Lily thought about her own contractions, how they'd come on so suddenly, how Mitch had helped her. In some ways, that night seemed eons ago.

After considering her options, Lily had decided to make Mitch something she had never cooked before. She'd found the recipe for chicken in wine in her favorite cookbook. It wasn't complicated. It just required a little time to prepare. Today she had the time. She'd brought along her favorite pan and started bacon frying in it. Rummaging in Mitch's cupboard, she found other pots and pans she could use. After she sorted her ingredients, she prepared the chicken to fry in the bacon drippings.

A half hour later, the chicken was browning nicely when she heard the garage door open. She took a quick look around the kitchen. She had managed to set the table before she'd started the chicken. She'd brought along two place mats, matching napkins, as well as a vase filled with pretty, hand-carved wooden flowers. Mitch's white ironstone dishes looked perfect on the dark green place mats.

Lily heard the door from the garage into the foyer open then Mitch's deep voice calling into the kitchen. "Something smells great."

And then he was there in the doorway, tall and lean, his almost black eyes taking in everything at a glance. He wore blue jeans, black boots and a navy henley. Skitters of sensation rippled up and down her spine.

They just stood there for a few moments, staring at each other. He assessed her white jeans and pink top with its scoop neckline. "Shouldn't you be wearing an apron?"

"The clothes will wash."

"Spoken like a mom."

Moving forward into the kitchen, he caught sight

of the table and stopped. "You've gone to a lot of trouble."

"Not really. You're just not used to a woman's touch." As soon as the words were out, she knew she should have thought first before speaking. Letting the thoughts in her mind spill free could land her in deep trouble.

Mitch didn't react, simply hung his keys on a hook above the light switch. "I don't know how long it's been since I walked into a kitchen with something good cooking. Do you want me to help with this?" He motioned to the stove and the sink. "Or do you want me to get out of your way?"

"You're welcome to help, but if you have something more important to do—"

"Nothing that can't wait," he said, washing his hands. "I worked in the yard earlier this afternoon."

"I like your house, and the way you've decorated."

His brows drew together as he dried his hands on the dish towel. "Maybe you can tell me the best way to set it up to entertain twenty to twenty-five people for the reunion weekend. I'm afraid space will be tight."

"What about a fire pit on the patio, depending on the weather, of course. It might draw a few people out there to toast marshmallows."

He studied her with one of those intense looks again and she knew it wasn't just the heat from the stove that was making her cheeks flame. "What?"

"You have great ideas."

Smiling to herself, she turned back to the chicken, deciding it was browned just right and that she had to concentrate on the meal so she wouldn't focus too much on Mitch. "My next great idea is that I'd better watch what I'm doing or your kitchen could go up in flames."

He chuckled. "What do you need help with?"

"Can you open the wine? I need a cup. I have everything else ready to simmer." She dumped in onions and celery, stirring to sauté them a bit, added carrots, chicken broth and the crumbled bacon. After Mitch loosened the cork and poured out a cup of wine, she took it from him, their hands grazing each other, hers tingling after they did.

Moving away from him, she poured the wine into the pot, put the lid on and set it to simmer, glad the major part of the meal was finished.

"Now what?" he asked.

"I need three apples peeled and sliced into that pie plate. I'll make the topping while you're doing that. Tell me about your meeting. Will you be able to reserve rooms at the bed-and-breakfast?"

When Mitch didn't answer, she looked up at him and saw him staring down at the apples. At that moment, she realized the request she'd made, as well as the mistake of asking him to do that kind of task.

"I've learned to do a lot of things with my left hand," he said matter-of-factly, "but using a knife to slice apples isn't one of them."

"Mitch, I'm sorry. I wasn't thinking."

"There's nothing to be sorry about. Why don't I look through my collection of DVDs and find something we would both enjoy?"

She wanted to put her arms around Mitch. She wanted to breathe in his scent and kiss him, letting him know the use of his fingers wasn't an issue between them.

"Okay," she said lightly. "I'll be there in a few

minutes." That was all the time she'd need to slice the apples, mix them with cranberries and pour on a topping.

Then she might have to decide just where she stood where Mitch was concerned.

Chapter Seven

Mitch knew he shouldn't have reacted as he had. It had been a very long time since something so simple had pushed his buttons. After Iraq, he'd been grateful he'd survived. He'd been grateful he could retrain in another specialty. He'd been grateful he had a life.

The truth was, he could have peeled an apple with his left hand, but those slices would have been chunky and choppy, maybe still bearing some skin.

At the practice, he spoke with couples, analyzed their needs, helped them decide which process was best. He calculated cycles, administered drug regimens, analyzed test results, sonograms, fluoroscopic X-rays. He could facilitate artificial insemination procedures. But he couldn't peel and slice an apple to his liking.

He could help bring life into the world, but he couldn't perform surgery to save a life.

Why had that fact hit him so hard just now?

He shuffled through the DVDs lying on the coffee table without paying attention to the titles. He was vaguely aware of the scent of cinnamon and apples baking, adding to the aroma of the chicken and wine. But when Lily stood in the doorway for a couple of moments before she took a step into the living room, he was elementally aware of her.

As she sat beside him on the sofa, only a few inches away, he wanted to both push her away and take her into his arms. It was the oddest feeling he'd ever experienced. Desire bit at him and he fought it.

"Dinner will be ready in about twenty minutes," she said, as if that were the main topic for discussion.

He could feel her gaze on him, making him hot, making him more restless. Facing her, he concluded, "Maybe this wasn't such a good idea."

"Eating dinner?" she asked, a little nervously, trying to make light of what was happening.

"Cooking together, eating together, watching a DVD together."

"I want to be here," she assured him, her eyes big and wide, all attempts at teasing gone. It was as if she were inviting him to kiss her.

He balled his hands into fists. "Lily—"

Reaching out to him, she touched the tense line of his jaw. "I don't know what's happening, Mitch, but being here with you is important to me. Maybe that first kiss wasn't as intense as we both thought it was. Maybe it was just an outlet—"

He was tired of analyzing and debating and pushing away desire that needed to be expressed. His hands slid under her hair as he leaned toward her, as he cut off her words with his lips. For over two years, he'd kept his desire for her hidden, locked away. Now, unable to resist, he set it free.

Passion poured out. Lily responded to it and returned it. For that reason, and that reason only, he didn't slam the door shut. He didn't throw the combination away again. She was softness and goodness and light in his hands. When his tongue swept her mouth, she wrapped her arms around his neck and held on. He was caught in the storm that had been building between them since the day he'd first held her. Warning bells clanged in his head, reminding him he should stop kissing her and pull away. But those warning bells seemed distant compared to the hunger that urged him on.

He sensed that same hunger had built in Lily. She wasn't holding back. Nothing about her was restrained.

The sounds of satisfaction Lily was making were driving Mitch crazy. His hand slid from her hair and caressed her shoulder. He could feel the heat of her skin under her knit top. Was she on fire for him as he was for her? Would she consider this kiss another mistake?

His hand slid to her breast. He knew if he didn't breathe soon, the need inside him would consume him.

Lily leaned away just slightly, as if inviting him to touch her more. His control was in shreds. He tore away from the kiss to nuzzle her neck as his hand left her breast and caressed her thigh.

When she turned her face up to his again, her eyes were closed. At that moment, Mitch knew this could be a very big mistake. What if she was imagining Troy loving her? What if she just needed someone to hold her and any man would take the form of her husband?

He leaned back, willed his heart to slow and found his voice. "Lily, open your eyes."

The few seconds it took for Lily to find her way back to the sofa seemed unending. She'd been so lost in pleasure that the sound of Mitch's voice—the request he'd made—seemed impossible at first.

When she did open her eyes, she was gazing into his. They were so dark and simmering, filled with the questions that took her a moment to understand. Until he asked, "Were you here with me?"

Her reflexive response was, "Of course, I was here with you." But as soon as she said it, she had to go back and think and feel. She had to be honest with Mitch and herself. As he didn't move an inch, she whispered, "*Mostly* here with you."

While she was kissing Mitch, had she been longing for Troy to be the one making love to her? Shaken by that question, as well as the aftermath of the passion that had bubbled up inside her like a well waiting to be sprung, she jumped when the cell phone in her pocket chimed.

Mitch seemed just as jarred. The resigned look on his face told her he knew she had to take the call. After all, Sophie or Grace might need her.

She checked the screen and then glanced at him. "It's Raina. She's in the hospital in labor. I have to find out if everything's okay."

Just then, the timer went off in the kitchen. Mitch rose to his feet. "I'll check on dinner," he said gruffly.

Lily closed her eyes and answered Raina's call.

Swallowing emotion that was confusing and

FREE Merchandise is 'in the Cards' for you!

Dear Reader,

We're giving away FREE MERCHANDISE!

Seriously, we'd like to reward you for reading this novel by giving you **FREE MERCHANDISE** worth over **$20**. And no purchase is necessary!

You see the Jack of Hearts sticker above? Paste that sticker in the box on the Free Merchandise Voucher inside. Return the Voucher promptly...and we'll send you valuable Free Merchandise!

Thanks again for reading one of our novels—and enjoy your Free Merchandise with our compliments!

Pam Powers

Pam Powers

P.S. Look inside to see what Free Merchandise is **"in the cards"** for you!

(S-SE-12/10)

W

e'd like to send you **two free books** to introduce you to the Silhouette **Special Edition**® series. These books are worth over $10, but they are yours to keep absolutely FREE! We'll even send you 2 wonderful surprise gifts. You can't lose!

REMEMBER: Your Free Merchandise, consisting of **2 Free Books** and **2 Free Gifts**, is worth over $20.00! No purchase is necessary, so please send for your Free Merchandise today.

Plus TWO FREE GIFTS!

We'll also send you two wonderful FREE GIFTS (worth about $10), in addition to your 2 Free Silhouette Special Edition® books!

Order online at:
www.ReaderService.com

YOUR FREE MERCHANDISE INCLUDES...

2 FREE Silhouette Special Edition® Books

AND 2 FREE Mystery Gifts

FREE MERCHANDISE VOUCHER

2 FREE BOOKS and **2 FREE GIFTS**

Please send my Free Merchandise, consisting of
2 Free Books and **2 Free Mystery Gifts**.
I understand that I am under no obligation to buy
anything, as explained on the back of this card.

*About how many NEW paperback fiction books
have you purchased in the past 3 months?*

☐ 0-2   ☐ 3-6   ☐ 7 or more
E9EY   E9FC   E9FN

235/335 SDL

Please Print

FIRST NAME

LAST NAME

ADDRESS

APT.#   CITY

STATE/PROV.   ZIP/POSTAL CODE

NO PURCHASE NECESSARY!

► Detach card and mail today. No stamp needed. ►

© 2010 HARLEQUIN ENTERPRISES LIMITED ® and ™ are trademarks owned and used by the trademark owner and/or its licensee. Printed in the U.S.A.

(S-SE-12/10)

The Reader Service - Here's how it works:

Accepting your 2 free books and 2 free mystery gifts (gifts valued at approximately $10.00) places you under no obligation to buy anything. You may keep the books and gifts and return the shipping statement marked "cancel." If you do not cancel, about a month later we'll send you 6 additional books and bill you just $4.24 each in the U.S. or $4.99 each in Canada. That's a savings of 15% off the cover price. It's quite a bargain! Shipping and handling is just 50¢ per book.* You may cancel at any time, but if you choose to continue, every month we'll send you 6 more books, which you may either purchase at the discount price or return to us and cancel your subscription.

*Terms and prices subject to change without notice. Prices do not include applicable taxes. Sales tax applicable in N.Y. Canadian residents will be charged applicable taxes. Offer not valid in Quebec. All orders subject to approval. Books received may not be as shown. Credit or debit balances in a customer's account(s) may be offset by any other outstanding balance owed by or to the customer. Please allow 4 to 6 weeks for delivery. Offer available while quantities last.

▼ If offer card is missing write to: The Reader Service, P.O. Box 1867, Buffalo, NY 14240-1867 or visit www.ReaderService.com ▼

NO POSTAGE
NECESSARY
IF MAILED
IN THE
UNITED STATES

BUSINESS REPLY MAIL
FIRST-CLASS MAIL   PERMIT NO. 717   BUFFALO, NY

POSTAGE WILL BE PAID BY ADDRESSEE

THE READER SERVICE
PO BOX 1867
BUFFALO NY 14240-9952

exhilarating, as well as terrifying, Lily cleared her throat. "Raina?"

"It's a girl, Lily! We had a *girl*." Her friend's voice broke.

"That was pretty fast."

"Once we got here, it was like she couldn't wait to get out. You've got to come see her, Lily. I know you... understand."

Lily did understand Raina's history, the loss of her husband and dreams unfulfilled. Now she'd captured those dreams again. "I'm at Mitch's."

Raina didn't miss a beat. Her joy was too big and broad. "Bring him, too. Shep could use a little distraction. He's hovering over both of us. Eva's here with the boys but she's going to leave in a few minutes. They're so excited about their new sister that they're getting a little rowdy."

"I'll call you back after I talk to Mitch."

"If I interrupted something, I'm sorry. You can wait to visit tomorrow."

Yes, she could. Yet she knew the joy Raina was feeling. She knew this was a once-in-a-lifetime experience for her.

After she and Raina ended the call, Lily went into the kitchen, where Mitch had taken the apple dessert from the oven and set it on the counter.

"Raina had a baby girl," she announced brightly.

"I bet she and Shep are ecstatic."

She remembered Mitch had met Shep the night of the awards dinner that now seemed forever ago. "She'd like us to come see the baby."

"Now? She wants company?"

"You know how it is with new moms. They're so

proud, so full of life. And Raina and I, we have a special bond. She says we can wait until tomorrow, but I don't want to let her down. The chicken should be finished. Do you want to have dinner first?"

Mitch glanced at the kitchen clock. "Visiting hours will be over soon. Let's put it in a casserole. We can warm it up when we get back."

"I can go alone."

"Would you rather go alone?"

Their intimacy on the sofa was still fresh in her mind and in her heart. She wanted to stay with him...*be* with him a little longer.

"I'd like you to come along."

He gave her a hint of a smile. "Then let's put this away and get going."

Lily thought she'd jump out of her skin every time Mitch glanced at her in his SUV. Their awareness of each other was so acute, it was almost uncanny. She suspected Mitch was feeling the same way when he flipped on the CD player. Both of them had agreed to go to the hospital because that was the easier thing to do. She'd almost gotten naked with Mitch, almost let him make love to her. Then what would they have had to say to each other?

At the hospital, alone in the elevator as they rode up to the maternity floor, Mitch turned to her. "I don't feel as if I belong here."

"Here?"

"The maternity floor. With your friend."

"My guess is Shep will be glad to see a friendly male face. He's not real comfortable with the softer things in life, if you know what I mean. But I think Raina's changing that."

"Softer things in life, meaning women having babies, pink blankets, nurses cooing?"

"You've got it."

Mitch almost smiled. "That does take some getting used to."

"I guess the transition from trauma surgeon to fertility specialist wasn't always easy for you."

"Fortunately I was able to rely on some of the research skills I'd acquired while I was in med school. I was a teaching assistant for a professor studying T cells, so analyzing data and studies wasn't foreign to me. I think the hardest part was learning to act as a counselor sometimes to couples who were stressed out because they'd been trying for years to have a baby and couldn't. All kinds of things popped up. I suppose that's why we have Dr. Flannagan as an adjunct."

"Vanessa is good. I've sent couples to her who are indecisive or who can't agree on what they want to do. Do you know Vanessa well?" Lily asked.

"No. We had lunch together once to discuss a case. She doesn't like to skate on the surface and I didn't want to be psychoanalyzed, so let's just say we didn't socialize after that—we stuck to business."

Lily was surprised to find herself relieved that Mitch hadn't gotten on well with the pretty psychologist. She admonished herself that she had no business being possessive. She had *no* rights where Mitch was concerned.

After Lily and Mitch signed in at the desk, Lily caught sight of Shep in one of the family waiting rooms. Joey and Roy, Shep and Raina's older boys, stood in the doorway as if ready to leave. Eva, their nanny, had one arm about each of them while Manuel, Shep and

Raina's almost three-year-old, was throwing a tantrum, his arms tightly holding Shep around the neck, his tears as heartbreaking as his sobs.

"Daddy, you come home, *too*," he wailed.

Shep spotted Lily immediately and said above Manuel's wails, "Don't you tell Raina about this."

"She'd understand."

"Hell, yes, she'd understand. She'd want me to bring them all into the room so they could sleep with her."

Lily had to chuckle because she knew Shep was right. "She'd call it a birthday sleepover," Lily joked.

Mitch groaned. "I think you're going to have to do better than that to cheer this little guy up. So your name's Manuel?" Mitch asked, bending down to him, looking into his eyes.

At first Lily thought the little boy would play shy. Instead of hiding in Shep's shoulder, though, he pulled himself up straighter and studied Mitch. "What's your name?"

"My name's Mitch." He pointed to Lily. "You know her, don't you?"

Manuel nodded vigorously. "She and Mom are BFFs."

The adults all looked at each other and broke out into laughter.

"Who'd you hear that from?" Shep asked.

"Joey. He knows."

"Yes, he does know lots of things," Shep agreed with a grin he couldn't suppress.

"Maybe you should go home and make sure everything's ready for tomorrow when your sister comes home," Mitch suggested. "I bet your mom and dad would both be surprised."

Eva stepped in. "We could cut some roses and put them in pretty vases. Your mom would love that. We can make sure everything in the baby's room is just right."

Manuel stared at Eva.

Adding another incentive, she offered, "I can turn on the new baby monitor and you can watch the lights flicker when we make noise in the room."

Swiveling toward his dad again, Manuel screwed up his little face. "Okay."

Shep tapped the pocket of his shirt. "I'll give you a call before bed and you can say good-night to Mom. How's that?"

"That's good," Manuel assured him, climbing off his dad's lap and taking Eva's hand.

After hugs and kisses from all his boys, Shep watched them leave the maternity floor with Eva.

"Man, that's tough," he muttered. "It breaks my heart when they're sad."

Lily patted Shep's arm knowing that before he met Raina, he never would have been able to admit that.

"I'm going to visit the new mom," Lily said.

Shep studied Mitch. "You want to get a cup of coffee with me?"

"Sure," Mitch answered, exchanging a look with Lily that told her she'd been right about Shep needing a break.

"See you in a bit," she said with a wave, and headed for Raina's room.

When she entered her friend's room, she stopped short. This was a woman who had her world together.

The head of the bed had been raised and Raina was holding her infant daughter. She looked abso-

lutely radiant and Lily almost envied her calm sense
of satisfaction.

"Hey, there," she called softly from the doorway.

"Hey, yourself. Come on in. Meet Christina Joy
McGraw."

"What a beautiful name! Did you and Shep decide
on it together?"

"He just said he wanted something pretty and a
little old-fashioned. I added Joy because that's what
she's going to bring us." After passing her hand over
her baby's head, Raina looked beyond Lily. "Where's
Mitch?"

"He's keeping Shep company for a cup of coffee."

"This is a rough day for Shep, but if he drinks more
than two cups, he's not going to sleep tonight."

Lily laughed. "I don't think he's going to sleep anyway. You *do* know he's going to stay here with you."

"He said something to that effect, but I thought he
was kidding."

"Uh-uh. He's not letting you or that baby girl out of
his sight for very long."

After they both stared down at the infant, Lily taken
with her raven-dark hair and eyes, Raina asked, "Did
I interrupt something when I called? I never imagined
you'd be with Mitch."

"Oh, I just decided to make him a thank-you dinner.
It was easier to do at his house."

"Did you eat?"

"No, we put it in a casserole for later. It will be
fine."

"I have lousy timing," Raina murmured.

"No, actually you have very good timing."

The two women exchanged a look.

"Do you want to tell me what's going on?" Raina asked.

"Not here. The men could come back. Besides, I'm not sure anything is going on. Nothing should be going on, right?" If there was one person to ask about this, that person would be Raina.

"I waited nine long years to find love again. You don't have to wait that long."

"But what if it isn't love? What if I just miss Troy so much, long to be held so much, that I mistake something else for real emotion?"

"Is that what you think is happening?"

Lily sighed. "I don't know. When I'm with Mitch, I actually can't think sometimes, let alone figure out the best thing to do."

"Then don't do anything until you're ready to do whatever's right for you."

"You make it sound so easy."

"Yeah, I know," Raina said with a wry smile. "If I'd taken my own advice, I wouldn't have this little girl in my arms right now. Do you want to hold her?"

"You bet I do."

Shep sat across from Mitch at the cafeteria table, staring down into his coffee. "When Raina went into labor—" He shook his head. "I don't think I've ever gone into such a panic."

"I know what you mean," Mitch said, thinking about that night at the banquet, Lily's contractions, knowing the twins would be premature.

Shep didn't say anything for a moment, but then remarked, "So you felt that way when Lily went into labor?"

What kind of trap had Mitch just walked into? He kept silent.

"You being a doc and all," Shep went on, "I would think you'd be more matter-of-fact about it."

He would have been with anyone else, but not with Lily. No way was he going to admit that out loud. Then it didn't seem he had to. Shep was giving him a knowing look that made Mitch feel uncomfortable. One thing Mitch never thought he'd be was transparent. He expected another question, but it didn't follow.

Instead, Shep took another sip of his coffee and set it down again. "Raina and Lily have become really good friends. They have a lot in common."

"Raina's been a great support for Lily since Troy died." He might as well just get the subject out there so they weren't trampling around it.

"I heard you've been, too."

"You heard?" Mitch tried to keep the defensiveness from his voice, but he was worried that gossip was spreading about him and Lily.

"That night at the banquet when you carried Lily off. Raina told me Troy had left a letter asking you to look after her. That's why you're with her again tonight, right?" Shep inquired blandly.

Lily had told Mitch about Shep's background and why he'd wanted to adopt. She'd always spoken admiringly of him and Mitch knew her to be a good judge of character.

So when Shep stopped beating around the proverbial bush and added, "When I met Raina, nine years had passed since her husband died. Even so, we had a few bumps in our road because of it."

"Lily and I aren't—"

"Aren't serious? Aren't involved? Only friends? I get that. No one's judging you…or Lily."

"Maybe *you're* not, but Troy's sister is and I can't blame her for that. Even *I* know Lily's still vulnerable and I should watch my step. But how do you keep a promise to protect someone and step back at the same time?"

"That's a tough one," Shep admitted. "But if you care about her, you'll figure out the right thing to do, without interference from anyone else." Shep drank the last of his coffee. "Thanks for coming down here with me. I want to be with my wife and baby, but I needed a little break just to settle down a bit."

"I understand."

Shep nodded. "So are you ready to meet my daughter?"

When Lily and Mitch returned from the hospital, they warmed up dinner and ate at the table Lily had set. She called Ellie to see how the twins were doing and to give a report on Raina.

After she closed her phone, Mitch asked, "Ready for dessert?" and brought the apple crumble to the table.

"I have to get back home. Sophie and Grace are okay but I don't want Ellie and Angie to feel as if I've abandoned them."

"You haven't. A couple of hours away will do all of you good."

"I know, but—"

"You don't have to run off because you think I might kiss you again. I won't, if you don't want me to."

Lily felt her heart start hammering. "That's the problem, Mitch. I think I want you to."

Although another man might have acted on that subtle invitation, Mitch didn't. He set the dish on the table and started scooping dessert out for both of them.

"You don't have anything to say to that?" she asked quietly.

"Shep thinks we're involved."

Lily felt rattled that the subject had come up between the two men.

"I didn't start that conversation, if you're wondering," Mitch assured her.

"No, I wasn't. I guess I was just surprised."

"Everyone who cares about you is worried about you. It's natural that they're going to watch what you're doing."

"I hate to think I'm being watched," Lily murmured.

"In a good way."

After Mitch took his seat again beside her, she confessed, "Raina thinks we're involved, too."

"And what do *you* think?" he asked, his dark gaze penetrating, assessing, questioning.

"I think I'm scared. I think a kiss means more than I want it to mean with you."

"We did more than kiss," he reminded her.

She couldn't look away, didn't look away, wouldn't look away. She had to be as honest as she could with him. "I'm not sure where we're headed, Mitch. A lot of hormones are still driving me. What if we go up in flames? How much damage will that do to either of us? I've never had affairs, even before Troy. I was always in committed relationships. So what's happening between you and me—"

"Isn't a committed relationship."

"We're really on sandy footing," she said with a shake of her head.

He didn't disagree.

"But I like being with you," she continued. "I feel so alone sometimes, but not when I'm with you."

"We're back to the friends-versus-more question," he said.

Suddenly Lily was tired of the seriousness of it all. She was a widow with two babies to raise and sometimes she just wanted to scream. "Why do we even have to decide? Why are we worried about affairs and committed relationships? I mean, why can't we just enjoy being together?"

A light smile crept across his lips. "You couldn't be saying we're analyzing too much."

"I'm saying I need to take some deep breaths and not worry so much, and maybe *you* do, too. Yes, I think about Troy all the time, and how much I miss him, and how much the babies would love to have him as a father. But he's not here, and I can't pretend he will be again."

"You still love him a lot."

"Yes, Mitch, I do. But that love can't fill up my life twenty-four hours a day anymore. I have to start making room for a different life."

"And?" Mitch prompted.

"And," Lily repeated, then hesitated a moment.... "And Ellie and Angie are going to a concert in Amarillo tomorrow. They're going to stay overnight. So why don't you come over around four and we'll take the babies for a walk. Then maybe we can toss around some ideas for your Christmas weekend. That will be looking ahead and it should be fun. I can plan a menu. You can decide who will be Santa Claus. We'll just hang out."

His gaze was still on her, seeing into her and through her. They had to both figure out what they wanted and maybe the only way to do that would be to spend some time together.

"You just want some help with Sophie and Grace," he teased.

After considering what he'd said, she shook her head. "No, I want to hang out with you."

If she thought Mitch had ignored her invitation earlier, she could see in his eyes now that he hadn't.

Leaning toward her, he reached out and moved a stray wave from her cheek. Then he rubbed his thumb over her lips, leaning even closer. "Does hanging out involve kissing?"

"Maybe," she said with a little uncertainty.

His lips came down on hers and the rest of the world fell away.

Chapter Eight

Mitch pushed the double stroller down the street, noticing the darkened gray sky and the storm clouds that had gathered. He felt a similar storm inside of himself, agitating to be set free.

We're just going to hang out together, he repeated in his mind like a mantra.

Strolling beside him, Lily bent to make sure Sophie and Grace were happy under their canopies. Lily wore a yellow sundress with strawberries appliquéd around the hem. He wondered if she'd dressed up for him or if he was reading too much into her choice of a simple dress on a warm June day. She'd tucked her hair behind her ears and held it in place with two pretty mother-of-pearl combs. She was a vision that plagued his dreams and unsettled his days.

When she straightened, she flashed him a quick smile. "You're staring."

"Caught in the act," he joked. "You look pretty today. But more than that. Freer somehow."

"It was nice being in the house alone with the babies the few hours before you came. Don't get me wrong. I'm so grateful for how Angie and Ellie help. I love being housemates with them. But I also like the feeling that I'm Sophie and Grace's mother and no one means as much to them as I do. Isn't that silly?"

"Not at all. But you don't have to worry. Their eyes are starting to follow you. They know you're their mother, no matter who takes care of them. You have an innate bond with them, just as they do with each other. Nothing will change that."

"Not even me going back to work?"

"Not even."

The breeze suddenly picked up, tossing Lily's hair across her shoulders. "Uh-oh," she said, looking up. "We might not make it back before it rains."

"The rain could hold off," he assured her, yet he knew it probably wouldn't. Once the weather cycle was set in motion, nothing could stop it.

"I'm not wearing running shoes. *You* are."

"I promise I won't race ahead of you. Sophie and Grace are protected by the state-of-the-art stroller your friends gave them. So I don't think we have to rush on their part."

Still, he rolled the stroller around in a half circle and headed back the way they'd come.

Lily stepped up her pace beside him. "I don't like sudden storms."

"You'd rather have planned storms?" he asked, amused.

She cast him a sideways glance. "I know you think that's funny, but just imagine. What if you knew ahead of time about the crises in your life? You could prevent them."

"Maybe. Or maybe fate would just find another way to get you to the same spot so you'd have to make the same kind of decisions."

"Oh my gosh! You're a philosopher and I never knew it."

Mitch had to laugh. "That's one title I've never been given."

"It's a compliment," she assured him, with a teasing tone in her voice that made him want to tug her into his arms and kiss her right there and then on the street. But in Sagebrush, that would almost be a spectacle.

She must have guessed what he was thinking because she slowed for a moment. He didn't stop, and she took a couple of running steps to catch up.

The wind buffeted them with a little more force now and large, fat drops of rain began to pelt them. Lightning slashed the sky not so far away and thunder grumbled overhead. The flashes and booms reminded Mitch of faraway places. He fought to keep memories at bay. Even though he was practically jogging with the stroller, he took deep, even breaths, reminding himself where he was and what he was doing.

A half block from the Victorian, the rain became steadier, rat-a-tatting on the pavement, pelting the leaves of the Texas ash trees blurred in Mitch's peripheral vision. The thunder became a louder drumroll.

Mitch blocked the sound as best he could.

Almost at the front yard of the big, blue house with its yellow gingerbread trim, Lily's sandal caught on the uneven pavement. Mitch sensed rather than saw what was happening and training took over. He reached low for Lily, catching her around the waist before she fell. Her body was warm, her shoulders slick with the rain dripping down. One of her arms had surrounded his waist as she'd steadied herself to keep from falling. His face was so close to hers he could almost feel the quiver of her chin as emotion and desire ran through them both.

Yet they seemed to recognize where they were and what they were doing at the same time because in unison, they murmured, "The twins."

Mitch tilted his forehead against hers for just a moment then released her and pushed the stroller up the walkway to the porch.

Lily unlocked the door while he easily lifted the stroller, carrying it up the steps and into the foyer.

Moments later she switched on the Tiffany light to dispel the shadows while he rolled the twins into the living room and stooped down at Sophie's side of the stroller to see if any pelts of rain had made their way to her.

Lily did the same on Grace's side. "They're dry," she said with amazement.

"At least their clothes are," he returned with a wink.

When Lily laughed, he felt as if he'd done something terrific. He also felt as if the lightning strike had sent supercharged awareness through *him*. When his eyes met Lily's, he knew she felt the same way.

Ducking her head, she lifted Grace. Her pink-and-yellow playsuit with the dog appliquéd on her belly was a little big. It wouldn't be long until she grew into it, Mitch knew.

Grace cooed at Lily and Lily cooed back. "You're a happy girl today. How would you like to sit in your swing?"

Grace's little mouth rounded in an O and her very blue eyes studied her mom's face.

Mitch held Sophie in the crook of his arm. "Do you want to join your sister?"

Sophie's outfit was pink-and-green with a cat appliquéd on the bib of her overalls. When she waved her arms and oohed and aahed in her baby language, Mitch chuckled.

He and Lily set the girls in their swings and wound the mechanism that would start the motion. Then of one accord, she and Mitch seemed to come together, standing close behind the twins.

He brushed his hand down her arm. "I think you need a towel." She was wet from the rain and he was, too. The result of that seemed to be steam rising from both of them.

"I need to change," she murmured but didn't move away.

He fingered one of her combs. "I like these in your hair."

"They were my mother's," she replied softly. "I haven't worn them very much. I was afraid something would happen to them. Suddenly today I realized she wouldn't want me to just leave them in my jewelry box."

Lily's skin was lightly tanned as if she'd taken the babies for walks many days in the sun. He clasped her shoulders and ran his thumbs up and down the straps of her dress. "I've been wanting to kiss you since I got here."

"I've wanted you to kiss me since you got here."

She tilted her head up and he lowered his. He told himself to go easy, not to scare her with too much need. He didn't want to need her at all. But the moment his lips settled on hers, he couldn't keep the hunger at bay. The feel of her in his arms was exquisite, the soft pressure of her lips was a temptation that urged him to claim her. When his tongue thrust into her mouth, her gasp was only a preliminary response. She followed it with a tightening of her arms around him. A return taste of him became a chase and retreat that had them pressing their bodies together.

Outside, a bright flash of light against a darkening sky was soon followed by thunder that seemed to crawl up one side of the roof and down the other. The crackle and boom sounded very close.

All at once the light in the foyer went out and the hum of the refrigerator ceased.

Mitch held Lily tighter, ended the kiss and rubbed his jaw against her cheek. "The electricity." Huskiness hazed his words. "The lightning must have hit a transformer."

After a few moments, she leaned away from him. "I'd better find the oil lamp in case we don't have power for a while. I had a stir-fry planned for supper."

"We'll have to make do with lunchmeat and cheese."

"I made a coconut cake. We don't need power to eat that."

"You have flashlights and candles?"

"I think they're under the kitchen sink. The oil lamp's upstairs. I'll get it when I change."

"Go ahead. I'll watch Grace and Sophie until you come back down. Then you can stay with them while I rummage."

After a last longing look at him, sending the message their kiss had ended much too soon, she ran upstairs.

Mitch took a hefty breath.

Sandwiches eaten, candles and oil lamp lit, Lily forgot about time and just lived in the moment. She and Mitch had talked as they'd sat on the sofa and exchanged fussy babies. They'd played patty-cake and peekaboo with Sophie and Grace in between talking about books they had read, movies they'd seen, first experiences swimming, diving, surfing, hiking. There seemed to be so much to talk about. Yet underneath it all, whenever their gazes met or their fingers brushed, memories of their kisses danced in her mind.

After a few hours, Lily breast-fed Grace while Mitch bottle-fed Sophie. Sophie finished first, and he laid her in her crib, starting her mobile.

They'd brought the oil lamp to the babies' room while they fed them. A flameless candle Mitch had found in a cupboard glowed in place of a night-light. Shadows were heavy in the room and Lily could see Mitch caring for her daughter, gently making sure she was settled, watching her for a few moments, then touching his fingers to her forehead.

He would make a wonderful father.

Turning from the crib, he stooped to pick up the bottle he'd set on the floor. "I'll wash this out."

Grace had stopped suckling and her eyes were closed.

Lily raised her to her shoulder until she heard a little burp, and then she carried her to her crib, settling her in for the night, then she took the oil lamp to the bathroom where she set it on the vanity. A small candle burned next to the sink where Mitch was rinsing the bottle. He'd rolled up his shirtsleeves and for the first time, Lily saw the scars on his right forearm. She didn't look somewhere else, but studied the lines that still looked raw...the gashes that had healed but would never fade away.

Slowly she raised her eyes to his.

He turned off the spigot and blew out the candle.

He was about to roll down his sleeve when she stopped him, her hand clasping his. "You don't have to hide them from me."

"They're ugly."

"No, they're a badge of honor." Without thinking, only feeling, she bent and kissed one of the welts.

"Lily." He said her name in a way he never had before. His words were thick with need, with desire that needed to be expressed.

Her lips lingered on his skin for a few seconds, maybe because she wanted to anticipate what might happen next, maybe because she was afraid of what might happen next.

When she straightened, he took her face in both of his hands. "Do you know what you're doing?" he asked, his voice raspy.

"I'm feeling," she said without apology.

"Damn," he growled, wrapping his arms around her, possessing her lips with his.

His kiss was long and hungry, wet and wild. Lily felt like someone else, like a woman who could throw caution to the side and be free from the chains of what she should and shouldn't do. She kissed Mitch with a fervor that shocked her, yet gave her hope.

Lily's breasts pressed into Mitch's chest. Instead of trying to touch her with his hands, he let their bodies communicate. His breathing was as hot and heavy as hers. They fit together with perfect temptation, perfect anticipation, perfect exhilaration. He seemed to wait for some sign from her that she wanted more and she gave it, pressing even closer. She felt his hardness, the desire he'd been controlling up until now. There would be no turning back from this.

She didn't want to turn back. She wanted tonight with Mitch. Did he want her as badly? Would he let his scars be an issue?

She lowered her hand from his shoulder and insinuated it between their bodies, cupping him, leaving him with no doubt as to what she was ready to do.

Still holding her securely, Mitch backed her out of the bathroom...across the hall...into her bedroom. The area was pitch-black, the glow from the oil lamp in the bathroom the only light, reaching just inside the door. But that didn't stop them. The dark seemed to hold some comfort for them both. Once they were enveloped by it, their mouths sought each other, their arms embraced, their fingers touched. The dark held more excitement than anything else.

Mindlessly, Lily reached for Mitch's shirt buttons.

He searched for the edges of her top and somehow managed to pull it up and over her head.

After he'd tossed it, she asked, "Do you have a condom?"

His hands went still on her waist. "Yes, I do." He

reached into his pocket, pulled out the foil packet and dropped it on the nightstand.

They'd both known this night was coming, hadn't they?

"I'd hoped," Mitch said honestly. "That's why I brought it."

His hands slid to her bra and unhooked it. She shrugged off the straps quickly and leaned forward, kissing his chest. She couldn't see but she could feel hot skin against her lips. Her hands became her eyes as she ran them down his flat abdomen and stopped at the waistband of his jeans. His belt was pliant but fought her hands as she tried to unfasten it. He helped her with it. A few moments later, he'd shed his sneakers, jeans and briefs. She'd flicked off her sandals. Now he slid his hands into the waistband of her shorts, sliding them down her hips along with her panties.

She knew he couldn't see much more than shadows, either, and she asked, "Should I light a candle?"

"No time," he muttered as he pushed her hair aside and kissed her neck, trailing his lips along her collarbone. His foray to her breast made her restless, flushed and needy.

"Mitch," she moaned, but he didn't stop. He just kept kissing lower, down her belly to the mound between her thighs. She couldn't let him be that intimate. She just couldn't. The reason why eluded her.

She grasped his shoulders and said again, "Mitch."

This time she felt him shift, felt his head tilt up. He straightened, flung back the covers, and climbed into bed, holding his hand out to her.

Thunder grumbled again outside and she thought fleetingly of Grace and Sophie and whether or not they'd awaken. She listened as the sky rolled but heard nothing from the babies' bedroom.

As if he read her mind, Mitch asked, "Do you want to check on them?"

She knew she'd hear them if they awakened, even without the monitor. "They'll let us know if they wake up," she replied, crawling in beside him, moving closer to him.

He wrapped his arm around her and stroked her back. "You'll have to tell me what you like."

She suddenly couldn't speak and didn't know why. So she tilted her head against his and finally managed, "I want *you,* Mitch. Kiss me and everything else will be okay."

His lips were searingly hot, his tongue an instrument of pleasure that urged her to caress his back, his sides, his manhood.

"Lily," he gasped. "Are you ready?"

"Yes, Mitch. I am."

Reaching to the nightstand, he grabbed the packet and ripped open the foil. After he slid the condom on, he stretched out on top of her, letting her feel his weight. He spread her legs and lay between them. As he braced himself on his elbows, she tensed a little. He must have felt it because he kissed her again until all she wanted was him filling her, giving her pleasure, helping her to forget.

Forget what? a little voice inside her head whispered, but she ignored it, not bothering to find the answer.

When Mitch entered her, she *was* ready. Each of his thrusts made her call his name, asking for more. Mitch's body was as slick as hers with their passion. His chest slid against her breasts as they rocked, tempting each other, provoking each other to the next level of pleasure. Lily held on tightly as a strong orgasm overtook her, shaking her world until it was upside down. Mitch's shuddering release came moments later.

She felt as if the storm had somehow come inside. Stunned by the pleasure still tingling through her, she also felt overwhelmed by the intimacy she'd experienced with Mitch. She wobbled on the verge of feelings that terrified her and she didn't know whether to run or to hold on to Mitch for dear life.

After Mitch collapsed on top of her, he whispered in her ear, "Are you okay?"

She didn't know how to answer him, but gave him the response that would be easiest. "Yes, I'm good."

He kissed her cheek then rolled onto his side, taking her with him, their bodies still joined. "Do you want me to check on Sophie and Grace?"

"In a minute." She was still catching her breath, still trying to absorb what they had done, what she had done.

"Talk to me, Lily."

"Just hold me, Mitch. Just hold me."

"I shouldn't fall asleep with you. I could have a nightmare."

"It doesn't matter, I don't want you to leave."

So Mitch stayed and she held on, unsure what morning would bring.

Lily snuck glances at Mitch as they made breakfast the next morning. The night before, the first time the twins had awakened, Mitch had climbed out of bed quickly. Lily wondered if he'd slept at all because he'd seemed so wide awake as they fed Sophie and Grace and settled them once more. Afterward, Mitch had kissed her and she thought they might make love again. Instead he'd said, "Get some sleep. I'm going to bunk on the couch. When the electricity clicks back on, I'll make sure everything's working okay."

"Mitch, you could sleep with me."

But he'd shaken his head and she'd known better than to argue.

The twins had slept later than usual this morning, so it was almost ten o'clock as she scrambled eggs and Mitch fried bacon. Sophie and Grace faced each other and babbled in their swings.

She hadn't talked to Mitch about last night. They'd been too busy changing, dressing, diapering and now making breakfast. What she wanted to ask most was, *What did last night mean to you?*

However, as she was about to begin the discussion, the front door swung open and Angie and Ellie charged in, overnight cases in hand. They gave some attention to the babies and then stopped short when they saw Mitch.

Cheerfully, Angie tried to set the tone. "Good morning."

"I didn't expect you back so soon," Lily remarked. "How was the concert?"

"It was wonderful," Angie replied. "I felt like a teenager again. Brad Paisley is one hot dude."

Lily forced a laugh because Ellie was being so quiet.

Angie slipped a CD from her purse. "I got his new one."

"Did you have a good time?" she asked Ellie. Mitch silently listened, forking the slices of bacon.

"Yeah, it was great. But we heard you had storms last night and a lot of the electricity was out. We were worried. That's why we got up early and drove back. I tried to call but the phone must not be working. It just kept ringing and you didn't answer your cell, either."

"Oh, I'm sorry you worried," Lily apologized. "My cell was out of power when the electricity went down and I unplugged the charger so it wouldn't get damaged if there was a surge." She felt as if she were overexplaining and Ellie was eyeing her and then Mitch. Lily felt uncomfortable.

"Did you have any trouble getting back?" Mitch asked. "Trees down? That kind of thing?"

"Just a tree down on Alamo," Angie answered when Ellie didn't. "Branches here and there. We heard a tornado went through Odessa. That's why we were worried. How did Sophie and Grace do with the storm?"

"They didn't seem to mind," Mitch said with a smile.

"How long have you been here?" Ellie inquired.

Mitch looked to Lily, obviously deciding to let her answer. She felt suddenly unsettled, as if what had happened with Mitch last night was definitely all wrong. She was the mother of three-month-old twins. What was she doing having an affair? What was she doing making love with a man when Troy hadn't been gone a year? What was she doing trying to find a life when her old one still seemed so real?

Suddenly plagued by doubts, she answered, "Mitch came over last evening to visit. While he was here, the electricity went off. He stayed to make sure we were all safe. He slept on the couch and when the power came back on, he made sure everything was working right again."

She sensed Mitch's body tense. With a sideways glance at him, she saw his jaw set and his mouth tighten. She didn't dare look into his eyes.

"I see," Ellie responded.

Silence shrouded the kitchen until Angie broke it. "We bought donuts at the convenience store. I left them in the car with the souvenirs. I'll go get them."

"I can throw more eggs into the pan," Lily offered. "We have plenty of bacon and toast."

Mitch switched off the burner, fished the bacon from the pan and let it drain on a paper towel on a dish. But then he said, "I think I'll be going. Everything's back to normal here and the three of you can catch up."

Lily reached out a hand to him. "Mitch, you don't have to go."

His gaze locked to hers. "Yes, I think I do."

Lily felt her heart drop to her stomach. The look on Mitch's face told her that her explanation to Ellie hadn't been what he'd expected her to say. She slid the eggs from the pan onto a serving dish and set it on the table.

"I'll be right back," she told Ellie. "I'm going to walk Mitch out."

Mitch stopped by Sophie and Grace, jiggled their feet, gave them a last long look, then went to the living room. Making sure the timer on the swings would keep the babies content for a little while longer, Lily bent down and kissed them both. She passed Angie in the living room and saw that Mitch had already gone out the door.

"What's up?" Angie whispered to her.

"We'll talk later," she told her friend, not knowing what to expect when she went outside.

Lily had never seen Mitch angry. A sense of calm always seemed to surround him. But now, even though he was still, he wasn't calm. His brown eyes simmered with an emotion she didn't understand. She thought he was accusing her of something and she went on the defensive.

"You could stay for breakfast."

"If I stayed and Ellie asked what happened last night, what should I tell her?"

Maybe the emotion she was witnessing in Mitch's eyes wasn't anger. It was something worse. It was betrayal.

Her hands suddenly felt clammy. "I couldn't tell her what happened."

"I understand you want to keep your life private. I understand you're afraid you'll hurt her feelings. I understand that you feel she'd be upset if she thinks you're moving on. What I don't understand, especially after last night, is that you gave her the impression I was like a security guard seeing to your safety. Why are you afraid to admit to yourself what happened last night. We were *intimate,* Lily, as intimate as two people can be. Do you want to erase that from your memory?"

The breeze tossed her hair across her cheek as she self-consciously looked around to make sure no one was walking anywhere nearby. Glancing over her shoulder, she needed to be certain neither Angie nor Ellie were in the foyer, listening.

"I don't know what to think about last night," she admitted. "I'm not like that, Mitch. I don't seek pleasure to wipe out—"

"Loss and grief and memories?"

"Why are you so angry?"

He ran his hand over his face and considered her words carefully. "I don't think I'm as angry with you as I am with myself. I should have known better. I should have known you weren't ready."

She remembered him asking her last night, "Are you ready?" He'd meant so much more than the physical. Deep down, she'd known that.

"The dark made it easy," he decided. "The dark let you think, subconsciously at least, that you were with your husband again."

She wanted to protest. She wanted to scream that he was wrong. Yet how could she? She didn't know if he was wrong or right. She didn't know if last night had been about her and Mitch, or if it had been about her needing a man to hold her. She felt awful. She felt as if she *had* betrayed him.

"I'm going to leave before I say something else I shouldn't," he muttered. "It's probably better if we don't see each other for a while."

For a while? How long was that? She'd be going back to work in November. He didn't mean that long, did he? But she had her pride and he had his. She'd hurt him badly and now she had to suffer the consequences.

He took his car keys from his pocket. "Take care of yourself, Lily."

Moments later, he was driving down the street away from her.

Taking a deep, shaky breath, she tried not to think or feel and went inside to Grace and Sophie.

Chapter Nine

Late November

Lily sat across from Mitch in his office, hardly able to bear the awkwardness that had developed between them.

She'd been back at work for two weeks and had only caught glimpses of Mitch. He had definitely made himself scarce. The only reason they were in the same room together now was because they had to discuss a patient. "Joan Higgins has high levels of FSH, which definitely lowers the quality of her eggs. I think further testing is indicated."

Mitch nodded, keeping his gaze on the notes on his desk.

After he'd left the Victorian that morning in June, he'd emailed Lily every few weeks to inquire about her health and her daughters'. *Emailed.* He was doing his duty and keeping his promise to Troy without truly getting involved.

Could she blame him?

Lily desperately wanted to blurt out to Mitch, "I miss you," yet she knew she couldn't. She'd hurt him greatly by making love with him while she grieved for her husband. But he'd hurt *her* by walking away as he had. If he could leave her life so easily, what had that night meant to him? What if they'd continued the affair? Would he eventually have opened up to her? Would he have been ready to care for her and the twins out of more than duty?

"I'll order further tests," he agreed, ending their discussion of the patient.

They sat in awkward silence.

Finally Mitch laid down his pen. "How does it feel to be back at work?" His expression was neutral and he could have been making polite conversation with any of their colleagues.

"It feels good to be back. But I miss Sophie and Grace," she added honestly, as if he were still the old Mitch. "I miss not being able to hold them whenever I want. I mostly miss not hearing every new baby word first."

"You could come in part time," he suggested, as an employer might.

"I might be able to do that for a month or so, but I need my salary. I can't just think about the moment, I have to think about the future."

When their gazes collided, they were both thinking about taking pleasure in the moment, and the night neither of them would forget. At least, Lily hoped Mitch wouldn't forget it. She knew *she* never would.

Mitch pushed the papers on his desk into a stack, clipped them together and tossed them into his in-box. "It's getting late. I won't keep you any longer. I know you want to get home."

"Sophie and Grace are really growing and changing."

He looked surprised she'd started up the conversation again.

Reaching into her lab coat pocket, she drew out a small picture portfolio. "These are the latest pictures... if you'd like to see them. I can't believe they're already nine months old."

Maybe she was making it difficult for him to refuse to look, but right now she needed to see emotion from him, something more than a polite facade meant just for her. She'd ached for him all these months, but she hadn't been able to do more than answer his emails in the same tone he'd sent them—politely and with pertinent information. Yet seeing him and working with him again, she realized how much she'd lost when he'd walked away.

As she slid the little booklet across the desk to him, she confessed, "I need to keep their faces close by."

He stared at the small album for a couple of seconds and then picked it up. After he leafed through it, he stood and handed it back to her. "They're beautiful kids, Lily. I imagine in a few weeks, you'll have their picture taken with Santa Claus."

Yes, the holidays were coming and she found she didn't want to celebrate them without Mitch. Did he feel anything when he looked at Sophie and Grace's photos?

Did he wonder if the monitor was still working? If the sun rose and set now without her feeling grief twenty-four hours a day? What could she say to him to bring warmth back into his eyes?

She returned the photos to her pocket and rose to her feet. Obviously, he wanted her to leave. She could feel the figurative miles he was trying to shove between them. She'd let him do that for the past five months because she hadn't known what else to do, what was fair, what was necessary. But she couldn't merely leave things like this, emotions all tangled up, words gone unsaid, desires left unfulfilled.

"Mitch, what can I do to fix this?"

He didn't pretend to not know what she was talking about. "I don't think there's anything to fix."

It had taken courage on her part to bring it up, but he had shot her down without a glimmer of understanding…without a glimmer of hope that they could reestablish the connection they once had. She felt foolish and embarrassed. She should just go home to the people who loved her and wipe from her memories everything that had happened with Mitch.

She'd almost reached the door when she felt his hand on her shoulder. That simple touch brought back everything—the long, wet kisses, his hands on her body, the orgasm that had swept her to another realm. She hoped the naked feelings weren't showing in her eyes.

"I don't know how to fix it," he admitted. "We crossed the line and we can't go back."

The five months that had passed had seemed like a lifetime. If she told him she was ready now, would it be the truth? Would he believe her?

"We could start over," she suggested.

"As what? Colleagues who once had sex and now are trying to renew a friendship?"

His words hit her solar plexus squarely, just where he'd intended. Yet she couldn't give up. "Maybe," she answered truthfully. "We can't deny what happened, but I hate this...wall between us. You were there when Grace and Sophie were born, and now you've just dropped out of their lives."

"I thought the emails—"

"Mitch, you sent them from a sense of duty, because you made a promise to Troy. I didn't know if you really cared. I didn't know whether to email you pictures or describe how I rolled their strollers through the sprinkler and they loved it, or how their hair was finally long enough to put little bows in."

He dropped his hand from her shoulder as if he could see the pictures, too, the pictures of *them* as they'd been, not just the twins. "I walked away because it was the right thing to do."

"For *me* or for *you?*"

"For both of us."

He didn't look or sound as if he had any regrets. That hurt—a lot. She shook her head and accepted what seemed to be inevitable. "If you want to just be colleagues, that's fine. We'll figure out eventually how to relate on that level."

She would have gone again, but this time the huskiness in his voice stopped her. "Lily."

When she swung around suddenly, she saw a flicker of something on his face...and she waited, hoping.

"What did you have in mind?" he asked.

If that wasn't a loaded question! But she did have

something in mind. She just didn't know if he'd go for it.

"How are you celebrating Thanksgiving?" Lily asked. It was only three days away. If he had plans, so be it. She'd figure out something else.

"I plan to pick up a turkey dinner at the Yellow Rose."

She noticed the lines around Mitch's mouth seemed deeper. "And take it home and eat it alone?"

"I guess that's not how most people celebrate Thanksgiving, but afterward I was going to make some phone calls, to make sure everyone was still coming next weekend."

His reunion weekend. The one she'd thought she'd be involved in. "Would you like to come along with Ellie and me to Raina and Shep's?"

Considering that for a few heartbeats, Mitch finally answered, "Are you sure they wouldn't mind having an unexpected guest?"

Her heart seemed to jump against her chest. "Shep said Eva bought a turkey big enough to fill the entire oven. I'm sure they won't mind."

"You already checked this out with Raina, didn't you?" he asked suspiciously.

"Actually, it was her idea. I mentioned things were strained between us here."

"Women," he said with a bit of exasperation. "Do you have to tell each other *everything?*"

"Not everything," Lily assured him quickly.

There was a darkening of Mitch's eyes and she knew he'd caught her underlying meaning.

"Ellie might not like the idea," he pointed out.

"No, she might not. And for her sake, it might be better if we meet at Shep and Raina's ranch."

"Doesn't this take us back where we started?" he asked with such soberness she realized much more was going on under the surface than he was revealing.

"No, it doesn't. Because I'll tell her I invited you. I'll make that clear."

It was easy for her to see that Mitch was debating with himself.

Although she didn't want to say acceptable words just because he wanted to hear them, she did. "If you don't want to come, that's okay. I understand. I just thought maybe we could ease back into…friendship."

"With a crowd around?" he asked, the corner of his lip quirking up.

"Sometimes conversation comes more easily that way."

"And kids are always great buffers."

"Yes," she agreed, now holding her breath, waiting for his answer.

He gave it in the form of another question. "What time does Thanksgiving dinner start?"

When Raina pulled Mitch into a bedlam of bubbling voices, running kids and chattering adults, he knew he must be crazy. He could be sitting home alone, in front of a takeout turkey dinner—

His gaze found Lily right off. At the stove, she was testing the boiling potatoes. Her hair was arranged in a wispy version of a bun that made his fingers tingle to pull it down. She was wearing a calf-length suede skirt with tan boots, and a long multicolored blouse with a concho belt slung low on her slim waist. When she turned to wave at him, he could read her apron that proclaimed in block lettering, I'd Rather Cook Than Clean.

As Shep came toward him, Mitch offered him a bottle of wine. To Raina, he handed a bouquet of colorful mums.

"You didn't have to do that," she said.

"I wanted to." He really had. It was nice of them to include him.

How much did Lily want him here? Maybe she just wanted them to work together without snubbing each other. That would be a far cry from becoming friends again. Friends like before Troy had died? Or friends like after the twins were born?

Lily's babies were sitting in play saucers in the kitchen so she could keep her eye on them. Eva was conversing with Ellie as they made a salad together. Ellie had given Mitch a glance and lifted a hand in his direction, but that was about all.

This could be one interesting Thanksgiving dinner.

Although he knew it wasn't in his best interest, he did want to see how Sophie and Grace had grown.

It had been more than difficult to stay away from Lily and her daughters all these months. But he'd felt it was the right move to make. She'd needed time to recover from Troy's passing. And even now he doubted enough time had passed. But today was about getting a real look at her life again. If he had to try to watch over her without getting involved, then somehow he'd manage that.

He hunkered down at Grace's play saucer, helping her ring a bell, spin a wheel and study her face in the mirror. She giggled at him and reached out to touch his jaw. That tiny hand on his chin made his heart squeeze uncomfortably, so he gave it a gentle pat and moved on to Sophie, who seemed a little more sedate. After all, she was the older sister, even if it was only by two to three minutes. She was slower to let Mitch join in her private game, but eventually she welcomed the intricacies of his set of keys and would have kept them if not for her mom intervening.

"She'll put them in her mouth," Lily said. "I try to keep her toys as sterile as possible, but you know how that is."

"Actually, I don't, but I can imagine with their crawling all over the floor." He looked around at the saucers and stroller and the high chairs. "You must have brought a truck."

Lily laughed.

"The high chairs and stroller fold. Ellie stowed them in the back of her car." She glanced back at the potatoes. "I'd better finish those if we want them ready with the turkey."

"Do you need help with the pot?" It was huge and, he imagined, quite heavy.

"Sure. That would be great."

As he stepped around her, his hip brushed hers. That minor connection of their bodies threw him more than he wanted to admit. He stood in front of the stove and reached for the pot. As always with Lily, physical contact sent his system into a rush forward toward something out of his reach. He thought that might have diminished in their time apart.

It hadn't.

Coming here today had been stupid. He avoided her gaze as he drained the potatoes into a colander in the sink, steam billowing up all around them. *This isn't the first time,* he thought ironically.

"Into the mixing bowl?" he asked, looking at the bowl on the counter.

She nodded, avoiding his gaze, too.

They were a pair. No, *not* a pair, he corrected himself. Just two individuals with wants and needs that couldn't be fulfilled.

He saw Lily go over to her daughters and consult with Raina, who was playing with them, her own five-month-old cuddled close on her lap. Then Lily returned to the mixer.

"Raina said I could put in whatever I want, so here goes."

"Whatever you want?" he asked. "I thought they just got butter and milk."

"That's the plain version," Lily explained with a smile, starting the mixer. "I like to add a little pizzazz."

She added pizzazz all right. With fascination, he watched her add sour cream, milk, chives and a blob of butter for good measure.

"No cholesterol there," he muttered.

She jabbed him in the ribs. "It's Thanksgiving."

He liked the feel of her friendliness again. He'd missed her a lot over the past five months. In his email inquiries, he'd wanted to ask question after question—about the babies and about her. Yet he'd known he had to, in large part, leave her alone. He should have done that to begin with. Today, however, with her close by his side, within kissing distance, inhaling the familiar scent of her perfume, he saw keeping a wall up between them was either very smart...or very stupid. What would an affair do to them? Was she even open to one? Were either of them really ready to move on?

After whipping the potatoes into a delicious white frenzy, Lily stuck in a spoon, took a fingerful and poked it into her mouth. She rolled her eyes. "Just right. Try some?"

He'd watched that finger go into her mouth. He'd watched her lips pucker up. He'd watched her lick it. If there weren't so many people in the big kitchen, he'd kiss her. But there were and he didn't. Instead he put his finger on the spoon, curled potatoes onto it and popped it into his mouth.

"Just right," he agreed, his eyes locking to hers, his gut telling him they weren't finished and might never be.

Mitch barely heard the sound of scraping chairs and laughter and the clatter of silverware.

He *did* hear the doorbell ring. Soon after, the door opened and he heard a woman's voice call, "We're here."

Shep picked up the turkey on its platter and carried it to the table, explaining to Mitch, "It's Raina's mom and brother. Ryder just got off his shift."

Mitch knew Raina's brother was a cop.

Ryder and Sonya Greystone came into the kitchen and were introduced to Mitch. Sonya said to him, "I hope you're a big eater, like Shep. I made pumpkin, apple and cherry pies, and I don't want to take any home."

Shep gave her a bear hug. "You don't have to worry about that."

Mitch had never experienced anything like this Thanksgiving celebration—so many people who seemed like family and really cared about each other. Then he realized that conclusion wasn't true. When he and his buddies and families got together, it was a similar feeling. Family meant something different to everyone, and he was suddenly glad he hadn't stayed home today and eaten dinner in front of a football game.

In the next few minutes, he helped Lily transfer the potatoes from the mixing bowl to a beautiful serving dish embellished with roses and gold trim. He stared at it for a second and Lily asked, "Mitch?"

In the midst of the holiday chaos, he said in a low voice, "This dish reminds me of one my mom used when she tried to make the holidays a celebration for the two of us."

"Holidays are supposed to be about memories and traditions and loved ones, even when they're not still with us."

He'd walked into that one. When his gaze met Lily's, he expected to see sadness on her face. Instead, he saw an emotion more poignant.

She said, "If you'll put those on the table, I'll set the twins in their high chairs."

In the next few minutes, everyone was seated around the huge, rectangular table. Even Joey and Roy seemed awed by the amount of food in front of them.

In the moment of quiet, Shep said, "Let's all give thanks for being together today."

Mitch didn't know where the chain started—maybe with Shep's children—but everyone held hands and bowed their heads, remembering Thanksgivings past, grateful for the opportunity to be together like this with more than enough food for everyone to eat.

Lily had taken Mitch's hand. He intertwined his fingers with hers and she looked over at him, her eyes questioning. He didn't have the answers to those questions. They'd have to just see where today took them.

After dinner, Mitch and Shep played a board game with Roy and Joey while Eva recorded everything she could on a video camera. Every once in a while Mitch glanced over at Eva, who was sitting on the floor beside Manuel as he rode a high-tech rocking horse. The letters of the alphabet appeared on a little screen in front of him the longer he rocked back and forth. Grace and Sophie crawled around Lily and Ellie's feet, while Raina played with her daughter in one of the play saucers.

Roy shouted, "I won," and everyone cheered as he moved his marker into the winning block.

Mitch moved to the sofa while the boys ran to the playroom for another game. Aware of Grace crawling over to him, he smiled when she sat before him and raised her arms. He knew what that meant. It had been a while since he'd held one of the twins, a while since he'd felt as if he should.

A baby's needs always trumped overthinking, so he bent and lifted her up to his lap. At nine months she was a heartbreaker. He could only imagine how beautiful she'd be as a teenager, when someone would have to protect her from overeager guys who would date her.

Grace grinned up at him and snuggled into his chest as if she were just waiting for a place to enjoy a comfortable nap.

Ellie, who'd been talking to Raina's mother and Eva across the room, came to sit beside him. She patted Grace's leg. "Tired, little one?"

"The day's celebration has wiped her out," Mitch said amiably. He didn't know what Ellie thought about his being here today.

"She only had a short nap this afternoon before we came."

Mitch touched Grace's name embroidered on the front of her pale green overalls. "Did you make this?"

"Yes, I did. I finally got the website up and running last month, and I have orders."

"So you're thinking about staying in Sagebrush?"

"That depends on Lily. Mom asked her to come back to Oklahoma and raise the twins there. That way she and my dad could see them more often and give her all the help she needs."

Mitch remained silent. Finally he said, "Lily seemed happy to get back to work. She'd have to find a practice in Oklahoma City or start her own."

"That's true. But Oklahoma City is a medical center. I don't think she'd have a problem starting over there."

Grace's tiny fingers rubbed up and down against Mitch's sweater as if it were a security blanket.

"What if Lily decides to stay in Sagebrush? Will you support that decision?" Mitch asked.

"Do you think you can convince her to do that?" Ellie asked in return.

"This isn't about convincing. It's about what Lily wants and where she wants to raise her daughters."

"You sound so removed from it. Don't you care?"

Oh, he cared. More than he wanted to admit—more than he dared to admit. "I won't persuade Lily one way or the other. She has to make up her own mind. If she doesn't, she'll have regrets."

"She asked you here today." Ellie's voice was almost accusing.

"I'm not sure why she did. As you know, we haven't seen each other for a while." Ellie was the type of woman who wanted the cards on the table, so he might as well put them there.

"You two have a connection," Ellie said softly. "One anyone can see."

"Anyone can?"

"You can't hide it, even though you both try."

Mitch smoothed his hand over Grace's hair, tweaking the little green bow with his finger. "And how do you feel about that?" he asked Ellie.

"I don't think it matters how I feel."

"Yes, it does." Mitch could tell Ellie that she was the reason he and Lily hadn't been in real contact since June. On the other hand, she wasn't actually the root of the problem.

"Lily asked you here today without my input," Ellie confided.

Mitch gave Ellie a regarding look. "What would your input have been?"

Ellie kept silent.

So he said something he probably shouldn't have. "I think Lily feels she needs your permission to move on."

That widened Ellie's eyes. "You're not serious."

"Yes, I am. We probably shouldn't even be having this conversation, but I thought it would be better if we cleared the air. I don't know what's going to happen next, but I do know Lily deserves to be happy."

He'd said too much. He'd tried to take himself out of the equation as much as possible, but that was difficult when he thought he had a stake in it. It was difficult when he felt as if Lily and the twins owned a piece of his heart.

Seeing them talking, Lily crossed to the sofa with

Sophie in her arms. Sophie was rubbing her eyes and her face against Lily's blouse. "I think we'd better get these two home. In a few minutes they're either both going to be asleep or fussing because they're tired."

Mitch carefully picked up Grace and stood with her. "I'll help you pack the car. I should be going, too."

"I can take Grace," Ellie said, reaching for the little girl.

Mitch aided in the transfer, wondering just how seriously Lily might be thinking about moving to Oklahoma City.

While Ellie watched the twins, Lily and Mitch took baby paraphernalia outside to Ellie's car. The weather had turned colder. The late-November wind blew across the parking area and through the corral across the lane. Lily opened the car door while Mitch slid the high chairs inside, along with a diaper bag. At the trunk, he adjusted the stroller to lay flat.

After he shut the lid, he regarded Lily in the glow of the floodlight shining from the back of the house. "Ellie tells me Troy's mother wants you to move to Oklahoma City." He'd never intended to start like that, but the question had formed before he could think of anything else to say.

Although she wore a suede jacket, Lily wrapped her arms around herself as if to ward off a chill. "I'm surprised she told you that."

"Were *you* going to tell me?"

"I don't know. After the past few months..." She trailed off. "If I went to Oklahoma City, you wouldn't have to worry about your promise to Troy."

"Is *that* why you'd move?"

She turned away, as if making eye contact was too difficult, as if she couldn't be as honest if she did.

But he clasped her arm and pulled her a little closer. "What do you want, Lily? A different life in Oklahoma?"

"I'm thinking about it. I have good friends here, but Troy's parents are Sophie and Grace's grandparents. I'm not sure what the right thing to do is."

"Whatever makes you happy."

She gave a short laugh. "And how do we ever really know what that will be?"

He'd meant it when he'd told Ellie he wouldn't try to persuade Lily one way or the other. They'd have to set aside the question of her moving...for now. "I'm glad you asked me to come today," he said after a long pause.

"Are you?" Lily's voice was filled with the same longing Mitch felt. They'd been apart and he'd hated that. He just didn't know if they should be together.

"I never experienced a holiday quite like it," he explained. "I haven't had a place to go for holidays in a long time."

"I think Sophie and Grace remember you. They're so comfortable with you."

"And how comfortable are you with everyone watching?" He swore under his breath. "That didn't come out right."

"Yes, it did. I know what you mean. But we weren't really together today, were we?"

He had to make a decision now, which way was he going to go with Lily. He could just cut her out of his life. But wasn't that in itself making a decision for her?

"How would you like to go to the tree-lighting

ceremony on Sunday at the library? We can show the twins all the lights and let them listen to their first Christmas carols."

She only hesitated a few moments. "I'd like to do that."

He didn't ask her if she'd ever been to the tree-lighting ceremony with Troy. He didn't want to know. Although he longed to take her in his arms and kiss her, he didn't. This time, they were going to take small steps toward each other to find out if that's where they wanted to be.

Maybe Sunday would be a beginning. Maybe Sunday would be an end.

At least he'd know one way or the other.

Chapter Ten

"It pays to have connections," Mitch said with a grin as he stood inside the library, peering out the long window with Sophie in his arms. Raina's mother was the head librarian and had told them they could settle inside for as long as they wanted.

Lily was holding Grace, peering outside beside Mitch. Her arm was brushing his. Every time it did, he remembered everything about their night together—everything about her hands on his body and the shake-up of his soul. Not for the first time he wondered if he wanted Lily simply because he shouldn't have her.

Mitch suddenly felt a hand on his shoulder and tensed. As he turned, he relaxed. "Hello, Mr. Fieldcrest. Are you and your wife going to enjoy the tree-lighting ceremony?" Tucker Fieldcrest and his wife owned the

B&B where his friends would be staying this coming weekend.

"We surely are. I was going to call you this week, but now I don't have to. I just wanted to tell you, we're all ready for your guests."

Mitch introduced Tucker to Lily. They all chatted for a few minutes and then Tucker motioned to the crowd gathering outside. "They're almost ready to light the tree. You'd better get your place. I'll see you Friday night." With a wave, he left through the library's huge wooden double doors.

"He seems very nice," Lily said, after the older man had gone outside.

"He and his wife Belinda are good people. They're cutting us a break, only charging half the normal room rates. They insisted they'd be empty this time of year anyway, and our veterans deserve more than reasonable room charges."

"Absolutely," Lily said emphatically, and Mitch knew what she was thinking about. Yet she surprised him when she asked, "So, do you still need activities for the kids? Would you like me to come over and paint faces?"

"I roped Matt into playing Santa Claus and I was hoping that would take up the whole afternoon. But if you're still willing, I'm sure everyone would appreciate it."

"I'm still willing."

To do more than face paint? he wanted to ask. All the words that passed between them seemed to have an underlying message. When he'd asked her to come along tonight, he'd thought of it as a sort of date. But did she think about it that way, too? Did having the twins along make it merely an outing they could enjoy together?

He'd drive himself crazy with the questions, especially when Lily looked at him with those big, blue eyes and a smile that again brought back their night together in vivid detail. It was ironic, really. They'd had sex in the dark but every moment of it was emblazoned in his mind in living color. Sometimes he thought he could see those same pictures running through Lily's thoughts, but that could be wishful thinking.

"Let's get Sophie and Grace bundled up so we don't miss their expressions when the tree lights glow. Do you have your camera?"

Lily patted the pocket of her yellow down jacket. "Right here. But I don't know how we're going to hold them both and take their picture at the same time."

"We'll figure out something," he assured her. Sophie suddenly took hold of his nose and squeezed it a little, babbling new consonant sounds as she did. He laughed. "Getting impatient, are you? Come on, let's cover that pretty blond hair with your hat and hood so you stay warm."

Once the girls were dressed, Mitch and Lily pushed the stroller down the side ramp to the sidewalk. A fir tree stood on the land in front of the eighty-year-old, two-story brick library. The storefronts farther up the street were all lit up with multicolor lights, more than ready for Christmas shoppers. Grady Fitzgerald owned a saddle shop in the next block and Mitch thought he caught a glimpse of him and Francesca with their little boy on the other side of the tree. Lily waved to Tessa and Vince Rossi, who'd brought their children, Sean and Natalie, to watch the ceremony.

"Gina and Logan are here somewhere," Lily said to Mitch, leaning close to him so he could hear her amidst the buzz of people talking.

She pulled the camera from her pocket. "You hold the stroller and I'll take your picture."

"Lily, I don't think—" But before he could protest, before he could say he hated to have his picture taken, she'd already done it. Turnabout was fair play, so he motioned her to the back of the stroller, snagged the camera from her hand and took more than one of her with her girls. Sophie and Grace seemed to be mesmerized by the people passing by, the stand with the microphone where the mayor stood, the wind carrying the smells of French fries, corn dogs and hamburgers from the food cart parked not far away.

As the mayor, Greta Landon, came to the mike and started her remarks, Mitch handed the camera back to Lily. He swooped Sophie out of the stroller and said, "If you hand me Grace, I can hold them both up, and you can take their picture when the lights go on."

After Lily lifted Grace from the stroller, she transferred her to Mitch. As she stood close, she tilted her chin up and was almost near enough to kiss. She said, "This was a great idea. Maybe we'll start a tradition."

If you don't leave Sagebrush for Oklahoma City, he thought. He believed he was so good at not giving anything away, but he must have been wrong about that. Because Lily backed away as if she couldn't reassure him she would be staying in Texas. Her impulsive exclamation had been just that—impulsive.

Just like their night together.

At that moment, the mayor announced, "Let this

year's Christmas tree glow brightly for all the residents of Sagebrush."

The tree came alive with blue, red, green and purple balls. Strand after strand of tiny white lights twinkled around those. Mitch witnessed the expression on Sophie and Grace's faces, and their wide-eyed awe was priceless.

Instead of looking at the tree when the Christmas carols began playing, Lily's face was Madonna-like as she gazed at her girls. Then her eyes locked to his. Something elemental twisted in his chest.

The twins already seemed to be developing their own language. They babbled to each other and the gibberish was almost in a cadence that Mitch thought of as language.

Lily leaned in and kissed both of their cheeks, then snapped a picture of Mitch holding them. "What do you think of all those lights?"

They waved their hands at each other and at her.

All of a sudden, Hillary was at Lily's side, carrying her own daughter. "Look who's here," Hillary said, taking in Mitch, Lily and the twins. "Since when are you two seeing each other outside of the office?"

"Since tonight," Mitch answered, matter-of-factly. "We're sharing some Christmas cheer. How does Megan like all this?" If there was one thing Mitch knew, it was that talking about someone's children always took their mind off anything else.

Still, Hillary gave him a knowing look. "She loved it, but now I think she's ready for bed. Besides, I don't want her out in the cold too long. How about you? Are you going to go back into the library for some complimentary hot chocolate?"

He and Lily hadn't discussed that, but he imagined what her answer would be. "We're headed home, too."

Hillary shifted Megan to her other arm. "Well, it was good to run into you without your lab coats on. I'll see you tomorrow." Then as quickly as she'd appeared, she was gone.

If Lily was going to take issue with what he'd told Hillary, this wasn't the time or place. He said, "Let's get them into the stroller and roll them to the car, unless you really would like some hot chocolate first."

As Lily took Sophie from him, she replied, "We can make hot chocolate back at the house."

Hmm. They just might be in for that discussion after all.

Lily had been surprised tonight at what Mitch had said to Hillary. For all those months he'd seemed as far away as the North Pole. But when he'd asked her to come along with him tonight, he seemed to have established a now-or-never attitude. However, everything was unsaid. Everything was up in the air. Everything was up to them.

How should she feel about his proprietary statement? Were they going to be a couple? Could Mitch make a lifelong commitment if that's where they were headed? What if she decided she shouldn't stay in Sagebrush? All the questions were terrifying, along with the life changes they could provoke.

But for tonight?

The warm and fuzzy feelings from the tree-lighting ceremony lingered as they drove home.

After they pulled into the drive, gathered the girls and the stroller and rolled them up the front walk, Mitch asked, "How will your housemates feel about us coming back here?"

"I guess we'll find out."

Her flippant reply almost seemed like a challenge.

Once in the living room, he found Angie and Ellie watching a forensic drama on TV while they strung popcorn to use as garlands.

"You're getting ready for Christmas?" he asked as a hello.

Ellie looked up, shot him a forced smile, then went back to stringing.

Angie responded to his question. "We all like to do home-crafted decorations, so it can take a while."

Without thinking twice, he took Sophie from her stroller, unzipped her coat, took off her mittens and hat and picked her up.

"Ma-ma-ma-ma," she said practically, as her sister chimed in with the same syllable.

He laughed and asked Lily, "Two bottles upstairs?"

She nodded.

"If you need some help..." Ellie called.

"You look like you're busy," Mitch said. "We'll be okay." Taking the lead was second nature to him. Would Lily mind? She didn't give any indication that she did.

"I put bottles together," Angie said. "They're in the refrigerator in their bedroom."

Mitch glanced over his shoulder as he carried Sophie upstairs, right behind Lily with Grace. He wasn't surprised to see Ellie's gaze on them.

In the twins' bedroom, Mitch and Lily stole glances at each other while they fed the girls and readied them for bed. They'd been super-aware of each other all night, but hadn't been able to act on that awareness. Now they still couldn't, with Sophie and Grace to care for and Ellie and Angie downstairs. The whole situation was frustrating, titillating and exciting. Mitch knew he'd thrown down a figurative gauntlet tonight, and Lily had to make the decision whether or not she wanted to pick it up. She could deny their bond as she had once before. Maybe he was just waiting for her to do it again. Maybe he wanted the safer route. Maybe living alone was preferable to caring about a family. Maybe he didn't think he deserved a family. Because he had come home but others hadn't?

It was a lonely route, yet he was used to it.

Once the twins were comfortably settled in their cribs, once Lily had kissed them both and he'd simply laid a protective hand on each of their foreheads, Lily and Mitch left them to sleep by the glow of the night-light and stepped into the hall. This was about the most privacy they were going to have.

At least that's what he thought until Lily said, "I need to turn on their monitor in my bedroom."

Lily's bedroom. Visions raced through his mind.

Lily went ahead to her nightstand and switched on the monitor. He stepped over the threshold and shut the door.

She didn't move and neither did he for a moment. Then he saw that flicker in her eyes, the memory of what it was like when they were together. He covered the two steps to her, lifted her chin and looked deep into her eyes. "I told Hillary we were dating."

"I know."

"Do you have an opinion about that?"

"I didn't protest."

"No, mainly so you wouldn't embarrass us both."

"That wasn't the reason."

"What was?" he demanded, tired of waiting, yet knowing that with Lily all he could do was wait until she was truly free of yesterday.

"Because I want to spend time with you, Mitch—*with* the twins…*without* the twins. I can't tell you everything's going to go smoothly. I still miss Troy." She looked down at her hand, and he did, too. Her wedding ring glistened there, as real now as the day Troy had slipped it on her finger.

"And *I'm* used to being alone," he admitted.

"Do you like that?" she asked with the spirit that was all Lily.

He almost laughed. Almost. But the question had been a serious one. "I used to think being alone was the only way I could deal with my life on my terms."

"And now?"

"I'm open to finding out differently. That's all I can give you right now."

The expression on her pretty face said she didn't know if that was enough. He didn't, either. But as he bent his head, kissing her seemed a lot more important than the future.

He brushed his lips against hers, maybe to test her, to see how much she wanted. But the test became his to pass or fail. She responded by twining her arms around his neck and slipping her fingers into his hair. He'd wanted to take everything slowly with Lily. This time they'd take it easy. This time he'd make sure she knew what she was doing. This time, she wouldn't want to deny what was going on between them.

But the moment her fingers tugged at his hair as if

she wanted more, undeniable desire rushed through his body.

Making himself slow down, he kissed her neck, and asked, "How much time do you think we have?" He leaned back to check her expression, to see if she felt guilty about being in her room with him, to see if what her housemates thought mattered.

"A few minutes," she responded. "Ellie and Angie will wonder if everything's all right."

A few minutes wasn't enough time. So he didn't waste a moment more of it. His mouth came down on hers possessively, coaxing, teasing, plundering. Still the moan that came from Lily's throat gave the kiss more power as they both gave in to the primal quality of it. He thrust his tongue into her mouth, felt her soft, full breasts against him, and knew he was more aroused than he'd ever been. His hands slid down her back and he pressed her into him. She shivered and the trembling of her body made him wonder what he was doing. Their kisses awakened him to the raw need inside him. What if that need could never be satisfied? What if Lily, too, turned away from his scars? After all, the last time, they'd made love in the dark. What if he had a nightmare while he was lying beside her? How would she react?

The questions flooding his brain doused the far-reaching, fiery tendrils of his desire. A good thing, too, because he might have pulled her onto that bed, undressed her and joined their bodies no matter who was downstairs.

Tearing himself from her and the kiss, he stood away so he wouldn't reach for her again.

Looking a bit dazed, she said, "Wow! Those few minutes sure went fast."

He rubbed his hand over his face. "You get to me."

Smiling, she replied, "*You* get to *me*."

What bothered Mitch was that, despite the rush of passion that had enfolded them, the smile on Lily's face and in her voice didn't touch her eyes. Neither of them seemed happy about it.

"I'm looking forward to this weekend, Lily, but if you don't want to take the time away from Sophie and Grace, I'll understand. I'll be busy playing host, so I don't know how much time I'll have for...us."

Her hands fluttered as if she didn't know what to do with them, so she stuffed them into her front jeans pockets. "Why don't we just play it by ear? I'll see what kind of day the girls are having and then decide."

"Fair enough," he responded. Yet what he'd suggested didn't seem fair at all. He'd just given her an out, and she might take it...just as she might still move to Oklahoma City and leave her life in Sagebrush behind.

Midweek, Lily softly descended the steps into the living room, not wanting to awaken anyone. Sophie and Grace were snuggled in for the night. Angie, on day shift now, had turned in around the same time as Ellie after the evening news.

But Lily couldn't sleep. The decision whether or not to go to Mitch's on Saturday was gnawing at her. Every time she ran into him during the course of the day, she knew he was wondering if she'd be there or not. She felt that if she decided to go, she would be making a commitment.

A commitment to Mitch when she still wore her wedding ring?

She'd had lunch with Raina today, who had given her

a DVD copy of the video Eva had recorded on Thanksgiving. Lying in bed, feeling more alone than she'd ever remembered feeling, Lily decided she needed to watch that DVD.

After she inserted the disk in the machine, she sat on the sofa, perched on the edge of the cushion, pressing the buttons on the remote. The video sprang to life and she watched Thanksgiving Day come alive for her all over again. The living room at Shep and Raina's had been full of lively chatter. Mitch sat on the floor with Joey and Roy, his long legs stretched out in front of him, crossed at the ankles. The boys said something and Mitch laughed. He had such a deep, rich laugh and she rarely heard it. But he'd laughed often on Thanksgiving Day. Because he'd been relaxed? Because kids surrounded him? Because the two of them were together with friends in a way they hadn't been before?

The moment Grace raised her arms to Mitch and he'd lifted her onto his lap brought tears to Lily's eyes. He was so caring and gentle with the girls. Yet Lily sensed he still withheld part of himself. He didn't want to get too attached. Because in being attached to them, he'd be attached to her?

"You should be asleep," a soft voice scolded.

Startled, Lily dropped the remote.

"Sorry," Ellie said, coming to sit beside her. "I didn't mean to scare you."

Bending to the floor, Lily found the remote and hit the stop button.

"This is Thanksgiving," Ellie noticed, staring at the freeze frame on the TV, the still image of Mitch holding Grace.

"Raina gave me a copy today. She thought I'd like to

have it for posterity," Lily said with a small, short laugh that she had to force out.

"You don't have to stop it on my account. I was there, remember?"

"I know, but I thought—"

"Stop tiptoeing around me, Lily. You don't have to. I know how I reacted at the beginning of the summer when Mitch was around. I'm sorry for that."

"You had every right to feel whatever you were feeling."

"I had no right to dictate who you should or shouldn't see."

"You didn't."

"Then why didn't I see Mitch around for almost six months?"

"That was *my* fault, not yours. I wasn't ready to open my heart to another man."

Ellie pointed to the screen. "It looks as if you're trying to figure out if you're ready now."

"If I have to figure it out, that means I'm not?" Lily asked, in turmoil about it. Yet that's what she was feeling.

"I don't know, Lily. Troy is still real to me. He's still my brother. I talk to him, and I listen for his advice. Is that crazy or what?"

"I don't think that's crazy at all. I still do that, too."

"Then maybe you should ask him about this," Ellie advised her.

The two women sat there for a few moments in the dark, with the silence, staring at the frozen picture on the TV in all its color and high definition.

Now that she and Ellie were having an open talk about this, Lily went to her purse on the foyer table and removed her camera. It had been in there since Sunday night.

"I want to show you something," she said to Ellie, sitting beside her sister-in-law again.

She switched on the camera, pressed the review button and brought up a picture. She was standing in front of the town's Christmas tree with the twins in their stroller. Then there were a few shots of Sophie and Grace by themselves, their faces filled with awe, the excitement of their first Christmas shining from their eyes. The miracle of Christmas was starting to unfold for them. She wanted the holiday to be filled with kindness and love and sharing so they'd never forget the importance of giving all year.

The final picture was Mitch holding Sophie and Grace, gazing into the camera with the intensity that was all his. Even though he was smiling, she knew he had questions about what the future held for all of them. Their attraction to each other couldn't be denied. But it muddied the already stirred-up waters. As Lily studied his face, her heart tripped. Her gaze fell to his smile and her stomach somersaulted. Staring at him holding her twins, she felt as if she could melt.

Lily flipped again to the photo of herself with Sophie and Grace, then the other one with Mitch. She said in almost a whisper, "I'm falling in love with him, and it terrifies me."

"Why?"

"Because I've lost everyone who loves me. Because Mitch has an area of his life he won't open to me. Because I'm still attached to Troy and afraid to let go."

"So what are you trying to decide?"

"Mitch's reunion with his buddies from Iraq is this

weekend. Saturday they'll be at his place most of the day and he asked me to come over. I'll be setting foot in an area of his life he kept closed off to me. He said we won't have much time alone, but after everyone leaves, we might."

"Are you asking my permission?" Ellie asked with a hint of a smile.

"No. I guess what I'm asking for is your blessing."

Ellie's gaze dropped to the end table by the sofa where a picture of Lily and Troy stood. Then she lifted it to the TV screen. "Go, Lily. You have to. It's the only way you'll know for sure if you're ready to move on. That's the best I can do."

Lily switched off the DVD player and set the camera on the coffee table. "Let's have a cup of hot cider. I want your opinion on what I'm thinking of giving to Angie and Raina for Christmas."

"You want to be distracted from what's really going on in your mind."

Ellie knew her too well because she was right.

Chapter Eleven

Mitch opened his door to Lily, trying to adjust his thinking about today to include her in it. His gut always twisted a little when he saw her...when her blue eyes looked at him with so many questions he wasn't sure he'd ever be able to answer. "I wasn't sure you'd come."

She had a cake holder in one hand, a paint case in the other. "I told you yesterday that I'd come to help."

Yes, she had. They'd been passing in the hall and she'd stopped him with a touch of her hand on his elbow. He'd felt the heat from it the rest of the day, though he'd told himself that was impossible. Had his caresses branded her the same way?

Stepping aside so she could enter, not sure what her presence meant, he pointed to the far end of the kitchen.

"I put the desserts on the table. The deli trays are in the fridge and the barbecued beef is in the slow cooker."

"It sounds as if you have all of the bases covered."

Except the base with her on it. He nodded to her carrying case. "Paints?" The mundane conversation had to get them through, although the question he wanted to ask was—would she stay the night? Too much to expect?

"Yep. And I have some board games and puzzles in the car. Along with Santa Claus, you should have the kids covered."

"I have a table set up for you in the sunroom."

After she unzipped her parka, he moved behind her, taking it from her shoulders. He hadn't been *this* close to Lily all week, though each time he'd passed her in the hall he'd wanted to haul her over his shoulder, carry her to a closet for privacy and kiss her. She'd left her hair loose today and he caught the scent of it as his hands closed over her jacket and red scarf. She was wearing a Christmas-red sweater with black jeans, dangling gold earrings and black shoe-boots with tall heels. She looked incredible.

When she glanced over her shoulder, their gazes collided and he bent his head to kiss her.

But that kiss wasn't to be. His doorbell rang and he swore under his breath. Not that he didn't want to see his visitors. But every private moment with Lily was precious.

"I'm nervous," she admitted with a shaky smile, as he hung her jacket and scarf over his arm.

"Why?"

"Because these are your friends and I'm not sure I belong here."

"I felt that way at Thanksgiving until Raina and Shep made me feel comfortable. Relax, Lily. These are just families who share a common bond. *You* share it, too."

His words didn't seem to reassure her. He wanted to wipe the anxious look off her face with a touch…with a few kisses. But he couldn't. His guests were arriving and he had to play host.

The next half hour passed in a whirlwind of guests entering and introductions being made. Lily had no trouble making conversation, as Mitch had known she wouldn't. She was easily drawn to the moms with kids, and to one of Mitch's best friends, Matt Gates, who was an ER doctor in Houston. After everyone else had arrived, Jimmy Newcomb's wife, Robin, drove their van into a space the guests had left for them in Mitch's driveway. All of the guys went outside in case Robin needed help. But the Newcomb's van was equipped with a wheelchair lift and, fortunately, Mitch's house had only one step to navigate to push the wheelchair inside.

"I don't want to make tracks in your carpet," Jimmy said to Mitch as he wheeled into the kitchen.

"You can go anywhere you want to in my house," Mitch assured him.

Robin and Maya, Tony Russo's wife, set up the kids in the sunroom with games and puzzles, drawing paper, pencils and crayons, while Lily arranged her face paints on a small table. The children began asking questions right away and she explained what she could do. Soon they were lined up, pleading with her to paint a Christmas tree or an angel, a reindeer or a butterfly on their faces. Once when Mitch looked in on her she was telling them about Christmas traditions around the world.

Another time, the children were explaining how they celebrated Christmas. He realized how much he wanted Lily to stay tonight. It had to be *her* decision. As she took a few breaks, he suspected she was calling Ellie to check on Sophie and Grace.

In the course of the afternoon, he attempted to spend time with everyone. He lit a fire in the fireplace, pulled bottles of beer from a cooler, made pots of coffee. When darkness fell, he set out the food. He'd ordered more than enough, and he was glad to see all his guests looked pleased to be there, sitting near the predecorated Christmas tree he'd bought at the last minute. Reunions could bomb. But this group had too much in common. Feelings ran deep and so did loyalties.

Matt had brought his Santa paraphernalia and stowed it in a spare bedroom where Mitch had stacked presents for the kids.

As most of the guests enjoyed dessert and Lily sat on the couch deep in conversation with Robin, Matt beckoned Mitch to follow him into the hall.

"Ready to sweat in that Santa suit?" Mitch asked with a grin.

Matt grimaced. "You're going to owe me for this one."

"Not if I can help it. You're going to love doing this so much you'll want to do it every year. If the gifts are too heavy in that flannel sack—"

"Do you think practicing in the ER is making me soft?" Matt inquired with a raised brow.

"Not for a minute," Mitch assured him.

"Before I forget, I want to give you something," Matt said, taking out his wallet and slipping out a business card.

"What's this?" Mitch glanced at it and saw the name, address and telephone number of a doctor—the head of the Hand and Trauma Surgery division at the hospital where Matt practiced.

"Eric Dolman is good, Mitch. The best I've ever seen. He's performed nerve grafting and conduits, as well as nerve transfers, with success. If you want to return to surgery, you might want to fly to Houston to see him. I could probably get you in on short notice."

Mitch's gut tightened. "I have a new career now. I was told surgery could cause more damage than I already have." He flexed his fingers just thinking about it.

"Look, Mitch. I know about survivor guilt. Most of us carry it. Maybe it's time to lose it and reach out for something you deserve to have. If you don't want to go back to trauma surgery, that's your decision. But Eric might be able to restore full use of your hand."

Mitch heard a noise and swung around. Lily was standing there and had obviously cleared her throat to make her presence known. She was holding her cell phone and probably looking for a quiet place to make her call.

"I didn't mean to interrupt," she told both of them. "I was just trying to find—"

"A little quiet?" Matt filled in with a smile. "That's hard to do around this crowd." His grin faded, then he became serious. "Tony's wife told me you lost your husband to Afghanistan. I'm sorry."

"Thank you," Lily replied, looking down at her phone where a picture of her twins stared up at her.

Matt tapped the card Mitch was still holding. "Don't lose that. Call him anytime. Just mention my name." Then he strode down the hall to the bedroom.

Lily's blue eyes found Mitch's. "I really didn't mean to interrupt. I overheard a little. This doctor could repair the damage to your hand?"

If Mitch was going to even think about doing this, he had to run it through his own mind first. "The risk could be greater than the rewards."

"But if you could return to surgery—"

"Lily, I don't think this is the time or place to have this discussion. Can we just table it for now?"

"Does that mean you'll want to talk about it later?" she challenged.

Not only was Mitch hesitating to start a serious relationship with Lily because of her memories...but also because of his. She might want too much from him, a closeness he didn't know how to give. She was pushing him now, and that made him restless and uncomfortable. So he was honest with her. "I don't know. I need some time to think about what Matt said. I might want to research this doctor. I might not want to discuss surgery at all."

He saw the hurt on Lily's face, and he knew he was closing her out. But this was sacred territory to him. She didn't understand the ramifications of everything surgery could stir up. Not only memories of his time in the hospital and rehab, working to change his specialty to endocrinology, but also the cause of it all. He didn't talk about *that* to anyone.

More gently, he told her, "I'm going to set up the kindling in the fire pit. After Santa leaves, we can toast marshmallows with the kids."

"I'm sure they'll like that," Lily said, much too politely.

He left her in the hall, believing that after the marshmallows were toasted, she would leave.

Lily opened one side of the French doors and stepped outside onto the red-and-gray brick patio. It was huge, running along most of the back of Mitch's house. But three high stone walls framed the outside of the patio, giving it a protective feel. Mitch, Jimmy and Matt sat by the fire, talking, mugs of hot coffee in their hands.

She walked over to them, zipping her parka. "The kids want to come out and sing Christmas carols before they all go back to the bed-and-breakfast."

"Tell them to come on," Mitch said, rising to his feet.

Lawn chairs were scattered across the bricks, where after Santa's arrival and departure some of the older children had toasted marshmallows for the younger ones under their parents' watchful eyes. Now the fire had died down and short flames licked at the remaining logs under the mesh fire screen.

Lily didn't have to convey Mitch's invitation to the guests inside. As soon as she turned toward the door again, all the children and adults who had gone for their coats poured out. Light from inside shone on the closest section of the patio. The rest was lit by a half moon and so many stars she couldn't count them all if she tried. For Mitch's guests who lived in cities, this had to be a treat. Those who lived in more rural areas knew how to appreciate the beauty of the winter night.

Jimmy's little boy, who was eight and had Rudolph painted on one cheek, grabbed Lily's hand and pulled her toward his mom and dad. "Stand over here," he told her.

She did and found herself beside Mitch.

The night was turning colder and a light wind blew over the stone walls, but she felt protected in the cocoon of the patio, although her breath puffed white vapor in front of her.

Beside her husband, Robin suggested, "Let's take hands."

A hush fell over the group and even the little ones reached for a hand on either side of them. Lily found one of her hands in Mitch's, the other holding Jimmy's. She was emotionally moved in a way she couldn't even begin to express, especially when Maya's sweet voice began "Silent Night." Lily's throat closed as she tried to sing along with the words.

All is calm. All is bright.

How these men deserved calmness and bright.

Instead of holding her hand now, Mitch swung his arm around her shoulders.

What was he feeling at this moment? What had this night meant to him? Would he talk to her about it? Would he talk to her about the possible surgery?

Sleep in heavenly peace. Sleep in heavenly peace.

She suspected all the men were thinking about fallen comrades and maybe how lucky and grateful they were to be alive...to be here together. She thought about the Purple Heart medal tucked away in her jewelry box and how well Troy would have fit in here tonight.

After the last verse of the Christmas carol, moms and dads herded up children and one by one thanked Mitch for his hospitality. She heard him say, "It'll be your turn sometime. Then I'll be thanking you."

He'd gone to a lot of trouble to put this weekend together and it showed.

Inside the house again once more, Mitch saw his guests to the door. Lily stowed food away while he made sure Jimmy accessed his van without difficulty.

"You don't have to do that," Mitch told Lily when he returned to the kitchen.

Actually she'd been grateful for something to do. She knew what *she* wanted to happen next, but she wasn't sure how Mitch felt. "There's not much left. A few pieces of chocolate cake, a half dozen cookies. Some guacamole and a bag of corn chips."

She covered the remainder of the cake with plastic wrap and set it on the counter. "Matt was a great Santa."

"He's always the life of the party," Mitch replied.

The echo of "Silent Night" and the picture of the group gathered outside would be lasting. "Jimmy's a remarkable man. Robin explained a little of what their life is like since he became paralyzed. They're both courageous people."

"She stuck by him when he wasn't sure she would."

"She loves him."

"Sometimes love isn't enough."

Mitch's decisive words seemed to echo in the kitchen. Lily didn't know if he was going to ask her to stay the night, but if he wasn't, she wanted to discuss the surgery on his hand.

He was standing by the counter perfectly still as she moved closer to him. "Nothing can change what happened to Jimmy in Iraq." She took Mitch's hand and ran her thumb over the top of it. "But maybe you can change some of what happened to you."

Mitch pulled away from her, his expression closed. "I told you—surgery could have repercussions."

"I understand that. But a consultation would do no harm."

"I'd have to take time off."

"The practice slows down over the holidays," she reminded him.

His jaw became more set. "I don't want to be a guinea pig. I don't want to be given false hope or become a statistic."

"You haven't even *met* this doctor. You don't have the information you need to make an informed decision."

He blew out a frustrated breath. "Lily, I don't want to argue about this."

"Fine," she said agreeably. "We don't have to argue. I'm merely making a few observations." Then stepping even closer to him, laying her hand gently on his tight jaw, she whispered, "I care about you."

The tension in his body was obvious in his granite-like expression, the squareness of his shoulders, his legs defensively widened. Did it come from more than this interchange between them? After all, although he'd never admit it, this had to have been an emotional day for him.

Looking deeply into her eyes, he seemed to try to see to her very essence. She stood silent, holding her breath.

Then he covered her hand with his. They stood that way for what seemed like hours. The ice maker in the freezer rumbled as it made new ice. The heating system pinged as it battled against the cold night. Lily could feel the pulse in Mitch's jaw jumping under her palm.

Finally he dropped his hand and wrapped his arms around her. When he kissed her, his raw hunger excited her need, ratcheted up the desire that had been building between them, told them both that coming together again would be an explosion of passion.

After Mitch broke the kiss, he leaned away slightly and asked, "Will you stay tonight?"

"I thought you'd never ask," she replied a bit shakily.

Moments later, sitting on the corner of the bed in Mitch's room, her earrings in her palm, Lily ended her call with Ellie. She'd switched on one of the dresser lamps when she'd entered. Now as she glanced around, she saw Mitch's minimalist taste reflected here, too. The bed's headboard was dark pecan, as were the dresser, chest and nightstands. The lamps were a combination of wood and black iron, with the dresser top uncluttered. Yet the multicolored rug beside the bed looked handwoven. The afghan on top of the brown suede-like spread seemed to be hand-knitted.

Rising to her feet, she walked to the dresser and laid her phone and earrings there. She hadn't packed an overnight bag. Because she hadn't wanted to think tonight was a sure thing?

When Mitch entered the room, her body knew it. She didn't turn around but rather raised her gaze in the mirror.

He came up behind her, his eyes on hers. "Everything's okay at home?"

She nodded.

Sliding his arms around her, he pulled her tight against him. "We both smell like wood smoke," he growled against her ear.

Feeling him strong and hard against her body, excitement coursed through her. Her breaths became more shallow, and already she was tingling in the places she imagined he might touch.

"Wood smoke can be sexy," she teased lightly.

"*You're* sexy," he returned, his hands covering her breasts.

Lily trembled from head to toe. At that moment her need for Mitch was go great, she felt she could melt in his hands. Even though she'd stopped breast-feeding, her breasts had remained larger than they once were. Now as they lay cupped in Mitch's palms, she was grateful for every sensation, every nuance of feeling. Yet she understood that feeling would be so much greater with her clothes *off.*

"Undress me," she requested with an urgency that Mitch could obviously hear.

His low chuckle vibrated against her back. "Sometimes making out can be more scintillating with your clothes on." His hands moved down her stomach to the waistband of her jeans.

"Aren't we going to do more than make out?" she asked.

His answer was rough against her ear. "Eventually."

Mitch's foreplay was driving her crazy. All she wanted to do was crawl into bed with him, their bodies naked and exposed to each other's hands and mouths.

Before she realized what Mitch was going to do, her jeans were around her hips, held up by his thighs. His hands slid inside her panties and cupped her. She'd never felt like this—on the verge of an orgasm without even a kiss.

"Do you know how often our first time together

plays in my mind?" he asked with an erotic rasp to his words.

She had those same pictures in her mind. The continuous loop the visions made came to her at odd times and could make her blush.

His finger slipped inside of her and she moaned, needing to turn and face him.

But he wouldn't let her. "Watch in the mirror," he commanded.

There was something so sensual about what they were doing, and the way they were doing it. She'd never watched herself enjoy pleasure. When she lifted her gaze to his and stared at their reflection, his fingers started moving again. Her breath caught. She stared into his eyes as her body tensed and then released in swirls of muscle-melting sensations.

After the orgasmic release, she lay her head back against his shoulder. He held her tightly.

After a few moments of letting her catch her breath, he said, "Let's take off those boots. They make your legs look like a million bucks, but I think they could be dangerous in bed."

They undressed each other beside the bed, and this time—unlike the first—they did it by the glow of the lamp. If Mitch had given her pleasure to blunt the experience of what she was about to see, it hadn't worked. All of her senses seemed even more sensitive to everything that was revealed. His body was hard and muscled and strong, attesting to his workouts. Silky black chest hair formed a Y, arrowing down his flat stomach, around his navel. But red scars from surgery streaked his side. The heel of her hand slid over them as she sifted her fingers through his chest hair.

"Lily," he breathed, "we can just get in bed—"

"No."

She wanted to see. She wanted to know. She needed to feel.

His shoulder and arm were mottled with zigzagging scars, bumps and ridges, and she could only imagine the pain of his injury. She kissed the arm that he kept covered the whole way down to his wrist. Then she took his hand in hers and brought it to her lips.

He again murmured, "Lily—"

He'd undressed her first, but now she finished undressing him. When he kicked his jeans and briefs aside, she rested her hands on his hips and gazed up into his eyes.

Then he was kissing her and his tongue was in her mouth and hers was in his. She couldn't seem to reach far enough to explore or hold him tight enough against her to hear the beat of his heart. She wasn't even sure how they managed moving, but they fell or rolled onto the bed, so hungry for each other they didn't have enough words or touches to express it. Mitch's fingertips stroked her face. Her hand passed down his thigh and cupped his arousal. They were frantic to kiss each other all over, to explore erogenous zones, to stoke their desire to the limit. Mitch's scent had become familiar to her and now it was like an aphrodisiac she couldn't get enough of. The intensity of their foreplay made her body glisten, her heart race, her limbs quiver in anticipation of release. She didn't want to admit how, at that moment, Mitch blotted out everything else in her world. She didn't want to admit to having this mindless passion she'd never felt before. Yet she had to face what was happening, how deeply she was falling, how inexorable their attraction was.

"I need you," she confessed with sudden tears closing her throat.

Mitch reached for a condom, prepared himself, then rose above her. He took her hands, one on either side of her head, and interlocked his fingers with hers. When she raised her knees, he entered her with a thrust of possession that made her gasp. Her climax began building from the first stroke. She wrapped her legs around him, swimming in pleasure that was bigger than the ocean, wider than the universe, higher than heaven.

"Open your eyes and look at me," Mitch commanded, and she knew why. He wanted her to make sure she knew who he was.

"Mitch," she cried, assuring him she did.

His rhythm became faster. She took him deeper. The explosion that rocked them both should have blown the roof off the house.

But it didn't. It simply left them both breathless and gasping and exhausted from a union that had been months in the making.

Lily lowered her legs, loving the feel of Mitch's body on hers. She wanted to postpone the "where do we go from here" moment for as long as she could.

At first, Lily didn't know what had awakened her. A shout. Groans.

Mitch wasn't in bed with her.

Another shout and she finally was alert enough to know what was happening.

She grabbed Mitch's flannel shirt from a chair and slipped it on as she ran from his bedroom to the guest bedroom next door. Mitch was thrashing in the bed, calling a name—Larry. He was drenched in sweat, breathing hard, eyes open but unseeing.

Lily had learned about post-traumatic stress disorder but didn't know whether to awaken him, or whether to get too close. She'd read about the cut with reality that occurred when flashbacks became more real than life itself. What had triggered this? Being with fellow servicemen who knew what war was about? Sitting around the fire? Talking about surface life yet never going too deep?

Grabbing the metal waste can, she banged it against a tall, wrought-iron floor lamp. The noise was loud and seemed to penetrate Mitch's nightmare. He sat up, eyes open with awareness now, and stared at her still holding the waste can.

When he passed his hands down his face, rubbed his eyes and forehead as if to try to erase everything he'd just seen, she slid into the bed beside him and attempted to fold her arms around him.

He prevented her from doing that and pushed away.

"Everything's fine now, Mitch. I'm here."

"Your being here doesn't change what happened over there." His voice was gravelly with regret, sadness and too many memories.

"Maybe it's time you tell me about it."

"You don't want to hear this, Lily."

When she clasped his shoulder, he flinched, but she didn't remove her hand. "I might not want to hear it, but you need to say it out loud. You need to talk to somebody about it, and right now I think I'm the best person. Just stop fighting your subconscious, Mitch, and let it out."

"Do you think talking about it is going to take away the nightmares? Get *real*, Lily."

"I don't know if talking about your experience will take away anything. I suppose it could make memories worse for a while. But suffering in silence isn't the answer, either."

In that silence Lily could hear Mitch's breathing, still not quite as regular as usual. She could feel his doubt, as if revealing *anything* could make his nightmares worse. But she sat there steadfastly, her hand on his shoulder.

His voice was detached when he said, "I got used to the scud alerts, the bunkers, the MREs. It's amazing what can become normal. I not only cared for our soldiers, but for Iraqis too, many of them children with shrapnel injuries. The sound of artillery shots and mortars coming back at us became a backdrop."

Stopping, he seemed to prepare himself for remembering. Sending her a look that said he didn't want to do this and he was going to get it over with quickly, he continued, "We had spent a couple of days cross-training with ambulance teams, going over procedures. We slept when we could catch minutes, sometimes an hour."

After a quiet so prolonged she didn't know if he'd continue, he did. The nerve in his jaw worked and she could hear the strain in his voice when he said, "I was traveling in a convoy when RPGs came at us. The next thing I knew we'd hit an IED."

Lily was familiar with the military speaking in acronyms. RPG stood for rocket propelled grenade...IED, improvised explosive device.

Mitch's face took on a gray pallor as he forced himself to go on. "Blood was *everywhere*." His voice lowered. "The man beside me was...gone. At that point I didn't realize the extent of my injuries, because adrenaline raced so fast I didn't think about anything except helping anybody who was hurt. My ears rang, though. And rounds were still bouncing off the Humvee even though it was burning. I helped two men from the vehicle, but I saw others who'd been tossed out by the explosion. There was fire all around. I spotted Larry and somehow reached him. He had a hole in his thigh—the femoral vein—" Mitch closed his eyes. "Tony covered me with an M16. All I could think of was that I had to stop the bleeding. I *had* to stop it. What seemed like wild shots zinged over my head. Everything was on fire," he said again. "So I threw my body over his. I heard a muffled yell. I finally saw part of the Humvee had been blown away from the fire. I dragged Larry behind it. Someone handed me a piece of a shirt. I tried to staunch the blood. Then I…must have blacked out."

Mitch took a deep breath…stared away from her…into the past. "I had recollections of the medevac, but other than that, the next thing I knew I was waking up in a hospital in Germany, my spleen gone, internal injuries repaired, a pin in my shoulder and another in my leg."

By the time Mitch finished, tears ran down Lily's cheeks. She hurt *for* him and *with* him and couldn't even fathom living with his memories. She wrapped her arms around him, and he was rigid with resistance. Yet she kept holding on and wouldn't let go.

"Larry died," he said, his voice rough. "Larry died."

Leaning her head against his, she didn't even breathe. After what seemed like an eon, she murmured, "Don't send me away. Let me sleep here with you."

Whether Mitch was too exhausted to protest, too

awash in the past to care, he slid down under the covers, letting her hold on.

She didn't fall asleep again until she heard the deep, even rhythm of his breathing. Then she let herself slumber with him, knowing morning would come sooner than they both wanted.

Chapter Twelve

In the morning everything always looked different.

That's what Lily thought as she awakened, reached across the guest room bed and found that Mitch was gone.

He'd slept in the bed with her most of the night. She'd awakened a couple of times and cuddled close to him with her head on his shoulder. He'd been asleep then... she could tell. But something had made him leave now and she had to admit to herself that that was her biggest fear—that he would leave. If not physically, then emotionally.

Their physical reunion last night had been spectacular. What he'd shared with her about Iraq had been wrenching. Did he have regrets about that now? Was that why he'd left the bed?

She glanced at the clock and saw that it was 7:00 a.m.

She knew he was meeting his friends at the bed-and-breakfast for brunch, but that wasn't until ten o'clock. She caught up the flannel shirt she'd discarded last night and slipped it on. She'd shower and dress after she found out where Mitch had gone.

After she buttoned his shirt from neckline to hem, she realized how silly that was. She certainly hadn't been so modest last night. She'd never felt so wanton or so free...so hungry or so sexual.

Sunlight poured in the hall skylight, a new, bright December day with Christmas right around the corner. What gift could she get Mitch?

She hated feeling uncertain like this. She hated not knowing how deep his feelings ran. Were they just having an affair?

That possibility made her heartsick.

She smelled the aroma of coffee and heard Mitch's voice before she saw him. He was pacing the kitchen, talking on his cell phone. He went to the French doors and looked out as he listened.

Spotting his jacket around the kitchen chair, a mug of coffee half gone, she wondered if he'd sat outside this morning in the cold before he'd come in to make his phone call. Who was he talking to? Jimmy? Matt?

Then she heard him say, "Dr. Dolman, I appreciate what you're saying. I searched your articles online this morning." There was a pause. "Yes, that too. I trust Matt. But I wanted to check out your credentials for myself."

Dr. Dolman. The surgeon who could possibly repair Mitch's hand. If Mitch was going to talk to him, why hadn't he discussed it with her? Why had he disappeared from the bed without a "good morning" or a kiss? Last night had meant the world to her. Decisions they each made would affect the other's life. Unless they weren't really "together." Unless last night hadn't meant what she thought it did.

She felt hurt and knew she shouldn't. This was *his* life. This was *his* decision. But she did feel let down. She'd thought last night they'd gotten closer than any two people could get.

Mitch sensed her presence and turned, finding her in the doorway. For a moment their gazes met, but then his mind was on the conversation again and he looked away, shutting her out.

At least that's the way it felt. She wouldn't eavesdrop if he didn't want her there.

She returned to the master bedroom and bath, catching the scent of Mitch's soap still lingering in the shower. She'd thought maybe they could shower together this morning. She'd thought—

Stop it, she chastised herself. Disappointment pressed against her heart as she showered quickly, found a blow dryer under Mitch's sink and blew most of the wetness from her hair. She'd dressed and was picking up her own phone to call the Victorian when she heard Mitch coming down the hall.

She closed her phone and waited.

He saw her standing there with it in her hand. "How are the twins?"

"I don't know. I haven't called yet."

The intimacy they'd shared last night seemed to have been lost. The electric buzz between them was still there, but there was nothing comfortable about it. She kept quiet to let him choose the first topic for discussion.

He asked, "You overheard some of my conversation?"

"Not much. Just the name of the doctor Matt told you about last night."

"Dr. Dolman."

She nodded.

"I was up early, went outside and did a ton of thinking."

She wanted to ask, *About us?* But that obviously wasn't what was on his mind.

"I thought about everything Matt said. He thinks I have survivor guilt."

"Do you?" she asked.

"Hell, I don't know. But I did think about why I wouldn't want to get my hand fixed. Yes, there could be more damage. But it also has to do with the life change I made."

"In other words, why rock the boat?" she inquired.

"Exactly. Yet I've never been a half-measure person. Why in this?"

There were only about three feet between them but it seemed like so much more.

He went on. "Dr. Dolman's success rate is outstanding. I made an appointment with him for Tuesday afternoon."

Tuesday was Mitch's day off. He could reserve an early flight and be in Houston before noon.

"I see," she said.

Tilting his head, he studied her. "I thought you'd be happy about it."

She *was* terrifically pleased he'd made the decision. "I am. But why didn't you wake me up to talk about it? Why did you leave and cut off the closeness we'd shared? Why didn't you think I'd want to be part of whatever you decided?"

His back became straighter, his stance a little wider, as if he had a position to defend. "Why do you think?"

"I'm not at all sure."

"You're insightful, Lily. Take a guess."

"Mitch…"

"No woman has ever touched my scars. *You* did. No woman has ever seen me in the throes of one of my nightmares. *You* did. I never told a civilian back here what happened over there. But I told *you*. If I had stayed in that bed this morning and you'd opened your eyes and I'd seen pity or worse yet, dismay, that even after all these years I still haven't gotten a handle on my own subconscious—" He stopped abruptly. "I just didn't want to have to deal with that."

She didn't know what to say. There were so many levels to his statement. She didn't know how to separate it into all the aspects they needed to examine.

So she stated what was obvious to her. "Why would I feel pity? Mitch, you're a decorated hero. You were awarded a Silver Star, a Purple—"

"I'm *not* a hero. I didn't save Larry's life."

"No, but you tried. You risked *your* life."

"Results matter…in surgery, in helping couples conceive, in life."

Shaking her head, she sank down onto the corner of the bed, hoping he'd do the same. "You expect too much of yourself. And maybe you don't expect enough of me."

"Maybe that's because I think in your mind you're still married."

His words struck her hard and stole her breath. "Did I act like I was still married last night?"

"Did you feel guilt afterwards?"

"No, I didn't," she said almost angrily.

Then he looked down at her hand in her lap. "Then why are you still wearing your wedding ring?"

"This is about my *ring?* You're jealous because I can't forget my husband?"

"I'm *not* jealous," Mitch protested with a vehemence she almost believed. "It's not about that," he concluded. "It's about your ability to let go of Troy so you have something with me."

The thought of letting go of Troy absolutely panicked her! If she let go, didn't that mean their love hadn't been very strong? If she let go, didn't that mean Sophie and Grace would never know their real dad? If she let go, and Mitch left, what would she have then?

He must have seen the color drain from her face. He must have seen how shaken she was, because he covered the few feet between them and clasped her shoulder.

But his touch, which still sent scalding heat through her body, activated her. She stood and pulled away from him. "I have to go home to Sophie and Grace."

"I know you do." His voice had lost its edge and was gentler than she expected. "But this is something we've needed to discuss and haven't."

"I thought we were discussing your surgery." Her feelings for Mitch had been simpler when the focus was on *him*.

"If I have surgery, I'm doing it to move on. You say you want to move on, but I don't know if that's really true."

She was stymied for a response and didn't know what he wanted from her.

"Why don't you go home, get the twins and meet me at the bed-and-breakfast for brunch?"

"I don't think that's a good idea." The words reflexively spilled from her.

"Why not?"

"Because...because I don't know what kind of night they had. I don't know if they're fussy or content. I should have called first thing and I didn't."

"Why didn't you?" he probed.

Because you were on my mind, she thought. "Because you left and I didn't know why."

"I only went as far as the kitchen."

Maybe that was true, but it hadn't felt that way at the time.

"I need to go," she whispered. More than anything, she needed to hold Sophie and Grace. To kiss them. To feel the bond she had with them.

Seeming to understand that, Mitch nodded. "Okay. I'll help you carry your things to the car."

Lily felt shell-shocked...as if her whole world had just crashed in. Mitch had turned the tables so effectively she didn't know who was more conflicted...or which one of them could figure out where they could go from here.

On Tuesday evening Lily sat at the kitchen table with evergreen boughs, ribbon and gold bells spread across newspaper. She was making a wreath for the front door while Angie and Ellie added more Christmas touches to the rest of the house. The last time she'd looked they were arranging a nativity set on the table by the sofa.

When the phone rang, she called into them, "I'll get it," went to the counter and picked up the cordless. The caller ID simply read Out of Area without a number.

"Hello," she answered, afraid to hope the caller was Mitch. Yesterday he'd been busy at the office tying up loose ends, cramming appointments together, going over histories of his patients with Jon and Hillary in case he got tied up in Houston. When she'd asked him about the brunch, he'd said everyone hated to leave the bed-and-breakfast, but they all had to get back to their lives. He'd given her one of those "Mitch" looks that was intense and full of meaning.

But then Jon had buzzed him and he'd rushed off. He didn't seem to be shutting her out, yet he didn't seem to be waiting for anything from her, either.

Before she'd left for the day, she'd placed a note on his desk, wishing him luck.

"Lily, it's Mitch. Are you tied up?"

She wanted to say, *Yes, my stomach's tied in knots and I'm worried about you.* Instead, she replied, "Sophie and Grace are sleeping. Ellie, Angie and I are decorating."

"I wanted to let you know Dr. Dolman believes I'm a good candidate for surgery. He has a slot open on Friday afternoon, so I'm going to stay, have some tests and then let him operate."

"That soon?" she murmured.

"I had to make a decision, Lily. This surgery will either work or it won't. One way or another, I'll know, and I'll adjust my life accordingly."

That's what Mitch did. He adjusted his life to fit whatever happened to him. His history had shown her that. He was a decisive, confident man who didn't stall or procrastinate or wait…unless waiting fit into the big picture. How long would he wait for her? Maybe his patience had already come to an end.

"Anyway, I'm staying at the Longhorn Inn. Matt said I could crash at his place, but he's starting a three-day rotation and will be tied up. I wanted to give you the number where I'll be in case my cell is out of reach. Got a pen and paper?"

She grabbed a pen and tablet from the counter. "Go ahead." She jotted down the number he gave her. "How long will you be in Houston after your surgery?"

"I'll be discharged the next day, but Matt wants me to give it forty-eight hours until I fly. If all goes well, I'll be back Monday. I can do physical therapy in Lubbock."

If all goes well.

"What about after you're discharged? Doesn't someone have to be with you?"

"I'll be fine, Lily. Matt said he'll have one of his doc friends check on me."

She hated the fact Mitch was going through this practically alone. Like most men, he probably didn't want anyone to see him when he wasn't at his best. But she didn't like the idea he'd be alone after surgery. She didn't like the idea that he was in Houston alone now.

After a long silence, Mitch asked, "So, did you put up a Christmas tree?"

"Yes, we did. Complete with a lighted star on top. Sophie and Grace haven't seen it yet, though. When they wake up they won't know what to think."

"You're lucky they're not walking yet. You can still keep most things out of their reach."

"Except for the tree. Angie hung ornaments that wouldn't break on the bottom. I have a feeling they'll have a few tantrums until they realize they can't touch it."

"They have to learn boundaries."

There was a commotion on Mitch's end. "Someone's at my door, Lily. It's probably room service."

"You're just having dinner?"

"After the consultation, I talked to Matt and then drove around for a while. I needed to…think. I wasn't hungry then. But after I got back and showered, the idea of food sounded good."

"I won't keep you then."

"I'm sorry you're going to have a heavier load this week because of my being away."

"Don't be concerned about that, Mitch. Hillary and Jon and I will be fine."

"Okay, then. If you need anything, or have any questions about my patients, just call."

"I will. And Mitch, I'll be praying for you…that everything goes well."

"Thanks, Lily."

When his phone clicked off, she set down hers, the hollow feeling inside her seeming to echo with Mitch's voice.

Angie came into the kitchen and saw Lily standing there, staring at the phone. "What's going on?"

Lily told her about Mitch's consultation and surgery. "He shouldn't be there alone," Lily murmured when she was finished.

"Who should be with him?" Angie asked.

Lily knew what Angie was suggesting. "I have Grace and Sophie to think about. And the practice."

"Take them with you."

Suddenly Lily heard a cry from the baby monitor.

"That's Grace," she said. "I'll find out what's wrong." On her way out of the kitchen, she glanced back at Angie. "I feel pulled in so many directions. I can't think about going to Houston. At least not tonight."

"Tomorrow will come soon enough," her housemate suggested.

Lily knew she was right.

On the way home from the office on Wednesday, Lily took a detour. After arriving at the outskirts of Sagebrush, she turned down a road where she hadn't driven for over a year...almost sixteen months. Mid-December darkness had already fallen and she glimpsed farms along the road with Christmas decorations and lights twinkling from eaves, gables and shrubs in front yards.

Eventually Lily reached an illuminated lane where a security guard was housed in a cupola before a high fence. She presented ID to him and a key. After a few taps into his computer, he okayed her, opened the gate and let her drive inside.

She passed row upon row of storage compartments, some looking more like closets, some the size of a garage. The area was well lit and there were no other cars around. It didn't take her long to find the row, and then the storage compartment that she was looking for. She didn't think as she parked in front of it. She tried not to feel. If she let herself feel now, what would happen after she went inside?

She did check her watch and knew she couldn't spend a whole lot of time here. Not today anyway. Sophie and Grace were waiting for her.

After she unlocked the combination, she inserted the

key into the padlock. Two levels of security. Now both were just barriers, locking her out of memories that she'd stored because they were too painful to see, listen to or handle.

The roll-up door stuck and she wondered if she'd have to call the security guard to help her heave it up. But then it gave way and rolled open, revealing the remnants of her marriage. At least the physical ones.

Stepping into the past, she looked around and her eyes burned. It was the cold, the staleness of the compartment, the boxes upon boxes that almost sixteen months ago she couldn't bear to donate or toss away. Moving to the Victorian had accomplished more than giving her an economical place to live, friends to support her, room for her twins to grow. Moving there so quickly after Troy had died had removed her from a good dose of the pain of losing him. She'd been nearly numb when she'd packed up her belongings and his. She'd sent a lot of Troy's things home to his mother, knowing she'd treasure them. But the rest was here in front of her, making her eyes go misty with the remembrance of what was inside the boxes.

She could sit here and go through them one by one. They were labeled and she knew what she'd find. But she hadn't come here to open a box with souvenirs from her Caribbean honeymoon with Troy or CDs they'd once listened to together. She'd come here to find something that would tell her whether she could meld the past with the present…if she *could* really move on. Besides cartons, she had to step over and around Troy's saws and metal boxes that held sets of chisels or a Dremel tool. Finally, after she'd moved a circular saw housed on its own table, she found what she was looking for in the corner.

She had asked Troy to make this for her. It was a multi-tiered plant stand fashioned in oak. Almost finished, it simply needed a last smoothing with fine sandpaper, polishing and then a coat of acrylic.

At least three feet high, the plant stand was bulky as she pushed it from its protected place to the front of the storage compartment and ran her hands over it, imagining Troy doing the same. Now tears really pressed against her eyelids. Giving in, she let them come and didn't even try to brush them away.

When she heard a sound, she realized an airplane was buzzing overhead. At the edge of the compartment, she lifted her gaze to the sky. The moon was bright, almost full, and brought back the memory of standing at the fire pit on Mitch's patio singing "Silent Night." Her nose was numb. Her fingers were stiff. Her feet were cold in her high-heeled pumps. But the cold didn't matter now as she stood still, just letting every feeling in her life wash over her.

Her gaze lifted to the moon and she suddenly saw something to the east of it—a shooting star. It glowed, streaked, then vanished.

Like Troy?

Turning away from the sky, she ran her hands over the solid wood again. She heard the question in her head as if someone were standing in the compartment speaking to her. *Do you love Mitch?*

Searching for the answer here, in the midst of her past life, she knew she did.

Why? that little voice asked again. *Because I asked him to look out for you?*

Reverently she slid her hands over the oak grain, straight and crooked, with imperfections and beauty despite that. She and Troy and Mitch had imperfections and beauty, too. No, she didn't love Mitch because Troy had asked him to watch over her. She loved Mitch because of who he was, and who she was when she was with him. She loved him because he was passionate and intense, and tender and caring. She loved him differently than she'd loved Troy. Whether or not that was because of Sophie and Grace, she didn't know. All of a sudden she just knew her love for Mitch was right.

Yes, it had come along at a time when she was still grieving. And maybe she'd miss Troy for the rest of her life. Loss wouldn't go away merely because she wanted it to. But Troy had so often told her, *There are no coincidences.* On and off, over the past nine months, she'd tested what she'd felt for Mitch. And every time, the desire, the aching to be with him, the dreams that appeared when she let herself think about the future couldn't be denied.

With one hand on the plant stand, she looked down at her other hand, where her wedding ring gleamed in the white moonlight. She slipped it off her finger and set it on the top shelf of the stand.

It was then that she felt warmth seeping into her body, as if someone had given her a giant hug. The sensation only lasted a matter of moments. Then once again she felt her cold nose, her stiff fingers, her numbing feet. She picked up the ring and slipped it into a zippered pocket in her purse. Then she pushed the plant stand out of the storage compartment, determined to fit it into her car.

She had to get home to Sophie and Grace and make an airline reservation to Houston.

Chapter Thirteen

The nurse ran the IV and Mitch watched the drip. This surgery was really going to happen.

Although Matt had stopped in a little while before, the one person Mitch wanted to talk to was Lily. But she was back in Sagebrush.

When the nurse left Mitch's cubicle, he flexed both hands, staring at his right one. Someday in the future, if not able to perform surgery, he might have fuller use of his fingers. Would he feel whole if he did?

He doubted it. Because he realized now he didn't need the use of his fingers to feel whole. He needed Lily. That need had been supremely evident the night of the reunion when they'd made love. Somehow, on that night, attraction and chemistry had transformed into something else entirely.

It had transformed into love.

He hadn't had the courage to admit it or the courage to feel it until he'd awakened the following morning holding her. Yet at that same moment he'd had doubts about Lily's ability to love again…doubts about her ability to freely make any kind of commitment to him. If he pushed her, he'd lose her.

He'd almost lost her when his ego had slid between them in June and his pride had convinced him to put time and distance between them. He'd almost lost her again when he'd prodded her about her wedding ring on Sunday morning.

Would she cut and run? Would she decide loving Troy for the rest of her life was enough? Were her feelings not deep enough to allow a future to develop between them?

He wanted her here to talk about all of it—his past mistakes, his future possibilities, her independence, their passionate hunger that went deeper than pheromones. He hadn't asked her to come, because she had Sophie and Grace to consider first. He hadn't asked her to come, because he knew if he pushed too hard she'd slip away entirely.

Turning away from the IV stand, he closed his eyes and tried to blank his mind.

Lily rushed down the hospital corridor hoping she wasn't too late. She had to see Mitch before he went into surgery. She *had* to.

The past three days had felt like a global marathon.

When she'd returned from the storage unit, Ellie had helped her carry in the plant stand. She'd also noticed the absent wedding ring. When Lily had explained what she wanted to do, Ellie had offered to take care of Sophie and Grace while she went to Houston. Angie had been at home, too, and when Lily couldn't find available seating on a flight, she'd called her brother-in-law, billionaire Logan Barnes. He'd booked Lily first-class seats. Both Angie and Ellie convinced her the twins would be well taken care of. Lily didn't have to worry about anything… except what Mitch was going to say and do.

Now as Lily headed for the information desk in the surgical wing, she was afraid. She loved Mitch Cortega with all her heart. But what if he'd lost patience with her? What if she was too late? What if he rejected her and she'd made a fool of herself?

She kept going anyway, almost at a jog. If she made a fool of herself, so be it.

When she reached the desk and inquired about Mitch's whereabouts, the woman asked, "Are you family?"

Lily said blithely, "I'm his fiancée."

Narrowing her eyes, the clerk asked if Lily knew his date of birth.

"I do. It's January twenty-first."

A tad less warily, the gatekeeper of this surgical unit next asked for his home address and telephone number.

Resigned to this delay, Lily rattled them off.

Finally the clerk pointed her in the direction she should go, advising, "Follow the yellow floor line."

Doing so, Lily almost ran toward the surgical waiting area, found cubicle number six and peeked around the curtain.

There Mitch was, lying on a gurney, an IV line attached to the hand that wouldn't be undergoing surgery.

She wondered if he'd already been given medication to relax, if he'd even be aware that she was here.

Crossing to the bed, she stood beside it and asked softly, "Mitch?"

His eyes opened. They were clear, alert and totally flabbergasted. "Lily? What are you doing here? My surgery was delayed an hour and they haven't given me anything yet. So I know you can't be a hallucination." He sat up and looked ready to climb out of the bed.

She laid a hand on his shoulder, stood as close as she could without jumping into bed with him, then plunged in. "I had to see you in person. I had to tell you before you went into surgery."

"What? Did something happen to Sophie or Grace?" The lines on his forehead cutting deep, his expression showed his extreme worry.

"They're fine. Ellie and Angie are taking good care of them."

Now he just looked totally perplexed.

She took his hand, stroked the scars on his arm and gazed deeply into his eyes. "I love you, Mitch. I couldn't let you go into surgery not knowing that. You've been so patient and I don't know if that patience has run out or not. But I do love you. I want to be with you. I want a future with you."

He didn't look as ecstatic as she thought he might, as she'd *hoped* he might. Instead, he looked troubled. "What happened, Lily?"

He didn't believe her! In fact, he seemed to consider her appearance as impulsive, that she might change her mind tomorrow. She stayed close to him, her hand still on his arm. Somehow she'd make him understand. "I went to the storage compartment where I kept everything

I didn't move into the Victorian. Troy's tools are there, and the plant stand he made for me before he was deployed."

Mitch began to say something but she didn't give him the chance. She rushed on. "The stand isn't finished and I'd like to finish it. And then I want to put it in your sunroom where it can hold plants or flowers and remind me of the love Troy gave me. It's part of my past, Mitch. Troy is part of my past. And I'll always hold his memory dear in my heart. I don't think it was a coincidence he chose you to look after me. He used to say, 'There are no coincidences,' and I believe he was right. When I was standing there looking at the moon and spotting a shooting star—I'd never seen one before in my life—I remembered standing by the fire pit with you and singing 'Silent Night.' My whole being just understood I should finally admit what I've been feeling. I *do* love you, Mitch Cortega. I'm ready to commit to you for the rest of my life. If you aren't ready, that's okay. We'll figure things out as we go. *Together.*"

She could see that what she was saying and feeling and meaning took a few moments for Mitch to absorb. But then he opened his arms to her. "Come here."

She didn't hesitate. If someone came in to take him to surgery, they could just take her along, too!

On his lap, with his arms around her the best he could manage it, he kissed her with such soul-stirring passion she thought she'd melt right into him.

But then he broke the kiss and lifted his head. "When we made love Saturday night, I was forced to admit to myself I was doing a hell of a lot more than watching over you. I hadn't tried the word *love* on what I felt. But on Sunday, I did. I guess I was embarrassed after the bad dream. I woke up thinking I had to do *something*. If you weren't ready, then I had to prepare myself for whatever life dealt. The best way to do that was to see if I could have my hand repaired."

"I was hurt you didn't talk about it with me," she admitted, knowing she had to be honest with him about everything.

"I'm sorry. I guess I thought I'd given you too many pieces of myself and this was one I had to take control of."

Stroking his face, she said, "I want all of you, Mitch. Not just the strong parts or the perfect parts. I'll support you no matter what happens, whether we return to our practice or whether you want to go back to trauma surgery. And I have no intention of moving to Oklahoma. I'm staying in Sagebrush with *you*."

Taking Lily's hand, Mitch smiled. "This isn't the place I'd imagined we'd be talking about this. I want to give you romance and flowers and music to remember the day by, not the clanging of hospital trays. But it seems like I've waited for you for so long, and I don't want to wait a second longer. Will you marry me?"

"When?" She'd be ready today if that's what he wanted.

"Soon. As soon as we can fly back to Sagebrush and arrange it. I don't want to wait a minute more than I have to to be your husband. And," he hesitated, then continued, "a stepfather to Sophie and Grace."

"You're not going to be a *step*father. You're going to be their dad. Troy would want that. I know he would."

Mitch kissed her again, just as the nurse swung back the curtain.

They were oblivious, lost in passion and promises they yearned to share.

Epilogue

"This is as unconventional as it gets," Mitch murmured to Lily, folding his arm around her in her cream wool cape. As long as she was in his arms, the world was good and he slept peacefully during the deep night hours. Marriage would gift them with the future they both wanted and needed.

Twinkle lights were strung around the border of Mitch's patio. The fire pit was lit, giving off warmth. The minister from Lily's church had agreed to perform the service. He'd told her early evening was fine. Afterward, he could return to his congregation for Christmas Eve midnight service.

Fortunately, the weather had cooperated and even Mitch had to admit his patio looked wedding-ready. The stars were crystal clear and the slice of moon glowed with silver-white light. An arbor, also decorated in

evergreens and twinkle lights, housed the minister as
Lily and Mitch stood before him, ready to say their
vows.

Lily cast a glance at Ellie, who was holding Grace,
and at Angie, who was carrying Sophie. The twins were
bundled up in their pink snowsuits and mittens, their
noses barely peeking out from their hoods. Gina had
dressed Daniel similarly in blue, and Logan held his son
so he could see what was going on, too, as Eva stood
with Hannah ready to help with the kids. Shep and Raina
had brought along Joey, Roy and Manuel. Tessa and her
husband, Vince, held their children's hands, while Francesca and Grady as well as Emily and Jared stood by
with their children. Within driving distance, Tony and
Jimmy had brought their wives, children and Christmas
along with them. Beside them, Lily and Mitch's colleagues watched from along one stone wall where the
twinkle lights flickered high above them.

Lily had wanted them all here to witness this joyous
celebration. She loved Mitch so much she wanted everyone who could to share their joy. They'd only be outside
for about ten minutes and then they'd go inside for their
reception, which would be homey and all theirs.

In a low voice beside Mitch, Matt said, "You two
couldn't wait until spring, could you?"

Mitch shook his head. "Not a chance. You and I both
know each day is a precious gift, and I want to spend
them all with Lily."

Lily cuddled closer to Mitch, not at all cold, just
wanting to feel him near. He was wearing a black,
Western-cut leather jacket. His hand and wrist were
still bandaged. After Christmas they would fly back to
Houston for an exam by the doctor and decide whether

Mitch was ready for physical therapy. The surgery had gone well, but it might take time for him to have use of those fingers again.

Reverend Allbright made some opening remarks and then said, "I understand the two of you have vows to make to each other."

"We do," they said in unison.

"Whoever wants to go first," the kindly older man invited.

Lily took Mitch's hands, one bandaged and one not, in both of hers. "I know how important vows and promises are to you. I promise to love you from morning till night and every minute in between. I vow to be your partner, lover and friend and I will always respect your opinion in raising our girls. Each and every day, I will try to bring happiness into your life and will be proud to call you my husband."

Mitch cleared his throat and held on to her as tightly as she was holding on to him. "I was broken when I met you, in ways I didn't even understand. Your acceptance, passion and caring have changed that. Having you and Sophie and Grace in my life has healed past wounds. I want nothing more than to be your husband and their dad. You are everything I've ever wanted, the woman I didn't even know I hoped to find. I love you, Lily, and I will cherish you, protect you, honor and respect you every day of our lives."

The minister opened his hand to Lily. Raina handed her a wide gold band and Lily placed it in the minister's hand. Matt handed Mitch a circle of diamonds and Mitch placed that in the minister's palm, also.

Reverend Allbright said, "These rings embody the circle of love that you have promised each other. I give them to you now to slide onto each other's fingers in memory of this night, the vows you have made and the love you will share."

Lily took the ring again and slid it onto Mitch's finger. "I thee wed," she said solemnly.

Mitch took the ring from the minister's hand and slid it onto Lily's finger. "I thee wed," he echoed, just as solemnly.

They held hands and faced forward again.

Reverend Allbright smiled. "I now pronounce you husband and wife."

Mitch took Lily into his arms and she lifted her face to his. Their kiss was an embodiment of everything their ceremony had entailed.

When Mitch raised his head, he said loud and clear, "I love you."

She kissed him again and buried her nose by his ear. "I love you, too."

Everyone around them was applauding and they realized they weren't alone in the universe. With her husband beside her, Lily went to Grace and lifted her into her arms. Mitch did the same with Sophie and they came together for a group hug.

"Can we cut the cake now?" Joey asked.

"We can cut the cake," Mitch announced happily, tickling Sophie.

After more hugs all around, they headed into Mitch's house, ready to begin their lives and the future they would build together.

* * * * *

*Look for Karen Rose Smith's REUNION BRIDES
series,
Coming soon to Silhouette Special Edition!*

**Silhouette®**

COMING NEXT MONTH

Available December 28, 2010

SPECIAL EDITION

SSECNM1210

HARLEQUIN®

A *Romance*

FOR EVERY MOOD™

Spotlight on

Classic

Quintessential, modern love stories
that are romance at its finest.

See the next page
to enjoy a sneak peek from
the Harlequin Presents® series.

*Harlequin Presents® is thrilled
to introduce the first installment of
an epic tale of passion and drama by*
USA TODAY *Bestselling Author*
Penny Jordan!

*When buttoned-up Giselle first meets
the devastatingly handsome Saul Parenti,
the heat between them is explosive....*

"LET ME GET THIS STRAIGHT. Are you actually suggesting that I would stoop to that kind of game playing?"

Saul came out from behind his desk and walked toward her. Giselle could smell his hot male scent and it was making her dizzy, igniting a low, dull, pulsing ache that was taking over her whole body.

Giselle defended her suspicions. "You don't want me here."

"No," Saul agreed, "I don't."

And then he did what he had sworn he would not do, cursing himself beneath his breath as he reached for her, pulling her fiercely into his arms and kissing her with all the pent-up fury she had aroused in him from the moment he had first seen her.

Giselle certainly *wanted* to resist him. But the hand she raised to push him away developed a will of its own and was sliding along his bare arm beneath the sleeve of his shirt, and the body that should have been arching away from him was instead melting into him.

Beneath the pressure of his kiss he could feel and taste her gasp of undeniable response to him. He wanted to devour her, take her and drive them both until they were equally satiated—even whilst the anger within him that she should make him feel that way roared and burned its resentment of his need.

She was helpless, Giselle recognized, totally unable to withstand the storm lashing at her, able only to cling to the man who was the cause of it and pray that she would survive.

Somewhere else in the building a door banged. The sound exploded into the sensual tension that had enclosed them, driving them apart. Saul's chest was rising and falling as he fought for control; Giselle's whole body was trembling.

Without a word she turned and ran.

Find out what happens when Saul and Giselle succumb to their irresistible desire in

THE RELUCTANT SURRENDER

Available January 2011 from Harlequin Presents®

REQUEST YOUR FREE BOOKS!
2 FREE NOVELS PLUS 2 FREE GIFTS!

SPECIAL EDITION
Life, Love and Family!

YES! Please send me 2 FREE Silhouette® Special Edition® novels and my 2 FREE gifts (gifts are worth about $10). After receiving them, if I don't wish to receive any more books, I can return the shipping statement marked "cancel." If I don't cancel, I will receive 6 brand-new novels every month and be billed just $4.24 per book in the U.S. or $4.99 per book in Canada. That's a saving of 15% off the cover price! It's quite a bargain! Shipping and handling is just 50¢ per book.* I understand that accepting the 2 free books and gifts places me under no obligation to buy anything. I can always return a shipment and cancel at any time. Even if I never buy another book from Silhouette, the two free books and gifts are mine to keep forever.

235/335 SDN E5RG

Name _____ (PLEASE PRINT) _____

Address _____ Apt. # _____

City _____ State/Prov. _____ Zip/Postal Code _____

Signature (if under 18, a parent or guardian must sign) _____

Mail to the **Silhouette Reader Service:**
IN U.S.A.: P.O. Box 1867, Buffalo, NY 14240-1867
IN CANADA: P.O. Box 609, Fort Erie, Ontario L2A 5X3

Not valid for current subscribers to Silhouette Special Edition books.

Want to try two free books from another line?
Call 1-800-873-8635 or visit www.morefreebooks.com.

* Terms and prices subject to change without notice. Prices do not include applicable taxes. N.Y. residents add applicable sales tax. Canadian residents will be charged applicable provincial taxes and GST. Offer not valid in Quebec. This offer is limited to one order per household. All orders subject to approval. Credit or debit balances in a customer's account(s) may be offset by any other outstanding balance owed by or to the customer. Please allow 4 to 6 weeks for delivery. Offer available while quantities last.

Your Privacy: Silhouette is committed to protecting your privacy. Our Privacy Policy is available online at www.eHarlequin.com or upon request from the Reader Service. From time to time we make our lists of customers available to reputable third parties who may have a product or service of interest to you. If you would prefer we not share your name and address, please check here. ☐

Help us get it right—We strive for accurate, respectful and relevant communications. To clarify or modify your communication preferences, visit us at www.ReaderService.com/consumerschoice.

SSE10R